The Chronicles of Nymeria

Xalis

Journey into Uncertainty

Author Eric Hawrylak

Special thanks

At this point, I want to express my deepest gratitude to two special people without whom this book would not be the same.

First, I would like to thank Lisa Block. As I ventured into uncharted territory as an author, you were my beacon. Your invaluable support, helpful tips and constructive suggestions paved my way. You were not only my mentor but also a patient beta reader, whose keen eye and honest feedback greatly enriched this work. Thank you, Lisa, for your tireless support and belief in me.

An equally big thank you goes to Kathrin Berlin. Your commitment as a beta reader and your detailed feedback were invaluable. Your constructive criticism and encouraging words helped me elevate my manuscript to a new level. Your comments were always precise and full of valuable insights, which have made this book what it is today. Thank you, Kathrin, for your time, your care and your open ear.

Without both of you, this book would not be the same. Your faith in me and my work has motivated and inspired me. I thank you both from the bottom of my heart.

Bibliografische Information der Deutschen
Nationalbibliothek: Die Deutsche Nationalbibliothek
verzeichnet diese Publikation in der Deutschen
Nationalbibliografie; detaillierte bibliografische Daten
sind im Internet über dnb.dnb.de abrufbar.

Verlag: BoD · Books on Demand GmbH, In de Tarpen 42,
22848 Norderstedt

Druck: Libri Plureos GmbH, Friedensallee 273, 22763
Hamburg

ISBN: 978-3-7597-7918-2

Prologue

In a world full of magic, mythical creatures and diverse peoples, Nymeria spans two great continents: Lurandis in the west and Thaloria in the east. This world is rich in history, cultures and mysteries that manifest in every corner. The inhabitants of Nymeria include a variety of races, such as humans, elves, dwarves and many others, each possessing their own form of magic or unique abilities.

Magic in Nymeria is as diverse as the peoples who inhabit it. Humans are particularly skilled in elemental magic, mastering the forces of fire, ice, air and, rarely, lightning magic. Elves, on the other hand, are deeply connected to nature and practice primarily nature magic, allowing them to communicate with plants and harness the powers of earth and water. Dwarves, known for their craftsmanship and warrior nature, are not capable of conventional magic. Instead, they have developed the art of runic magic, a form of sorcery based on engraving magical symbols and patterns onto weapons, armor and artifacts. These runes grant items special powers, making dwarves formidable warriors and esteemed craftsmen.

It is the year 856 of the Nymerian World Calendar. Particularly Lurandis is experiencing an era of peace and prosperity. The peoples live in relative harmony and trade routes between the continents are thriving. The exchange of knowledge and culture has led to a golden age, where discoveries and advancements in magic, science and art have improved the quality of life for all inhabitants.

Our story unfolds on the continent of Lurandis, a land known for its majestic mountains, dense forests and vast plains. Here, humans live in cities, elves in ancient forests and dwarves in the depths of the mountains, where they operate their mysterious runic forges.

Yet, in the shadows of this peace, a new threat is brewing. Unrest is growing and dark forces are beginning to stir. The fragile peace that has lasted so long is at stake and the signs of an impending crisis are unmistakable.

Chapter 1: A Dark Prophecy

Our story begins in a small, picturesque village surrounded by majestic mountains and dense forests. This small paradise exuded an aura of peace and was surrounded by fertile fields and lush meadows. The people in this village were hardworking, having built their modest homes from the materials of the surrounding nature.

The environment around the village was rich in wildlife and plants that were of great importance to the community's survival. They hunted in the forests that stretched around the village and gathered berries and herbs in the fragrant meadows. The river that flowed through the village provided ample fish and water for the fields and gardens. The water sparkled in the sunlight, reflecting the clouds in the sky.

Overall, harmony prevailed in this village and the people lived in harmony with the nature they depended on. The community was closely connected and neighbors helped each other in good times and bad.

In the midst of this idyllic village, a young woman made her way to a secluded house on the edge of the settlement. The golden rays of the rising sun bathed the scene in warm light as she reached her destination.

Determined, the young woman knocked several times on the wooden door. "It's me. Open the door," she called out in a familiar voice. Inside the house, a robust man lay on his bed, still lingering in a half-sleep. The knocking and familiar voice at the door slowly reached him.

As he heard the noises, the man finally opened his eyes. A slight smile crossed his face as he recognized the voice. With a sigh, he got up, stretched briefly and made his way to the door. "Yes, wait. I'll open the door for you," he called back as he navigated his way through the cozy house.

After the man opened the door, he greeted the young woman with a friendly smile. "Good morning, Fiona." She returned the greeting and looked up at him. "Oh, Gronak, you've overslept again," she noted with a slightly mischievous smile.

Gronak laughed heartily and waved it off. "Oh, come on in. Let's have some breakfast first and then we can head out." Fiona entered Gronak's house and took a seat at the table. Gronak went to the pantry, fetched bread, cheese and sausage and joined Fiona at the table. Together, they began to enjoy their breakfast.

While they were eating, Gronak looked at Fiona with a questioning expression. "What's on the agenda for today?" Fiona looked up at him while eating a piece of bread and replied, "We're supposed to go see Walter. He has a task for us." Gronak nodded as they finished their meal.

After they had finished their meal, Gronak and Fiona stood up and cleared the dishes. They then prepared to head out to Walter. The sun was now higher in the sky and the village was slowly coming to life. Gronak donned his armor and Fiona checked her bag one more time.

Gronak, a formidable warrior of impressive stature, was blessed with a massive physique. His muscular arms and legs gave him immense strength and his broad shoulders conveyed an impression of invincible power. His skin was tanned and marked by numerous scars, testifying to the battles he had fought.

His wild black hair framed his striking face, which was accompanied by a distinguished full beard. His eyes shone in an icy blue, revealing his unwavering determination. They were windows to a soul filled with fighting spirit and love for his homeland.

Gronak wore heavy leather and chainmail armor that provided excellent protection. The armor was adorned with intricate engravings that told the history of his people. Various weapons hung from his belt, including a powerful broadsword, its blade shining in the sunlight and a heavy axe with a dark ebony handle.

Despite his imposing appearance, Gronak had a big heart. He always stood up for the weak and oppressed and was ready to sacrifice his life to protect his friends and family. His bravery made him a true hero, always ready to fight for the good.

Fiona, on the other hand, was a young and talented magician who played a crucial role in Gronak's life with her magical abilities and sharp intellect. Her grace and elegance radiated a special aura that drew attention. Her long dark hair was often tied into a braid, while her emerald-green eyes had a captivating allure.

Fiona wore an elegant robe of fine fabric, with complex runes and symbols in bright colors representing her affiliation with the Order of Mages. The robe gently conformed to her figure, emphasizing her graceful form. Around her neck, she wore a silver necklace with a sparkling gemstone that seemed to glow upon closer inspection.

Fiona was distinguished not only by her outer beauty but also by her extraordinary intelligence and sharp mind. She had discovered her magical abilities at a young age and had eagerly begun to explore and develop them. Her magical skills ranged from manipulating the elements to healing living beings. Her knowledge of magic was impressive and she used it with great care and precision.

Proud of her abilities, she often relied on her knowledge and experience to support her friends in difficult situations. Fiona also had a strong personality and a pronounced sense of justice. She was deeply committed to the needs of the weak and oppressed and never hesitated to use her magical powers for the benefit of others. Although she could sometimes be impatient and stubborn, Fiona was a loyal and trustworthy friend, always ready to stand up for her comrades.

Since childhood, Gronak and Fiona had been inseparable friends and had already experienced many adventures together. They recognized that their abilities perfectly complemented each other and that as a team, they were unbeatable. While Gronak, with his physical strength and combat experience, formed the front line, Fiona protected and supported their group with her powerful magical abilities.

Gronak admired Fiona's magical prowess and was always amazed at how she could defeat enemies in seconds with her powers. He saw her not only as a friend but also as a trusted ally he could rely on in every battle. Fiona, in turn, trusted Gronak's tireless dedication and his ability to keep a cool head in any situation. His determination and bravery were an inexhaustible source of inspiration for her.

Gronak and Fiona left Gronak's house together and headed towards the marketplace, where Walter's tavern was located. The walk was short and within a few minutes, they reached the bustling village square.

On their way there, villagers who were already busy with their work greeted the two adventurers warmly. Some waved at them, while others paused their work to exchange a few words of greeting. The close-knit community of the village was evident in the friendly gestures and heartfelt interactions.

As Gronak and Fiona entered the marketplace, they noticed the lively activity. The vibrant marketplace, which formed the heart of the village, was a place of active trade where residents exchanged and sold their agricultural produce and handcrafted goods. There were also several craft businesses, including a blacksmith, a potter and a tailor. The blacksmith expertly hammered the glowing metal to forge weapons and tools, while the potter spun his wheel to shape intricate pottery. The tailor worked on elegant garments that shimmered in many bright colors.

At one end of the marketplace stood an ancient oak, serving as the village meeting place. Its strong trunk seemed to tell stories from centuries past and its branches stretched majestically into the sky. Important decisions were made here and it was also the site of joyful festivals where villagers gathered to laugh, eat and dance together.

There, they discovered Walter's cozy tavern, which drew attention with its inviting charm. The aroma of freshly prepared food and the soft murmur of guests gave the place a pleasant atmosphere. Gronak and Fiona entered the tavern. Walter, as usual behind his counter, was sorting beers and wines when the two adventurers walked in.

Gronak smiled and approached the counter. "Good morning, Walter." The innkeeper turned around and returned the smile. "Good morning to both of you. It's nice to see you." Walter reached for two clean mugs and filled them with a hearty beer.

As he poured the beer, Walter began to speak. "Tomorrow is the village festival and the mayor has asked us to handle the catering." Gronak and Fiona listened attentively as they took their mugs. Walter sat down at the counter with them and continued. "It's going to be a big celebration and we need to make sure that all the villagers are well provided for."

Gronak took a hearty sip from his mug and nodded in agreement. "Alright, Fiona and I will head out right away to hunt wild boars and deer." Walter laughed heartily and praised them. "Great, you two are my salvation. With your skills, you're the perfect choice for the job."

Fiona smiled with her friendly demeanor and responded. "Of course, Walter, we'll gladly do this for you and the village." The support of the village was important to the two adventurers and they were ready to contribute to the success of the festival.

After finishing their drinks, Gronak and Fiona left the tavern and set out towards the forest, which was not too far from the village. The sun was now higher in the sky and the birds chirped cheerfully in the forest as the two adventurers made their way through the green paths.

Gronak and Fiona began the hunt with concentration. Their experience and skill with the bow and arrow paid off and after some time, they had taken down two wild boars and a deer. They loaded the game onto the small cart they had brought for this purpose.

As they secured their trophies, a traveler approached the trade road. He appeared exhausted and was clearly seeking help. The stranger approached Gronak and Fiona and greeted them politely. "Greetings. I'm on my way to the nearest city; I have an important message to deliver."

Gronak and Fiona paused their activities and focused their attention on the traveler. "Greetings, traveler. You look quite worn out. Is everything alright?" Gronak asked with concern.

Fiona, also worried, offered the weary traveler her water bottle. "Drink some first and tell us what happened," she suggested as Gronak and Fiona watched him attentively.

The traveler gratefully took a few sips of water and then spoke. "Thank you, I needed that. But time is pressing, I will tell you everything once we reach your village." Gronak and Fiona exchanged puzzled glances but recognized the urgency in his voice and agreed.

The three of them made their way back to the village with the hunted game and the traveler. The small cart, laden with the fresh trophies, trailed behind them as they walked through the green paths of the forest back to the village. The atmosphere was tense and Fiona could sense an unease that troubled her.

Once they reached the marketplace, the traveler requested to be taken to the mayor. Gronak and Fiona nodded in agreement and led him through the bustling streets of the village to the mayor's impressive house. The traveler thanked the two adventurers warmly and departed with a promise to reveal more about the urgent message later.

The two returned to the marketplace and headed to Walter's tavern to deliver the game. Walter was pleased with the wild boars and the deer and praised them for their hunting skills. After the game was stored, Gronak and Fiona took a moment to sit at the counter and relax.

A while later, as they were still contemplating their next plans, the loud market bell suddenly rang. An unmistakable sign of important events. Gronak and Fiona exchanged puzzled glances before leaving the tavern and heading towards the marketplace.

There, the other villagers had already gathered. The atmosphere was tense and people whispered excitedly among themselves. Gronak and Fiona joined the crowd and waited eagerly to find out what had caused the ringing of the market bell.

At the marketplace, the villagers gathered, eager for the mayor's words. Gronak and Fiona stood amidst the crowd, their eyes fixed on the mayor as he positioned himself at the base of the large tree.

"Listen to me, my friends!" the mayor began in a serious tone. "A traveler came to me earlier with a terrible announcement." The villagers perked up their ears and the mood in the marketplace grew restless.

With a grave tone, the mayor continued. "A Dark Mage, a demon in human form who calls himself Xalis, has appeared in the northern part of the country, spreading fear, death and destruction. He has already reduced several villages and cities to rubble and his cruelty knows no bounds."

A murmur of concern and excitement spread through the crowd. The villagers spoke over each other and their anxious faces testified to the seriousness of the situation.

The mayor raised his voice to regain attention. "Listen to me! Although the situation seems frightening, the threat is still very far away and brave warriors will surely appear to defeat this Xalis."

Gronak felt the tension in the air. Fiona also looked serious, her thoughts racing. The mayor's words lingered as the villagers whispered among themselves, exchanging skeptical glances. Gronak and Fiona exchanged a look, not of fear but of determination.

The mayor concluded the assembly with these words. "We must remain vigilant and stand together. The village festival will still take place, to strengthen and encourage ourselves in these dark times." The villagers returned to their tasks, but the tension still lingered.

The sun was setting and it was getting late. Gronak and Fiona sat, as almost every evening, at their usual spot in Walter's tavern. Despite the grim news, the atmosphere in the tavern was lively. The waitress, Thea, brought them food and beer and the people in the tavern laughed with joy.

Gronak looked at Fiona, his forehead creased with worry. "What do you make of the story about this Xalis?" Fiona met his gaze with concern and replied, "I find it terrifying, even though the danger is far away. Sooner or later, it could come to us and destroy everything we hold dear."

Gronak nodded in agreement. "That's exactly what I thought." The realization that even in their remote village, the threat of unrest and danger was not out of the question weighed heavily on their shoulders.

At that moment, the traveler entered the tavern. Gronak looked at him and waved him over. The traveler, whom

Gronak and Fiona had met earlier on the trade road, approached them. "Have a seat," Gronak invited him.

The traveler smiled warmly. "Thank you and thank you for your help earlier. I haven't introduced myself yet. I'm Dietmar," he said sincerely. Gronak and Fiona returned the smile. "Nice to meet you, Dietmar. We were just discussing the news you brought," said Fiona.

Gronak turned to Dietmar. "You certainly caused quite a stir in the village today." Dietmar grew calmer and his face showed a look of distress. "I would have preferred to bring better news. But what is happening in the Northlands is simply dreadful."

A moment of silence fell over the table as Gronak and Fiona looked at each other with concern. Fiona broke the silence and asked gently, "Can you tell us more about this Xalis? We'd like to hear more."

Dietmar looked deeply into his mug and began to recount. "I was a resident of the Northlands. One day, we were attacked by monsters that destroyed the land and the villages one by one. They slaughtered the people without mercy. Everyone who fought was killed. Our only option was to flee. My wife and daughter were killed in the process."

A heavy silence fell over the tavern as Dietmar recounted the dreadful events in the Northlands. The loss of his family and the cruel actions of the monsters left deep marks on Dietmar's face.

Dietmar took a short pause before continuing with a trembling voice. "These creatures were accompanied by powerful monsters. They kept repeating that their master, Xalis, had returned to destroy the world. They said these words over and over again. That's why I'm traveling through the land, trying to warn as many people as possible, hoping that there are brave warriors who will stop this monster Xalis."

As Dietmar spoke, Gronak's face was set in anger. He could hardly imagine the destruction and suffering in the Northlands. He looked at Fiona, who was very concerned.

Dietmar stood up from his seat and looked at the two of them. "I think I'll go to bed now. The day has been very exhausting." Gronak and Fiona bade Dietmar farewell and wished him a restful night.

Gronak looked at Fiona with excitement, his eyes shining with determination. "Do you think the same thing as I do, Fiona?" Fiona nodded with resolve and replied, "Of course, we can't just let this mage Xalis continue like this."

A grin spread across Gronak's face. "That's exactly what I wanted to hear from you. Let's prepare everything tonight and leave first thing tomorrow morning." Fiona agreed, her eyes reflecting the same resolve. "That's exactly what we'll do. I can't stand the thought of Xalis killing so many innocents. We must stop him, not just for our village, but for the entire land."

Filled with concern and a strong sense of responsibility, Gronak and Fiona decided that they could not stand idly by while the world was falling apart. They knew their strengths as a warrior and a mage were needed to confront this dark threat. Their village, their friends and their homeland were in danger. They were prepared to do whatever it took to protect them.

Gronak and Fiona stayed in Walter's tavern for a while longer, discussing all the details for their spontaneous departure the next day. They considered which route to take, what resources they would need and how to effectively deal with Xalis and his monsters.

As it grew late, Gronak and Fiona bade farewell to Walter and headed home to prepare for the next day. The stars shone in the sky and the air was filled with a mix of excitement and tension.

In their homes, they gathered their equipment, checked their weapons and armor and wrote short letters to their families and friends. The concern about the upcoming journey and potential dangers occupied their thoughts. But their motivation to defend their homeland gave them strength.

With a mix of excitement and a certain heaviness in their hearts, Gronak and Fiona went to bed. The night before their spontaneous departure was short, but the anticipation of the challenges ahead and the hope for a victorious end filled their dreams.

The sun was still low on the horizon the next morning and the morning mist enveloped the village in a mysterious silence. Birds chirped in the trees and the gentle rustling of the brook was like a soothing melody.

Gronak and Fiona checked their gear and bags one last time for the journey ahead. Fiona spoke softly to Gronak. "The task before us will not be easy," she whispered, her voice tinged with seriousness. "Xalis is a powerful mage and he has already brought so much suffering to this world."

Gronak looked at her calmly, his gaze full of hope. "But we have something he doesn't. Our friendship and our determination. We can rely on each other, just as we always have. Together, we are unstoppable."

Together they left Gronak's house and walked to the edge of the village. Gronak glanced back at the village he loved so much one last time. The houses still rested in the morning mist and only a few birds chirped in the trees. A touch of melancholy rose within him as he knew he would be leaving his home for a long time. Yet, he was also aware that it was necessary to stop Xalis and save the world.

Fiona stepped beside him and smiled encouragingly. She felt Gronak's nervousness and wanted to reassure him. "We will make it, Gronak," she said quietly, her eyes shining with confidence. "We are ready for this journey and will do everything to stop Xalis."

Gronak nodded and placed his hand on her shoulder. "You're right, Fiona. We need to stay strong and keep our goal in sight. Our village, our friends and the entire land are counting on us."

With a determined gaze and full resolve, Gronak and Fiona stepped into the future together, facing the darkness of Xalis and igniting the light of hope in a dark world. They knew their journey would be fraught with dangers and challenges. But they were ready to do whatever it took to defeat evil and save the world from Xalis is dark plans.

With their unique abilities and deep friendship, they were the ultimate team to defy the darkness. They were prepared to face any obstacle in their path. Thus, they set out to explore the unknown and defend the good, hoping their actions would make the world a better place.

Chapter 2: The Journey Begins

Gronak and Fiona had spent their entire lives in the idyllic countryside. But now fate had called them to leave their roots and embark on the path of their destiny. Both were aware that this could be a dangerous adventure. Yet with determined will, they were ready to face the challenges.

In the early morning light, they left their familiar village, their steps leading them northward. The air was filled with a pleasant coolness, while the cloudless, bright blue sky stretched overhead. The morning birds sang their harmonious songs and the grass, gently rustling beneath their feet, swayed in the morning breeze.

After a few hours, they finally reached the edge of the dense forest. The trees stood in close formation, their branches artfully covered with moss and ferns.

Fiona gazed at the majestic trees, their height seeming to touch the sky, as she looked up with a hint of awe. "The forest looks so ancient and mysterious. They say strange things happen here. I wonder what adventures await us."

Gronak turned his gaze to her and smiled. "We'll find out soon enough, Fiona. Be ready for anything." His smile radiated confidence as they took their first step into the shadows of the old forest together.

The two of them moved forward bravely. The forest canopy was dense and the sunlight only occasionally filtered through the leaves. The atmosphere was filled with a slight tension and the surroundings seemed to vibrate with secrets. They were aware that the forest was full of dangers and that they could encounter a trap at any moment.

Suddenly, a deep growl broke the silence, seeming to come from the impenetrable bushes. "Did you hear that, Gronak?" Fiona whispered anxiously, her eyes widening with alertness.

Gronak cautiously peered into the shadows of the bushes. "Yes, it could be a wild animal. We need to be careful and stay alert." His gaze penetrated the darkness as they prepared to confront the forest's mysteries and the potential dangers hidden in its shadows.

The dark forest was a grim and impenetrable place, avoided by many creatures. The trees were so closely packed that only little sunlight penetrated through and an eerie green glow filtered through the canopy. The ground was covered with dense moss and mushrooms, which squeaked and cracked with every step of the travelers.

Fiona whispered, her voice tinged with uncertainty. "I have a very uneasy feeling, as if someone is watching us, Gronak." The forest shadows seemed to close in around them as Gronak held his axe firmly in his hands.

"It could be that we are not alone. Keep your eyes open; we might be surprised at any moment." His tone suggested caution as they moved through the opaque thicket together.

They felt uneasy in the eerie forest, their senses heightened and Gronak's weapon at the ready. The sounds of the wilderness had suddenly become very loud and threatening. The underbrush rustled and they repeatedly heard strange cries and noises that sent shivers down their spines.

Fiona turned to Gronak, her face reflecting a slight fear. "Have you ever seen such a creepy place, Gronak?" The darkness of the forest seemed frightening in her eyes.

Gronak shook his head and replied seriously. "No. This forest is unlike anything I've experienced before. It feels somehow unnatural and very menacing." His gaze pierced the darkness as they ventured further into the opaque depths of the forest.

The darkness of the forest was pierced by a creepy humming, accompanied by a scraping noise that seemed to come from deep within the trees. A ghostly whisper permeated the air as the ground beneath Gronak and Fiona's feet suddenly began to tremble. Hairy legs twitched between the tree trunks and a sinister presence seemed to manifest within the impenetrable tangle of the forest.

"What the hell was that?" Fiona cried, her voice filled with panic as the unusual apparitions threw her senses into turmoil.

Gronak directed his axe toward the sound. "I don't know, but we need to be prepared for whatever awaits us!" The darkness seemed to thicken with an impenetrable aura as they braced themselves to face the invisible dangers of the forest.

Then the horror appeared in full. Monstrous spiders with bodies as large as ox carts. Wrapped in hairy, flexible legs that spread out from their joints in every direction. Their eyes glowed red in the dark and their jaws were so large that one could easily fit a head inside them. The spiders moved smoothly and swiftly toward their prey, ready to tear apart anyone who got in their way with their razor-sharp claws and venomous fangs.

Fiona let out a terrified scream as she spotted the giant spiders and called to her companion. "Those are giant spiders! I hate spiders! What do we do now?"

Gronak prepared for battle, fixing his gaze on the foremost spider. "We fight, Fiona. Stay behind me and let's drive these creatures away!" With firm resolve, he faced the threat as the spiders relentlessly charged at them.

The spiders' legs clattered against Gronak's weapon as he skillfully deflected their attack. Fiona conjured a whirlwind that drove the spiders back, giving them precious time to regroup.

Fiona called to Gronak. "These creatures are really disgusting. We need to kill them quickly before more show up!" Together, they fought against the spiders, skillfully combining their weapons and abilities to keep the creepy creatures at bay.

Gronak fought with all his strength against the spiders. He slammed his axe hard against the ground, creating a shockwave that knocked the spiders to the ground. Fiona seized the opportunity and summoned powerful lightning bolts down upon the spiders. The monsters convulsed and screamed in pain, but they were not yet defeated.

The creatures lunged at Gronak, trying to grab him with their claws, but he managed to dodge and struck them with his axe. Fiona shot fireballs at the spiders, which ignited in flames. The spiders shrieked and writhed in pain, but they still held their ground.

Fiona gasped, exhausted. "I hate spiders and now they're so huge! But we can't give up, Gronak! We can do this together!"

Despite their exhaustion, they continued fighting, each strike and movement accompanied by great effort. The spiders proved stubborn, but after a long and grueling battle, Gronak finally managed to sever the last spider's head. They looked at each other, sweat and spider silk sticking to their bodies, as they took deep breaths. It had been a fierce fight, but they had succeeded together.

Silence gradually returned to the forest, with only the soft rustling of leaves and the chirping of crickets heard. Gronak and Fiona, still tense, sank to the ground and exchanged nods of acknowledgment.

Gronak and Fiona were completely worn out. Their clothes were torn and bloodstained, remnants of the fierce battle with the giant spiders. The need to recover quickly to continue through the opaque forest was urgent.

Fiona began gathering herbs and medicinal plants, while Gronak set up the camp and started a fire. Together, they cleaned their wounds, treated them with healing ointments and carefully bandaged them. Every movement revealed their exhaustion, but their determination to overcome the injuries quickly drove them on.

"Fiona, how are your injuries?" Gronak asked with concern, as he carefully wrapped a bandage around his own bloody arm. Fiona sighed, took a deep breath and replied, "It's getting better, but it will take a while before I'm back to full strength. How about you?"

Gronak grinned, his face showing happiness despite the pain that Fiona was doing okay. "I've been through worse. We need to stay strong, Fiona. The forest surely has more dangers in store for us."

As the fire burned and they had rested a bit, they considered how to continue their journey through the forest. The air was heavy and damp and there was no sign of civilization nearby. The trees around them were dark and eerie and there were sounds they couldn't identify.

Gronak stared into the impenetrable darkness of the forest. "We should move on, Fiona. The longer we stay here, the more dangerous it becomes."

Fiona nodded in agreement. "You're right, Gronak. Let's continue on our way. I hope we don't encounter those disgusting creatures again." The two gathered their weapons and armor, preparing to venture once more into the uncertain darkness of the forest. Their senses were heightened, constantly alert for potential threats. Each step was measured and their eyes searched relentlessly for signs of danger, ready to defend themselves at any moment.

Amidst the quiet forest atmosphere, cries suddenly pierced the air. Gronak and Fiona immediately reacted, turning toward the direction from which the desperate sounds came. Their eyes fell on a man running toward them with bleeding wounds. His face was marked by pain and fear.

The man was completely exhausted as he panic-strickenly cried out, "Help me, the witch is after me!" With his last strength, he collapsed before Gronak and Fiona, who quickly rushed to his side. Fiona knelt beside the injured man and asked with concern, "What happened? Which witch are you talking about?" The man gasped heavily, summoning his remaining strength to respond.

The man looked at Fiona with terrified eyes and spoke in a labored voice. "The Forest Witch, she captured me and my group many days ago. Since then, she has been tormenting us and using dark magic against us. I somehow managed to escape. But before I could free my friends, the witch found me and I had to flee."

Gronak looked seriously at the injured man. "Where is this witch? We will rescue your friends!" The man pointed into the dense forest. "Her house is hidden along that way. You must be careful."

Fiona tended to the man's most severe wounds while Gronak prepared himself. "This should be enough for now. You stay here and we will go to the witch's house," Fiona said firmly. Gronak agreed and they set off in the direction the man had indicated. The forest seemed to grow even more menacing, but they were determined to help the man's friends and defeat the witch.

As they ventured deeper into the forest, they heard the laughter of an old woman. They knew they were in danger and prepared for a fight. Suddenly, they were attacked by a dark figure. It was the old witch of the Dark Forest that the man had spoken of.

The old witch in the Dark Forest was a grim figure who slinked between the shadowy tree trunks. Her face was etched with deep wrinkles and her eyes glowed with an eerie green. Her hair was matted into wild strands and her tattered dress concealed various magical items and dark secrets.

Gronak whispered to Fiona, "That's the witch. She must have been searching for the man. Be careful." Fiona nodded in agreement and replied, "Of course! Watch out for her magic. Dark magic is very dangerous."

The Dark Forest Witch immediately reacted by hurling several fireballs at the two adventurers. Gronak acted instinctively and managed to block the fireball with his shield. Meanwhile, Fiona quickly cast a protective spell that shielded them from the witch's deadly attacks.

Gronak breathed heavily as he exhaled the smoke from the deflected fireball. "That was close. This witch means business, Fiona." The witch, skillfully using the trees and underbrush of the forest, moved swiftly and attacked from ambush. She continued to throw fireballs at Gronak and Fiona.

Fiona quickly realized that the witch was hiding behind a nearby tree. Gronak did not hesitate and charged toward the tree to confront the witch. The branches rustled as Gronak fought his way through the foliage to locate and neutralize the witch.

The witch laughed menacingly and taunted, "You cannot escape me, fools! I am the ruler of this forest and you will feel my power!" With these words, she attacked Gronak with a malevolent curse that weakened him and clouded his senses.

The witch grew furious and screamed, "You will regret standing against me!" In another act of rage, she threw a fireball at Gronak, which this time hit its mark. Gronak was engulfed in flames and roared in pain. Fiona rushed to him, desperately trying to extinguish the flames as the witch laughed triumphantly.

Fiona fought with all her might against the flames and Gronak gritted his teeth to endure the pain. The witch laughed mockingly, but her joy was short-lived. Dark clouds gathered in the sky and rain began to drench the leaves of the trees. Fiona seized the opportunity and concentrated her magic for a powerful attack. A loud thunderclap shook the forest, followed by a lightning flash that struck the witch directly. Her ominous figure began to blur and a pained scream escaped her lips.

Fiona had managed to significantly weaken the witch. Gronak, who had been extinguished by the rain, took the chance to deliver his final blow. "Die, you wretched witch!" he shouted in fury. As Gronak delivered the killing blow, something strange happened. Instead of dying, the witch vanished in a swirling mist that quickly dissipated.

Fiona stared at the spot where the witch had stood. "It seems she was just a phantom." Confusion was in her eyes as the rain continued to wash away the remnants of the battle.

Still, Fiona sensed a magical presence in the area and they knew the danger was not over. The raindrops splashed on their tattered clothing and the forest seemed to glow with a ghostly light. They decided to find the witch and finish her off for good.

"We should continue searching in the forest," Gronak suggested, casting his gaze through the gloomy trees. His breath steamed in the cool air and his muscles were tense from the previous battle.

Fiona nodded in agreement. "Yes, we can't give up. The witch must be hiding her true form somewhere here." Rain dripped from her nose as they made their way through the forest, searching for the witch.

They followed a dark path deeper into the forest and eventually came to an old, dilapidated house. The witch's house loomed deep in the dark forest, as if it had been swallowed by the darkness itself. The house's exterior gave off a creepy and morbid impression, making anyone who saw it shudder.

Gronak looked at the witch's house, its dark contours looming before them and muttered, "This must be the place where the witch practices her dark deeds." His gaze pierced the forest's darkness as he took in the house's grim aura.

Fiona nodded, her eyes cautiously fixed on the house. "Let's be careful. Who knows what traps await us here?" A hint of tension was in her voice, ready for any challenge that might lurk in the mysterious witch's house.

The building was marked by time and seemed to have stood in this enchanted forest for eons. Its weathered wooden planks were covered in thick moss and vines, wrapping around the house like green shackles. The moss seemed to be swallowing the building, pulling it back into the earth, giving the house an eerie greenish glow.

Gronak surveyed the surroundings carefully, his eyes narrowed at the dark witch's house. "The house looks as grim as the forest itself. I hope we find the witch and the abducted travelers here." A slight hint of concern was in his voice as he analyzed the dark contours of the house, searching for clues about the witch's malevolent activities.

The tall chimney of the house loomed threateningly into the sky and dense, gray smoke was rising from its weathered chimney. This smoke seemed to indicate that dark rituals were being performed or dangerous potions were being brewed.

Fiona looked worriedly at Gronak. "The witch is here. I can feel it. Let's proceed with caution."

The windows of the witch's house were small and dirty and their curtains were torn and discolored. It seemed as though dark secrets and eerie activities were hidden behind these windows, things no one should see.

Gronak whispered to Fiona. "Let's go in, Fiona. We don't know what awaits us inside, so please be prepared for anything." With cautious steps, they approached the entrance of the gloomy witch's house, ready for what they would find within.

The house's door was made of massive, weathered wood and looked like the entrance to another world. Above the doorframe hung a rusty iron sign bearing strange symbols and signs that only the witch herself could decipher. Gronak took a deep breath. "Ready, Fiona? We are about to enter the heart of darkness."

The witch's house radiated an ominous aura that shrouded the surrounding forest in a mysterious darkness. It was a place of terror and power where the witch plotted her dark schemes and practiced dark magic. A place only the bravest would enter and even they did so only in the direst necessity.

The interior of the small witch's house was as gloomy and eerie as its exterior. As Gronak and Fiona entered, a world of secrets and magic opened up before them, permeating the space and creating a mysterious atmosphere.

Fiona looked at the countless bookshelves in the room. "These books look very old and valuable. We should search through them, Gronak." The dim light of the flickering candles cast shadowy shapes on the dusty book spines, which seemed full of knowledge and perhaps also dangers.

Gronak scanned the shelves, his fingers carefully gliding over the dusty covers. "Perhaps we'll find useful clues about the witch or other valuable things here." The silence in the room was only interrupted by the faint rustling of pages as they began exploring the mysterious writings and searching for answers and possible solutions.

The room they were in was small, but it seemed filled with countless bookshelves. The shelves reached up to the ceiling and were crammed full of dusty, outdated books dealing with witchcraft, spells and dark rituals. Many of the books were written in a language completely foreign to the two adventurers and their pages were yellowed and worn from many years of use.

Fiona searched through a shelf and pulled out an old, dusty book. Her fingers brushed over the yellowed pages as she murmured, "It looks like this is a book on healing magic. The knowledge could be very useful to us in the future." The writing in the book seemed to preserve centuries of secrets and Fiona eagerly showed Gronak the book.

They exchanged their findings and continued their search. Everywhere in the room, dense cobwebs spanned from the ceiling, making the space even more eerie. The fine threads shimmered in the pale light of the few candles placed on weathered tables and shelves, giving the room a ghostly ambiance.

Fiona spotted an old chest hidden under a table. She carefully opened it and found strange potions and herbs inside. With shining eyes, Fiona said excitedly, "This chest contains magical potions that could help us in our fight against the witch." Gronak nodded in agreement. "Well done, Fiona. We should take everything that might be useful."

In the center of the room stood a large black cauldron, suspended on a rusty tripod over an open flame. The cauldron was bubbling and hissing and a mysterious mist was rising from its interior. What was being cooked inside was undefinable, but the stench rising from the cauldron was acrid and unpleasant.

Gronak cast a skeptical glance at the cauldron and wrinkled his nose. "It looks like a magical potion. But with that smell, it's likely a poison." The fumes rising from the cauldron were pungent, making the danger in the air almost palpable.

Strange objects and artifacts that seemed to testify to unimaginable power were hanging on the walls. Skulls, ornate candleholders and cursed amulets adorned the dark walls of the room. The faint light of the candles cast eerie shadows on the morbid decorations.

Fiona carefully examined an ornate skull. "These objects might possess magical powers. But I sense dark energies emanating from them. We should stay away from them." The grim atmosphere of the room intensified her warning.

Gronak looked at the artifacts and nodded in agreement. "We should really be cautious and not underestimate any of these items. Who knows what the witch has done with them. Her dark dealings might lurk in each of these objects." Awareness of the potential danger sharpened their senses as they continued to explore the mysterious room.

The two adventurers thoroughly searched the small witch's house and it seemed that every corner and crevice revealed another dark secret. Gronak accidentally stepped on a loose floorboard while inspecting a corner of the room. With a firm pull, he revealed a hidden cellar door. The door creaked open and a cold, musty draft met them.

Without hesitation, they descended and found themselves in a dark, winding secret passage. The walls of the passage were made of weathered stone and filled with a damp, clammy atmosphere. The passage led them deeper into the bowels of the house and their way was lit only by flickering candles set in wall niches. The faint sounds of the forest gradually disappeared as they immersed themselves in the silence of the underground.

Eventually, they reached a massive wooden door. As they opened it, an astounding sight unfolded before them. The room was enormous and extended far beyond what they could easily discern. It was lit only by a few candles that flickered faintly.

Fiona whispered, awed by the size of the room, "This is incredible, Gronak. This room is huge." Gronak nodded but remained alert, looking ahead with concern. "Yes and it's full of magical items and strange artifacts. We must be careful." His eyes scanned the room, searching for potential dangers or clues about the witch.

The walls were covered with countless shelves, on which magical artifacts, alchemical potions and mysterious objects were arranged in disordered fashion. The dim light from a few flickering lanterns revealed sparkling crystals, ornate boxes and ancient scrolls. Each shelf seemed to tell its own story and the air was filled with a hint of mysterious magic.

Fiona examined the shelves closely. "There are so many things here. I can't even imagine how long it must have taken to collect all this and how many must have suffered for it." Her gaze wandered over the numerous items, some of which shone in gilded boxes while others were hidden in dark shadows.

Everywhere were cages containing the remains of monsters and creatures, whose sight would frighten even the bravest. Fiona could almost feel the suffering in their empty eye sockets and a shiver ran down her spine.

Gronak said with a grim expression, "These creatures were abused by the witch for her dark purposes. We need to ensure no one else suffers under her control." His gaze lingered heavily on the cages and his resolve to put an end to the witch's deeds was palpable.

In the corners of the room, bony remains were stacked as if used by the witch as part of her eerie rituals. The remains gave the impression that this room had been used for dark purposes for centuries. The musty smell of old decay permeated the air and the grim ambiance heightened the dark shadows that lay over the history of this mysterious place.

Fiona shuddered and felt slightly nauseous at the sight. "This is atrocious. This witch has done terrible things and taken so many lives. But I don't see the travelers anywhere. Perhaps they are further down the passage." Her gaze swept over the cages containing the mutilated remains and she was filled with deep sympathy for the victims.

Gronak firmly gripped his sword and whispered to Fiona, "Over there, Fiona. I think there's something back there." His gaze was fixed on a dark corridor leading deeper into the room. The darkness seemed to intensify there and an ominous crackling filled the air. The two adventurers exchanged a concerned look before making their way to further investigate the dark magic and secrets of this mysterious place.

In the distance, at the end of the room, they spotted the witch. She stood before a large, ancient cauldron suspended over an open flame, brewing strange potions. When she noticed them, she turned around. Her eyes glowed with an eerie green light and a malevolent smile appeared on her altered face.

"Look at that. What little rats have sneaked into my house?" the witch cackled into the room. "You must be the adventurers who defeated my phantom," she continued. The witch laughed wickedly and stared deep into Gronak and Fiona's eyes. "I hope you realize what predicament you're in. You will never leave this place."

The atmosphere in the room was tense and the confrontation with the witch seemed inevitable. Gronak and Fiona had ventured into this dangerous place to defeat the witch once and for all. They were ready to conquer this dark place and its sinister inhabitant.

Fiona whispered to Gronak, "Be ready and watch out for her magic. This will be no easy fight." Gronak nodded confidently. "We will defeat her, Fiona. For all those who have suffered under her dark power."

Gronak took a step forward and said in a firm voice, "Witch, your dark deeds have caused enough havoc. We will stop you and free the land from your malevolent schemes!"

The witch, however, grinned and drank a strange green potion from a vial. "So you want to eliminate me? Don't make me laugh. I will kill you and gnaw your flesh from your bones." Her laughter was shrill and piercing, while dark energy seemed to surround her.

Fiona watched the witch closely. "Be on your guard, Gronak. Her magic has become stronger after the potion." The witch's grim aura intensified and her eyes glowed with an eerie green. Gronak drew his sword, ready for the impending battle, as the tension in the air became almost palpable.

Suddenly, the witch began to change. Her form grew grotesque, larger and more distorted. Her limbs stretched out, becoming longer and more skeletal, covered with bizarre blisters and warts. Her skin seemed to harden and sharp claws extended from her fingers. A foul-smelling mist enveloped her as she began to murmur in an ancient, unintelligible language. Ominous roots shot up from the ground, their twisted forms reaching for Gronak and Fiona as if they had a life of their own.

The roots hissed and creaked as they approached the adventurers. Some had thorny tips to inflict additional damage. The witch's dark aura seemed to merge with the ancient magic of the forest and nature itself appeared to turn against the intruders.

Gronak swung his sword at the attacking roots. But even when he severed them, they seemed to regenerate. The roots coiled around his legs, holding him in an iron grip.

Fiona reacted swiftly, conjuring a powerful fire spell that set the roots ablaze. "Burn, you cursed roots!" she shouted. The fire hissed and crackled and for a moment, the danger seemed to be averted.

However, the witch skillfully used this distraction. In a dark ritual, she cursed Fiona, severely weakening her magic. Fiona gasped as she felt the sudden loss of power. "My magic has been weakened, Gronak!" she warned, her eyes full of concern for the impending fight.

The witch laughed maliciously. "You wanted to stop me? You bothersome rats will die here!" Her voice echoed through the gloomy room, accompanied by a sinister cackle.

Filled with rage, Gronak charged at the witch head-on. With all his strength, he swung his sword at her. But the witch focused her dark magic and unleashed a massive pressure wave that struck Gronak like an invisible blow. The warrior was thrown across the room and crashed into a shelf with a pained cry. Books fell to the ground before the shelf collapsed and buried Gronak.

Fiona screamed in distress. "Gronak! Gronak, are you okay?" Her voice was piercing, filled with fear for her companion.

Gronak struggled painfully from under the debris of the collapsed shelf, his body marked by severe, bleeding wounds. Every breath seemed to make him gasp and moan in pain, but he kept his gaze fixed firmly on the witch.

The witch laughed again, a diabolical melody echoing through the room. "You're quite resilient," she mocked. "I could certainly do some interesting experiments with you. But you've caused me too much trouble and that ends now!"

The witch began to channel her magical energy and a powerful fireball manifested in front of her hands. The air around her crackled with magic and the witch's dark intentions seemed to unfold within the burning sphere, a threatening glow that filled the room.

Gronak took the initiative. His voice cut through the silence of the room as he shouted, "Fiona, throw me some of the potions we found!" His words sounded panicked as he kept his gaze fixed on the witch.

Fiona didn't hesitate for a moment. With deft movements, she reached into her belt, pulled out some of the mysterious vials and threw them with practiced precision towards Gronak. The vials glinted in the dim candlelight as they flew through the air.

Gronak caught the vials skillfully and could almost feel the magic pulsing within them. A surge of hope filled him as he realized these vials might be their last chance to defeat the witch.

With impressive strength, Gronak hurled the potions at the fireball the witch had conjured. The vials sliced through the air and struck the flames precisely, resulting in an immediate and massive explosion. A blinding flash of light filled the room, accompanied by a deafening roar that made the air tremble.

The force of the explosion hurled the witch back with great intensity and a bone-chilling scream erupted from her mouth, echoing through the room. Sparks flew in all directions as the witch's magical energy was overwhelmed by the power of the explosion.

The walls of the room shook as the explosion unleashed a staggering force. Dust and debris swirled through the air, enveloping the room in a dense cloud.

Gronak and Fiona were caught in the relentless force of the explosion, thrown backward and crashing heavily onto the hard floor. The dull sound of the impact resonated through the room.

Gronak gasped heavily, feeling the effects of the explosion in every fiber of his body. "That was close, Fiona. I thought that was it. This witch was truly a tough opponent."

As the smoke slowly cleared, the witch became visible amid the devastation. Her body was now marked by burns and wounds. She appeared severely weakened and struggled to stay on her feet.

Fiona looked at the injured witch, her eyes analyzing the situation. "She survived the explosion, but she looks badly hurt, Gronak. This might be our chance."

The once-powerful smile of the witch had vanished, replaced by an expression of defeat. Fiona sensed that this could be the decisive moment.

Gronak approached the witch with a grim look, his hand tightly gripping the hilt of his sword. Fiona began to feel the witch's curse weakening. She started to regain her magical strength, preparing to use it in the crucial moment.

Gronak directed his words at the witch. "It's over, witch. Your dark deeds end here and now." The tension in the air was palpable as the confrontation between light and darkness approached its climax.

The witch, though gravely injured, stared at them with a last spark of madness in her green, glowing eyes. "You will regret my wrath, you little maggots!"

Filled with deep fury, Gronak relentlessly attacked the witch. His sword sliced through the air with precise movements, landing several good hits. But the witch, despite her injuries, did not retreat and struck wildly. Her powers were still unbroken.

Amidst the battle, Gronak shouted at the witch. "That won't help you now, monster! We're going to bring you down!" His words echoed through the room as he relentlessly struck the witch.

But the witch did not give up. With a malevolent grin, she generated another sudden shockwave, sweeping through the air with great force and hurling Gronak away with brutal violence. The impact was devastating and Gronak found himself severely injured on the ground, while the witch triumphed in her madness.

Fiona, visibly weakened, glared angrily at the witch. However, when she noticed a crack in the stone ceiling caused by the previous explosion, she acted instinctively and cast an ice spell to fill and expand the crack with ice. Fiona roared at the witch in fury, "This is your end, you damned monster, you won't harm anyone ever again!"

The ceiling could not withstand the enormous pressure exerted by the ice and huge boulders crashed down on the witch with a thunderous noise. In that devastating moment, the witch realized her hopeless situation as she looked up. But it was too late. The witch was struck by the falling rocks and screamed in pain. She lay on the ground, buried under the weight of the stones and seemed defeated.

Gronak gasped heavily and tried to get up, while Fiona sank exhausted to the ground. With his last strength, he slowly moved towards the witch. The witch, in her desperate state, pleaded for her life. "Spare me, please! I will never harm anyone again, I promise you." But Gronak, filled with an unshakable resolve, ignored her pleading words and completed his mission. He raised his sword and struck the witch in the head, bringing her dark deeds to a final end.

Gronak went over to Fiona, who was exhausted and kneeling. The room was filled with a strange mix of triumph and exhaustion. Gronak grinned at their victory.

"We did it together, Fiona. This witch will never cause harm again."

Fiona, relieved by the successful fight, nodded in agreement. "Yes, but it was a tough battle. I'm glad we got through it." She stood up, her muscles aching from the intense fight, but a sense of satisfaction flowed through her.

Fiona looked around the room in bewilderment. "Now we need to find the travelers. I hope they're alright." Together, they decided to search the room for clues about where the prisoners might be.

As they inspected the remains of the witch and the magical artifacts in the room, Gronak discovered a door in one of the dark corners. His attention was immediately drawn to it. "Fiona, look over there. That could be the way to the prisoners."

Gronak and Fiona entered the room behind the door. But what they saw there took their breath away. A horrific sight unfolded before their eyes. The room was filled with corpses, both of creatures and humans, that the witch had used for her cruel experiments.

The remains of beings of various kinds and origins were scattered across the cold stone floor. The stench of decay hung heavily in the air and Fiona felt nauseated by the dreadful sight. "This is abhorrent; I've never seen anything so horrible," she whispered in disgust.

Gronak looked around the room with frustration. "We're unfortunately too late. No one survived." His voice sounded grim and his gaze swept across the horrific scene. The witch had clearly left a trail of destruction that had consumed all who crossed her dark path.

Gronak and Fiona left the crypt, filled with the dark memories of the witch and stepped back into the night. Outside the witch's house stood the traveler, who had regained his strength thanks to Fiona's herbs. His gaze was anxious and full of expectation as he addressed the two adventurers.

"Did you kill the witch and what about my friends?" the traveler asked with a hint of hope in his voice.

Gronak shook his head regretfully. "We killed the witch. But your companions, unfortunately, did not make it." His words were tinged with a mix of sorrow and resignation. It was clear that the news was a heavy blow for the traveler.

The traveler bowed his head in sadness, while Fiona empathetically added, "We're sorry we couldn't get here in time to help them." The traveler was visibly affected by the news. "I understand. But thank you for killing that wretched creature and avenging my friends."

After a brief moment of silence, the three decided to raze the witch's house to the ground. Together, they set the witch's house on fire. The flames illuminated the night and consumed the grim building that had once been a place of terror.

As the embers slowly died down, the traveler bid farewell to Gronak and Fiona. "Thank you again. I will make sure that my friends stories are not forgotten. May they now rest in peace." With those words, the traveler went on his way, while the two adventurers turned back to the dark forest.

Gronak and Fiona continued on their path, their goal clear: to stop Xalis. The darkness of the forest surrounded them, but their determination remained unshaken. Together, they walked through the shadows to tackle the next phase of their adventure. The path ahead was still unknown. But they knew their journey was far from over.

Chapter 3: The Crystal Cave

Gronak and Fiona wandered through the dense forests, their steps accompanied by the silence of the woods. The trees seemed to lean over them, as if warning the two adventurers.

"Fiona, these woods are really eerie," Gronak said, casting a wary glance at the surrounding trees. "I have the feeling that someone is watching us," Fiona replied, keeping her hand firmly on the strap of her bag.

Eventually, they reached a gloomy cave hidden deep within the rugged mountains. The rock walls surrounding the cave were rough and uneven and the stone seemed to be made of dark gray granite. The silence was oppressive. Only the faint dripping of water flowing from the cave broke it. The cave itself appeared dark and oppressive. The darkness within seemed threatening and the air smelled damp and musty.

Fiona wrinkled her nose in disgust. "Ugh, this stench is really terrible."

The massive cave entrance was completely surrounded by a thick spider's web hanging from the ceiling. The eerie shadows seemed to move in the darkness and ominous sounds reached their ears.

"Are you also wondering if we should fight our way through this spider's web?" Fiona asked worriedly, examining the web more closely.

Gronak furrowed his brow as he surveyed the surroundings. "It seems like we have no other choice. Be prepared to react to whatever awaits us inside."

Gronak and Fiona felt a sinister aura around the cave, as if they were surrounded by something evil. Yet, they felt an inexplicable fascination pulling them irresistibly into the depths of the cave, as if an invisible hand was guiding them. With fascination, they continued forward, ready to uncover the mystery of the darkness.

As they approached, they heard a loud growl and grunt from inside the cave. They knew they had to be extremely cautious, as a dangerous creature might be lurking within. Slowly, Gronak drew his weapon, ready for a possible fight.

As they cautiously entered the cave, the biting stench of rotting flesh and moldy fruit hit their noses immediately. The air was thick and unpleasant and Fiona had to suppress a gag reflex. "This is really disgusting," she whispered softly. "I hope the stench doesn't get any worse."

The darkness in the cave was suffocating and they could hardly see anything. But the growling and grunting of a creature was unmistakable and echoed off the rock walls. With every step, it felt as though they were plunging deeper into a nightmarish world.

Fiona pressed close to Gronak and whispered to him, her voice barely more than a faint murmur. "We're not alone here," she said, peering tensely into the cave's darkness. Her eyes searched for movement while her heart raced in her chest.

The ground was uneven and littered with sharp rocks, making movement extremely difficult. Their feet stumbled over stones and creaked on dry branches. The darkness seemed to engulf them and they had to rely on their sense of touch to avoid falling.

Suddenly, a torch flared up. Its flickering light revealed the outline of a massive creature emerging from the shadow of the cave wall. Fiona recoiled in shock, her eyes widening in horror. "Gronak," she gasped, "there's a giant ogre!"

Gronak reacted immediately, tightening his grip on his sword as he faced the beast. "We can't back down now, Fiona," he said. "Let's defeat this monster and clear our path."

The ogre towered over them, at least three times the size of an average man. Its skin was covered in scars, most of which seemed to be from battles fought over the years. Its eyes glowed an eerie red, as if it could breathe fire and its teeth were yellow and broken, giving it a terrifying grin. It wore torn trousers and a vest made of animal hide, looking as wild and unkempt as the ogre itself. Its enormous hands were smeared with dirt and dried blood.

The tension in the cave was palpable as Gronak readied his sword for battle. Fiona began to raise her hands in an intricate gesture to prepare her magic.

The ogre approached menacingly, its massive body moving with a thunderous rumble through the cave. Its enormous fists swung through the air like sledgehammers, casting powerful shadows on the uneven cave floor.

"Fiona, cover my back!" Gronak shouted over the noise, his voice resolute and battle-ready. He faced the ogre bravely, his sword firm and ready in his hands.

Gronak barely dodged in time as the ogre's colossal fist slammed into the ground, leaving a crater that sent stones and dust flying. The impact's shockwave even made their bones shiver.

"Fiona, watch out for its blows! They could crush us," Gronak yelled, his voice piercing and filled with concern as he prepared for a counterattack. His grip on the sword tightened, muscles tensed and ready to face the ogre.

Fiona unleashed a powerful fire spell that struck the ogre. The fire seared through its skin and the ogre roared in pain as smoke and fumes billowed into the cave. Its massive body glowed with heat and it flailed wildly to extinguish the flames. But the fire, fueled by Fiona's mighty magic, raged on unabated.

"Great hit! That landed! We almost have him!" Gronak shouted triumphantly, his face set in a determined expression as he launched another attack.

The ogre swung its arm again and this time it landed a powerful blow on Gronak. He staggered back, but his courage remained unshaken. Adrenaline pumped through his veins as he quickly recovered, gripping his sword tightly and charging once more at the enraged ogre.

Fiona did not hesitate and continued her magic. "We can do this, Gronak! We must not relent!" Every fire spell she hurled at the ogre was a fiery assault. The flames swept over the ogre and he seemed trapped in the blaze that bathed the cave in a hellish glow. The thunder of the fire spells mingled with the ogre's wild roars as it tried to put out the roaring flames consuming its massive body.

Unfazed by the heat and the burning flames, Gronak deftly ducked under a devastating blow from the ogre. His body moved like a dancer as he elegantly avoided the ogre's attack.

With a lightning-fast maneuver, Gronak drove his sword deep into the creature's body. The metallic clang and the ogre's muffled roar echoed like a grim response through the cave, followed by a dull thud as the ogre fell to the ground.

"That was fantastic, Gronak!" Fiona praised. Her voice full of admiration as she tirelessly continued to use her fire magic to keep the ogre at bay.

The ogre roared louder, its body convulsing in pain as it desperately tried to strike Gronak with its massive fists. "We mustn't let up, Gronak! He won't give up easily!" Fiona shouted tensely, launching another fire spell at the ogre to weaken it further.

Gronak deftly dodged the ogre's wild swings, his grip firm on his sword. The fight was a breathtaking interplay of skill and raw strength. "We need to find a way to defeat him once and for all, Fiona. Keep him occupied as long as you can," Gronak replied, continuing to attack the ogre.

Fiona realized that the time had come for the decisive blow. With a powerful lightning strike, she stunned the ogre, which seemed momentarily paralyzed.

"Now, Gronak! This is your chance!" Fiona shouted excitedly, watching as Gronak prepared for the final attack. His eyes were filled with determination and his sword ready to finally overcome the ogre.

Gronak seized the opportunity and drove his sword with all his might deep into the ogre's torso. The giant roared one last time, its body trembling in agony before collapsing to the ground. The impact was so tremendous that the ground quaked and stones fell from the ceiling. Gronak and Fiona stood there, breathing heavily as they looked at the fallen ogre.

"We did it together, Fiona," Gronak said, his breath labored and his voice marked by exhaustion, but his face shining with satisfaction.

Fiona nodded in agreement, her eyes glistening with pride and her smile radiant. "Yes, Gronak," she responded gently, her voice full of conviction. "Together, we are unbeatable."

They had won the brutal battle, but it had been a grueling and dangerous dance with fate. The exhausted bodies of Gronak and Fiona trembled with fatigue, their clothes soaked with sweat and blood.

"Fiona, that was incredibly close," Gronak panted, wiping the sweat from his forehead, his breath still heavy and irregular.

Fiona nodded in agreement, her lungs burning from the effort as she responded breathlessly. "I definitely agree, but we made it. The damned beast is dead." A hint of relief and triumph was in her voice as she slowly straightened, her muscles protesting painfully with every movement.

The darkness of the cave surrounded them as they got back on their feet and looked at each other, the triumph over the beast still in their eyes. But then, just as they thought the danger had passed, the unexpected happened.

A loud, rumbling noise broke the silence, followed by a tremor that made the ground beneath their feet shake. It was as if the mountain itself were awakening and the cave seemed to quake as though it were about to collapse at any moment. An overwhelming terror surged through their bodies, making their hearts race as time seemed to stand still for an infinite moment.

"Damn it, what's happening?" Fiona shouted, her voice filled with panic as she desperately searched for answers in the darkening cave. Every sound seemed more threatening than the last and the certainty that they were trapped in the midst of a new danger pressed relentlessly into their thoughts.

Gronak and Fiona knew they couldn't waste a second. They ran as fast as their exhausted legs would carry them, but the way back to the entrance was now blocked by fallen rocks. Panic surged within them as they were forced to delve deeper into the cave, searching for another way out.

"We need to find another way, Fiona! Quickly!" Gronak shouted, his voice urgent as they rushed forward, their steps hurried and uncertain.

The darkness in the cave was so dense that they could barely see their own hands in front of their faces. A suffocating sense of dread enveloped them and their fingers clung to each other as they desperately searched for an exit, each breath filled with fear and effort.

"Can you see anything, Gronak?" Fiona asked with a trembling voice. Her hands touched the cold rock walls in search of any hint of direction in the darkness.

Suddenly, a massive boulder fell from the ceiling and crashed down directly towards Gronak. Fiona's heartbeat quickened and she screamed, pulling Gronak aside at the last moment to save his life.

"Gronak, are you okay?" Fiona called out anxiously, her gaze searching for signs of injury, her hands trembling with adrenaline and fear as they both slowly recovered from the shock.

Gronak breathed heavily, his body shaken by the near brush with death, but he nodded slowly. "Thanks, Fiona," he managed to say. "That was damn close." His voice sounded brittle with relief as he took his friend's hand and slowly stood up, the darkness around them seeming even more menacing and unreal than before.

As they hurried forward, the mountain's rumbling still echoed in their ears and the ground continued to shake beneath their feet. They reached a junction and without hesitation, Gronak took the path to the right. It was an instinct, a fleeting intuition that guided them.

But it proved to be the wrong choice. The path ended in a gloomy dead end and the terrible realization hit them like a lightning bolt. The rumbling of the collapse was getting closer.

"Gronak, we're stuck! We can't go back; the way is already collapsed!" Fiona cried, her voice full of panic. She closed her eyes and focused on her last magical reserves. "I have to find a way to get us out of here," she whispered to herself. Her inner strength surged and with a desperate effort, she fired a powerful magical beam at the wall, hoping to break through to the outside world.

The wall trembled and shattered, just moments before the cave would have engulfed them. The sounds of the collapse grew louder and louder and the cave around them seemed to be collapsing with a tremendous crash. The ground seemed to tear apart and Gronak and Fiona suddenly found themselves in free fall.

"Damn it, we're falling!" Gronak shouted, his voice filled with fear.

The darkness swallowed their screams as they plummeted at breathtaking speed. The rush of adrenaline and the pitch-black void made their senses whirl.

In a moment of unreality, they finally landed in another large cave. The impact was harsh, making their bodies shudder. Yet, they were fortunate in their misfortune. For they didn't land on solid ground, but in a large underground lake.

The icy water surrounded them and Fiona struggled desperately to reach the surface. Her heart pounded wildly in her chest and the darkness of the water seemed to suffocate her.

"Gronak, I can't hold on! Help me!" she thought, her emotions filled with panic and exhaustion as she gasped for air and her lungs burned.

But Gronak was there, his muscles tensed with adrenaline as he reached for her. Together, they managed to reach the surface, gasping and drenched by the icy flood. "We made it, Fiona! We're safe," Gronak said, relieved, pulling her to the shore.

As they finally reached the shore, they collapsed on the ground, exhausted. The cold seeped deep into their bones and they struggled to breathe. But they were alive and that was all that mattered.

"That was really close, Gronak. I thought I was going to drown! Thank you so much for getting me out of there," Fiona said with a trembling smile, her teeth chattering from the cold, but her eyes shining with gratitude.

Gronak smiled back tiredly but relieved. "I'm glad you're okay. I was really scared for you," he confessed quietly as he hugged Fiona tightly.

"Who could have expected the whole cave to collapse like that?" Fiona murmured in astonishment. As she snuggled close to Gronak, she was grateful for his presence and unwavering support in this life-threatening situation.

As Gronak and Fiona oriented themselves in the new surroundings, they were overwhelmed by a scene that left them speechless. The cave they had landed in was a true natural wonderland. Everywhere they looked, breathtaking crystals of various shapes and colors stretched out. "Fiona, look at this! It's incredible," Gronak whispered, his eyes wide with wonder.

The cave's ceiling was adorned with massive amethysts that shimmered in purple and reflected the surrounding light. The walls sparkled in a mosaic of emeralds, sapphires and rubies, as if created by a magical artist. The crystal-clear reflections on the surface of the lake bathed the entire scene in a magical, shimmering glow.

"Fiona, I've never seen anything so beautiful. It's like a gift from nature," Gronak said, his voice filled with awe.

Fiona could only agree as she admired the magical surroundings. "Yes, Gronak, this is truly unique. We've found something truly special here."

The crystals seemed almost alive, as if they were telling the story of millennia while they had slowly grown. A sense of awe and admiration overtook Gronak and Fiona in the face of this natural beauty. The danger they had just escaped faded into the background for a precious moment as they gazed in fascination at the shimmering formations.

It was as if they had plunged into another world, a world where time seemed to stand still and the beauty of nature was experienced in its purest form. In this cave, they felt

53

both tiny and infinitely happy to be witnesses to such a wonder.

But necessity soon brought them back to their senses. They knew they didn't have time to linger in this wondrous crystal cave, no matter how fascinating it was.

"Gronak, we need to move on. We can look at the crystals later, but first, we need to warm up," Fiona said, looking at the glittering crystals.

Gronak nodded in agreement. "You're right, Fiona. Our priority is to get out of here alive."

Together, they set up a makeshift camp on the shore of the sparkling lake. With the few supplies they had, they prepared a simple meal to strengthen their exhausted bodies and rest.

"This isn't the worst place to spend a night," Gronak remarked as he skillfully arranged the wood for the campfire and lit it. The warm flicker illuminated the dark surroundings and provided warmth.

Fiona nodded in agreement as she warmed herself by the fire. "Yes, you're probably right," she agreed and made a small joke to break the tension of the past events. "It's at least safer than the cave we were in before. Though I must admit, that adventure also had its charms," she added with a soft laugh.

The camp was rudimentary but served its purpose. They used some of the larger crystals as natural light sources, casting a gentle, soothing light in the cave. The soft rippling of the lake and the occasional glitter of the crystals on the cave walls accompanied their conversations and thoughts.

The next morning, they awoke from a peaceful sleep, their bodies refreshed and ready to escape the cave and return to freedom.

"Fiona, we need to find a way out before we run into an ogre or something even worse," Gronak said seriously as he prepared and checked his equipment.

Fiona nodded in agreement as she sat up and stretched. "Yes, you're right," she agreed and added, "We should continue on our way and hope to find a safe exit. Caves like these can be like giant mazes, but together we'll find a way out."

As they moved through a narrow tunnel, they suddenly heard metallic noises coming from the darkness. The sounds were unfamiliar and eerie and they exchanged worried glances.

"Gronak, do you hear that too? It sounds like someone is hitting metal," Fiona whispered quietly.

With weapons drawn, they continued on their path, the tension in the air palpable as they prepared to face another uncertain danger.

The curious and unsettling noises eventually led Gronak and Fiona to a significantly larger chamber within the cave. As they entered, they were met with a scene that seemed straight out of another world. In this expansive room, numerous mining machines and equipment were meticulously arranged.

"What the hell is this? Where did these machines come from?" Gronak muttered as he inspected the strange contraptions.

Fiona stared in disbelief at the apparatuses. "I have no idea, Gronak. But this doesn't look like it's naturally here; it looks like mining equipment."

There were massive drills with rotating blades ready to dig deep into the rock. Conveyor belts snaked through the room, seemingly poised to transport valuable resources. The walls were lined with shelves full of tools and gear, including pickaxes, shovels and heavy mining hammers.

The floor itself was littered with a variety of ores and minerals, from gleaming silver to gold. But the most striking detail was a gigantic pile of sparkling crystals, stacked in various shapes and colors. The light from the crystals reflected off the metallic surfaces of the mining machines and equipment, bathing the room in a mysterious glow.

The scene in this room resembled a treasure from a long-forgotten era when miners sought the earth's riches.

"This is incredible, Gronak. I've never seen anything like this," Fiona whispered as she admired the astonishing setup.

Gronak nodded in agreement. "Yes, these crystals and metals are truly impressive. But who could be mining so deep in this cave?"

The two adventurers couldn't help but marvel at the brilliance of the crystals, even as they wondered who was responsible for the mining activities in this deep cave and what the metallic noises were about.

Fiona excitedly grabbed Gronak's arm and pointed ahead. "Gronak, look! Those are dwarves!" she whispered excitedly, her eyes shining with the thrill of the unexpected encounter.

The dwarves moved like busy ants around their work, their figures standing out clearly against the backdrop of sparkling crystals and metals decorating the cave walls. The metallic clinking of their tools mixed with their animated voices as they excitedly discussed their plans.

"Probably the dwarves are responsible for all of this," Gronak said, his eyes widening in surprise at the unexpected encounter.

The scene was both fascinating and surreal as the industrious dwarves worked in their natural setting, surrounded by the rich treasures of the earth they so passionately mined.

Fiona couldn't contain her curiosity any longer and cautiously approached the group of dwarves. "Excuse us, gentlemen. We happened to stumble in here. Could you explain what's going on and how we can get out of here?"

The dwarves, gathered around the mining machinery in the impressive cave chamber, presented a fascinating sight. These stout beings exuded an aura of experience and determination.

The dwarves had muscular bodies and rough skin from years of hard work underground. Their beards ranged from shining white to deep black and were as significant as their weapons. They wore practical clothing and heavy leather boots suited for the cave terrain.

Their faces were marked with character and their eyes, surrounded by deep wrinkles, radiated strength and wisdom. They had broad, angular noses and strong jaws, indicating their stubbornness and survival instinct.

Their movements spoke of decades of mining experience, as their hands skillfully handled their tools. Overall, they emanated toughness, wisdom and a mysterious aura that made them captivating in the underground world.

The dwarves were visibly surprised by the sudden visit from Gronak and Fiona. One of the dwarves, stocky with a beard that almost reached the ground, stepped forward and asked with a mix of suspicion and curiosity, "Who are you and how the hell did you get here?"

Gronak stood beside Fiona and stepped forward confidently. "We're not here by choice. We ended up stranded in this cave and are trying to find a way out," he explained calmly.

Gronak and Fiona quickly explained their unusual situation, recounting their fierce battle with the ogre and the subsequent fall into the cave. They emphasized that they had no ill intentions and had no desire to intrude on the dwarves' mining operations. Instead, they stressed that they were desperately seeking a way out to escape the collapsing cave and return to the surface.

The dwarves, deeply impressed by Gronak and Fiona's story, withdrew for a brief, subdued consultation. In the flickering light of the crystals, the seriousness of their deliberations was reflected on their faces and it seemed as though the dwarves' already heavy beards grew even heavier with contemplation.

Recognizing the sincerity and urgency in Gronak and Fiona's eyes, the atmosphere among the dwarves became more reflective. Their heavy beards moved in a slow, deliberate rhythm as if they were making a significant decision for the future.

Finally, the leader of the dwarves stepped forward and introduced himself to the two strangers. His appearance radiated authority and his beard, which reached halfway down his chest, spoke of a long history and experience.

"Hello, I'm Hemli, the leader of this mining expedition. We are very impressed by your story and we have a proposal for you," he began in a calm yet serious voice. "We have discovered a vast chamber filled with valuable crystals and ores. However, this cave also houses a colossal golem. The golem attacks immediately if anyone comes too close. We have already made several attempts to defeat it, but so far without success."

Gronak and Fiona's brows furrowed with concern. A golem, a living being made of stone and earth, was a powerful and dangerous creature. They understood the dwarves' concerns, as the golem would block access to the precious resources and endanger the miners.

Hemli continued, his voice calm yet serious. "We have no idea how to defeat the golem, so we need your help. We are not inexperienced fighters, but this golem is particularly strong and resilient. With your strength and magic, we might have a chance to defeat it and retrieve the treasures in the chamber. In return, we will guide you safely out of the cave."

Hemli's words hung heavily in the air and the dwarves awaited Gronak and Fiona's response with bated breath as the glow of the crystals illuminated the scene.

Gronak and Fiona withdrew to a secluded corner of the cave, where the crystal light was dimmed, to confer in private. The decision to assist the dwarves with the dangerous task of defeating the golem weighed heavily on their shoulders. They knew it was not only a bold but also a life-threatening task. Nevertheless, they understood that it was the only way to escape the cave.

"Alright, Gronak, we need to help the dwarves. It's our best chance to get out of here alive," Fiona said with determination in her voice.

Gronak nodded in agreement. "You're right, Fiona. We will fight alongside the dwarves to defeat this golem."

In the silence of the cave, they exchanged looks and thoughts and after a brief discussion, they finally agreed to assist the dwarves. It was a decision marked by hope and solidarity. They knew that together with the dwarves, they had a chance to defeat the mighty golem.

When the dwarves heard Gronak and Fiona's agreement, cheers erupted among them. The miners were relieved and grateful for the help. They immediately began preparing for the impending battle. "Let's all work together and defeat this golem!" Hemli called to the dwarves, Gronak and Fiona.

Weapons were sharpened, magical artifacts were readied and the dwarves gave their heroes looks full of hope and trust.

Together, Gronak, Fiona and the dwarves made their way through the complex tunnel system of the cave. Fortunately, the dwarves were well-acquainted with this labyrinth and they navigated securely and purposefully to the chamber where the mighty golem rested.

In the chamber, the golem sat majestically, motionless and bathed in the surreal light cast by the cave's sparkling crystals. Its body, a monumental sculpture of solid stone, loomed high and towered over the onlookers. The stone from which it was formed seemed to bear centuries of weathering and life within the cave. Its surface was marked with fine cracks and fissures, like scars from past battles it had endured.

The golem exuded an aura that seemed to merge nature and magic. Its imposing exterior embodied the strength and mysteries of the ancient world. The sparkling light of the crystals surrounding it cast an otherworldly glow. It almost seemed as if it was the guardian of this magical place, having rested within the mountain for centuries and now facing a new threat.

Fiona stepped forward and explained calmly. "Golems are immune to heat and electricity but vulnerable to cold. At the same time, they have a massive stone hide." Her words lingered in the air and the dwarves and Gronak listened attentively, understanding the gravity of the task ahead. The crystals in the chamber cast sparkling reflections on the golem's gleaming, stone body, as if emphasizing its power and invulnerability.

Gronak and the dwarves listened intently as Fiona laid out her plans with great precision and detail. Together, they developed a clever tactic to defeat the golem. They knew that any mistake could have devastating consequences. After the plan had been thoroughly discussed, the group took the crucial step and entered the room where the mighty creature rested.

The golem's eyes glowed and with a tremendous quake, the massive creature rose. The ground shook so violently that the group was thrown to the floor. The start of the battle against the golem was anything but gentle and they felt the sheer power of the golem shaking the cave.

The golem, a colossal monstrosity of stone and earth, moved menacingly toward the group and its enormous steps left deep impressions in the ground. Fiona, despite the overwhelming threat, called to the dwarves to begin their preparations. The dwarves did not hesitate for a moment and threw their homemade bombs, normally used in mining, at the golem. The explosions of the bombs created deafening noise and caused the golem to stagger back as dust and rock fragments swirled through the air.

"Now's our chance, use everything and attack him!" Gronak shouted to the dwarves and they charged at the staggering golem.

Fiona seized this opportunity skillfully and invoked her powerful ice magic. Frosty energy flowed from her hands and enveloped the golem. Gradually, the golem began to freeze as icy layers covered its massive form. However, freezing the entire golem would take some time and the group knew they had to stay alert in the meantime.

The golem, despite its icy shell, was not easily defeated. A menacing roar echoed through the cave as it extended its massive hand and fired sharp stone projectiles like deadly missiles from a giant crossbow. The sharp projectiles sliced through the air with a dangerous hiss and seemed to fly straight at Fiona. In that ominous moment, where time seemed to stand still, Fiona felt at the mercy of the golem's overwhelming power.

But in an act of boundless bravery, Gronak and some of the bravest dwarves positioned themselves between Fiona and the incoming projectiles. Gronak, armed with his mighty shield, positioned himself in front of Fiona and held it up in a protective gesture. The dwarves simultaneously raised their tools pickaxes and hammers to deflect the stone projectiles and shield Fiona from certain death.

"Let's stand together, protect Fiona and defeat this beast!" one of the dwarves shouted and the others joined in, as they deflected the projectiles and faced the golem.

The teamwork between Gronak, the dwarves and Fiona was marked by impressive determination, but the golem's unimaginable strength was still overwhelming. The stone projectiles ricocheted off Gronak's shield and the dwarves' tools and despite their unwavering courage, some of the dwarves were severely injured. Their cries and screams of pain filled the cave, yet they heroically stood their ground to buy Fiona the precious time needed to continue channeling her ice magic against the golem.

Fiona herself worked tirelessly on her spell. The frosty energy emanating from her hands continuously enveloped the golem, turning piece by piece of its mighty body into ice. Meanwhile, the shimmering light of the crystals in the cave seemed to reflect and amplify the desperate struggle between magic and brutal force. It was an epic battle, a duel between the forces of nature and the hope of the group.

Gronak and the dwarves continued their attack with even more strength and fury. Gronak swung his mighty axe with impressive force in a wide arc and struck the golem with tremendous impact. The axe dug deep into the golem's stony skin and the impact created a deafening sound that echoed through the cave.

"We must not relent!" Gronak shouted to his companions. "Together, we will defeat this golem and be victorious!"

The dwarves, inspired by Gronak's bravery, worked diligently and fearlessly against the golem. Their pickaxes and hammers came into play as they struck at the golem's stone shell, chipping away at it piece by piece. Sparks flew as the tools hit the hard stone and the dwarves gave their all to overcome the golem.

Gronak encouraged them. "Don't falter, my brave friends! Together we are strong and this golem will fall!"

The dwarves responded with a loud battle roar and struck the golem with renewed determination. It was an unrelenting fight, in which the dwarves proved their strength and endurance.

The golem, despite its enormous power, desperately resisted the attacks. With a powerful swing of its massive arms, it hurled some of the dwarves into the air, who flew through the cave and crashed painfully back to the ground. The dwarves were valiant, but the physical superiority of the golem was undeniable.

Meanwhile, Fiona had fully deployed her ice magic and the golem was now encased in a thick layer of ice that restricted its movements. The battle reached its climax as Gronak climbed onto the frozen golem and lifted his enormous axe. With all his strength, he struck the golem. The ice trapping the golem shattered into a thousand glittering shards.

The golem now lay in many shattered pieces, defeated on the cave floor. The group had successfully vanquished the dangerous foe and cleared the way to the precious crystals and ores. Exhausted but relieved, they looked at the result of their brave fight. They had achieved something great together and overcome the challenge of the golem.

The dwarves erupted in jubilation and the cave echoed with their loud cheers. They hugged each other joyfully and patted each other on the back as they celebrated their victory over the mighty golem. The relief of finally gaining access to the valuable crystals and ores was evident. Hemli, the leader of the dwarves, stepped forward and warmly shook hands with Fiona and Gronak.

"We can't thank you enough for your help," Hemli said with a broad smile. "You saved us from a very tricky situation. You are true heroes." Hemli's recognition and the dwarves' gratitude deeply touched Fiona and Gronak.

The group decided to celebrate their successful fight and victory over the golem in style. They gathered around a crackling campfire, whose flames cast a warm, soothing light in the glow of the sparkling crystals. Together, they enjoyed a festive meal from the dwarves' supplies. The dwarves shared stories from their world of mining and underground adventures, of glittering treasures and dangerous tunnels.

Gronak and Fiona, in turn, shared stories of their travels and the thrilling encounters they had experienced. The dwarves listened attentively to their tales and a lively exchange of adventure stories ensued.

"Once, we got lost in the depths of an enchanted forest," Fiona began. "The trees were alive and spoke to us and we had to earn their trust to continue on our way."

A dwarf named Durgin, with a broad grin, responded. "That reminds me of the time we were trapped in a labyrinth of underground passages and had to fend off hungry cave creatures. But in the end, we found the exit!"

The stories flowed abundantly, accompanied by hearty laughter and applause. It was an evening of friendship and camaraderie and the group enjoyed each other's company in this fascinating cave, now a place of victory and togetherness.

As the hours passed, the atmosphere grew merrier. The dwarves sang songs from ancient times and danced around the fire, while Gronak and Fiona joined in the dance with joy. Together, they celebrated their victory and their friendship.

The last hours of the day went by and darkness slowly spread through the cave. The final sparks of the campfire glowed like stars in the night sky before they extinguished.

The next morning, Gronak, Fiona and Hemli reached the cave's exit, with the shimmering light of the sparkling crystals following them step by step, as if the stones were bidding them farewell on their way out. The echo of the joyful songs and the image of the dancing dwarves accompanied them to the cave's threshold.

At the cave's entrance, they lingered for a moment as Hemli, the leader of the dwarves, once again thanked the two adventurers warmly. His eyes sparkled with gratitude. "You saved us today and opened a new door to riches. We will be forever grateful."

Gronak smiled and responded. "It was an honor to help you. You are brave and generous friends and your stories and company have brightened our day. If you ever need our support, don't hesitate to call on us."

Fiona added. "Yes, we are always ready to stand by friends. May your mines yield rich returns and your underground adventures be safe and successful."

To emphasize his words, Hemli pulled out two rings from his pocket. The rings were masterfully adorned with magical dwarf runes that gleamed in their silver settings. Hemli handed the rings to Gronak and Fiona and they immediately felt the presence of the enchanted runes.

They knew these rings would be of use in their future adventures.

"These rings are a symbol of our deep appreciation," Hemli continued. "May they enhance your powers and increase your skill. Wear them with honor."

Gronak and Fiona accepted the rings with smiles and put them on their fingers. The magic of the runes coursed through them and they felt their powers strengthening. Their eyes met and they knew that these rings were not just a gift from the dwarves but also a symbol of the friendship and cooperation they had found in this unexpected encounter.

"Thank you very much, Hemli," Gronak said warmly. "These rings are truly precious gifts and we will treasure them."

Fiona agreed. "Your generosity and friendship mean a lot to us. We will think of you as we continue our adventures."

Hemli nodded with satisfaction. "May you always be safe and successful on your journeys. The depths of the earth will always be a home for you, should you ever return."

With these words and a heartfelt handshake, they bade a final farewell to the dwarves and stepped out into the freedom. The sun shone above them and the magic of the runes accompanied them on their onward journey.

Their adventure continued and the memory of the brave battle against the golem and the friendship with the dwarves would forever remain in their hearts. They bid farewell to Hemli and the sparkling crystals, knowing that on their journey, they were not alone, but could always count on the support and magic of friendship.

Chapter 4: The Swamp

Gronak and Fiona had traveled for days through dense forests and rugged terrain to reach the toxic swamp. When they finally arrived, they were greeted by a thick fog rising from the murky waters of the swamp. The ground was muddy and slippery, teeming with venomous creatures. The air was heavy and stuffy, filled with the stench of decay and rot.

Gronak and Fiona set up their camp on a small rise to shield themselves from the poisonous fumes and creatures. They lit a small fire and sat down wearily to rest.

When they woke up the next morning, they decided to cross the swamp and reach their goal. They pulled their hoods low over their faces and covered their noses and mouths to protect themselves from the toxic fumes.

They moved cautiously through the swamp, carefully planning each step to avoid falling into a poisonous trap. They heard the eerie hissing and growling of creatures nearby, but they remained calm and focused as they continued on.

"This swamp is really creepy," Fiona remarked quietly, casting a nervous glance at the murky water. "I can barely breathe with this stench."

Gronak nodded in agreement and replied just as quietly. "Yes and these ominous sounds from the creatures here don't make it any easier. We need to stay alert."

As they continued through the swamp, they began to hear loud chirping and hissing coming from the underbrush. Gronak stopped and drew his axe, while Fiona prepared her magical powers. "Something's coming toward us," Gronak muttered, focusing on the direction from which the sounds were coming.

Suddenly, they were attacked by a group of venomous lizards. The toxic lizards in the swamp are a threat to any traveler daring to traverse their territory. With scaly green bodies and yellow eyes that shine like sparkling gems in the dark, they can move almost silently through the dense reeds.

Their long tongues shot out quickly to snatch their prey and crush it with their powerful jaws. When they attack, they also spit a corrosive poison from their mouths that attacks the skin and flesh of their victims, causing deadly wounds within seconds.

The lizards often lie in wait in small groups in the mud and under the roots of fallen trees, waiting for their prey to pass by. The swamp lizards are a deadly danger that even experienced fighters must approach with caution.

The creatures were fast and cunning, their sharp teeth glinting in the dim light of the swamp. Gronak and Fiona drew their weapons and attacked the lizards. Fiona used her lightning magic to weaken the lizards while Gronak swung his mighty axe, killing one of the creatures.

However, the lizards were not easily defeated. Some of them spat deadly poison from their mouths. Fiona felt the poison entering her body, weakening her muscles. Gronak, on the other hand, had a higher resistance to the poison, but it still gradually affected him.

The lizards were fast and agile, attacking from ambush. Gronak and Fiona could see the green lizards moving quickly and silently through the swampy water towards them.

Fiona reacted swiftly, casting a spell that created a shield of magical energy around them both. Gronak attacked, swinging his axe to strike one of the lizards, but it dodged skillfully and attacked him from the side. Gronak swung wildly, but the lizards were too fast for him.

"Fiona, watch out!" Gronak called, trying to keep the lizards away from her.

Fiona focused on her magic and launched a lightning bolt at the lizard threatening Gronak. The bolt struck its target and the lizard convulsed in pain. Gronak seized the opportunity to deliver a powerful blow, knocking down the lizards.

"Watch out, Gronak!" Fiona shouted, pointing at a group of lizards approaching from behind.

The two fought desperately against the lizards as they slowly made their way through the swamp. The air was filled with flashes of lightning and the sounds of battle as they fought the venomous creatures blocking their path.

Fiona conjured a fireball and hurled it at a group of approaching lizards. The lizards screeched in pain as the fire burned their scales. Gronak took the chance to strike one of the lizards, severely wounding it. The lizard tried to attack again, but Gronak withdrew his axe and struck again. This time, he hit his target and killed the lizard. The remaining lizards fled into the protective mist of the swamp.

Gronak and Fiona breathed heavily, gasping as they pulled themselves out of the murky water. Their bodies burned and ached from the venomous bites of the lizards that had attacked them. Fiona shivered from cold and pain, while Gronak continued to try to catch his breath.

"That was damn close," Gronak panted, wiping the sweat from his forehead with a trembling hand. The strain of the battle was evident on his face.

Fiona, also out of breath, nodded in agreement. Her gaze rested on the slain lizards as her heart continued to pound. "Yes, those damn lizards are more dangerous than I ever thought," she replied with a hint of admiration in her voice. "But we defeated them," she added proudly.

As they rested for a moment, Fiona gathered a handful of herbs growing nearby and crushed them between her hands. The scent of mint and sage filled the air as she applied the crushed herbs to their wounds. Gronak winced in pain as Fiona treated his wounds with the herbs. But soon he felt the burning in his body gradually subside.

Fiona worked carefully and methodically as she applied the herbs to her own wounds and continued treating Gronak. Healing took time, but gradually the pain and inflammation began to decrease.

Eventually, they both leaned back, exhausted and took deep breaths. Fiona looked up at Gronak and smiled at him. "It will get better soon," she said. "We just need a little patience and rest."

Gronak nodded and closed his eyes while Fiona continued to focus on her wounds. Slowly but surely, their wounds began to heal and after a while, their bodies felt strong enough to keep moving. With one last look at the dead lizards that had attacked them, they set off.

Through the dense swamp, Fiona and Gronak trudged forward laboriously. Each step was accompanied by the humid air and the penetrating smell of decaying plant matter. The heavy moisture in the air weighed down on their shoulders, as if invisible hands were holding them back.

They kept an eye out for any small trace that would bring them closer to their goal. Every overgrown path, every slightly moved plant caught their attention as they fought their way through the swampy thicket.

"Do you think we're on the right path, Gronak?" Fiona asked, carefully avoiding a mud puddle, her boots heavy and muddy from the struggle with the terrain.

Gronak hesitated for a moment before replying, his brow furrowed in deep concentration. "I hope so, Fiona. But in this cursed swamp, it's easy to get lost. We need to stay alert."

The ground beneath their feet was muddy and slippery and they had to move cautiously to avoid stumbling or falling. Each step was a balancing act between avoiding mud pits and making progress in the right direction.

The sounds of the swamp surrounded them like a constant companion. The chirping of insects, the croaking of frogs and the occasional rustling in the underbrush heightened their tension as they relentlessly pursued their goal.

Suddenly, Gronak stumbled into a deep hole he hadn't noticed in the muddy ground. With a muffled cry, he fell in and quickly sank into the boggy depths of the swamp.

"This cursed swamp, damn it!" Gronak's voice was filled with panic and frustration as he desperately tried to free himself from the clinging mud. "Fiona! Help, I'm stuck!" His words echoed through the swamp as he struggled with all his might against the suffocating grip of the swamp.

Fiona rushed to him immediately, her eyes wide with worry. She knelt beside the hole and reached for Gronak's hand to pull him out, but the mud was too deep and too thick. She pulled and tugged with all her strength, her fingers gripping his hand, but he did not move.

"Gronak, hang on! I'm not going to leave you behind!" Fiona's voice trembled with strain as she fought against the rising panic. Her heart pounded in her chest as she desperately tried to find a way out of this hopeless situation.

Gronak sank deeper and deeper, his movements slowing as the mud relentlessly pulled him down. "Fiona, I can't go on..." Gronak whispered, his voice barely more than a choked breath in the dense air of the swamp. The hopelessness of his situation weighed heavily on him as he resigned himself to the seemingly inevitable fate.

But Fiona was not discouraged. With frantic hands, she reached for her herbal pouch, which she always kept close at hand. Her fingers trembled with excitement as she pulled out a handful of herbs and sprinkled them into a bottle containing a yellow, shimmering liquid. This liquid was part of her emergency gear, a gift from an old herbalist Fiona had once met on her journey.

Fiona poured the liquid into the mud around Gronak and immediately an amazing transformation began. The mud that had trapped him became softer and more slippery and Gronak was finally able to rise and breathe freely. He coughed and spat out mud, his lungs grateful for the air.

"Fiona, you saved my life," he said gratefully, his voice filled with deep relief and gratitude.

Fiona gave a faint smile, her eyes shining with relief and unhidden affection. "I'm so glad you survived," she whispered, her voice trembling with emotion. "I don't know what I'd do without you."

Exhausted and covered in mud, Gronak and Fiona lay on the swampy ground. Their bodies were weakened by the terrifying ordeal, but they were alive. They took deep breaths and tried to regain their strength while their hearts still pounded from shock and effort.

However, just as the tension of their struggle for survival seemed to be subsiding, a faint rustling pierced the silence of the swamp. It was barely more than a whisper in the dense grasses, but it was enough to pull both fighters from their exhaustion.

Gronak and Fiona snapped upright. Their bodies tensed like bowstrings as they strained their senses to determine what was approaching. The sounds of the swamp seemed to suddenly fall silent as they focused on the unknown in the gloomy surroundings.

"What was that, Gronak?" Fiona whispered, her eyes wide with alertness.

Gronak reached for his axe while Fiona prepared her magical abilities. In this dangerous environment, one could never know what might come next. Gronak called out in the direction of the sound. "Who's there? Come out!" His voice echoed through the thick mist of the swamp.

Fiona felt the tension in the air as she prepared to channel her magical energy. Her palm glowed softly as she shaped the energy into a fireball, ready to defend against an attack if necessary.

The response to Gronak's call came in the form of a timid voice from the swamp grass. "Please don't attack me," the voice pleaded with a hint of desperation. "I'm not an enemy." A small swamp gnome emerged slowly, his figure blurry and fragile in the faint light of the swamp.

Gronak and Fiona exchanged a glance, regarding the stranger with suspicion and caution. Gronak stepped forward slowly, still vigilant, as he addressed the gnome. "Who are you, little friend and what are you doing here in the swamp?" His voice was firm but not unfriendly as he tried to ascertain the stranger's intentions.

The gnome was small, even for a gnome and his green skin shimmered in the dim light of the swamp. He had a shy expression on his face and his delicate hands trembled slightly as he approached the two fighters, his eyes full of fear and uncertainty.

He cleared his throat and introduced himself in a quiet voice. "My name is Doro. I live here in the swamp. I usually hide from strangers, but I saw you fight against the venomous lizards and I thought maybe you could help me."

Gronak and Fiona exchanged a concerned glance before they lowered their combat stances. They could see a genuine plea for help in the little gnome's eyes.

Fiona approached the young gnome, Doro, who still bore the traces of terror in his eyes. She bent down and asked gently, "Doro, has something terrible happened?"

The small gnome swallowed hard and nodded before answering softly. "Yes, something terrible has happened. A dreadful creature came to our village and destroyed everything. My tribe and my family they are all gone. I am the only survivor."

Fiona and Gronak felt sympathy for the young gnome. They could see the pain and desperation in his eyes. Together, they decided to start a small campfire to warm up and give Doro a chance to tell his story.

As they sat around the campfire, Doro began to speak. His voice trembled as he recounted the terrible creature that had plagued his village. He described it as a monstrous beast that had emerged from the depths of the swamp. With shimmering eyes, he spoke of its fearsome claws, its terrifying roar and its hungry gaze.

Fiona gently placed a hand on Doro's arm and said softly, "That must have been horrifying, Doro. We're so sorry you had to go through that."

"It destroyed everything," Doro said with tears in his eyes. "Houses, trees and gnomes. Nothing and no one was spared. I barely escaped and since then, I've been hiding to avoid being found by that creature. But when I think of that day, all I can think about is revenge."

Gronak and Fiona listened attentively, deeply moved by Doro's story. The determination with which the young gnome wanted to avenge his tribe impressed them.

Gronak stood up and placed a reassuring hand on Doro's shoulder. "You don't have to fight this creature alone, Doro. We will help you. Together, we will avenge your tribe and drive this beast away."

Doro looked at Gronak and Fiona with a glimmer of hope in his eyes, his lips trembling slightly as he spoke. "Really? Would you do that for me?"

Fiona met his hesitant gaze with a warm smile that reflected a trace of compassion. "Yes, Doro," she answered gently, trying to soothe his fear. "We can't stand injustice and we won't leave anyone in need alone. Together, we'll find and defeat this beast. Don't worry."

Doro looked up at Gronak, his face showing a mix of concern and fear. He was grateful for the offer of help. But the thought of facing the creature again frightened him deeply.

Gronak noticed Doro's worries and said compassionately, "We know this won't be an easy task, Doro. But we will stick together and protect each other. You're not alone in this fight."

Fiona handed Doro a cup of warm tea to comfort him. "You're not alone, Doro. We're with you. Together, we'll come up with a plan and defeat this creature. You don't have to be afraid anymore."

Doro smiled faintly and nodded. For the first time since the attack on his village, he no longer felt alone. With the support of Gronak and Fiona, there was a chance to seek justice for Doro's tribe and defeat the terrifying creature that had destroyed his life.

The gnome felt bolstered by Fiona's and Gronak's words. They rested for a while and discussed their next steps. After some time, they set out towards the tower in the swamp that Doro had mentioned.

As they traveled, Doro told them more about the tower and the creature that lived there. He explained that the tower was a gloomy and decaying place, surrounded by dense fog. The creature they sought had made the tower its lair. Doro had seen the tower from a distance and warned again that approaching it could be dangerous.

Fiona glanced at the ominous tower and asked with concern, "Can you tell us anything about this creature, Doro? We need to know what we're dealing with."

Doro hesitated for a moment before replying. "This creature is a monstrous figure with claws as sharp as knives and an insatiable hunger for destruction. It has the power to manipulate nature itself and turn the swamp into its ally."

Gronak growled softly in anger. "Then we have no choice. We need to stop this creature before it causes any more harm. But we need to be cautious. If what you say is true, we're dealing with a dangerous opponent."

Eventually, the group reached the tower. It loomed from the swampy ground and appeared to be overgrown with moss and brambles. The tower was surrounded by a sinister aura that shrouded the entire area in darkness. A green mist hung around the tower, giving it a ghostly appearance.

"This place has a foreboding aura," Fiona noted, feeling an ominous chill in the air. She pulled her hood tighter around her, as if trying to hide from invisible eyes lurking in the darkness.

Gronak nodded in agreement, his eyes scanning the murky outlines of the swampy landscape with suspicion. "Yes, there's something evil here and I don't like it one bit," he added.

The tower itself was tall and slender, with weathered stones and broken windows. The doors appeared to be locked and there was no obvious way to get inside. However, Doro knew of a hidden entrance that he had used in the past to enter the tower.

"We need to find the hidden entrance at the back of the tower," Doro said, searching for the secret passage. Shortly afterward, he found it behind a bush and called to Gronak and Fiona. "Over here is the entrance, come quickly."

With Doro leading the way, they ventured through the passage revealed by the hidden side door of the tower. A faint squeak accompanied their entry into the dark domain. The interior of the tower revealed an atmosphere of abandonment and decay that was as threatening as the outer appearance.

The walls of the tower were threaded with cobwebs that fluttered like fine veils in the dim light. Each step on the moss-covered floor was accompanied by a slippery sensation spreading beneath their boots. The air was filled with a musty odor that smelled of damp rot.

"This darkness is oppressive," Fiona whispered as she looked around uneasily in the gloomy surroundings. Her voice echoed softly through the space, as if swallowed by the shadows.

Doro nodded in understanding and led them further through the dim corridor, his face an expression of silent determination. "We're almost there," he assured them quietly, though his tone betrayed a slight uncertainty as they ventured deeper into the heart of darkness.

The group carefully ascended the decaying stairs, their footsteps accompanied by somber echoes. The darkness inside the tower was suffocating, only occasionally broken by dirty windows through which a faint light filtered. Their hearts beat faster as they progressed further into the tower.

"Stay alert," Gronak said quietly to his companions, his voice swallowed by the dark walls of the tower. "We don't know what awaits us here, but we must be prepared."

Fiona whispered softly to Doro, her voice barely a breath in the oppressive silence. "Do you have any idea where we might find this creature?"

Doro hesitated for a moment, his eyes searching the darkness for answers. "I'm not sure," he finally replied. "But the highest room in the tower is the most likely place. Be prepared for anything, Fiona. This creature is unpredictable."

Gronak tightened his grip on his sword. "We're ready, Doro," he said, his gaze filled with determination. "We'll find it and stop it, no matter the cost." His words sounded like a vow, echoing in the threatening darkness of the tower.

As they moved forward, they felt the presence of the creature drawing closer. A deep, menacing growl emerged from the darkness, followed by a chilling draft. The decision to enter the tower was irreversible and the true challenge now lay ahead. The confrontation with the terrifying creature waiting inside this grim place was drawing ever closer.

On the top floor of the gloomy tower, Gronak, Fiona and Doro encountered the horrifying creature Doro had spoken of. The sight before them was terrifying and fearsome.

The creature standing before them was a Soul Slime. A humanoid form composed of a strange combination of slimy substances and bones. Its body seemed to be in constant flux, as if it had no fixed shape. The slime that enveloped it glittered in a sinister, iridescent play of toxic green and gloomy black.

Gronak spoke up, his tone firm. "So this is the creature you spoke of, Doro? Truly a horrifying sight."

The head of the Soul Slime was grotesquely distorted and appeared to consist of a mass of skulls and bones that constantly shifted and changed. Dark, glowing eyes seemed to peer out from the slime, without pupils or visible emotions.

Its limbs were long and thin, almost like slender tentacles extending in all directions. At the ends of the tentacles were sharp claws, ready to cause harm. The Soul Slime seemed capable of changing its shape at will and fluidly adapting its bodily structures.

The eerie creature stood in a gloomy corner of the room, surrounded by a thick sludge of greenish slime that moved slowly, drawing pulsating patterns on the floor. The room was filled with a suffocating sense of despair and horror emanating from the creature.

Fiona looked at the creature. "We won't be intimidated by your terror. Together, we will defeat you and free the swamp from your reign of terror."

Doro trembled with fear as he gazed at the creature and both Gronak and Fiona felt they were facing a powerful and dangerous foe. The Soul Slime, Doro explained, fed on living souls and had already consumed his entire village. Its mere presence exuded an aura of evil and corruption.

The group knew they had no choice but to fight this horrifying creature to avenge Doro's people. Their hearts pounded with excitement and fear as they prepared to confront the Soul Slime and drive the darkness from the tower.

Gronak and Fiona readied themselves for battle against the dreadful Soul Slime. Fiona concentrated her magic, preparing a lightning spell, while Gronak gripped his massive sword tightly. The tension in the air was palpable as they braced for the impending confrontation.

Fiona spoke quietly to Gronak without taking her eyes off her magic. "We need to be cautious, Gronak. I sense a strong and dark magical energy emanating from the Soul Slime."

Gronak nodded in agreement and responded quietly. "I understand, Fiona. We should be prepared for anything. This creature will certainly have some dreadful abilities."

But suddenly, something completely unexpected happened. Doro, the gnome they had considered an ally, pulled out a knife and treacherously stabbed Fiona in the back. A bone-chilling scream escaped Fiona's lips as she staggered from pain and surprise.

Gronak, who had been preparing to attack the Soul Slime, turned around in shock to see Doro still holding the knife. His heart pounded wildly in his chest as he tried to grasp what had just occurred. The air was filled with oppressive tension as Gronak stood frozen in a moment of disbelieving silence.

Gronak glared at Doro with anger, his eyes filled with disappointment and confusion as he forced the words out. "Why, Doro? Why did you do this?" His voice was a thunder that echoed through the room, filled with a mixture of rage and despair.

Doro lowered his gaze, his face contorted with remorse and suffering as he replied in a trembling voice. "I'm sorry, Gronak, but the creature controls me. I couldn't help it." His words were a soft whisper in the oppressive silence of the tower, his eyes filled with pain and self-reproach.

Fiona struggled with the pain, her voice a faint whisper. "Gronak, let's defeat the Soul Slime," she said insistently. "Then we can help Doro. He's not himself, I can feel it." Her words were a gentle plea of hope amid the darkness, a promise that still hung unfulfilled in the air.

The Soul Slime itself laughed maliciously, its nauseating voice filling the room and piercing the silence. It turned to Doro with a repulsive grin on its distorted face and thanked him for his betrayal. "Ah, Doro, you have done well in your task," the slime hissed with a sinister undertone. "You are only here because the gnome lured you. You are nothing more than food for me." Its words were like an icy breeze sweeping through the darkness, sending a shiver down the spines of those present.

Fiona lay on the ground in pain, her teeth clenched tightly as she tried to rise and complete her spell. But the stab wound in her back had weakened her and her movements were labored and slow. Gronak stood beside her, angry and desperate, his body tense with what was to come. Yet he knew he could not save Fiona as long as the Soul Slime threatened her.

The Soul Slime began to move closer. "You can do nothing to stop me," it mocked with a voice that echoed in the companions' ears. "Your souls belong to me!"

Driven by rage and despair, Gronak pushed the frightened gnome Doro aside and rushed to Fiona, who was bleeding heavily and groaning in pain. He carefully lifted her into his strong arms and felt her warm blood flowing over his hands. Fiona fought bravely against the agony, but the stab in her back was severe.

"Gronak, don't let me die here," Fiona whispered with tears in her eyes, her voice a quiet cry of desperation. She fought valiantly against the pain, but the wound in her back was grave and darkness threatened to consume her. Slowly, she lost consciousness, her eyelids growing heavy as she succumbed to the call of the abyss.

Gronak nodded, his gaze full of fury as he fixed his eyes on the slime. "Don't worry, Fiona," he promised in a firm voice that resonated in the oppressive silence of the tower. "I won't let you die here."

Meanwhile, the slime was preparing a black energy sphere, which obviously contained destructive power. Gronak was desperate; he didn't know how to confront such a powerful enemy. Fight or flee, that was the agonizing question that plagued him in this critical moment.

With one last look at the unconscious Fiona, Gronak decided that her safety was the highest priority. He knew he could not defeat the Soul Slime alone and that they had no chance if they stayed.

Gronak reached into his bag and pulled out a smoke bomb, which he had once received from the dwarves. Without hesitation, he threw the bomb towards the Soul Slime. The bomb exploded in a swirl of dense, impenetrable smoke, enveloping the entire room in an opaque darkness.

The room was filled with the acrid smell of smoke, clouding his senses. The Soul Slime could see nothing and began to roar angrily as it lost itself in the thick fog.

Gronak seized the opportunity and managed to lift Fiona onto his shoulders. He whispered encouraging words to her as he carried her out of the room. The two fought their way through the dense smoke and eventually reached the staircase leading down.

"Fiona, hang in there," Gronak said softly as they reached the first steps. "We need to get out of here and come up with a new plan."

Gronak, with Fiona in his arms, ran down the tower stairs as quickly as he could. Each step was accompanied by a dull echo and his fear for Fiona drove him forward. Upon reaching the bottom, he searched for the exit but instead encountered an unexpected barrier.

The exit was sealed by a powerful magical barrier. Gronak knew he had no chance of breaking the seal without the proper skills and knowledge. Panic seized him as he looked helplessly at the locked door.

At this critical moment, the small gnome Doro called out to Gronak. "Come, Gronak, follow me! I can help you save Fiona!"

Gronak hesitated; his mistrust of Doro was understandable after the betrayal in the tower, but he had no other choice. He couldn't leave Fiona in this dire situation. With Fiona in his arms and a heavy heart, he followed Doro into one of the nearby rooms.

"Fiona, stay strong," Gronak whispered to her, his voice a gentle comfort amidst the darkness. "I will find a way to help you."

The room Gronak and Doro entered was larger than expected and told a grim tale of suffering and oppression. Along the walls were cages containing gnomes of various ages, their faces marked by fear and hopelessness. It was a terrifying sight, showing that the Soul Slime had captured numerous innocent villagers.

"This is dreadful," Gronak murmured, his gaze filled with horror as he saw the prisoners. "This perverse bastard will pay for this, but first, we need to take care of Fiona."

The cages were cramped and small and the gnomes inside looked frightened and desperate. Some were children, others were elderly. They huddled together in their tight confines, their clothing torn and their faces showing the marks of hunger and suffering. Their eyes were filled with hopelessness.

Gronak slowly approached one of the cages and spoke to the gnomes inside, his voice firm and reassuring. "We are here to free you. Hold on, we will get you out." His words were a promise that resonated in the oppressive silence of the room.

An older gnome gave a weak smile, his eyes full of gratitude and responded with a voice marked by exhaustion. "You are our salvation. Thank you, stranger." His words were like a breath of hope in the oppressive darkness of the room, a ray of light amidst the gloom.

Gronak breathed heavily, his heart weighed down by the burden of the suffering he saw before him and turned to Doro with a look of anger in his eyes. "What the hell is going on here, Doro?" His voice was a quiet cry of desperation as he tried to understand the reasoning behind the Soul Slime's cruel act. "Why are all these gnomes imprisoned here?"

Doro lowered his gaze and explained in a sorrowful voice. "The Soul Slime has captured them all to feast on their souls. He has drained their life energy and kept them in these cages. I tried to save them, but I am powerless against him alone."

Gronak felt anger rise within him, but he could not simply leave the imprisoned gnomes behind. "We need to find a way to free them, Doro. And then we must defeat the Soul Slime before he causes more havoc."

Doro led Gronak to one of the cages, where the village shaman was imprisoned. He stared at Gronak with tired eyes. He looked at Fiona, who lay unconscious in Gronak's arms. "Bring the young woman to me," he demanded. "I can perform healing magic to save her."

Gronak moved closer to the shaman's cage with Fiona and gently laid her on the ground. Through the bars, he felt the shaman applying healing magic to Fiona. A soft, glowing light surrounded the girl and she slowly opened her eyes.

She carefully sat up and thanked the shaman for her rescue. "Thank you, esteemed gnome, this healing magic is truly amazing. I feel like I've been reborn." Fiona also thanked Gronak. "Thank you, Gronak, I couldn't have done it without you. But now let's finally kill that disgusting beast!"

The shaman, who introduced himself as Dreskor, was an impressive gnome of imposing stature, surrounded by a deep aura of wisdom. He had long white hair and an even longer white beard that almost reached the floor. His eyes, framed by wrinkles, radiated a profound calm. Dreskor's clothing consisted of sacred robes adorned with mysterious symbols and runes, underscoring his role as the village shaman.

Dreskor spoke with a calm and wise voice to Gronak and Fiona. "You are brave souls to face the Soul Slime. But this battle will not be easy. The creature is powerful and malevolent and it has already brought so much suffering to our village."

Gronak nodded in agreement. "We are aware of the danger, Dreskor. But we cannot allow the Soul Slime to continue devouring the innocent. We must defeat it to bring peace and justice for you and Doro's clan."

Fiona, having recovered from Doro's betrayal and the Soul Slime's attack, added, "We are ready to do whatever it takes to stop this creature and free the imprisoned gnomes. Please, Dreskor, do you have any information about the Soul Slime that could help us?"

Dreskor nodded thoughtfully and explained. "The Soul Slime used Doro to lure both of you here because he knew you couldn't easily leave this place," he began in his wise voice. "He is an extremely dangerous foe, but he will not come down to hunt you. Instead, he will wait until you come to him."

Dreskor took a brief pause and continued. "Only by defeating the Soul Slime will the seal surrounding the tower be broken and you will be able to leave the tower safely. It will not be easy, but you have already shown that you are brave."

Gronak and Fiona listened attentively and nodded. They were aware that they had no choice but to face the challenge and defeat the Soul Slime, not only to save themselves but also to rescue Doro's clan.

Gronak and Fiona sat with Shaman Dreskor, brainstorming feverishly on how to best defeat the Soul Slime. Dreskor knew that Soul Slimes were extremely resistant to physical damage and magic was their only weakness. Even then, it was not easy to get close to the slime.

Dreskor explained with a serious expression. "The key to destroying the Soul Slime lies in destroying its black heart within its chest. But to do that, you must get close enough to the creature, which is extremely dangerous."

Fiona, known for her intelligence and creative solutions, suddenly had a brilliant idea. A smile spread across her face as she turned to Gronak. "I think I have a plan, Gronak." Gronak looked at her expectantly. "What's your plan, Fiona?"

Fiona looked at Gronak and asked for his sword. With a trusting expression in his eyes, he handed her his mighty sword. Fiona held the sword firmly in her hands and began to channel her magic into it. The blade started to glow with a shimmering blue light and a magical aura enveloped it.

Gronak was fascinated by the sight. The sword he had wielded so many times in battle now seemed to be imbued with powerful magical energy. He could almost feel the energy emanating from the blade.

Fiona explained with a serious expression, "This sword will now deal magical damage when we attack the Soul Slime. However, the effect will last only for 2-3 strikes, so we need to use it wisely."

Gronak nodded, admiring the sword. He was impressed by Fiona's abilities and her clever use of magic. Together, they were now even better prepared for the upcoming battle.

Gronak looked at Fiona with renewed hope. "That's brilliant, Fiona. Let's surprise the Soul Slime with this and inflict as much damage as we can. We might only have one chance, so we need to make it count."

Determined and armed with their magical sword, Gronak and Fiona set off back to confront the creature. The tension in the air was palpable, but they were ready to defeat the Soul Slime and save Doro's clan. With united strength and a clear goal in mind, they climbed the tower stairs once more, ready for the final battle.

The Soul Slime, visibly pleased by the return of Gronak and Fiona, immediately began its attacks. Black energy spheres shot out from its slimy body and raced toward the two adventurers as they entered the room.

Fiona looked at Gronak tensely. "I'll handle the magic spheres, Gronak. You deal with the slime." With a determined look in her eyes, she focused her magic and sent sharp ice shards at the incoming energy spheres. The shards shattered the spheres into a thousand sparks, preventing a devastating impact.

Suddenly, the slime fired a massive energy sphere imbued with dark power at Fiona. The sphere hit her with full force and slammed her against the wall behind her. Fiona let out a cry of pain as she was struck and lay dazed, while the slime triumphed.

Gronak, who had witnessed the attack up close, was beside himself with anger and worry for Fiona. He knew he had no time left and charged at the Soul Slime, determined to use the magical sword to pierce the black heart of the monster.

Gronak skillfully dodged the remaining magic spheres and moved closer to the Soul Slime. His heart pounded with excitement and concern for Fiona. As he took the final few steps to reach the creature, the slime prepared another attack.

Fiona, slowly recovering from the severe attack, struggled to rise. "Gronak, watch out! The slime is preparing for another attack!" she called to him.

Gronak heard her warning and ducked just in time as the slime fired another deadly energy sphere. The sphere raced past him and slammed into the wall, exploding with a massive blast. Debris and dust filled the air as the force of the explosion shook the tower.

Gronak, having narrowly survived the attack, rolled skillfully to the side and got back on his feet. His body was pulsing with adrenaline. "Thanks, Fiona! That was close!" he shouted, his voice filled with a hint of relief as he kept his gaze fixed on the Soul Slime.

Fiona managed a weak smile, her face marked by pain, as she tried to pull herself together. "Watch yourself, Gronak," she whispered before preparing for her next spell.

Gronak charged at the Soul Slime, gripping his magical sword tightly and keeping his eyes firmly on his opponent. The slime reacted immediately, extending its slimy tentacles to grab and restrain Gronak.

Gronak swung his sword with all his might. The blade cut through some of the slime's tentacles, which seemed to burst in a spray of dark energy. But the creature was stubborn and not easily defeated. "Damn, this slime is stronger than it looks," Gronak grunted as he fought off the tentacles.

A powerful tentacle coiled around Gronak's foot and pulled him down with immense force. Gronak found himself on the slimy ground, trapped in the sticky and merciless tentacles of the Soul Slime.

The slime began to move slowly towards Gronak, its tentacles tightening around his body. The dark energy of the slime flowed through Gronak and he felt his strength waning. His air supply was cut off by the tentacles and he struggled desperately for every breath.

Fiona, having somewhat recovered from the attack, saw the horrific scene and called out Gronak's name, her voice a desperate cry amidst the chaos. But she could do nothing to help him, as she was still too weakened. Her muscles burned with effort and her body felt like lead.

Gronak fought desperately against the tentacles. But the tentacles grew stronger and refused to let go, their slimy embrace a prison of darkness and despair. The Soul Slime fed on his life energy and its dark eyes gleamed with greed and triumph.

Time seemed to stand still as Gronak battled in the Soul Slime's deadly grip, his thoughts a whirlwind of panic and despair. Yet he was not ready to give up. A spark of hope flickered in his eyes, a beam of light amidst the darkness, driving him to keep fighting.

Fiona, with tears in her eyes, called out again. "Gronak, hold on! You can't give up!" Her voice was a gentle call of encouragement and solidarity amidst the horror.

Gronak responded with a muffled voice, his breath a gasping whisper in the stuffy air. "I will not give up, Fiona! We must defeat this slime and rescue Doro!" His words were a promise he would not break as long as there was a spark of life left in him.

The Soul Slime laughed mockingly, its voice a gurgle of darkness as it continued to hold Gronak captive in its tentacles. "You can't do anything against me," it taunted, its eyes glowing with triumph. "Your powers are too weak and your souls belong to me." Its words were an echo of the horror surrounding them, a whisper of despair amidst the chaos.

Fiona felt the anger rise within her and gathered her remaining strength. With a trembling hand, she tried again to cast a lightning spell to weaken the slime. She managed to ignite a spark of magic that hit the slime, but it seemed to have little effect.

Gronak, trapped in the deadly embrace of the Soul Slime, fought desperately for his survival. The cold of the sticky tentacles encased his body, threatening to suffocate him. In this moment of desperation, he drew upon his last reserves of strength. His fingers searched for his magical sword, though it seemed nearly unreachable in his precarious position.

With a desperate jerk, Gronak managed to grasp the sword. His hand trembled with effort as he drove it deep into the Soul Slime's chest. A bone-chilling shriek filled the room as the sword pierced the slime's black heart. Dark energy sprayed in all directions as the slime slowly dissolved and vanished into nothingness, leaving only its bones, silent witnesses of the final desperate battle.

Gronak fought his way free from the remaining remnants of the slime and stood up, exhausted but victorious. He ran to Fiona, who was still dazed and injured.

Fiona, slowly recovering, smiled gratefully at Gronak. "You saved us, Gronak. You're the greatest."

Gronak returned the smile and responded with a touch of pride in his voice. "We did it together, Fiona. And we saved Doro."

With all caution and concern, he carried Fiona down the stairs to the gnomes and shamans. The steps were heavy, but Gronak gritted his teeth and showed no sign of his struggle.

"Gronak, are you okay?" Fiona asked softly with a worried glance as she lay in his arms. Gronak nodded and replied with a weak smile. "Yes, Fiona, I will make it. Don't worry."

Upon arriving in the tower's lower level, Gronak and Fiona were already expected by the gnomes. The gnomes' joyful faces beamed with relief and gratitude.

"We did it!" cried one of the gnomes. "The tower is finally free!"

After the death of the Soul Slime, the magical seal surrounding the tower was finally broken. The shaman, Dreskor, stepped forward and immediately began healing Fiona and then Gronak from their injuries. His healing magic surrounded them like a gentle breeze and the pain and injuries of the two adventurers began to fade.

"Thank you, Dreskor," Fiona said with relief as the pain eased.

The gnomes cheered for the two of them, their voices filling the room with joy and relief. They were endlessly grateful to their saviors for defeating the Soul Slime and freeing their village. "We will carry you forever in our hearts," said one of the gnomes.

Once the healing was completed, Gronak and Fiona, along with the gnomes, left the gloomy tower. The daylight welcomed them outside and they felt liberated from the oppressive darkness that had surrounded the tower.

"Finally, we are free," Gronak remarked, smiling at Fiona. Fiona nodded in agreement. "Yes and we achieved this together, Gronak."

The villagers led the two of them to the village, where they were greeted with cheers and celebrations. Gronak and Fiona had not only saved the village but also won the gnomes' hearts. The gnomes clapped and cheered as Gronak and Fiona were led to the center of the village. The two adventurers smiled and waved to the gnomes.

Together, they celebrated this victory over darkness and the end of a terrible threat. The sun was slowly setting as the celebrations continued and Gronak and Fiona could finally share a moment of peace and contentment with each other.

"It was a tough trial; I thought it might be the end for us," Gronak said. He took Fiona's hand and smiled. "But we made it." Fiona smiled and squeezed his hand. "And we managed to free all the gnomes, which makes me very happy," she said with joy.

They had gone through unimaginable challenges together and emerged stronger from this trial. Together, they had defeated evil and reunited the village and their friendship was stronger than ever before.

The next day, Doro and Dreskor came to Gronak and Fiona to express their gratitude and farewell words. Dreskor stepped forward and spoke on behalf of the entire gnome village. "On behalf of our village, I want to thank you from the bottom of our hearts, Gronak and Fiona," Dreskor began his speech. "You saved us from a terrible threat and freed our village. Your bravery and willingness to sacrifice will never be forgotten."

Gronak and Fiona nodded modestly, grateful for the shaman's words. It had felt right to help the village and the gnomes' recognition meant a lot to them. "It was an honor to help you," Gronak replied. "We will always remember you and this village fondly." Fiona added, "And we are sure that your village has a bright future ahead."

Doro also stepped forward and bowed his head humbly. "I want to sincerely apologize to both of you for putting you in this dangerous situation," he began. "It was my fault for luring you into the clutches of the Soul Slime. But I also thank you from the bottom of my heart for saving me and my tribe. You are true heroes."

Gronak placed his hand on Doro's shoulder and said kindly, "Doro, you did your best to help. It wasn't your fault; you were just a victim of the slime. We are glad we could help you and your tribe."

Fiona added, "And your apology is accepted. We are now friends and will always be there for each other."

Doro smiled with relief and thanked them again. After the farewell words, Doro led Gronak and Fiona out of the swamp where they had experienced so many adventures. The swamp, which had once been ominous and dangerous, now seemed less dark and unwelcoming.

"Where will your adventures take you next?" Doro asked curiously.

Gronak thought for a moment. "We don't know exactly, Doro. But we will be ready to face any adventure and drive away any darkness. We will rest only when Xalis and his minions have been defeated."

Doro smiled and wished them good luck on their journey. Gronak and Fiona continued on their path, strengthened by the friendship of the gnomes and the certainty that they could achieve great things together. The swamp might be full of dangers, but they were ready to face any adventure and drive away any threat that stood in their way.

Chapter 5: The Elven Forest

Gronak and Fiona had had a long and exhausting day. They had traveled through the swamp, fought dangerous creatures and covered many miles. But finally, they had found a suitable place to rest. In the midst of the dense forest, they discovered a small clearing surrounded by majestic trees. Here, they set up camp.

Gronak gathered dry wood and lit a fire, while Fiona set up the tent and organized their belongings. The crackling of the flames and the warming heat of the fire enveloped them. Fiona began preparing a simple meal of dried meat and bread that they would share.

Gronak leaned back comfortably and looked into the flames. "What a day," he said with a slight smile. "Those creatures in the swamp were really persistent and that Soul Slime was a tough opponent."

Fiona nodded in agreement and added, "Yes, but we defeated them. You were excellent in the fight against the Soul Slime, Gronak."

Gronak laughed modestly. "And your magical abilities often paved the way for us. I'm glad to have you by my side."

Fiona gazed thoughtfully at the sky. "Thank you for your words, but I've realized that I need to become stronger. Dreskor's healing magic was very impressive." Fiona pulled out the old magic book from her bag that she had found in the witch's house and held it up to Gronak. "But with this book, I'll soon master healing magic too," Fiona grinned, full of determination.

They continued discussing their journey so far and their plans for the future. They laughed over amusing anecdotes and enjoyed each other's company. After finishing their meal, they relaxed and enjoyed the peace and quiet of the night. Fiona read from the old book while Gronak relaxed and gazed at the starry sky.

The stars sparkled brightly in the sky and the moon cast its gentle light. The fire crackled softly, casting fascinating shadows on the trees surrounding the clearing. The forest was completely silent, as if honoring their presence.

Despite their exhaustion, they both felt content and grateful. The campfire had not only provided warmth and light but also a moment of rest and relaxation amid their thrilling adventures. After a while, they decided to go to sleep to rest and regain their strength for the coming day.

Gronak and Fiona were in the process of breaking down their camp early the next morning when suddenly the silence of the forest was shattered by distant cries. Fiona furrowed her brow, her worried gaze turned to Gronak and she said with a concerned voice, "Did you hear that, Gronak? It sounded like cries for help."

Gronak nodded in agreement. "Yes, those were definitely screams and they came from nearby. We should find out what's going on."

In a flash, Gronak packed his weapons while Fiona carefully gathered her magical artifacts. Together, they set off, their steps leading them deeper into the forest. They fought their way through thorny underbrush and over fallen trees, always following the cries. The screams grew louder and more desperate the closer they got.

Finally, they reached a small river that wound its way through the forest. The screams led them to the riverbank, where they saw a young elf on the opposite side. Her eyes were wide with fear and she trembled with panic.

The elf was slender and of breathtaking beauty. Her long hair, which fell in gentle waves over her shoulders, shimmered in a delicate shade of blonde and framed her fine features in a captivating manner. Her eyes were almond-shaped and a deep blue, glimmering in the sunlight and reflecting the color of the clear sky.

Her skin had a pale complexion, marking her origin from the elven forest. She wore light armor made of green leather and fabric, protecting her from enemy attacks without hindering her graceful agility. Her belt was adorned with various tools and weapons, including an intricately crafted longbow, indicating her skill with ranged weapons and a long dagger resting at her side.

Gronak and Fiona didn't hesitate for a second. They recognized that the elf was in great danger and without hesitation, they jumped into the river to reach her. The icy water nearly reached their chests, but they were undeterred. The current was strong, yet with combined strength, they finally reached the shore where the desperate elf stood.

Fiona approached the soot and ash-covered elf cautiously, who was completely distraught and on her knees. In a gentle tone, she asked, "Who are you?" The elf looked at Fiona, tears streaming down her cheeks. "My name is Lea," she sniffled, trying desperately to wipe away her tears.

Fiona knelt compassionately beside the elf, Lea. "What happened? Why are you crying for help, Lea?" The elf responded with a trembling voice, "It's terrible... Our village was attacked."

Fiona gently placed a comforting hand on Lea's shoulder, encouraging her to continue. At that moment, she felt the despair and pain in Lea's eyes. The ash on Lea's face hinted that she had fled from the ruins of her village.

Lea sobbed and began to recount in a broken voice, "I woke up that morning and heard the loud cry of a creature echoing through the village. I immediately knew we were in danger and ran out of my house to see what was happening. What I saw was horrifying. Our village was being attacked by a large hellgriffin, destroying everything we held dear."

Her gaze grew sadder as she continued her story. "I ran to my bow and quiver, which always lay beside my bed and prepared to fight the hellgriffin. I ran through the village, which was ablaze and filled with the terrible screams of the villagers. I could see the hellgriffin in the distance, slashing its claws into the houses and turning them into rubble."

Fiona listened intently and asked worriedly, "That's truly awful, I can hardly imagine how terrible that must have been for you. Did you hit the hellgriffin? Were you able to hurt it?"

Lea sighed and replied, "Some of my arrows hit its wings, but it seemed unfazed and continued to fly over the village. I realized that I couldn't fight such a powerful creature alone and ran into the forest to seek help."

Fiona looked into her eyes with compassion. "We're here to help you," she said calmly and gently. "Gronak and I will protect you and make sure that this griffin causes no further harm."

Lea looked up and saw Fiona's deep green eyes, filled with determination and strength. She felt a wave of relief wash over her, sensing that she was in good hands. Fiona had a calming effect on her and she knew she could trust her words to guide them to safety.

Gronak stepped forward and placed his massive hand on Lea's other shoulder. "We will find this griffin and face it," he said firmly. "You are not alone, Lea. We will stand by you and together we will overcome this threat."

Lea felt her fear gradually subside, allowing her to refocus on her mission. She was grateful for Gronak and Fiona, who gave her hope and a sense of security. Together, they set out to find and defeat the griffin.

Lea smiled faintly. "Thank you both. I truly appreciate your help. The griffin is dangerous, but together, we will stop it."

Gronak, Fiona and Lea reached Lea's devastated village, which had been attacked by the hellgriffin. As they approached, they saw the destroyed houses and buildings engulfed in flames, with villagers desperately trying to hide from the griffin. The air was filled with the piercing screams of the terrified villagers and the animals surrounding the village.

As they ventured further into the village, the oppressive heat from the searing wind, emanating from the blazing flames and the glowing heat of the burning buildings, became increasingly palpable. The smoke rising from the flames hung thick in the air, making breathing a strenuous effort.

Fiona's brow furrowed with concern as she took in the devastating scene before them. "We must act immediately! The villagers urgently need our help!"

Gronak, with a serious expression on his face, nodded resolutely. His hand gripped the hilt of his sword tightly, ready for battle. "Stay close to me and watch out for each other. We can't waste any time."

Lea, with a determined look and a powerful expression, drew her bow. "Let's stop the griffin and save the villagers from this danger."

The three knew they had no time to lose. They rushed into the village to fight the hellgriffin and rescue the villagers. As they suddenly saw the hellgriffin in the sky, the same creature that had attacked their village, Lea drew her bow. "Watch out, he's coming back!"

The hellgriffin is a creature that strikes fear into the hearts of the bravest. Its body is covered in black feathers that shine like tar. Its eyes are blood-red and seem to pierce through the darkness. Its claws are as sharp as blades and its wings span over ten meters.

Its cry is a bone-chilling screech that makes the ground tremble. When it spreads its wings to rise into the air, it generates a strong wind that churns everything around it. Its attacks are swift and deadly. With its claws and beak, it can tear its enemies to pieces and devour them.

Its appearance and powers pose an unprecedented threat to anyone who faces it. Those who wish to fight it must prepare for the worst and be willing to risk their lives.

Gronak shouted urgently to the villagers, "Stay in cover! We will stop the griffin!" The panicked villagers sought shelter and remained hidden as the three faced the approaching hellgriffin.

Gronak, with his mighty sword firmly in hand, charged towards the hellgriffin. His armor clanked with each step as he approached the winged beast. The hellgriffin, its black feathers glinting in the light, let out a bone-chilling screech and spread its enormous wings to take flight.

Fiona stood beside Gronak, her eyes glowing with concentration as she prepared her lightning magic. Her fingers began to sparkle and sparks flew as she started to channel the energy of the lightning. The hellgriffin, noticing the imminent attack, attempted to turn in the air and dive towards Gronak.

Fiona looked up and shouted in concern, "Watch out, Gronak, he's diving at you!"

Gronak deftly dodged the hellgriffin's attacks and swung his sword. The metallic clash of his blade striking the griffin's feathers echoed through the air. The hellgriffin screeched in pain, losing some of its feathers, but quickly counterattacked, trying to slash at Gronak with its sharp claws.

Lea called out in worry as she kept a keen eye on the griffin. "Gronak, watch out for his claws! If they catch you, they'll slice you open!"

Gronak raised his massive shield to protect himself from the relentless strikes of the griffin. The immense force of the blows pushed him back, but he held his ground. Fiona, having unleashed the power of her lightning, fired a powerful bolt at the hellgriffin, sending a jolt through the demonic creature. The griffin convulsed in pain and let out a deafening scream.

Lea, with steady hands, drew her bow and desperately tried to bring the hellgriffin down. However, the griffin maneuvered deftly, twisting its massive body in wild aerial maneuvers to avoid the deadly arrows. In a moment of precision, Lea aimed carefully and released an arrow. The arrow pierced the air and struck the hellgriffin directly in the eye.

The hellgriffin roared in agony and momentarily lost control of its flight. Gronak seized the opportunity and delivered a powerful strike, hurling his axe. It struck the griffin with such force that it plummeted to the ground, crashing with a tremendous impact that shook the earth.

Fiona, still surrounded by magic, unleashed another bolt of lightning on the wounded hellgriffin, which roared in pain and fury. The battle raged on as the griffin desperately tried to rise, clawing and biting at its attackers.

Gronak shouted, gripping his sword tightly, "We must finish it now before it gets back up!"

As the hellgriffin lay on the ground, wavering and weakened, Lea and Gronak seized the chance to defeat it together. The griffin struggled desperately to rise, but its strength was rapidly fading.

Lea, endowed with incredible agility and dexterity, dodged the griffin's final desperate attacks. With her dagger in hand, she cautiously approached the demonic creature. Her eyes flashed with determination as she focused on the griffin's heart. Lea whispered with inner fury, "This is your end, you damned monster."

Sensing its impending doom, the griffin roared in pain and desperation. But Lea was swift, driving her dagger deep into the griffin's heart. A bone-chilling screech filled the air as the hellgriffin took its last breath.

Wasting no time, Gronak seized the moment and swung his mighty sword with all his strength. The deadly blow severed the griffin's neck and its head was cleaved off.

Gronak roared with adrenaline, "We did it! For Lea's village!"

The griffin's body convulsed one last time before lying lifeless on the ground. The heroes stood breathless over the fallen hellgriffin, which had once been an unstoppable threat. Their courage and teamwork had saved the day. The dangerous griffin was defeated and the villagers of Lea's home could finally breathe a sigh of relief and hope again.

Lea smiled wearily, gratitude shining in her eyes. "We did it, we really did it. Thank you, Gronak and Fiona. You've saved my village."

Her words were filled with deep appreciation and respect for her companions. Lea had an extraordinary ability with both the bow and her dagger. With her skillful hand and sharp eye, she could make precise shots to defeat her enemies. Gronak was impressed by her skill and Fiona admired her bravery.

Gronak said to Lea, nodding appreciatively, "Your combat skills are truly remarkable, Lea. How you dodged those attacks and your prowess with the bow just incredible."

Lea smiled modestly and replied, "I only did what was necessary to defend my village. And I could only do it because you both were by my side."

After Gronak, Fiona and Lea had defeated the hellgriffin and saved the village from further harm, the surviving villagers gathered around them. Most were still in shock and mourning the loss of their homes and loved ones, but there was also a sense of relief in their eyes.

An elderly man with gray hair, who introduced himself as the village elder, stepped forward and bowed deeply to the three adventurers. "I am the village elder and speak on behalf of all our villagers. We are infinitely grateful for your help and bravery. You have saved us from destruction and we will never forget what you have done for us."

Gronak and Fiona nodded respectfully to the village elder. Gronak responded, "It was our honor to help you. We're glad we arrived in time to stand by your side."

The villagers echoed the elder's words, expressing their gratitude. Some embraced the adventurers, others shook their hands, assuring them that they would remain forever in their hearts.

Finally, the village elder invited Gronak and Fiona to stay in the village and rest to recover from the ordeal of battle. The two gratefully agreed, ready to take a well-deserved break in the village's community.

The next morning, the sun had just risen when Gronak and Fiona decided to set out early. They were determined to continue their journey to stop Xalis. The two had already packed their belongings and were ready to face the dangers of their adventures once more.

As they opened the door to their lodging, they were surprised to find Lea standing outside. Lea, whom they had met the previous day while saving her village, had a determined expression on her face. She stepped forward and spoke softly, "I heard you're planning to defeat Xalis. I want to join you on your journey."

Gronak and Fiona exchanged concerned looks. They knew this journey would be extremely dangerous and did not want to put Lea in harm's way. But as they looked into Lea's eyes, they saw the resolve within her.

Fiona spoke calmly to Lea, "Lea, this journey won't be easy. Xalis is an extremely powerful sorcerer and we don't know what lies ahead. It could be very dangerous and we don't want to put you at risk."

Lea, however, was undeterred. "I understand the dangers, but I want to help defeat Xalis to prevent other villages from suffering the same fate. Yesterday, you proved that you are brave and strong warriors and I want to fight alongside you."

Gronak and Fiona exchanged looks again, sensing that Lea's decision was unshakable. Finally, they nodded in agreement. "Very well, Lea," Gronak said with a hint of admiration in his voice. "If you wish to join us, then so be it. But be warned, it will be dangerous."

Lea beamed with joy and ran back to her house to pack her things. When Lea returned to Gronak and Fiona, the village elder unexpectedly stood before the two adventurers. The older man had a stern expression on his face and his presence was unexpected.

He addressed Lea directly, speaking in a serious tone. "Lea, you know the rules of our village. You cannot simply leave the forest without the blessing of the elder. There are laws and traditions of the elves that you must respect."

Gronak and Fiona were confused and asked for clarification. "What exactly do you mean, elder?" Fiona inquired politely. "What laws must Lea follow to leave the forest?"

The elder sighed heavily and explained, "In our community, it is forbidden to leave the forest without the blessing of the elder. The nature spirits that dwell in our forest are very important to us elves, you must understand. They grant us the power of nature magic, which gives us elves our abilities and magic. In return, we protect the forest and, thus, the nature spirits. Therefore, it is our highest rule to stay in the forest to protect it. Only with the elder's blessing may an elf leave the forest, so as not to anger the nature spirits. This rule is in place to ensure the safety of our village and to respect our connection to nature. Lea knows this very well."

He turned his gaze back to Lea and spoke to her sternly. "Lea, you know these laws. You know they cannot be broken lightly. Your duty is to stay here and protect the village and the forest, as our tradition demands."

Lea lowered her gaze, feeling torn between her desire to accompany Gronak and Fiona to defeat Xalis and her sense of responsibility to her village and her roots. She knew the elder was right and that she needed to respect the rules of the elves.

Gronak, who was naturally practical, asked the village chief, "Where exactly can we find the High Elder? We will go to him and ask for his blessing so that Lea can accompany us. Then it would be alright, wouldn't it?"

The village chief pondered for a moment and finally answered, "Yes, that would be alright. The High Elder lives about an hour's walk from the village, in a remote part of the forest. It's a place not many of us visit, as it is deep in nature."

Gronak and Fiona exchanged a thoughtful look and nodded to each other. "Then we will set out and ask the

High Elder for his blessing," Fiona declared. "We respect the importance of your community's laws and traditions."

The village chief observed the determination in their eyes and after a moment of contemplation, he agreed. "Be careful on your journey and may the High Elder look favorably upon your request. Lea, you have earned our respect for your courage. Follow your heart." Lea was pleased with the village chief's approval and thanked him warmly. She felt she was on the right path and that her dream was within reach.

The three companions continued their journey through the dense forest of the elves. The thick canopy of the tall trees above them formed an impenetrable net, filtering the sunlight and bathing the forest in a gentle, green light. The rustling of leaves and the song of birds accompanied them as they moved through the lush vegetation.

During their hike through the picturesque forest, Gronak couldn't contain his innate curiosity and turned to Lea with a slightly thoughtful look. "Lea, if you don't mind me asking, how old are you exactly?"

A gentle smile spread across Lea's face as she heard his question. "I'm just 89 years old."

Gronak, surprised by her answer, could barely conceal his astonishment. His eyes widened slightly as he processed her words. "Only 89 years?" His voice sounded incredulous and there was a hint of admiration for her youthfulness in his tone.

Fiona, who had been attentively following the conversation, patiently explained to Gronak, "Elves have a much longer lifespan than most other races. They can live for several centuries and age very slowly. In human years, Lea is about the equivalent of a young woman around 17 years old."

Gronak was fascinated by this knowledge. He could hardly imagine what it was like to live so long and age so slowly. "That's truly remarkable," he remarked. "You must have had many fascinating experiences."

Lea nodded and shared some of her adventures she had experienced over many years living in the Elven forest. As they walked through the forest, the bond between the three grew stronger and they exchanged stories and experiences. The journey to the High Elder became not only a quest for permission but also an opportunity to learn from each other and strengthen their ties.

After a long and challenging hike, Gronak, Fiona and Lea finally reached the sacred tree of the Elven forest, which also served as the main seat of the High Elder. The tree was undoubtedly a majestic and impressive wonder of nature. Its trunk extended several hundred feet into the air and radiated an aura of magic and mysticism that seemed to permeate the air around it.

The surroundings around the tree seemed as if they had sprung directly from a fairy tale. Soft, shimmering rays of light filtered through the dense canopy, bathing the ground in a warm, green glow. The atmosphere was filled with a calm and mysterious presence. All around and on the tree, one could see small tree spirits watching the visitors' arrival with curious but respectful eyes.

At the base of this enormous tree, an entrance led into the tree's interior. The entrance itself was an imposing passage framed by glowing plants and vines. This entrance seemed to invite one to step deep into the heart of the sacred tree, where the High Elder resided.

Fiona felt the tree's energy pulsing around them and whispered softly to her companions. "This place is truly amazing and infused with magic. We should conduct ourselves with respect and prepare for our upcoming visit with the High Elder." The reverence for this sacred place was palpable, filling the group with humility.

As they approached the entrance, they began to speak with each other to ease their nervousness. Lea, with a hint of uncertainty in her voice, addressed Gronak and Fiona. "I'm a bit worried about his response. I hope the High Elder will support our endeavor."

Gronak nodded in agreement, but his expression revealed a certain seriousness. "Yes, I hope so too. But we must be aware that he will thoroughly scrutinize our motives and our resolve before making a decision."

Fiona, with a thoughtful expression on her face, joined the conversation. "We should speak openly and honestly about our intentions. We need to show him that we are willing to do whatever it takes to defeat Xalis. Only then can we earn his trust and secure his support."

At the entrance to the Sacred Tree, two imposing elven warriors stood guard, their armor made of gleaming green metal. They examined the group of Gronak, Fiona and Lea and asked in a stern but polite tone, "What brings you to the sacred tree?"

Lea stepped forward with a firm stride, her posture and voice clear as she explained, "We seek an audience with the High Elder. It is of utmost importance that we speak with him."

Before the guards had a chance to respond, a wise and majestic voice from within the monumental tree cut through the silence. The words were like a gentle but firm

112

command. "Let them in." It was as if the voice carried the echo of ancient power and authority, embodying respect and obedience.

The guards immediately obeyed the command and stepped aside to allow Gronak, Fiona and Lea to pass. The group entered the sacred tree and felt the presence of ancient magic and wisdom permeating the place. They were eager to meet the High Elder and request his permission for Lea to accompany them on their perilous journey.

As the group entered the sacred tree, Fiona immediately sensed the overwhelming presence of nature magic that permeated the place. The interior of the tree was remarkably natural yet deeply infused with magic. Everywhere on the walls hung orbs entwined with roots, from which a pleasant, soft green light emanated, bathing the room in a soothing glow.

The orbs seemed not only to serve as decoration but also contributed to the overall magic of the tree. It was as if nature itself lived and breathed within this room and Fiona could almost feel the strong connection between the elves and their sacred tree. The harmony between magic and nature created a captivating atmosphere.

Gronak, impressed by the magic of the place, could not help but express his awe. He said softly to Fiona and Lea, "I've never seen anything so amazing. This magic is incredible. It's as if the tree is speaking to us."

Fiona nodded in agreement and replied, "Yes, Gronak, it is truly remarkable. This place breathes history and wisdom. We should conduct ourselves with respect. I am very curious to see what the High Elder is like."

Lea, admiring the fascinating surroundings, added, "The connection between the elves and nature is truly special. I hope the High Elder can understand and support our intentions."

At the end of the long corridor guarded by the sentries, the group reached a spacious hall. In the center of this hall stood a massive throne, intricately carved from wood and surrounded by a majestic aura. On this throne sat the High Elder, an elven elder of impressive size and age. His long silver hair fell over his shoulders and his face bore the marks of many centuries of wisdom and experience. His eyes were a deep green that seemed to reflect the forest itself, radiating an unparalleled depth. It was as if he carried the essence of the forest and the wisdom of the ages within him.

The group approached the High Elder's massive throne with respectful demeanor. The High Elder, whose voice sounded calm and wise, began the conversation with the words, "I have been expecting you."

The statement left both Gronak and Fiona astonished. It seemed as though the High Elder had known of their arrival in advance and this realization was as fascinating as it was mysterious.

The elven elder continued, "In this forest, there is a connection between all living beings and nature itself. I am closely connected with the events in my woods and can perceive much. I am aware of your plan to defeat Xalis and I know that you are here because of Lea."

Lea stepped before the High Elder's throne and lowered her head respectfully. "Esteemed High Elder," she began, "I ask for your permission to leave the forest and travel with Gronak and Fiona to stop Xalis. It is my destiny to fight this powerful enemy and I ask you to grant me this blessing."

The High Elder looked at Lea with a benevolent gaze and spoke with admiration in his voice. "I admire your determination, Lea. But that is not the only reason." His words were gentle and compassionate.

Lea lowered her head as if she knew what he meant. Gronak and Fiona, curious, glanced between Lea and the High Elder and finally asked, "What do you mean by that?"

The High Elder replied calmly, "It is about your sister, isn't it?" His eyes conveyed a deep understanding of Lea's situation.

Lea nodded sadly and then turned to her two companions. Her voice was tinged with sorrow as she recounted, "I'm sorry I didn't tell you earlier, but what the High Elder says is true. A few moons ago, my village was attacked. My parents were killed and my little sister Elena was taken by the attackers." The words came heavily from her lips and the memory of the painful loss of her family weighed heavily on her.

Fiona and Gronak looked at Lea with sympathy, now understanding the full extent of her motivation. Lea not only wanted to defeat Xalis but also hoped to find her sister and avenge her family.

The High Elder rose from his throne and approached Lea. "Your fate is closely tied to this mission and these two people, Lea. I give you not only my permission but also the blessing of the forest. May nature and the spirits of the forest assist you on your path."

Lea burst into tears at the High Elder's words. She knew that this journey would not only fulfill her own destiny but also provide a chance to find her sister and achieve justice for her family.

Fiona gently approached Lea, who had collapsed to her knees in tears and placed a comforting hand on her shoulder. "It's okay, Lea. You could have told us. We will help you find your sister and defeat Xalis."

Gronak nodded in agreement and added, "We will do everything in our power to help you, Lea. You are not alone in this mission."

The High Elder, who had been observing the scene, stepped forward again and spoke to Lea. "These two are good people; do not bring shame upon them, Lea. Trust them and let them stand by your side."

Lea agreed and promised to support the two of them as best as she could. She knew she had found allies she could rely on.

The High Elder then turned to Gronak and Fiona and requested, "Take good care of Lea. Her mission is of great importance and she will need your support."

Fiona and Gronak nodded and promised to protect and support Lea on her journey, no matter the challenges they faced. Together, they now had a clear mission and the support of the High Elder and the forest itself.

Once all the open questions had been addressed and Lea had shared her heart-wrenching story, the High Elder took on a very serious tone. He began to introduce the attendees to the world of Xalis, the Dark Sorcerer. The three brave adventurers listened intently as he began his narrative.

"Let us now speak of Xalis," began the High Elder, placing heavy emphasis on each word. The eyes of the three companions were fixed on him, filled with anticipation and a hint of concern.

The High Elder continued, unfolding the dark history of the dark sorcerer Xalis. "Xalis was already responsible for terror and destruction in this world 1200 years ago and his malevolent deeds know no bounds. Then as now, he sent forth his legions of demonic creatures to spread fear and terror and to bring the world to its knees."

The group listened intently to the High Elder's words, struggling to comprehend how a being could endure over such a long span of time and repeatedly bring ruin to the world.

The High Elder continued his account, delving into Xalis is cruel abilities and dangerous intentions. "Xalis is a dark sorcerer of immeasurable power. He has mastered dark rituals and spells that allow him to control his creatures and destroy his enemies in cruel ways. With the ability to create darkness and chaos wherever he goes, he is an unstoppable threat to the world."

The three adventurers listened in rapt attention as the High Elder further illuminated Xalis is sinister nature. In their hearts, their resolve grew stronger to defeat this dark sorcerer and free the world from his darkness.

The High Elder continued with a measured voice, his words carrying the weight of centuries of knowledge and concern. "One day, however, a group of brave warriors confronted Xalis. After a fierce and costly battle, they managed to seal Xalis forever with a powerful magical artifact." As he spoke, a faint glimmer of hope could be seen in the eyes of those present. The notion that Xalis had once been defeated sparked a quiet sense of optimism.

But then, as the High Elder continued, his gaze fell and his voice took on a sorrowful tone. "Unfortunately, no one knows how Xalis managed to break the seal and escape from his confinement." A deep sigh filled the room as the oppressive reality of this fact weighed heavily on the attendees.

Fiona, always seeking solutions, dared to ask a question. "Couldn't we try to seal Xalis again like before? Perhaps there is a way."

The High Elder shook his head regretfully. "That is unfortunately not possible. The unique artifact used in the sealing was destroyed during the ritual itself. There is no second artifact of that kind to seal Xalis again." The disappointment in his words was palpable and the prospect of defeating Xalis suddenly seemed even more grim.

Concern spread across the faces of Gronak, Fiona and Lea as they realized that Xalis could not simply be sealed again. But the High Elder sought to offer them hope.

He said with a gentle smile, "Xalis may be powerful, but he is not invincible. You can still defeat him, but you must become stronger than you are now."

The High Elder's eyes sparkled with hope as he continued, "I wish to contribute to this effort myself. I have the ability to focus and amplify a person's strength."

The group looked on eagerly at the High Elder, who evidently possessed a powerful ability that could aid them in their mission.

"With my help, you can maximize your abilities and challenge Xalis," the High Elder explained. "But you must also continue to develop your own skills and work as a team. Together, you can overcome the darkness."

The High Elder smiled and said, "Come to me then, so that I may strengthen you." Gronak stepped forward and approached him. The High Elder placed his hand gently on Gronak's head.

At the moment the High Elder's hand touched Gronak's head, an immense energy surged through his body. A wave of unparalleled strength and vital life force spread rapidly within him and he could feel his muscles growing stronger with each passing second. It was as if he was suddenly absorbing the essence of nature and the unstoppable energy of the forest itself.

Gronak could not contain his excitement and said to his companions, "This is incredible! I feel stronger than ever before. This energy will be extremely useful for our upcoming task."

Fiona also stepped closer to the High Elder, who gently placed his hand on her forehead. Instantly, she felt her magical abilities reach a level of strength she had never known before. Her control over the elements seemed to deepen and she could almost feel the untamed power of nature in her hands. She knew she was now capable of unleashing magical forces of unprecedented magnitude.

Fiona beamed with joy. "This connection to magic is overwhelming. I will make sure to use it wisely and responsibly."

Lea, who also approached the High Elder, experienced a remarkable increase in her physical and mental strength. Her senses seemed to sharpen dramatically and she felt as if she could perceive the world around her with even greater precision. Her movements became smoother and her reflexes sharper, as if she could now effortlessly tackle the most challenging obstacles.

Lea could not hide her gratitude and said to the High Elder, "Thank you from the bottom of my heart for this gift. I promise to use it wisely."

The High Elder withdrew his hand and smiled with satisfaction. "You are now strengthened and ready to embark on your journey. Remember to stay united and act as a team."

The three adventurers were overwhelmed by the sense of strength the High Elder had bestowed upon them. It was an incredible gift, which they accepted with great gratitude.

Lea, overwhelmed with emotion, addressed the High Elder. "We will do our best to justify your trust. Xalis will be defeated and my sister will be rescued, I promise."

Gronak found the right words and added, "We are deeply grateful for your support. Your magic will aid us on our path and we will use this gift responsibly."

Fiona, still feeling her newfound magic within her, said, "May the light of hope guide us and lead our mission to success. We will do everything in our power to defeat Xalis and rescue Lea's sister."

The High Elder smiled. "May it be of benefit on your journey and may the light of hope illuminate your path. Good luck on your mission to defeat Xalis and rescue Lea's sister. I place my full trust in your hands."

The three thanked the High Elder from the bottom of their hearts for his support and promised not to disappoint his trust. With renewed strength, they left the Sacred Tree and set out once again, determined to fulfill their mission and vanquish the evil.

As they reached the edge of the forest, Lea turned one last time and looked back at the majestic Elven Forest. It had been a place full of magic and mystique, her home. The green treetops reached high into the sky and the gentle rustling of the leaves was like a sweet melody. Gronak and Fiona felt the melancholy in Lea's gaze and spoke words of encouragement to her.

Gronak soothingly placed his large hand on Lea's shoulder and said compassionately, "We will return, Lea, once our mission is complete. You will see your home again and free your sister. The forest will be waiting for us."

Fiona added, her eyes full of confidence and her voice a gentle breath of encouragement, "We are by your side, Lea. Together we will defeat Xalis and find your sister. You are not alone in this dark time."

Lea smiled at both of them with hope, her eyes shining with optimism and she nodded firmly. "Thank you, Gronak. Thank you, Fiona. Let's set off and stop the evil." Her words were a vow, a promise she would not break as long as there was a spark of life within her.

With renewed determination and a hint of wistfulness in her heart, they set off. Their thoughts were filled with adventure and hope for a better future. Their journey would undoubtedly be dangerous, but they had the power of unity and the support of the Elder on their side, giving them hope for a better tomorrow, a world free from the threat of Xalis and his dark power.

Chapter 6: The Trading City

It had been some time since Gronak, Fiona and Lea had left the Elven Forest. The memories of the majestic forest and the Elder accompanied them on their journey. The days had turned into grueling hikes, the sun burned on their heads and the wind swept through their hair. Yet they were motivated to continue their mission, which drove them forward.

As they climbed a hill, they could see the outlines of a city in the distance. The city was nestled in a fertile valley and radiated a sense of calm and tranquility. Tall towers and massive city walls rose majestically against the blue sky.

Lea, who spotted the city first, could barely contain her curiosity. "Look, a city! This is a welcome change after all this hiking. Maybe we can gather some information about Xalis here."

Fiona nodded in agreement and said, "And our supplies could use a replenishment. It's a good place to get new equipment and rest for a bit."

Gronak, always on the lookout for a chance to rest, said with a grin, "And I could use a good meal and a tavern to quench my thirst."

As they approached the city, the activity grew more vibrant. The clattering of carts, the clatter of hooves on cobblestone streets and the singing of merchants peddling their wares filled the air. The enticing smell of fresh bread and exotic spices wafted into their noses, whetting their appetites.

The city gates opened before them and they were greeted by friendly residents who welcomed them with open arms. An older man with a friendly smile approached them. "Welcome to our city, travelers! You look exhausted. How can we assist you?"

Fiona responded gratefully, "Thank you for the warm welcome. We are on an important mission. We could also use a rest and some fresh supplies."

The man nodded understandingly and replied, "You are most welcome here. I will show you the way to the tavern where you can rest and refresh yourselves. And if you are looking for supplies and equipment, be sure to visit the merchant district."

Gronak, Fiona and Lea thanked the man for the information and set off to explore the city.

Gronak excitedly turned to Lea. "How about it, Lea? Shall we head to the weapon shop and see if we can find something good?" Lea looked up at Gronak and responded eagerly, "Sure, I'm curious to see what they have to offer."

Fiona smiled and said to both of them, "Feel free to explore. I'd like to check out a magic store. We'll meet up later."

Gronak and Lea wandered through the bustling streets of the city, their steps echoing on the cobblestone ground. The sounds of the city, the murmur of people and the calls of merchants filled the air. Their mission required equipment of the highest quality and they were in search of a blacksmith who could meet their needs.

After a while of searching, they finally found a small forge on the edge of town. The smell of molten metal and coal smoke hung heavy in the air as they opened the door and were enveloped by the warmth of the forge. Inside, numerous workbenches and anvils were in use by half a dozen blacksmiths. Sparks flew from the hearths as the blacksmiths heated their iron to work it.

An older blacksmith, his face marked by many years of hard work, turned to them and asked in a gruff voice, "What can I do for you, travelers?"

Gronak and Lea explained their intention to repair their equipment and look for new weapons and armor. The blacksmith nodded understandingly and led them to a rack full of weapons and armor. Everywhere, shiny swords, sparkling armors and other impressive weapons hung.

Gronak examined the swords and shields and eventually found a sword that suited his taste. He lifted it and made a few test cuts in the air. The blacksmith explained, "This is a sword made of folded steel. It's light yet strong and the blade retains its sharpness over a long time."

Lea, wanting to perfect her archery skills, searched for a suitable bow. The blacksmith showed her various models and explained the differences. She eventually chose a bow made of fine wood and some carefully crafted arrows. The blacksmith said, "This bow is specially made for precision. The arrows fly faster and hit more accurately."

As Gronak and Lea made their choices, the blacksmith began repairing and adjusting their equipment. With skilled hands, he worked on Gronak's axe, making it sharper and more resilient. Lea's dagger received some adjustments to give her better precision.

When the blacksmith was finally finished, he handed Gronak and Lea their new weapons and armor. Gronak felt the lightness yet strength of his new sword and Lea was impressed with the smoothness and precision of her bow.

They paid the blacksmith generously and thanked him warmly. "These are excellent works, Master Blacksmith. We are very grateful."

Lea added excitedly, "This equipment will be very useful for our mission. Thank you for your skills."

The blacksmith smiled with satisfaction. "It was a pleasure to help you. May your journey be safe and successful, travelers."

With their newly improved weapons and armor, Gronak and Lea left the forge and returned to the bustling streets of the town.

Fiona entered the magic shop located in the heart of the city. The door opened with a soft chime as she stepped inside. The shop was small and cozy, but its walls were lined to the brim with shelves and display cases holding a seemingly endless variety of magical items, crystals and books. The room was bathed in a gentle, dim light reflected from the many glass orbs and crystals. The scent of burnt sandalwood and exotic herbs lingered in the air, giving the room a mysterious atmosphere.

Fiona's footsteps echoed softly on the wooden-paneled floor as she browsed the shelves and display cases with curious eyes. Crystals of all colors and shapes glittered and shimmered in the showcases. Some seemed to radiate magical energies, while others were simply beautiful to behold. On the shelves, enchanting potions were displayed in bottles of various shapes and sizes. Some contained liquids of bright gold, while others had a mysterious, pale green liquid that Fiona couldn't immediately identify.

Behind the counter stood an older woman with gray hair, wrapped in a long, dark blue cloak. Her eyes had a wise expression and she greeted Fiona with warm friendliness as she approached.

"Welcome, young mage," she said to Fiona. "How can I assist you? Are you looking for something specific?"

Fiona returned the smile and explained, "I'm looking for magical artifacts and potions that might be useful for my upcoming adventures."

The woman nodded understandingly and began showing Fiona various items and potions. She took a necklace with a sparkling diamond from a display case and explained, "This is an amulet chain that can protect the wearer from evil spirits and demons. The diamond has been blessed by an ancient sorcerer."

Fiona looked at the diamond with fascination, then her gaze fell upon a magnificent wand adorned with sparkling gemstones. "What about this wand?" she asked.

The woman carefully took the wand in her hand. "This wand is embellished with gemstones that can enhance various magical abilities. It was created by a skilled mage and possesses a mysterious power."

Fiona nodded and then examined a small vial with a purple liquid. "And what is this?" she asked curiously.

The woman smiled and explained, "That is a concentration potion. It can improve mental clarity and enhance focus. A sip of it can be very useful in critical situations."

After Fiona made her selections, she paid generously for the magical potions and artifacts. She thanked the woman warmly and left the shop to rejoin her friends at the local forge. With her newly acquired magical items, she felt prepared for the upcoming adventures and challenges that awaited her.

When Gronak, Fiona and Lea met up at the forge, they began to show each other their new items. Gronak proudly displayed his new sword and gleaming shield, which he had acquired at the forge. The blade of the sword glinted in the sunlight and the shield was adorned with intricate designs.

Fiona showed her friends the magical artifacts and potions she had bought from the magic shop. The amulet chain with the sparkling diamond and the small vial with the purple liquid piqued their curiosity. She explained how each of these items could be useful in various situations and how she looked forward to further developing her magical abilities.

After admiring their new acquisitions, they decided to stroll leisurely through the streets of the city and enjoy the atmosphere. The city was bustling with life and they enjoyed exploring the various shops and stalls.

Suddenly, a small boy appeared in front of them and snatched Fiona's wallet from her pocket. Fiona immediately felt the theft and called after the boy, while Gronak and Lea quickly tackled him to hold him down.

The boy was barely older than ten and wore worn and dirty clothes. He struggled desperately against Gronak and Lea, but their superior strength gave him no chance. Fiona stepped closer and spoke to the boy in a gentle voice while he continued to flail. "Why did you do this?" she asked empathetically.

The boy stammered out a few incoherent words, but gradually the truth came to light. He told them that he was an orphan with no place to live. The streets of the city had become his home and he had learned to survive through theft. It was the only thing that had helped him so far, but he knew it was wrong.

Gronak and Lea slowly released the boy as Fiona kindly offered for him to follow them. She assured him that they would help him find a better way to survive. The boy, initially mistrustful, sensed that these strangers were different from most adults he had encountered. Their friendly and concerned tone piqued his interest and he eventually agreed to follow them.

The four of them went together to a nearby market, bustling with busy traders and curious buyers. Fiona bought food and clothes for the boy, who still seemed a bit shy and reserved. She asked him his name and he replied hesitantly, "My name is Kian."

Fiona, Gronak and Lea sat with Kian in a shaded spot at the market where they spread out their purchases. Fiona gently began to ask Kian about his story. Kian looked at her hesitantly, then lowered his gaze to the ground and began to speak quietly.

"My parents died when I was very young," he started. "I had no other relatives and was not taken in by anyone. So, I grew up alone on the streets of this city. The other children I live with are like my family, but it's hard to find food and stay warm. So, I learned to steal to survive."

As he spoke, the sadness in Kian's eyes, marked by deprivation and loss, was evident. He had experienced a harsh reality that was far too heavy for such a young child.

Fiona, Gronak and Lea listened attentively and empathized with Kian. They quickly realized that Kian was not a villain but was merely trying to survive in this harsh world. After a brief consultation, they decided to help him. Fiona gently placed her hand on Kian's shoulder and said, "Kian, you are not alone. We will help you find a better way to live. You don't have to steal to have food and a home."

Lea nodded in agreement and smiled at Kian. "You deserve a second chance, Kian. We won't let you down."

Kian, initially full of mistrust, began to slowly understand that there were people who offered him a second chance and showed him that there were better ways to shape his life. The boy, touched by their kindness, gave a slight smile and felt a sense of hope for the first time in a long while. "Thank you," he whispered, "I'll do my best not to disappoint you."

As they considered Kian's future, they came up with the idea of giving him a chance at honest work. They inquired around and learned that the owner of the local weapon shop was looking for an apprentice to learn the art of blacksmithing.

Determined, they took Kian to the shop and introduced him to the owner, an experienced weaponsmith with a serious demeanor. The blacksmith was skeptical when he saw the young boy, but Kian was eager to prove himself. He demonstrated his skills and interest in blacksmithing and spoke about his desire to become an honest craftsman and leave his former life behind. After the blacksmith asked Kian a few questions and examined his abilities more closely, he eventually agreed to take him on as an apprentice.

With his new job and the opportunity to work honestly, Kian began to flourish. He was grateful for the group's help and promised to change his life. The trio was pleased that they could help a young boy who was simply trying to survive and that they had contributed to changing his future.

In the evening, as the sun set and the sky turned a deep red, they sought out a tavern to rest and have something to eat. The tavern was a lively place, filled with loud voices and sounds. The scent of roasted meat, beer and wine hung in the air, attracting hungry and thirsty travelers.

As they entered the tavern, the walls were decorated with swords, shields and other weapons. Torches hung from the ceiling, casting flickering light over the scene. A large fireplace dominated the back wall, while long tables and benches filled the center of the room.

The patrons were a colorful mix of races and cultures. Humans, dwarves, elves and even a few halflings sat at the tables, enjoying a glass of beer or wine. Some played card or dice games, while others loudly discussed their adventures.

At the end of the tavern, there was a small stage where a bard played a lute and sang catchy songs. A small dance floor was in front of it and a few couples swayed their hips to the lively music.

The tavern keeper, a sturdy woman with red hair and a friendly smile, moved between the tables taking orders. She wore a white shirt and an apron and always kept a keen eye on the needs of her guests. The tavern offered a good selection of beers, wines and spirits, as well as hearty dishes like roasted chicken, sausages and ham. She recommended the local beer, known for its rich flavor.

Overall, the tavern was a cozy place where one could relax after a long day on the road and enjoy something to eat and drink while mingling with other adventurers and travelers. The warm atmosphere and cheerful mood of the guests invited them to stay.

As they sat together at a cozy table in the tavern and enjoyed their meal, Fiona, Gronak and Lea talked about their past adventures and the upcoming challenges that awaited them. The crackling fire in the hearth bathed the room in a warm, inviting light.

Fiona started the conversation, excitedly sharing her plans to visit an ancient library in search of a lost spellbook. "The library is said to hold hidden treasures of magical knowledge," she said eagerly. "I hope to finally track down that ancient spellbook I've been searching for so long."

Gronak, who was busy with a large piece of roasted meat, looked up and grinned as he began to recount his own tale. "I had my own adventure," he said. "A powerful wyvern was terrorizing a remote area and I was called to deal with the threat. After a grueling battle, I managed to defeat the wyvern and free the village."

After the meal, they relaxed by the hearth and shared stories with other travelers who were also staying in the tavern. The tales ranged from legendary treasure hunts to fascinating encounters with rare creatures. Each traveler had their own story to tell and the stories flowed in a continuous stream of adventures and mysteries.

The evening atmosphere, the warmth of the town's residents and the exciting stories from other travelers made their stay in the city an unforgettable experience.

After a night of storytelling and cozy camaraderie, Gronak, Fiona and Lea finally retired to their rooms in the tavern for sleep. The rooms were simple but comfortably furnished. The beds provided a restful night's sleep and the exhaustion from their long journey and the day's exciting events soon lulled them into a deep, restorative slumber.

The next morning, they awoke refreshed and full of energy. The first rays of the day's sun streamed through the windows, bathing their rooms in a warm, golden light. It was time to set out and continue their adventures. The anticipation of new discoveries and challenges was palpable.

As they descended the stairs into the tavern's common room, they immediately noticed something was amiss. Loud, unusual noises were coming from the kitchen. Screeching, shouting and the clattering of dishes could be heard. Curiosity led them towards the kitchen and when they opened the door, they were met with an unexpected sight.

The tavern keeper, an older woman in a crumpled apron dress, stood amidst a scene of chaos. She was wielding a broom and desperately fighting against a rat. But this was no ordinary rat. It was enormous.

The giant rat was about the size of a fully grown dog and had a thick, dirty fur. Its eyes were wild and glowing red and its sharp teeth protruded menacingly from its mouth. Its rat claws scratched wildly on the floor as it tried to drive the tavern keeper away.

The rat's fur was thick and its tail was longer than that of an ordinary rat. With every swing of the broom, the tavern keeper tried to drive the beast away, but the giant rat showed no fear and fought back with impressive aggression.

Its screeching and hissing filled the room and tables and chairs were overturned. The other tavern guests had retreated to watch the fight from a safe distance, with some daring to place enthusiastic bets on whether the tavern keeper or the giant rat would prevail.

Gronak, who had charged into the battle against the giant rat, acted swiftly. His massive muscles tensed as he swung his enormous axe and struck the creature directly on the head with a powerful blow. A deafening impact filled the kitchen and the force of the strike sent the rat creature crashing to the ground.

The rat creature twitched a few more times, its monstrous body writhing in final convulsions before it finally lay still. Gronak stood triumphantly over his defeated foe, breathing heavily but with a look of joy in his eyes at the victory.

The tavern keeper, who had been in grave danger, breathed a sigh of relief and approached Gronak. "Thank you so much," she said with a hint of admiration in her voice. "You've saved us. These rats are a true plague and are growing bolder. It was brave of you to come to my aid."

Gronak, still feeling the aftermath of the fight in his arms, smiled and replied. "It was a pleasure to help. But where do these giant rats come from and why are they so aggressive?"

The tavern keeper sighed and sat down at one of the kitchen tables as Gronak, Fiona and Lea listened attentively. She began to recount the strange events that had been occurring in the city.

"For weeks now, there have been repeated attacks by giant rats in our city," she began, her voice low and concerned. "Normally, they live in the sewers and don't cause any problems for the residents. But recently, they've been coming out of the sewers and onto the streets, behaving extremely aggressively."

Fiona frowned as she absorbed the information. "That sounds really strange. Have the city guards offered any explanation?"

The tavern keeper sighed again and shook her head. "The city guards have tried to push them back, but it seems they keep coming back. It's as if they are being driven by something, something that makes them extremely aggressive."

Lea, pondering the unusual circumstances, asked further. "Do you have any suspicions about what might have stirred up the giant rats? Are there any rumors or clues?"

The tavern keeper thought for a moment, resting her chin on her hand. Finally, she responded. "There are rumors about strange occurrences in the sewers. Eerie noises, unusual apparitions and unexplained phenomena. Some say there could be monsters involved, but no one knows for sure."

Fiona, who was reflecting on the mysterious incidents in the sewers, finally voiced her thoughts. "It seems like there's a serious problem in the sewers that no one has investigated so far. Even the city guards haven't taken any interest in it."

The innkeeper sighed again and nodded in agreement. "You're right," she said with a thoughtful expression. "The sewers are a dark and dangerous place and the city's residents usually avoid them. But lately, we have no choice but to confront this problem."

Gronak, always ready for a challenge, suggested to the innkeeper. "We could take a closer look and find out what's going on in the sewers. Maybe we can solve the rat problem and free the city from this threat."

The innkeeper was relieved by Gronak's suggestion and thanked him sincerely. "That would be wonderful!" she exclaimed. "If you can solve this problem, I'll prepare a feast for you that you'll never forget."

Fiona and Lea, who were not averse to good food, immediately agreed. Gronak laughed heartily at the reaction of his companions. They were ready to accept the innkeeper's offer of a feast and look forward to enjoying delicious food upon their return.

Gronak, who was always hungry and already thinking about the upcoming meal, couldn't help but ask the innkeeper. "That sounds great! But before we get excited about the feast, could you please tell us how we can get into the sewers?"

The innkeeper nodded understandingly and led them out of the tavern to the city wall. There was a narrow, descending staircase leading underground. "This is the easiest way into the sewers. The staircase leads directly to the main tunnels, from where you can investigate the rat infestation."

The three friends thanked the innkeeper warmly for her help and set off to uncover the mystery of the rat infestation in the sewers. The staircase led them into the darkness and they entered the grim tunnels of the city's underworld.

The group wandered for some time through the gloomy corridors of the city's sewers. It was a creepy and unpleasant place, marked by damp walls, rusty pipes and muddy puddles. The floor was covered with a layer of dirt and debris and the light from sporadic torches on the walls was weak and flickering. The stench of sewage and decay hung in the air and permeated every breath. The walls were covered with damp moss and the soft splashing of water accompanied them on their way.

In the gloomy surroundings of the sewers, they felt as if they had descended into a completely different world, far from the lively city above them. Gronak, Fiona and Lea stayed together, keeping an eye out for signs of the rat infestation as they ventured deeper into the darkness.

Fiona, who was not thrilled by the unpleasant environment, remarked with a disgusted expression. "This place is really gross. I can't believe we're down here in the sewers."

Lea, who was holding her nose, responded in agreement. "Yeah, it smells like hell here. Hopefully, we'll find the cause of the rat infestation soon."

Gronak, always with a sense of humor, laughed and tried to lighten the mood. "Think of the innkeeper's good food. That'll keep us going."

As they wandered through the filthy corridors, they were suddenly attacked by several giant rats. The rodents had red eyes and approached the group with bared teeth. With their newly acquired weapons, Fiona, Lea and Gronak successfully fought off the rats and then continued on their way.

After some time, as they continued strolling through the dark passages, Lea suddenly stopped and raised a finger. "Wait a minute, I hear something," she whispered, listening intently. A faint, rhythmic murmur and soft muttering seemed to be coming from afar.

The group froze in their tracks as Fiona asked with a curious tone, "What is that sound?" Her gaze searched the dim corridor as if trying to pinpoint the source of the noise.

Lea, still listening carefully, responded after a brief pause with a quiet whisper. "It's voices, I hear people. They seem to be very close." Her words carried a mix of curiosity and caution.

The three of them quietly crept toward the sound, carefully placing their steps to avoid being heard. Eventually, they reached an old wooden door that was slightly ajar, letting in a faint light. The room beyond seemed to be bathed in a pale, subdued light coming from a few flickering torches on the walls.

The group approached the door and peered through the crack. Inside the room, they saw several armed individuals deeply engrossed in a serious discussion. The walls were covered with grimy, peeling wallpaper and the room was furnished with old, dusty rugs. Large wooden shelves were filled to the brim with books, potions and strange artifacts. In the center of the room stood a large, ornate table covered with various maps and papers.

Surrounding the people were numerous crates and barrels, which obviously played an important part in their operation. Some of the individuals wore dark cloaks that reached to their feet, while others had on leather armor.

Their faces were serious as they spoke quietly but with an agitated tone about something evidently significant.

Gronak whispered quietly to consult the group. "This looks like trouble. We should proceed cautiously and find out what they're up to down here."

Fiona agreed and added, "Yes, but we shouldn't make our presence known until we know more about their intentions." The three of them kept a close watch on the situation and waited to gather more information before taking action.

The people in the room were talking quietly about smuggling goods and other criminal activities. They appeared to be involved in illegal operations and Gronak whispered to his companions. "These are smugglers, I'm sure of it." His gaze remained fixed on the suspicious figures as he tried to overhear their conversation.

Fiona asked quietly, her eyes also fixed on the group. "What do we do now?"

Gronak thought for a moment and replied. "We should first take a look around and find a good position to learn more about their plans."

The three of them continued to creep through the dark corridors of the sewer and entered additional rooms. In one room, they discovered more barrels, which were likely filled with illegal goods. In another room, they found a collection of weapons, indicating a dangerous undertaking.

Lea whispered with tension. "It seems like we're dealing with a well-organized gang. We need to be careful and find out exactly what they're doing down here."

Gronak was tense and nodded in agreement. "Let's go a little further and see if we can find more clues." The group moved cautiously through the gloomy sewer, searching for further evidence of the smugglers' activities.

The three brave adventurers dared to open the last door and were immediately overwhelmed by a beastly stench that nearly took their breath away. The room they entered was filled with darkness and dampness, illuminated only by a few weakly flickering torches on the walls. The smell of decay and stagnant water was so dense in the air that it was almost unbearable.

Slowly, their eyes adjusted to the darkness, revealing a horrific scene. Cages lined the room, containing children of various races. Their clothes were torn, their faces marked by fear and despair. The children huddled together tightly, their eyes full of dread as they looked at the newcomers.

But the most horrifying sight was the blood covering the floor and walls of the room. In a dark corner of the room, several corpses were stacked on top of each other. It was a scene of terror that shocked Fiona so much that she had to turn away and vomit.

Gronak, on the other hand, felt his anger boiling over. His fist clenched with rage and his voice sounded menacing as he quietly vowed, "These villains will pay for their deeds, I promise you."

Suddenly, a faint and weak voice came from the back of the room. "Lea, is that you?"

Lea's hair stood on end and she abruptly turned toward the sound she had heard and rushed toward it. Gronak and Fiona were surprised but didn't hesitate for a second and followed Lea. Their hearts pounded in their chests as they saw the grim cages and the sight of the imprisoned children.

When Lea finally reached one of the cages, she burst into tears and sank to her knees. "Elena, is that you?" Lea whispered with a trembling voice and tears in her eyes. Her voice trembled with emotion and her hands shook with excitement and fear.

Gronak and Fiona arrived at Lea's side and when they looked into the cage, they froze in shock. Elena, Lea's missing sister, lay in the cage, covered in blood and barely alive. Her condition was dreadful and it was obvious that she urgently needed medical help. The silence in the room was only broken by Lea's sobs and Elena's weak gasps.

Lea tried with trembling hands and tear-blurred eyes to pick the lock of the cage. But in her excitement and desperation, she couldn't unlock it. She cursed quietly and tried again, but time was running out and Elena's condition worsened by the second.

Gronak recognized the urgency of the situation and grabbed Lea's shoulder. "Lea, let me handle this." His voice was full of concern as he looked at the desperate Lea. Gronak drew his axe and with a precise strike, he shattered the cage lock, causing it to fall into pieces. Lea immediately ripped the cage door open and carefully pulled Elena out of her dreadful prison.

"Elena, can you hear me? I'm your big sister Lea," Lea whispered with tears in her eyes as she held Elena in her arms. Her voice trembled with emotion and her eyes were red. Elena responded weakly, "Please help me, Lea." The words barely made it past her parched lips.

Fiona, who was also by the cage, focused on her magic and tried to counteract Elena's severe injuries. Her forehead was creased with effort as she whispered incantations to cast healing spells. Her gaze was fixed on Elena and she did everything in her power to save Lea's younger sister.

Fiona sighed heavily. "Her injuries are extremely severe. I need a lot of time and absolute concentration to heal her," Fiona said with concern, turning back to Elena. Her heart ached at the sight of the suffering before her and she did everything she could to help Elena.

Lea gently held her sister and whispered comforting words. "Stay with me, Elena. We'll get you out of here and Fiona will do everything she can to heal you." Her tears fell onto Elena's face as she lovingly embraced her sister, determined not to let go.

Gronak stood watchfully nearby, his eyes on the room's door to ensure no one unexpectedly entered. His expression was grim with anger and his fists were clenched with rage. Time was short, but they had found hope in discovering Elena and they would do everything to save her.

Lea gazed at her sister and could hardly hold back her tears. With a trembling voice, she asked Elena, "Did these guys in the next room do this to you?" Her heart ached with grief and rage as she saw the confirmation in Elena's faint nod.

"Yes, but especially their leader has tormented and abused us day by day," Elena whispered with her last strength before losing consciousness again. The memories of the torment she had endured were still fresh and she struggled to stay awake.

Lea felt her anger and hatred boiling up inside her. She couldn't allow these villains to go unpunished after inflicting so much suffering on her sister. Her hatred grew and she vowed to take revenge and protect Elena.

Without hesitation, Lea, driven by vengeance, stormed toward the next room where the smugglers were. Her steps were quick and purposeful and her eyes burned with determination. She wouldn't rest until she had brought justice for her sister.

Fiona, still busy healing Elena, called out to Gronak. "Gronak, quickly, go after Lea!" Her voice was full of concern for her friend, but she knew she had to stay to stabilize Elena.

Gronak hesitated for a moment, his eyes on Fiona, who desperately tried to heal Elena. "Can you handle this?" he asked worriedly, his gaze shifting between Fiona and the corridor.

Fiona nodded with concern. "Yes, don't worry about me. But you need to help Lea before something worse happens." She knew that time was of the essence and that Lea alone stood little chance against the smugglers.

Gronak nodded and rushed after Lea, his heavy sword firmly in hand. The situation was extremely dangerous and they knew they had to stick together and rescue her sister, no matter the cost.

Lea flung the door to the smugglers' room open with a loud crash. The men in the room were startled and quickly drew their weapons as they saw the furious young woman before them. Her presence alone made the atmosphere in the room more tense.

With a voice trembling with rage, Lea shouted, "Which one of you pigs is the damn leader?" Her voice was piercing and filled with fury as she glared challengingly at the men.

A door at the back of the room slowly opened and two figures entered. The first was a burly dark elf warrior, his muscles visible beneath his armor. His dark gaze revealed that he was a seasoned fighter. The second was a smaller, but richly dressed man with an arrogant grin on his face. His self-satisfied demeanor suggested that he considered himself untouchable.

The smaller man stepped forward and asked sarcastically, "Who are you and what do you want here, little girl?" His voice was mocking and challenging.

Lea shouted in fury, her eyes blazing with hatred. "Are you the leader, you miserable bastard?" Her voice trembled with rage, but at the same time, it radiated an unwavering determination.

The leader of the smuggler group laughed defiantly and replied, "Yes, I am Olaf, the leader of the smugglers. What do I owe the honor of your visit, little elf?" His grin was smug and displayed his arrogance.

"What have you done with the children?" Lea screamed angrily at Olaf. Her voice quivered with rage as she stared at Olaf, as if her gaze alone could make him answer for his actions.

Olaf laughed mockingly and responded, grinning at Lea's enraged face, "Well, what do you think? I've sold them into slavery and some I've tortured for my own amusement." His words were like a cold slap to the face and his smug expression showed no remorse.

Gronak, who had joined Lea by now, was horrified by the revelation. The thought of innocent children falling into the hands of such cruel criminals filled him with dread and fury. He turned to Lea and said calmly, "Ready when you are." His words were a promise that they would bring these ruthless criminals to justice, no matter the cost.

The two of them charged at the smugglers, their hearts filled with rage and began a fierce battle against the merciless criminals. Every blow they delivered carried the weight of their anger and the quest for justice for the innocent children who had suffered.

Gronak, with his immense strength, fought bravely against two thugs at once. His sword whirled through the air and each strike was precise and deadly. The smugglers struggled to withstand his attacks and their defense crumbled under the force of his blows. With a swing to the right and another to the left, he forced them to defend themselves while simultaneously dodging their attacks.

Lea, on the other hand, deftly drew her dagger and charged at another smuggler. With swift movements, she evaded the smuggler's attacks and then delivered a fatal stab that sent her opponent crashing to the ground. Her face was a mix of anger and concentration as she skillfully wielded her dagger.

After she sheathed the dagger, Lea drew her bow and nocked two arrows simultaneously. With calm precision, she aimed and released the arrows. One arrow pierced the chest of a thug and the other struck another standing beside him. The two men collapsed with cries of pain as Lea readied another arrow.

Meanwhile, Gronak swept aside the remaining two thugs with his powerful sword. His muscles tensed with each strike and the sound of his sword slicing through the air was deafening. With a mighty blow, he finished one off and then prepared for the final strike against the last smuggler, who was desperately defending himself.

The air was filled with battle cries, the clanging of weapons and the thud of bodies hitting the ground as Gronak and Lea bravely faced the smugglers. Their fighting spirit was unbroken and they would not rest until justice was served for the innocent children and Elena.

By the end of the bloody battle, only Olaf and his dark elf partner remained. However, things took a sudden turn when the dark elf abruptly dashed into the room they had come from and locked the door behind him. Olaf, shocked and furious, pounded on the door and roared, "Open up immediately, you traitor!"

The dark elf turned calmly to Olaf. "I'm sorry, Olaf, but I believe our partnership ends here." With these words, he turned and left Olaf in his rage. The betrayal by his partner had completely caught Olaf off guard.

As Olaf turned to face Lea, he felt a surge of fear rise in his gut. He ran past her toward the exit, but before he could escape, Lea swiftly drew her knife and threw it with great precision. The knife pierced Olaf's leg and he collapsed to the ground, screaming in pain.

Lea approached Olaf slowly, her eyes burning with fury. Olaf, lying on his back and dazed from the impact, tried to struggle to his feet and turned desperately on the floor. He begged Lea for mercy, but her ears were deaf to his pleas. In her eyes, there were tears, but they were not tears of remorse, but of pure contempt and deep pain.

With a cry, Lea jumped on Olaf and roared at him as if she wanted to scream out all the repressed anger and despair of her soul. "Spare you? Like you spared my sister and all the other children! You miserable bastard!" Her voice trembled with rage and she clenched her fists. She struck Olaf with all her might. Each of her blows was filled with the unbridled power of her emotions. Blood splattered across the room and Olaf's screams were filled with pain. With each strike, she screamed louder, as if she wanted to declare her rage and sorrow to the universe.

The blows that Lea rained down on Olaf were brutal and relentless. Olaf desperately tried to defend himself, but he had no chance against Lea's unrestrained fury and unwavering resolve. His face and body were marked by her strikes and he screamed in pain and despair.

Gronak stood silently, his expression showing anger as he watched Lea release her emotions. After some agonizingly long minutes, he finally placed his strong hand on Lea's shoulder and said gently, "Lea, that's enough, it's over."

Lea, her fists covered in blood and her strength weakened by exhaustion, looked up at Gronak. Her tears mixed with the blood on her face. She was overtaken by her exhaustion and embraced Gronak as if seeking refuge in his arms. All her pent-up emotions burst out and it was a moment of release after all the suffering and anguish she and her sister had endured.

The anger and sorrow that Lea had endured for so long were now eased by the love and support of her friends. Yet the memory of the horrors they had experienced in that underground hell would remain in their minds and hearts for a long time.

Gronak reminded Lea that they needed to return to Fiona and Elena to ensure that everything was alright. Lea agreed and they set off on their way back.

The two of them entered the room where Fiona was waiting for them. As Fiona heard the sound of their footsteps, she turned with a beaming smile. In her arms, she held Elena, who, though still weak, was alive.

Lea could barely contain her joy and ran to Elena, kneeling beside her and hugging her sister lovingly, tears in her eyes. "Are you okay, Elena? It's me, Lea."

Elena slowly opened her eyes and smiled at Lea. "You came, dear sister."

"Of course," Lea replied gently. "I've been waiting so long for this day, to finally find you." The two sisters embraced warmly, as if all the time apart was forgotten in that moment.

Gronak smiled contentedly as he watched the reunited sisters. It was a moment of joy and happiness that made them forget all the horrors and dangers they had endured.

Elena closed her eyes and fell unconscious again. Fiona turned reassuringly to Lea, trying to dispel her concern. "Don't worry, Lea. She's just sleeping." Gronak carefully lifted Elena, being mindful not to wake her.

Fiona looked worriedly at Gronak. "What about the other children?" Gronak frowned. "There are still dangerous rats running through the sewers, so it's difficult to keep an eye on all of them at once. We'll get help as quickly as possible." Fiona looked anxiously at the children. "Don't worry, we'll get help so that all of you can get out of here safely. I promise you."

The group left the gloomy sewer, their steps accompanied by a haunting echo. As they emerged into the daylight, they were greeted by the warm sun and fresh air. They took deep breaths, relieved to have escaped the underground labyrinth.

After freeing themselves from the sewer, they returned to the tavern, where the innkeeper was shocked upon seeing the group. Her eyes widened in horror.

Gronak and Fiona sat down with the innkeeper and detailed their experiences in the sewer. They recounted the giant rats, the smugglers and the kidnapped children. They explained that the rats had only come to the city because the smugglers had disturbed their habitat in order to sell and abuse the children as commodities.

The innkeeper listened attentively, her face reflecting horror and concern. "This is dreadful," she said with a trembling voice. "I had no idea what was happening beneath the city. I thank you from the bottom of my heart for dealing with this matter and saving our town from this terrible problem."

The innkeeper immediately acted on the information from Gronak and Fiona. She summoned her young apprentice, Ruben, with an urgent gesture and instructed him, "Ruben, go straight to the city guard and report this incident. They need to free the remaining prisoners from the sewer."

Ruben nodded eagerly and hurried out of the tavern to inform the city guard about the situation.

The innkeeper led the exhausted group to one of the guest rooms in the tavern, where Gronak gently placed Elena in bed. Lea sat anxiously beside her sister and held her hand tightly. Tears were in her eyes and her worry for Elena was evident.

Fiona tried to calm Lea and said gently, "Don't worry, Lea. Elena will be fine. She just needs a lot of sleep to recover." Her gaze was full of compassion as she stroked Lea's shoulder to offer comfort.

After a few hours, Elena awoke from her sleep and Lea could hardly believe her luck. She hugged her sister warmly, tears of joy in her eyes.

Elena smiled at Lea. "Thank you for saving me, Lea." She then turned to Gronak and Fiona, adding, "And thank you both from the bottom of my heart." The words were filled with deep gratitude and Elena beamed with joy over her rescue.

The innkeeper entered the room with a beaming expression and was visibly relieved to see Elena doing well. "As promised, I have prepared a feast for you," she announced cheerfully. "After all, you are heroes." A warm smile spread across her face as she looked at the group.

The three women stared at the innkeeper with wide eyes when they heard about the feast. The anticipation of the delicious food made their stomachs growl and they could hardly wait to sit down at the festive table.

Gronak could not help but laugh heartily at the thought of the tempting dishes. "Well, I think we shouldn't delay any longer. Let's go down and indulge in this feast."

The innkeeper had set a festive table just for them, filled with a bounty of delicious dishes. There were juicy roasts, fresh vegetables, fragrant rice and delectable desserts. The four friends enjoyed the delicious meal throughout the evening, sharing stories and laughing heartily about their adventures and experiences.

As the hours passed and it began to get late, they eventually decided to end the evening. The group made their way to their room and settled into their beds, satisfied and ready to rest from the exciting events of the day. Together, they fell asleep, aware that new and thrilling adventures awaited them the next day.

The next morning, as the first rays of sunlight illuminated the city, the group was awakened by a loud knocking on their door. When they opened it, the city guards stood there in their splendid armor.

The leader of the city guard stepped forward and reported with a smile that they had successfully rescued the children from the sewer. His words were filled with gratitude and recognition for Gronak, Fiona and Lea, who had assisted in the rescue. The three heroes were visibly relieved and thankful for this pleasant news.

The leader of the city guard told them that the smuggler group operating in the sewer had long been sought by the authorities. Their criminal activities had finally come to an end. As a token of their gratitude, the guard handed Gronak a heavy bag full of gleaming coins. "This is the bounty for Olaf," he explained, "and I thank you again for bringing him down."

Gronak accepted the bag and nodded to the guard. "We only did our duty and are glad we could help. The safety of the city concerns us all."

Lea informed the city guards about Olaf's accomplice, the burly dark elf, who had managed to escape. The guard, pondering this new information, nodded and said, "That must be Reyve, the feared dark elf. He is a notorious mercenary leader and has already been responsible for numerous raids and murders in the land."

Gronak and Lea exchanged frustrated glances, as they had not captured Reyve while dealing with Olaf. Aware of this sentiment, the group thanked the city guard for the valuable information and said their goodbyes.

Several days had passed since Elena had gradually recovered from the terrible events in the sewer. Gronak, Fiona and Lea had engaged in countless discussions to determine what to do with Elena. It was clear that they could not simply take the young girl along on their dangerous journey to track down the dark mage Xalis.

The group's thoughts were filled with concern and indecision. Lea sighed deeply, her forehead creased and she appeared as someone burdened by a heavy weight. The responsibility of protecting her newly found sister Elena weighed heavily on her.

The attentive innkeeper, who had overheard the group's conversation, finally decided to step closer. Her face radiated compassion and consideration as she spoke. "Perhaps I could help you."

The three adventurers looked at the innkeeper questioningly and Lea responded cautiously. "How could you help us? We want to protect Elena, but our journey is too dangerous for her. We can't just leave her behind."

The innkeeper smiled warmly and continued, "I know you are on an extremely important mission, so I offer to keep Elena here with me. She can help me in the kitchen and will have a safe place to sleep. I will take good care of her, as if she were my own daughter."

Her offer was so heartfelt and selfless that the group of adventurers felt overwhelmed. Fiona couldn't suppress a smile as she looked at the innkeeper and Gronak nodded in agreement. They had just found someone who would lovingly take care of Elena while they focused on their dangerous mission.

The innkeeper winked at the group and laughed lightly. "This way, you can concentrate on saving the world from that strange Xalis."

Lea beamed with gratitude and hugged the innkeeper warmly. "Thank you so much, it means the world to us." The words alone couldn't express how relieved and thankful they were for this unexpected help.

Gronak and Fiona also thanked the generous innkeeper for her big heart and the offer to provide Elena with a safe place. The burden of responsibility for their reunited sister was lifted and they could set out with a sense of confidence to save the world from the threat of Xalis.

Lea immediately ran upstairs to Elena's room to bring her the news. When she opened the door, she saw Elena packing her things. The room looked warm and inviting, with cozy wooden furniture and soft sunlight streaming through the window.

"Elena, you're going to stay here and work at the tavern," Lea explained excitedly, her voice filled with confidence and relief. "The innkeeper will take good care of you."

Elena looked at her sister and nodded, a radiant smile of joy on her face. "I'm happy, Lea. I'll do my best and make you proud. You need to continue your mission; I'm so proud of my big sister."

Meanwhile, the innkeeper spoke privately with Gronak and Fiona in a secluded area of the tavern. This part of the tavern was quiet and dimly lit, underscoring the seriousness of the conversation. The innkeeper, with a concerned expression on her face, began to warn them.

"The journey will get much harder from this point on," she began, choosing her words carefully. "The further north you go toward Xalis fortress, the rougher and harsher it will become. His armies are spread everywhere and threaten many regions."

She pulled out a map and showed them a route off the usual paths. "Look here, if you go over the mountains and head north, you can bypass Xalis monstrous army. You will still encounter many dangers, but you'll reach his fortress without being detected."

Gronak and Fiona listened attentively, the innkeeper's words firmly anchoring in their thoughts. They thanked her and promised to do their best and protect each other. Their determination to complete their mission successfully and eliminate the threat of Xalis remained unshaken.

The next morning, Gronak, Fiona and Lea prepared for their upcoming journey. The room they stayed in at the inn was cozy and bathed in warm morning light. On a table lay the generously packed supplies from the innkeeper, including provisions, water bottles and bandages. All these items would be of great use on their arduous journey. The three friends looked at the supplies and felt grateful for the support they had received. They were determined not to disappoint the innkeeper.

Lea and Elena faced each other, tears in their eyes. The emotions were palpable in the air. Lea hugged her sister tightly and whispered softly, "Please take care of yourself, Elena. I will come back, I promise."

Elena smiled and wiped a tear from her face. "I will wait for you, Lea. And I will listen to the innkeeper and not bring you shame."

The two sisters embraced warmly, as if trying to hold onto the time they would be apart in that hug. Finally, Lea released the embrace and smiled at her sister once more.

Gronak, Fiona and Lea thanked the innkeeper again for her hospitality and generous help. The innkeeper smiled warmly and nodded, wishing them all the best and good luck on their dangerous journey.

The three friends left the tavern and stepped once more into the world beyond the trading city. They took one last look at the bustling streets as they bid farewell to the familiar surroundings.

Lea couldn't help but think of her little sister Elena and a hint of longing was in her gaze. She fervently hoped she would see her sister again soon, safe and sound.

Gronak noticed Lea's worried look and placed a comforting hand on her shoulder. "Don't worry, Lea. We'll see her again soon," he assured her with a firm voice.

Fiona also came to Lea's side and offered her comfort. "The innkeeper will take good care of Elena, I'm sure of it. She's a truly kind woman."

Lea struggled with her tears as she listened to her friends encouraging words. She wiped the moisture from her cheeks and forced a smile. "You're right," she said hopefully. "Let's move on."

Determination was evident in their eyes as they prepared to face the dangers and challenges that lay ahead. Their path led them further north and they were ready to complete their mission successfully and finally eliminate the threat posed by Xalis.

Chapter 7: The Lost Forest

Gronak, Fiona and Lea continued their trek through the increasingly dense landscape, the trees seeming to close in above them and the silence was broken by eerie sounds. The sense of foreboding grew stronger with each step. Suddenly, they reached the banks of a river, where an old fisherman was peacefully casting his line. The tranquility of this serene spot was in stark contrast to the grim surroundings.

The fisherman, surprised by their appearance, looked up and scrutinized the group. His voice was rough as he spoke to them. "You are brave to venture this path. The forest ahead is a place of malice and corruption. I have myself experienced terrible things within it, things from which I barely escaped alive."

Lea stepped closer and asked with a worried expression. "What horrors should we expect in the forest?"

The fisherman sighed deeply before recounting his experiences. "Strange beings and mystical creatures lurk in the shadows. They show no mercy and attack anything that ventures near. I have seen their ghastly eyes and heard the whisper of their malevolent voices."

Fiona, with a deep understanding of the dangers of traveling, nodded seriously and thanked him for the warning. "We appreciate your words, good sir. However, we have no choice but to cross the forest to fulfill our mission."

Gronak, who had been studying the fisherman for a moment longer, added. "We are in search of a dangerous mage named Xalis and we will not let a forest full of monsters stop us."

The fisherman nodded understandingly, though he looked concerned. "May fate be on your side. Take care of yourselves and may your luck protect you from the horrors of the forest."

With these words, Gronak, Fiona and Lea bid farewell to the old fisherman and stepped into the dense forest, ready to face the unknown dangers that awaited them.

As they approached the forest, they felt the air grow denser and more humid. The fresh breeze of the open land turned into a sweltering heaviness that clung to their clothing. The chirping of birds and the gentle rustling of leaves filled the air and for a moment, it felt as if it were just an ordinary forest stroll.

Yet beneath these everyday sounds were also unsettling noises that they couldn't place. A hoarse gasp here, a mysterious whisper there. The sounds seemed to come from the dense shadows between the trees, sending shivers down their spines.

Eventually, they took the plunge and entered the forest and it felt as though they were being swallowed by the darkness. The tall trees loomed like somber towers reaching into the sky, forming an impenetrable canopy that allowed barely a ray of sunlight through. The air was damp and heavy and the smell of decaying leaves and rotting wood lingered in the atmosphere.

Gronak, who had sharpened his senses to the utmost, could hear the scuttling of insects and the rustling of animals in the dense underbrush. The silence was only interrupted by the mysterious whispering of the leaves and the eerie sounds emanating from the darkness.

Lea, keeping her bow and arrows ready, looked worriedly at her companions. "This forest is truly a dark place and I'm afraid we won't find our way easily here."

Fiona frowned and added, "And these creepy noises don't make it any easier. I have no idea what creatures might be lurking here."

Gronak attentively observed the surrounding darkness. "We must be prepared for anything. We will traverse this forest, no matter the cost. But watch your steps and keep your eyes open."

The group continued their journey through the lost forest, knowing it was notorious for its many mysteries and enigmatic powers. The vegetation was high and dense, making it easy to get lost. Yet their determination to reach their goal drove them forward as they faced the dangers and secrets lurking in the depths of this gloomy forest.

Gronak, Fiona and Lea wandered deep into the lost forest when suddenly a strange, gentle glow in the distance caught their attention. Curiously and cautiously, they approached the light source. With each step they took closer, the glow became more intense until they finally discovered a group of night fairies. The delicate, elfin-like beings danced in a mysterious circle, waving their sparkling lights as they sang a soft, enchanting song.

Gronak rubbed his eyes in disbelief and whispered in astonishment, "Look at that! Night fairies! I thought they were just a legend."

Fiona watched the fairies with fascination and replied, "It is said that they possess magical powers and dance only for those they deem worthy. This is truly something special."

Lea, still overwhelmed by the surprising appearance of the fairies, asked, "What should we do? Should we approach them?"

Before they could decide, the fairies seemed to notice the strangers. Their delicate faces turned in their direction and the lights they waved grew brighter and more intense. The fairies floated gracefully towards the group, encircling them in a graceful dance.

Lea gasped in shock as one of the fairies circled her face in a swift trail of light, its delicate wings brushing against her cheeks. She trembled and stammered, "This is... this is really happening! They're real!"

Gronak drew his sword and held it protectively in front of him, watching the fairies with suspicion. "Be careful! It may be fascinating to us, but we don't know what they have in mind."

Fiona felt the magic pulsing in her fingers, ready to be used to defend her friends. "We should stay alert. Even the most enchanting things can pose a danger."

The fairies seemed unimpressed by the friends defensive attempts and continued their curious harassment as if they wanted to judge the strangers according to their own secret plan.

A small fairy tugged at Fiona's hair, making it float in sparkling strands. Another fairy danced around Gronak's head, chirping into his ear in her own bell-like way, while a third fairy tried to tickle Lea's ears with her tiny wings. The three friends tried to fend them off, but the fairies were too fast and agile. Their songs and delicate laughter filled the air as they enchanted the travelers with their unusual behavior.

Fiona finally dared to speak to the fairies. "Please stop! We are on an important journey and have no time for games." Her words seemed to hang in the air and the night fairies paused to look at her. A moment of silence ensued before they resumed their activity, but with more intensity and curiosity.

Eventually, Gronak yelled out in frustration. "Enough! We haven't done anything to you! Leave us alone!" But the fairies seemed to ignore his words and continued their harassment. Their dainty forms danced and fluttered around the three friends.

Gronak tried to scare the night fairies away by wildly swinging his sword, but they were too numerous and too quick for him. Fiona, in a desperate attempt to use her magic, raised her hands and began to murmur a spell. To her dismay, the fairies appeared to be immune to her magic. The lights of the fairies flickered brightly as they moved around Fiona's hands, as if absorbing her magic.

Lea, breaking free from a moment of panic, angrily exclaimed, "What the hell do these fairies want from us? They're really starting to get on my nerves!"

The night fairies seemed to enjoy teasing and irritating the group. They giggled and whirled in a chaotic dance around the friends, their sparkling lights illuminating the surrounding darkness.

Suddenly, Gronak, Fiona and Lea realized that the night fairies were leading them into a trap. The fairies ushered them towards a cliff. The ground beneath them gave way and they tumbled down a steep slope. They fell and fell, their screams echoing in the darkness, until they finally landed with a dull thud in a cave.

The smell of decaying flesh and blood pervaded the air as the heroes ventured into the dark cave. It took a few moments for their eyes to adjust to the darkness. Then they heard the menacing growling and hissing of many creatures.

Gronak whispered softly, "Be careful. We're not alone here. This is a claw wolf cave." His words echoed in the darkness.

The claw wolves, dark creatures larger than regular wolves, had sharp claws and teeth that glinted in the dark. Their fur was black as night and their eyes glowed like malevolent red embers. Fortunately, the wolves were deeply asleep and snoring in the cave's hollow.

Fiona whispered anxiously, "These wolves are dangerous. We need to be careful and try to move through the cave unnoticed." Her voice sounded nervous as she kept her eyes on the wolves.

The group began to move slowly and quietly, trying not to alarm the wolves. However, it was difficult to navigate the narrow and uneven cave without making any noise.

Suddenly, without warning, a claw wolf rose and let out a loud scream that startled the other wolves. The group was cornered and had no choice but to defend themselves.

The wolves got up and charged at the group, their sharp claws and teeth ready to attack. Gronak swung his sword and sent one wolf crashing into another, who fell to the ground with a bone-shaking growl. Fiona began to murmur a powerful spell that set another wolf ablaze.

Lea drew her bow and aimed precisely at the wolves coming too close. "Stick together, guys! We can do this!" she shouted to her companions.

However, the creatures were numerous and seemed to endlessly emerge from the shadows. A wolf lunged at Fiona, its teeth flashing in the dark, but Gronak came to her aid with a powerful blow, forcing the wolf back.

Lea shot arrow after arrow into the flanks of the wolves, but they seemed endless. A particularly aggressive wolf charged at her and she managed to fire an arrow just in time, bringing the beast down.

The pack was relentless and seemed like it would never stop coming. The group fought bravely, but they were outnumbered and their strength began to wane. They were pushed back by the wolves and driven to the edge of the cave.

In the cave's darkness, a sudden, deafening roar made the wolves fall silent for a moment. An impressive figure crashed into the cave and it quickly became clear that it was a massive bear. Its massive claws and sharp teeth made it a fearsome sight and it was ready to drive the wolves away.

Gronak, Fiona and Lea wasted no time taking advantage of this unexpected opportunity. Working closely with the mighty bear, they began to push the wolves back. The growling, hissing and howling of the animals filled the cave, but after a fierce battle, all the wolves were finally defeated.

Exhausted and covered in scratches and bites, Gronak, Fiona and Lea leaned against the rough cave wall. Their breaths were heavy and their clothes were torn. The relief of having survived the fight was evident on their faces.

Fiona looked at the bear and smiled gratefully. "Thank you, great friend. You saved our lives." The words were soft, but they spoke volumes about her gratitude.

The bear stared at them for a moment, then turned and left the cave with its prey. The group was now alone again in the darkness of the cave, but the threatening tension had eased.

They decided to spend the night in the cave to recover. Outside, it began to rain and the rain quickly intensified. Soon, a fierce storm developed, shaking the ground and lighting up the sky with bright lightning.

The cave remained dark and eerie, illuminated only by a few faintly flickering torches that Gronak had lit, casting uneven shadows on the walls. The smell of blood and sweat hung heavily in the air and the adventurers' bodies were tired and worn from the fierce battle. In the darkness of the cave, they sought comfort and rest.

Gronak sat at the entrance of the cave, keeping watch, while Fiona and Lea tried to start a fire to warm up and dry out. Fiona eventually managed to ignite a fire by gathering some dry twigs and leaves she had found in the cave and creating a spark.

The warmth of the fire slowly spread through the cave, easing the tension among the adventurers. Fiona and Lea had retreated to a corner of the cave, where they curled up in a few blankets to warm up and get some sleep.

Fiona yawned quietly and murmured, "The fisherman wasn't exaggerating when he warned us. I'm glad we made it through safely. This cave isn't exactly comfortable, but it serves its purpose. Hopefully, we'll have a quiet night."

Lea nodded in agreement as she snuggled into her blanket. "Yes, let's hope we don't have any unpleasant surprises waiting for us. I have a feeling we need to be ready for anything."

Gronak, keeping watch at the cave entrance, muttered to himself to stay awake. "This darkness is terrifying. I wish morning would come sooner."

The night passed slowly and the sounds of the rain and wind outside gradually faded until they finally ceased. The adventurers eventually fell asleep, tired and exhausted from the long day of dangers.

The next morning, as the first rays of sunlight pierced through the forest leaves, Gronak, Fiona and Lea began to prepare for departure. They had spent the night in the cave and were ready to continue their trek through the lost forest.

Gronak checked his gear and sharpened his sword. "The blades need to be sharp. You never know what we'll face in the forest."

Lea checked her bow and arrows and tightened the straps of her leather armor. "Our survival skills will be tested, Gronak, but we're well-prepared. It's good we could upgrade our gear in town."

Fiona prepared her magical potions and spoke to the others. "I hope today doesn't end like yesterday did. I can't handle another day like that."

Once they had finished their preparations, they continued their arduous journey through the lost forest. The trees stood close together and light barely penetrated the dense canopy. It was a constant up and down as they struggled through hills and valleys.

Gronak looked into the darkness of the forest and murmured, "This forest seems endless. I hope we find a way out soon."

Fiona, with a concerned look at the map she held, replied, "It's easy to lose your bearings here. We need to be very careful about where we're going."

Lea, gripping her bow tightly, nodded in agreement. "I have a feeling we'll face more challenges ahead. We need to be prepared for anything."

As they battled their way through the forest, they heard the sound of water in the distance. They followed the noise and eventually reached a wide river. The water flowed swiftly, forming a natural boundary between the forest and the even denser woods that rose behind it.

Gronak looked at the river and said, "The water looks pretty wild. Hopefully, we can find a safe way to get to the other side."

The three companions followed the river and eventually found a shallow spot where they could wade across. The current was strong, but with their combined efforts, they managed to make it to the other side, soaking wet.

Lea shook herself like a wet dog and laughed softly. "The water might have been cold, but at least we're on the other side. I'm definitely awake now after that bath."

After drying their clothes and gear, they continued on their way. The forest grew denser and darker and the fog hung heavily in the air. They heard the distant howling of wolves and quickened their pace.

Fiona wrapped her robe tighter around herself. "The howling of wolves is never a good sign. We should hurry and find a safe place to spend the night."

The group trekked on through the dense lost forest for several hours, but the trees seemed to shift around them and the fog became increasingly impenetrable. Suddenly, they realized they had lost their way. They decided to search for a safe place to rest for the night to regain their strength and reorient themselves.

Gronak, Fiona and Lea ventured deeper into the forest and stumbled upon an abandoned and decaying house hidden in the thick undergrowth. It had undoubtedly been magnificent once, but now it was in a state of near-total decay. The roof tiles had fallen off, the windows were shattered and the door hung crookedly on its hinges.

"Look at this," Fiona murmured as she surveyed the gloomy ruin. "This house looks like it's been left to decay for decades."

Ivy and wild vines had overrun the decaying facade, adding an extra layer of mystery and gloom to the building. The surrounding trees and shrubs seemed to be almost swallowing the house and it lay in an aura of neglect and decay.

The group approached the abandoned house and felt an eerie stillness and coldness. The air seemed heavy, as if the house was somehow registering their presence in a sinister way. No birds sang and the rustling of the wind was the only sound breaking the silence.

Lea dared to move closer to the half-open door. It creaked ominously at the slightest touch from the faintest breeze. The darkness inside seemed eerie and the entire atmosphere was filled with an oppressive weight. The walls were covered in mold and cobwebs and a musty smell lingered in the air.

"Maybe we should avoid going in," Gronak warned, casting a worried glance at the house's grim aura.

Fiona, undeterred by the house's mysterious allure, explained, "There might be clues or information that could help us get out of this forest. We should at least take a look."

Lea was also intrigued. "I agree with Fiona. We should be cautious, but it won't hurt to explore the house."

Gronak hesitated at first about entering the decaying house, but eventually agreed and the group stepped inside. The wood beneath their feet creaked ominously and the dull echo of their footsteps reverberated through the room. The eerie silence became even more oppressive and the shadows seemed to close in on them, as if the house itself was reacting to their presence.

Despite the oppressive atmosphere, the three friends were adventurous and ready to explore the house. They kept their weapons at the ready, gripping their handles tightly and sharpened their senses as they carefully moved through the dark rooms. Every step was taken with utmost caution, as they feared triggering a trap or encountering something terrifying lurking in the dark.

In the first room they entered, their eyes fell on a dusty table and a few dilapidated chairs. Everything was covered in thick cobwebs. On the table lay decayed books, with pages barely legible. Fiona bent down to pick up one of the books, but it crumbled into dust in her hands.

A door led to another room, littered with debris and rubble. The walls showed numerous cracks and the broken window panes had allowed the elements inside.

The ghostly silence was only broken by the occasional drop of water falling from the leaky ceiling onto the floor.

Lea stepped closer to the window and looked out into the forest. "This place seems to have been abandoned for ages," she remarked, surveying the bleak surroundings.

Gronak nodded in agreement and added, "It's hard to say what happened here, but it seems the house has its own secrets."

Fiona, always on the lookout for clues and knowledge, continued to search the room and eventually discovered an old diary hidden under a pile of debris. She picked it up and began leafing through it.

"Look, a diary," she said excitedly. "Maybe we'll find clues about the history of this house and why it was abandoned."

The group gathered around Fiona as she began reading from the diary. It contained entries about the lives of the house's former occupants, their joys and concerns, but also darker passages about mysterious occurrences and unexplained events that had taken place in and around the property.

The stories in the diary sent a chilling shiver down the adventurers' spines, intensifying the grim atmosphere of the house. Gronak turned to his companions. "It seems like the occupants of this house experienced terrible things. We should see what else we can find."

The grim atmosphere in the abandoned house seemed to intensify and Fiona felt a chill creeping over her arms. The question of the history of this place weighed heavily on her. What terrible secrets did the walls and dark corners conceal?

Gronak and Lea continued to search the room, their torch banishing the shadows. They moved a heavy, dusty shelf aside, revealing a concealed door. The discovery of this hidden passage sparked the group's curiosity and Fiona felt her initial fear give way to an insatiable curiosity. She wanted to know what lay behind this secret door.

Carefully, Gronak and Lea opened the door and the group entered another room shrouded in twilight. The walls were covered with old, faded wallpaper and in the center of the room stood a weathered bed with tattered sheets. Old paintings hung on the walls, depicting people long gone.

Fiona, fascinated by the paintings, approached one of the pictures and stared at the portrait of a young woman. "Who was she?" she murmured, more to herself than to the others.

Gronak and Lea continued further into the room, examining the dusty furniture. "It seems this room was once inhabited by someone, but it's been so long that time has erased its traces," Lea said to the others.

Gronak nodded in agreement and moved closer to an old writing desk. On the table lay yellowed letters, testament to a bygone life. He picked up one of the letters and began to decipher it. "It seems like someone here recorded their life and thoughts. Unfortunately, almost nothing is readable anymore," he said thoughtfully.

Fiona turned away from the paintings and joined the two. "It's as if time has stood still here, as if the occupants of this room suddenly vanished and left everything behind."

In the room, they eventually found an old, ornate wooden chest filled with dusty books and scrolls. Some

169

of the books had weathered covers, while others were adorned with magical symbols and formulas. The discovery of this mysterious collection made the adventurers pause again and fall into lively discussions.

Fiona could barely contain her excitement as she began to sift through the books and scrolls. Her fingers glided over the yellowed pages and she could feel the wisdom and knowledge of past times slumbering within these texts. "Look at this!" she exclaimed excitedly, holding up a book with faded runes. "These are ancient writings on magic and alchemy. There are magical formulas and rituals here that I have never seen before."

Gronak and Lea leaned in curiously over Fiona's shoulders to catch a glimpse of the discovered treasures. "This is truly amazing," Gronak agreed. "These scrolls and books could be of great use in our future adventures. They might hold secrets and powers we haven't even dreamed of."

Fiona sat down on the dusty floor and focused on a particularly old book buried in the corner of the chest. She pulled it out and sensed that it was something special. The book's leather cover was plain and worn, but adorned with golden ornaments that still sparkled amidst the dust and cobwebs.

With the utmost care, Fiona opened the book and immersed herself in the ancient writings that filled the pages. The characters and magic symbols were so complex and fascinating that she held her breath. Each page was covered with intricately arranged runes and symbols, many of which were completely unfamiliar to her.

"Fiona, what have you found?" asked Lea, who was also fascinated by the treasures they had discovered.

Fiona did not answer immediately, so engrossed was she in the texts. Finally, she looked up and said, "This is no ordinary book. It is an extremely valuable magical grimoire. The information contained in this book could grant us astonishing powers and knowledge. I will definitely take it with me."

With careful hands, Fiona placed the magical book into her backpack, feeling the presence of the magic contained within surround her. She knew that this discovery would profoundly impact her life and adventures in the future.

As Fiona carefully placed the magical book into her backpack, she felt the air in the room change. A strange presence seemed to envelop her and she could sense an odd energy in the surroundings. She turned around and could hardly believe her eyes. Floating before her was a small, transparent spirit. Its round head was crowned with large, sad eyes and its delicate hands moved like wisps of mist in the air. Its entire body shimmered, almost like a fragile smoke sculpture floating in the air.

The spirit was no larger than a small child and despite its otherworldly appearance, it radiated an eerie gentleness and kindness. It seemed more curious than threatening and looked at the three heroes with an expressive gaze that conveyed deep sadness.

Naturally empathetic, Fiona slowly approached the spirit. "Who are you, little one?" she asked in a gentle tone, trying not to frighten the small spirit. "What has bound you to this place?"

The little spirit lowered its head for a moment before opening its delicate lips and answering in a faint, smoky voice. "I was once a little boy playing in the forest. But one day, I was ambushed by a group of evil sorcerers. They captured me for a sacrifice, for one of their dark rituals and killed me. My body was hidden here and my spirit has been trapped in this old house. I have wandered restlessly for decades, never finding redemption."

The heroes listened intently as the spirit recounted its heartbreaking story. The darkness and mystery of the abandoned house began to clear before their eyes as they made a connection with this tormented spirit.

Gronak, Fiona and Lea looked at each other determinedly after hearing the little spirit's heart-wrenching story. They knew they could not simply walk away and unanimously decided to help the spirit.

Gronak said compassionately, "We can't just walk away if we can help someone find their peace." Fiona added empathetically, "You can count on us, little friend. We will help you."

The little spirit was overjoyed by the offer and nodded happily. His large, sad eyes seemed suddenly filled with a glimmer of hope. He beckoned the heroes to follow him as he led them through the dark and mysterious house. Each of their steps seemed to be surrounded by a mysterious aura as they ventured deeper into the heart of the abandoned estate. Finally, after traversing several narrow corridors and dusty rooms, the spirit stopped in front of an inconspicuous door in the basement of the house.

Gronak opened the door slowly and cautiously. A musty odor and darkness awaited them inside. The sight that greeted them was heart-wrenching. In a dimly lit room lay the decayed corpse of the little boy who had unjustly lost his life decades ago. Fiona knelt before the child's remains and began a mixture of prayers and ancient magical formulas. Her hands glowed with a soft light and the room filled with an exalted yet sorrowful atmosphere.

Lea noticed that Fiona was struggling and placed a comforting hand on her shoulder, whispering encouragingly, "You can do it, Fiona. We believe in you."

The little spirit hovered beside Fiona, looking at the body he had left behind with great anticipation. As the magical words reached their climax, the remains of the boy began to glow faintly. A delicate, gentle light permeated the room and the child's spirit beamed with joy.

Fiona addressed the redeeming spirit. "Your journey of unrest and suffering has now come to an end. You can now rest in peace and find the tranquility you have longed for." The little spirit nodded with a smile that warmed the heroes' hearts. His form began to fade as a warm, bright light filled the room. It was a magical moment when the heroes felt they had done something extraordinary by helping this poor spirit find the peace he had yearned for.

However, as they prepared to make their way back to the exit of the old house, they were stopped by mysterious figures. These ghosts seemed to have been trapped in the dilapidated estate and were now enraged that their disturbance had come from freeing the child's spirit.

Gronak, who was leading the group, froze as he saw the dark and eerie creatures that had suddenly manifested before them. They were ghosts draped in dark robes that gave their appearances a shadowy form. The hoods they wore concealed their faces, leaving only deep, empty eye sockets visible, conveying the sense that these beings were not of this world.

Fiona swallowed hard and whispered to her friends, "Stay calm. We need to find out what they want."

Their appearance was accompanied by an icy wind that caused the air around them to freeze. The temperature seemed to drop drastically near them and their mere presence sent shivers down the heroes' spines.

Lea dared to ask quietly, "Who are you and what do you want from us?"

The ghosts moved slowly and deliberately. Their movements were silent, as if they existed in another dimension. The menacing aura they radiated revealed an eerie power and an insatiable thirst for vengeance and retribution.

A spirit with particularly hollow eye sockets stepped forward and spoke in a grim, echoing voice. "You have disrupted the balance by freeing the boy. His suffering kept us bound here. But now that you have freed him, we must endure his torments!"

Gronak tried to clarify the situation. "We didn't know you were trapped here. We only wanted to help."

The spirits seemed filled with rage. "If you truly wish to help, you must take the boy's place. Therefore, we will now kill you all and bind your souls here."

The group was shocked by the ghostly figures and instinctively prepared for battle. Gronak drew his powerful sword and charged at the spirits, ready to confront the looming threat. But as he struck with all his might, his sword passed through the ghosts as if they were air. There was no resistance, no injury, no bleeding.

Absolutely nothing! An icy shiver ran through his body and frustration mingled with concern as he realized that his physical weapons were completely ineffective against these eerie spirits.

Fiona, quickly devising a plan, looked at the spirits threateningly approaching Gronak. She knew they couldn't use conventional weapons against these beings, but she had an idea. She swiftly raised her hands and began to murmur softly. Her fingers moved deftly as she recited a spell she had recently learned from an old book.

Suddenly, a bright green light flared up and enveloped Gronak's sword. It seemed almost as if the blade began to glow from within, with greenish sparks flying from its tip. The spirits recoiled in shock as Gronak swung his sword. Clearly, the enchantment had worked and his sword was now capable of harming the ghosts.

Fiona then turned to Lea and repeated the same process with her bow. Lea's arrows were now surrounded by a greenish aura and began to glow faintly. As Lea drew her bow and aimed at one of the ghostly intruders, the arrows flew and struck their target with eerie precision. The spirits flinched in pain and backed away as the green-glowing arrows inflicted physical damage on them.

Gronak and Lea marveled at the unexpected effect of the enchantment. Their eyes reflected both relief and hope. With their newly enchanted weapons, they suddenly had a real chance against the surrounding spirits. In silent agreement, they charged at the remaining ghosts to engage in battle and defeat the spectral beings. The spirits, which had previously seemed invincible, were now vulnerable and could be overcome.

Gronak and Lea gripped their newly enchanted weapons tightly and faced the approaching spirits once more. This time, their attacks hit their mark and the ghosts began to wail horribly. The dark hoods they wore fell from their shadowy forms, revealing disfigured faces marked by centuries of suffering.

Gronak skillfully parried the ghosts' attacks with his glowing sword and struck back forcefully. The ghostly substance of the beings faded and lost its form, as Gronak dissolved part of them with each touch. Fiona used her magical powers to hurl the ghosts back with a powerful shockwave. The ghostly creatures recoiled from the immense magical energy and seemed to scream in pain. Lea, having drawn her bow, shot arrow after arrow at the spirits, who had now gathered around the friends, hitting them with remarkable precision.

The battle against the ghosts was in full swing and the heroes fought with united strength against these eerie beings that had been trapped in the cursed house for so long. It was a fight not only for their own survival but also for the redemption of the tormented souls of the ghosts.

The ghosts attacked from all directions, with more and more emerging through the walls and ceilings of the old haunted house. The rotting floorboards creaked under their invisible feet. Gronak, Fiona and Lea fought fiercely against the supernatural intruders. They constantly shifted positions to prevent the ghosts from surrounding them. Dust swirled around them as they struck at the transparent attackers with drawn swords and notched bows.

Gronak, with a furious cry, drove the ghosts back and shouted to Lea, "Hang in there, Lea! We won't let them win!"

Lea nodded and placed a precise arrow on the string of her bow. "Together we can do this!" Her arrows whizzed through the air, decimating the ghosts. But more and more ghosts continued to emerge from every corner of the walls.

The ghosts charged at Gronak and Lea and the friends felt the icy touches of the malevolent figures. The ghosts seemed determined to end their lives. But Fiona, who had one last trick up her sleeve, did not hesitate.

She pulled a small amulet from her pocket that she had purchased from a mysterious magic shop. It was a delicate piece of jewelry adorned with a sparkling crystal. Fiona held the amulet up, her eyes shining with hope and began to concentrate her magic on it. The crystal started to glow brightly, its light permeating the entire haunted house.

The ghosts were struck by the blinding flash of light and their ghastly forms twisted in pain. A shrill wailing filled the room as they dissolved into glittering light. When the light faded, the ghosts were gone and silence returned.

Fiona lowered her arm and looked at the amulet resting in her hand. Her heart raced with excitement and a proud smile spread across her face. But as she examined the amulet more closely, she realized that the use of her magical powers had caused the crystal to crack. It had become useless.

Fiona sighed, both disappointed by the loss of the amulet and relieved that she and her friends had defeated the ghosts. She turned to Gronak and Lea. "The amulet is broken, but at least it saved us. I think it was worth the effort."

Gronak nodded in approval and patted Fiona on the shoulder. "You did a great job, Fiona. Now let's get out of this cursed place as quickly as possible."

Lea nodded in agreement and turned toward the door. "Let's leave before more trouble happens. Our mission isn't over yet."

The three adventurers left the abandoncd villa, their steps echoing on the creaking wooden floor as they approached the exit. The gloomy atmosphere of the house finally gave way to the fresh air outside.

Gronak took a deep breath and said with relief, "Finally some fresh air. It was really eerie in there."

Lea agreed and said, "You're right, Gronak. The mustiness was starting to get to me. I'm glad we're leaving that place behind."

Fiona added, still touched by the encounter with the boy's spirit, "But at least we were able to help the boy's spirit. I'm very happy about that."

Gronak and Lea nodded in agreement and they were all convinced that redeeming the tormented spirit had been a worthwhile endeavor.

Dusk began to fall and the heroes noticed that it was already night. The sky turned deep blue and the stars began to twinkle.

Gronak started joking, "We could spend the night in the haunted house. That would be an exciting adventure, wouldn't it?"

Fiona and Lea exchanged glances, their faces reflecting pure horror and they said in unison, "No way! We're never going back in there."

Gronak laughed heartily at their reaction and suggested they set off. "Alright, no ghost house sleepover. Let's find a safe place to spend the night."

The three friends made their way down the dark path as the stars shone in the sky and the shadow of the abandoned house slowly receded behind them.

They eventually reached a picturesque lake, its surface shimmering in the dark. The clear water sparkled under the gentle moonlight and the surrounding forest filled the air with soothing sounds.

Gronak, exhausted from the day, suggested, "We should set up camp here. It looks like a safe spot and tomorrow we can move on refreshed."

The others agreed and they began to set up their camp. Fiona spread out her findings, including the magical book with complex runes and symbols she had discovered in the haunted house. She delved into the ancient texts while Gronak and Lea prepared dinner by the campfire. The warm glow of the fire illuminated their faces as they focused on cooking.

Fiona looked up from her book, still fascinated by the ancient writings and said, "This book is incredible. I've never seen much of it before, but unfortunately, I don't understand many of the old runes."

Gronak and Lea exchanged a glance, clearly recognizing the potential of this discovery. Gronak asked curiously, "Can you perhaps translate some of the texts, Fiona? Who knows what secrets this book might hold?"

Fiona frowned and replied, "I'll try, but some of the runes are so old and complex that they seem puzzling. It will take some time before I can figure out more about them."

Once the meal was ready and everyone was satisfied, they leaned back by the campfire and enjoyed the calm of the night. The flames flickered, casting a warm, comforting light on their faces. The sounds of the forest surrounded them and they felt the tension of the past days slowly melting away.

But suddenly, as they looked over the lake, they saw a beautiful natural spectacle. Thousands of tiny fireflies rose above the lake. They danced in the air, forming sparkling patterns and casting a magical light over the lake. The water seemed to glow from within and the entire lake shimmered like a carpet of stars.

The three friends were overwhelmed by this breathtaking sight. Lea whispered excitedly, "This is simply enchanting. I've never seen anything like this before."

Fiona looked at the lake with wide eyes and added, "It's as if the lake is illuminated by a thousand stars."

Gronak gazed in wonder at the fireflies. "After days of torment through the forest, this moment of calm and peace is a welcome change."

They watched the spectacle for a while, enjoying the magic of the fireflies and leaving the stress of their past adventures behind. Nature showed its most beautiful side and it was as if the forest was showing them its gratitude.

The next morning, they awoke early, refreshed from a restful night by the lakeside. They packed up their camp and prepared to move on. The sun slowly rose over the horizon as they crossed the forest that had brought them so many secrets and dangers.

Finally, they reached the edge of the forest and stood once again in the daylight. The freedom and the certainty that they had redeemed the tormented spirit of the boy filled them with pride and satisfaction. Their adventure was far from over, but they were ready for whatever the future held.

Chapter 8: The Secret in the Mountains

The sun cast its warming rays on the group as they left the lost forest behind and stood before an imposing mountain range. The steep path that rose before them wound its way upward, while the majestic mountains surrounded them on all sides. The landscape around them gradually changed and the fresh mountain air was a welcome relief, even though the sun was already burning on their skin.

In the shadow of the mountains, a variety of trees and shrubs extended along the slopes, bringing life to the hills. Birds chirped merrily in the treetops and the gentle murmur of streams accompanied them on their ascent. Nevertheless, the path was rocky and challenging and the group had to exert considerable effort to advance.

Time and again, they were presented with breathtaking views. From the heights of the mountains, they could overlook the entire valley below. Rivers and lakes meandered through the green forests that stretched to the horizon. In the distance, at the banks of a majestic river, they glimpsed a city bathed in golden light. The scene was both awe-inspiring and fascinating.

The effort of the steep climb did not seem to discourage the group. On the contrary, they were full of motivation to continue their journey and face any challenges that lay ahead in the mountains.

"This is truly impressive," Fiona remarked as they took a short break and enjoyed the picturesque view. "This mountain landscape is so different from the dark forest we traversed."

Gronak nodded in agreement. "Yes, it feels like nature is rewarding us after we defeated the ghosts in the haunted house. Let's hope our further journey is just as exciting."

Lea, who was watching the horizon, said with some concern, "Look down there. That city by the river looks like the trading town where we rescued Elena. I hope she's doing well."

Gronak reassured Lea. "Of course, Elena is fine. The innkeeper is taking good care of her and she has enough food and a safe place to sleep. So don't worry."

When they finally reached the summit of the mountain, they were greeted with a breathtaking panorama. The setting sun bathed the sky in dazzling colors. A spectrum of orange, pink and purple stretched across the horizon, while the silhouettes of the mountains and valleys before them formed a majestic backdrop. The group stood there, feeling invincible at that moment.

Fiona could not take her eyes off the dizzying beauty of the scene. "It's as if we're on the roof of the world," she whispered, awestruck.

Gronak, proud of their achievement, nodded in agreement. "We've reached the summit and the view is the reward for all our efforts. This moment is unforgettable."

Lea joyfully added, "It reminds me that there's still so much to discover on our journey. The world is full of wonders and adventures and we've only just begun."

The three friends lingered for a moment to enjoy and absorb the magnificent view. The surrounding mountain peaks, stretching into the distance, seemed unreachable and majestic, yet their resolve to continue their journey and overcome all obstacles remained unshaken.

After leaving the summit, they continued their path through the rocky terrain. The landscape was rough and untamed, characterized by steep cliffs and deep ravines. The path was challenging and strenuous, but the group navigated it with bravery.

After traveling through the rugged terrain for a while, they eventually reached a small cabin off the main path. The cabin appeared old and dilapidated, with a crooked roof and weathered walls. It seemed uninhabited, but the group decided to investigate the cabin further as it exuded a certain allure.

As they approached, they noticed a delicate plume of smoke rising from a chimney. With a light knock on the door, the cabin opened, revealing an aged hermit who lived there.

The hermit was a friendly man whose appearance seemed in harmony with nature. His long silver hair was tied back in a braid and a thick gray beard reached his chest. His deep blue eyes radiated a certain wisdom. His clothing was simple, a brown tunic patched in places, sturdy leather sandals on his feet and a necklace of various stones and bones around his neck. Overall, the hermit had a very natural and earthy look, indicating that he had lived in the mountains for years and adapted to the elements.

With a warm smile, he invited the group into his cabin. "Welcome, travelers. My name is Sawil. You are in a rough area. Come inside, warm yourselves by the fire and let us share what nature provides us."

The group, touched by Sawil's friendly reception, entered the cabin and felt the warmth of the fire crackling inside. The cabin was small and simple, but it was evident that much time and care had gone into its arrangement. Shelves full of books and herbs in various stages of drying hung on the walls. A few old but well-maintained pieces of furniture were in the room, including an old wooden table, some chairs and a bed in the corner. Small sculptures, artworks and strange items, some of which seemed magical, were scattered throughout the room.

A delicious aroma of stew and freshly baked bread filled the air and the weary travelers found themselves in this hospitable place that sheltered them from the cold of the mountains.

Gronak thanked Sawil warmly. "We are on a long journey and saw the sight of your cabin. We appreciate your hospitality, thank you very much."

Fiona looked at Sawil happily and added, "It is a true blessing to meet such a kind and wise man like you."

Lea, admiring the hermit's simple life, asked curiously, "How long have you lived here in the mountains, Mr. Sawil?"

Sawil smiled and replied, "For many, many years, young lady. The mountains and nature are my home and I have learned much from them."

Sawil handed each of them a bowl of soup and a piece of fresh bread, which smelled delicious. The tired travelers sat around the simple wooden table in the middle of the cabin and began to eat together. The warming soup did them good and the crispy bread was a true delight.

The old hermit looked at the three attentively and finally asked, "Why have you journeyed to such a remote place? What drives you to travel here in the mountains?"

The group told Sawil about their adventurous journey and their quest to stop Xalis and protect the world from his dark magic. They spoke of the trials and dangers they had faced and their resolve to restore justice and peace.

As they ate, Sawil pointed to the many bookshelves in his cabin, where numerous old books and writings were carefully stored. He explained, "I have dedicated many years of my life to exploring and studying the secrets of the universe. These books contain knowledge about magic, natural forces and the hidden powers of the world. It is my duty to preserve this knowledge and pass it on to those who seek it."

The atmosphere in the small cabin grew increasingly tense as the group got to know the old hermit Sawil better. They found his way of life and his knowledge of nature and magic equally fascinating and there was a certain reverence in the air.

Fiona, always interested in magic and ancient knowledge, could not hide her curiosity. "That sounds fascinating, Sawil. Have you heard or seen anything about the dark magic of Xalis that could help us?"

Sawil nodded thoughtfully. "Yes, I have heard of Xalis and his dark magic. Many centuries ago, he already brought death and destruction."

Gronak, Fiona and Lea, longing for a way to stop Xalis, finally dared to ask the burning question on their lips. "Sawil, can you help us in our quest? Can you aid us in finding a way to defeat Xalis and his dark powers?"

Sawil looked at the group one by one before slowly nodding. "Yes, I will help you. I have heard much about the danger posed by Xalis and I cannot allow his darkness to grow further and consume the world."

Gronak could not hide his relief. "That's great, Sawil. We are very grateful for your support."

Sawil began to tell an old story. "There is an ancient shrine here in the mountains, known to few. It is hard to find and surrounded by many dangers, but within it lies a powerful rune crystal. This crystal is one of the strongest ever created. It has the ability to weaken and banish dark magic."

The three looked at each other skeptically and Gronak voiced his thoughts aloud. "That sounds too good to be true, Sawil. How are we supposed to find this shrine and what dangers will await us?"

Fiona added, "And how can we be sure that this rune crystal will really work against Xalis? There are so many myths and legends."

The hermit sighed and leaned back in his chair. "I understand your doubts. The shrine is hidden deep in the mountains and its exact location is a secret. It is said to be guarded by creatures that pose a formidable challenge even for seasoned warriors. But if you find the rune crystal and master its power, you might be able to defeat Xalis."

Fiona stared at Sawil with a mixture of hope and determination. "How can we use the rune crystal? What must we do to banish the dark magic and free the world from Xalis is influence?"

The hermit hesitated for a moment before replying. "That's hard to say. The crystal is a powerful tool, but it can only be wielded by someone with enough power and knowledge to control it. You will have to find the right way to use it against Xalis. Trust in your abilities and perhaps you can vanquish the darkness."

In the evening, they sat around the crackling fire, talking with Sawil. The hermit shared stories of his own adventures in the mountains and the wonders of nature he had discovered throughout his life. The group listened intently, feeling their bond with this mysterious place and its inhabitant grow stronger.

The group spent the night in Sawil's cozy cabin. The hermit offered them simple sleeping mats and warm blankets. It was a restful night after the day's hardships and they were able to recuperate well.

The next morning, as the first rays of sunlight illuminated the mountain peaks, the group was already up. Sawil had prepared a simple breakfast for them and they bid farewell to their host.

Gronak thanked Sawil sincerely and promised to honor his knowledge and wisdom by doing everything in their power to stop Xalis and save the world.

The three adventurers resumed their arduous ascent through the mountains, determined to find the powerful rune crystal and stop Xalis. The majestic mountain peaks loomed before them and the air grew thinner as they climbed higher. Sawil's words gave them the motivation needed to face the challenges ahead.

The path led them further into the wilderness of the mountains. Their steps grew slower as they struggled through steep and uneven terrain. The sun beat down mercilessly, drying their throats as they bravely pushed forward through the harsh landscape.

Fiona looked around and sighed. "These mountains are beautiful, but also unforgiving. Finding Sawil's shrine won't be easy."

Lea agreed and wiped the sweat from her forehead. "But we can't give up. We have a goal and we will find that shrine. That gives us the strength to keep going."

Finally, after hours of hiking, they heard a deep roar followed by a terrifying clattering of stones. The group froze and looked around frantically to identify the source of the noise.

Suddenly, they were taken by surprise as two massive boulders came hurtling toward them with considerable force. Gronak, closest to the oncoming rocks, reacted swiftly. With a powerful jerk, he pulled out his massive shield and held it protectively in front of him.

The boulders crashed against Gronak's shield with a deafening impact, but he stood firm, not letting the force knock him over. The massive rocks shattered into thousands of pieces, flying like shrapnel in all directions.

Fiona and Lea had taken cover behind Gronak, narrowly avoiding being hit by the flying debris. They looked up at Gronak, thanking him for his quick reaction.

Gronak lowered his shield and gazed at the rubble surrounding them. "That was close. I wonder what triggered those boulders."

The group looked around and froze in fear as they saw two mountain trolls charging toward them. These gigantic, hairy creatures with their yellow eyes were a terrifying sight. Each troll was at least twice the size of an average man, with muscular arms and legs equipped with razor-sharp claws. Their fur was so dense it looked like they were wearing a natural armor.

The mountain trolls had faces marred with scars and scratches and their pointed teeth gleamed in the eerie light. They roared and growled menacingly as they ran towards the adventurers. The ground shook under their heavy steps and their mere presence spread fear and dread. It was clear they had nothing but killing and devouring their prey in mind.

Gronak drew his mighty sword and positioned himself in front of Fiona and Lea. "Stay behind me!" he shouted, preparing for battle.

Fiona glanced at the creatures and quietly chanted a protective spell. An invisible shield formed around the group, meant to protect them from the attacking trolls.

Lea drew her bow and aimed at one of the approaching mountain trolls. "We have to defend ourselves. Watch out, Gronak!"

The mountain trolls roared again as they came closer and hurled boulders in the direction of the adventurers. Gronak swung his sword to deflect the projectiles while Fiona maintained the protective shield. Lea released her arrow and it flew with deadly precision toward one of the trolls. However, the troll blocked it with a rock.

Gronak charged at one of the trolls, his mighty sword held firmly in hand. With a thunderous strike, he attempted to hit the troll, but the creature was surprisingly strong and resisted the blow. The mountain troll's eyes sparkled with fury and it struck back, knocking Gronak to the ground.

Fiona summoned her magic and hurled fireballs at the other troll. Flames licked around the troll, but it remained unfazed and rolled to the side to avoid the attack. Its hairy body singed in places, but it advanced with a menacing growl.

Lea took advantage of the confusion in the battle and skillfully climbed a rock. She intended to attack from above and catch the trolls off guard. However, the rock she stood on proved unstable. With a terrified scream, Lea lost her footing and plummeted down.

Gronak immediately recognized the danger and ran to the cliff where Lea had fallen. With a quick and daring leap, he reached the edge and extended his strong hand. He caught Lea at the last moment before she could crash onto the sharp rocks below. She now hung in his arms, her heart racing and trembling with fear.

"Everything is alright, Lea. You're safe," Gronak said soothingly as he held Lea tightly.

Fiona refocused her magic and fired another fireball at the troll that was still advancing on them. This time, the fire hit its mark and the troll howled in pain and collapsed as its body was engulfed in flames.

The other troll rushed to its burning partner, trying to smother the fire with dirt and rocks. His powerful arms shoveled earth over the burning troll and the sand and stones rained down on the flames. Slowly, the fire died out and the injured troll managed to stand, though it was shrouded in smoke.

Fiona seized the opportunity to summon her powerful ice magic. With a sweep of her hand, she caused icy crystals to rise from the ground. The crystals converged in the air and encased the mountain trolls in a frosty cocoon. The icy cold crept into their limbs and the trolls froze, unable to move.

"Now, Gronak, push them over the edge!" Fiona called out, watching the two frozen mountain trolls with a stern gaze.

Gronak ran to the frozen trolls, his powerful muscles tensed and grabbed one of them firmly. With all his strength, he shoved the troll toward the nearby cliff. The troll, barely able to defend itself, let out an angry scream as it reached the edge of the cliff.

The troll lost its footing and the frosty shell surrounding it began to break as it tumbled over the edge. A mighty crash echoed from the depths, followed by a relieving silence.

Gronak hurried to the second troll and repeated the process. With a powerful shove, the frozen mountain troll was hurled over the cliff, its scream fading as it followed the first troll into the darkness.

The group breathed a sigh of relief as the danger was averted. The two mountain trolls were defeated and would no longer pose a threat. Gronak, Fiona and Lea exchanged looks of triumph and relief.

After defeating the mountain trolls, they noticed smoke rising from the direction where the trolls had attacked them. Gronak suggested investigating the smoke to find out what was happening there. Fiona and Lea agreed and they set off, following the rising smoke.

The path led them up the hill and as they reached the top, they were met with a surprising sight. In front of them, they discovered a campfire still burning. Lea said, "This must have been the trolls' camp." Gronak agreed, "Yes, we should look around and see if we can find anything useful."

The group cautiously approached the campfire. They saw that the mountain trolls had hoarded some stolen treasures and supplies here. There were weapons, armor and food taken from their victims. Fiona found an old but well-preserved book on magic and natural forces, which she carefully set aside.

Lea discovered some scrolls engraved with ancient symbols and runes. "These could be useful," she said, placing them in her backpack.

Gronak searched through the weapons and armor and found a powerful axe, which he decided to keep for his collection. "This axe might prove useful," he murmured contentedly.

Suddenly, Lea heard a faint calling in the distance. She hesitated for a moment, then excitedly said, "Wait, guys, I hear something!" She pointed to a row of crates hidden under some bushes.

Gronak and Fiona approached the crates and could now hear the desperate cries as well. "Help, get us out of here!" The cries came from the crates that Lea had discovered.

Gronak didn't hesitate and began opening the crates. With his impressive strength, he managed to lift the lids, revealing two people who were bound and obviously severely injured.

The two captives were exhausted and weakened, but they breathed a sigh of relief as they regained their freedom. Lea immediately stepped forward and began to untie their bindings. "You're safe now," she assured them.

Fiona also came closer and began treating their injuries. With her healing magic, she could alleviate their pain and slowly heal their wounds. The two captives looked at the adventurers with gratitude, overwhelmed by their rescue.

The two rescued individuals thanked Gronak, Fiona and Lea warmly and introduced themselves. The man stepped forward and said, "My name is Janon and this is my partner Anika. We are traveling adventurers and researchers of ancient cultures and knowledge." He added, "We were on our way to an ancient ruin when we were attacked by these mountain trolls and put into these crates."

Anika nodded in agreement and added, "Yes, it was truly a nightmare. We were completely overwhelmed by these trolls. But now we are so grateful that you rescued us."

Janon is characterized by his athletic build, shaped by many years of adventure and physical activity. He has wavy, dark brown hair that reaches his shoulders. His eyes are a deep brown and his tanned complexion shows the many hours he has spent outdoors. His face often bears a broad smile and sharp eyes, always looking for new adventures and discoveries. Janon wears practical adventurer's clothing that allows him to move freely and often carries a leather bag with his essential gear.

Anika is an equally robust adventurer. She has shoulder-length, straight blonde hair and her clear, blue eyes radiate determination. Her face shows signs of years of adventures and challenges. She wears practical yet feminine clothing that does not restrict her movement and is always ready for new discoveries and challenges. Anika's presence is a mix of strength and grace and she is as capable an adventurer as Janon.

Gronak, Fiona and Lea were equally shocked and amazed that the mountain trolls had not killed them immediately. It was unusual, as trolls were typically so merciless. But at the same time, they were relieved that the two adventurers had survived and were now safe.

Fiona suggested using the trolls' camp to spend the night. "We should take this opportunity to restore our strength and plan our next steps," she proposed. "It's safe here and we can use the information from Janon and Anika about the area to continue our journey."

The idea found unanimous approval and they decided to use the abandoned troll camp as a temporary base. The group gathered dry wood and lit a campfire to warm themselves and make the night more comfortable.

The five adventurers prepared the camp and cooked their dinner together. The warmth of the campfire and the aroma of the food filled the air as they gathered around the fire. Janon and Anika shared a wealth of thrilling stories about their shared adventures and discoveries. Everyone listened intently to the tales of forgotten ruins, ancient treasures and mysterious cultures they had explored.

Gronak, Fiona and Lea were equally enthralled by the stories and followed with tales of their own exciting journeys. They spoke of their mission to stop Xalis and how they had set out to find a shrine in the mountains with a powerful rune that could help them stop Xalis.

After the stories were exchanged, Janon suggested accompanying them to the ruin they had originally intended to explore. "Maybe there is information in the ruin about the rune crystal you're searching for," he proposed. "We can combine our knowledge and strengths to learn more about this rune and its potential effects."

Fiona didn't hesitate and enthusiastically agreed. "That sounds like a great idea. Together, we are stronger and who knows what we might find in that ancient ruin."

Gronak and Lea laughed at Fiona's joyful excitement but agreed as well. Gronak grinned and said, "Well, if the rune is as powerful as we think, we shouldn't waste any time. Let's explore this ruin together and see if we can find clues about this crystal."

Night quickly fell and darkness enveloped the adventurers' camp. Gronak suggested, "I'll take the night watch. Who knows what else lurks around here and it's safer if someone keeps watch." Janon nodded in agreement and said, "You're right, I'll stay with you, Gronak. It's safer with two of us."

The women, exhausted, slipped into their sleeping bags and prepared for a well-deserved rest. Gronak and Janon sat by the campfire, staring into the flames as the sounds of the night echoed around them.

Janon suddenly pulled out a small box from his bag and showed it to Gronak, who was filled with curiosity. His eyes sparkled as he asked, "What's in there, Janon?" Janon smiled, his eyes gleaming with excitement as he looked at the box and replied with trembling joy in his voice, "It's a ring. After this adventure, I plan to finally ask Anika to marry me."

Gronak couldn't hide his broad grin and said warmly, "That's wonderful, Janon! I wish you all the best and I hope she says 'yes.' How long have you known each other?"

Gronak listened attentively as Janon spoke about his connection to Anika. The flickering campfire cast gentle shadows on his features as he spoke of their deep bond. "I've known Anika since we were both little kids. It was in our village when I was being bullied by some other kids. She bravely stepped in and protected me. We quickly became friends and spent every day together. Our childhood was full of adventures and discoveries. As we grew up, we joined an adventurers' guild and embarked on many journeys together. Anika was always by my side and I was by hers. She is simply the right one for me."

A tearful smile crossed Gronak's face as he listened to Janon's story. He looked toward Fiona and said with a touch of nostalgia, "Yes, I understand exactly what you mean. Fiona and I have been friends since childhood as well. We've shared so many adventures together and she is very important to me. It's something truly special to have such deep connections with people." Gronak felt the memories of all their shared adventures flowing through his emotions.

As the last stars faded from the morning sky, Gronak and Janon had spent half the night exchanging stories about their beloved adventurers, Anika and Fiona. Their faces radiated friendship and trust as the first rays of sunlight greeted the day.

When the women awoke, they could smell the delicious aroma of a freshly prepared breakfast. The men had risen early to prepare the meal and the women fortified themselves for the day ahead. They sat around the campfire, enjoying the warmth of the rising sun and discussing their upcoming journey.

Anika excitedly explained, "It's not far from here to the ruin. I'm looking forward to finally learning more about the rune and its significance."

Lea nodded in agreement and said, "I'm really eager to see this ruin. Maybe this place will bring us one step closer to our goal."

Fiona joined in the anticipation and said, "It's exciting to gain new knowledge on such journeys. I hope the ruin provides us with some answers to our questions."

Gronak and Janon looked at each other and laughed. Once they had everything prepared, the five of them set off. The group was ready for the adventure ahead and together they would explore the secrets of the ancient ruin.

The group continued their journey and after hours of hiking, they finally reached the ruin, which turned out to be the remains of an old monastery. The buildings were heavily weathered and seemed to be suffering under the weight of centuries. However, as they approached, they noticed the weathered walls adorned with a variety of mysterious runes. These symbols stretched across the stones and appeared to carry a hidden message.

The excitement in Janon and Anika's eyes was evident as they saw the runes. Fiona, who had experience with such symbols, examined them with fascination and said, "These runes look familiar. I've seen them somewhere before, but I can't recall where."

Janon explained, pointing to one of the runes, "These symbols belong to an ancient culture that lived in this region many centuries ago. They might give us valuable clues, perhaps even the secret of the powerful rune you're searching for."

Together, they entered the former monastery and found themselves in a small garden amidst the crumbling buildings. Gronak looked around and said, "This must have been a beautiful place once, full of tranquility and peace."

Anika added, "Yes, it was said that this was a place of research and knowledge. Perhaps we will find clues here that could aid you in your journey or help us in our search for ancient knowledge." The thought that this decaying site might hold hidden secrets filled the group with excitement and curiosity.

As the group eagerly searched through the old ruin for important artifacts or writings, their peace was suddenly disturbed. An unknown and extremely arrogant voice broke the silence. "I see that the trolls didn't do their job very well; I guess I have to do everything myself," the voice called from above.

Startled and surprised, the group looked up and saw a man standing on one of the weathered buildings. His posture radiated arrogance and the adventurers realized they had encountered an unwelcome visitor.

Lea's eyes widened as she recognized the person and yelled angrily, "You're Reyve! What the hell are you doing here, you miserable coward?"

Reyve, the dark elf mercenary, is an imposing yet sinister figure. With his grace and strength, he embodies the mysterious and dark aura typical of his people. His appearance is marked by striking darkness.

He has a robust, shadowy figure. Reyve possesses a refined and sharply chiseled facial structure, dominated by his pointed, pale violet eyes. The eyes gleam with a coldness and hardness that reflect his character. His hair is deep black and reaches his shoulders.

Reyve wears a mix of light yet resilient clothing that allows him great freedom of movement. His attire is in dark colors and adorned with silver embellishments, showcasing his exquisite taste and attention to detail. Various pouches and bags hang from his belt, in which he keeps his tools and secrets.

Reyve responded irritably with a hint of arrogance in his voice, accompanied by a cynical smile. "Ah, it's you. You've ruined my business with Olaf."

Janon and Anika's eyes were filled with curiosity and concern about Reyve's identity. They turned to Lea for more information about this dangerous man.

Lea answered with an angry undertone that made her disdain for Reyve clear. "This is Reyve, a mercenary and a ruthless murderer. He helped Olaf kidnap my sister and many other innocent people, forcing them into slavery. He is dangerous and unscrupulous."

Reyve reacted to Lea's accusations with sarcasm, laughing cynically. His words cut through the air like sharp blades. "Oh yes, that's exactly what I did. It's always uplifting to kidnap people and see their despair in their eyes. But this time, I'm only here for this woman." He pointed at Anika, which unsettled the entire group.

Gronak could barely suppress his tension and asked through clenched teeth, his anger bubbling in his voice, "What do you want with Anika?" The tension in the air was palpable as the group realized with horror that Reyve had targeted Anika.

Reyve replied with a dangerous coldness in his voice. "You see, Anika is the daughter of a wealthy merchant and important men have hired me to kidnap her. I hired the trolls to do the job, but apparently, they failed. So, it looks like I have to do the dirty work myself."

Janon could no longer contain his fury and shouted, "I will never allow you to kidnap my Anika!"

Worried about the powers Reyve possessed, Fiona asked him, "How did you manage to command the trolls?"

Reyve laughed derisively and explained, "It's quite simple, my pretty lady. I have entered the service of the powerful ruler Xalis and he has granted me the ability to control creatures and give them orders. In his name, I am to spread terror and despair."

Gronak, Fiona and Lea were shocked by this information. Gronak responded with anger in his voice, "If you're working for Xalis, then we will do everything in our power to stop you!" The group was determined to protect Anika from this threat and confront Reyve and his dark plans.

Reyve grinned maliciously and raised his hand, snapping his fingers with a quick motion. A powerful roar suddenly erupted and behind Reyve, a mighty wyvern appeared. The group was equally surprised and shocked by this unexpected turn of events.

The wyvern, a majestic and dangerous creature, spread its enormous wings and emitted a bone-chilling scream that made the air tremble. Its scales gleamed in the blinding sunlight and its eye sparkled with danger. The wyvern's scales were a deep, shimmering green that glistened like emerald jewels. Its body appeared powerful and muscular and its wings spread majestically across its back.

Reyve laughed mockingly and spoke with an arrogant tone. "Since I still have a score to settle with you, I actually don't care about kidnapping my prey at this moment. Your desperate looks are reward enough for me." His malevolent grin made it clear how much he enjoyed the power that Xalis had granted him.

With another hand gesture, Reyve commanded the wyvern to attack. The colossal dragon obeyed immediately and launched a powerful, blue-glowing fireball at the group from the air. The adventurers watched in horror as the flames rushed toward them, feeling the heat and destructive force of the attack.

Gronak positioned himself in front of the others and raised his mighty shield to intercept the powerful fireball. When the blue-glowing sphere hit the ground, it exploded with tremendous force. Sparks and ashes flew through the air, searing into the ground. The shockwave was so intense that the ground beneath the group's feet gave way.

The earth collapsed as it was shaken by the immense explosion. Gronak struggled desperately to maintain his position and protect his friends, but the crumbling ground dragged them all down. Amidst the dust and darkness, the five adventurers fell into the void, the roar of the collapsing earth echoing in their ears. It felt as if they were plunging into an endless abyss while the earth around them quaked.

Reyve's derisive laughter echoed from above as he said, "This will teach you to mess with me and Xalis. You will pay for your arrogance."

Gronak awoke in the darkness and looked around anxiously. He saw the other four members of his group lying on the ground, unconscious and marked by the effects of the fall. The darkness surrounded them and only the faint light of some magical crystals allowed him to discern the situation.

Gronak first went to Fiona and Lea, who were slowly beginning to wake up in pain. He gently shook their shoulders and said with concern, "Wake up, you two. We need to get out of here."

The two women slowly opened their eyes and moaned in pain as they regained their senses. Meanwhile, Gronak attended to Janon and Anika.

Lea, feeling disoriented, held her hand to her head. "What happened?" Fiona, also still weak, replied, "The explosion created a hole in the ground and we ended up here. Fortunately, no one died."

With great relief in her voice, Fiona said, "I'll heal you." She focused on her healing powers and began to ease her friends injuries. The group's painful condition gradually improved and they were able to stand again.

Fiona smiled as she saw her friends slowly recovering. "Well, everyone's feeling better now," she announced with a hint of relief in her voice.

Gronak turned to Fiona and asked with concern, "How are you, Fiona?"

Fiona responded with a weak smile, "I'm feeling much better, Gronak. Thank you for your concern. Now we should figure out where we are and how to get out of this darkness."

Janon noted, "It seems we're in the catacombs beneath the monastery. It's a gloomy and eerie place, but perhaps we can find answers to our questions here."

The group first took a moment to recover from the exertion, pausing to regroup and consider how to escape the underground labyrinth.

Gronak, ever curious, turned to Anika and asked, "So Reyve had it out for you. Why, Anika?" His eyes reflected his desire for answers.

Anika looked down, her voice full of regret as she answered, "My father is a wealthy merchant, but he has made powerful enemies over the years. He never admitted it, but I knew he did many terrible things to get to where he is now. I always stayed out of his business and wanted to live my own life with Janon and experience adventures. But it seems my past has caught up with me. Reyve's employers likely wanted to weaken or blackmail my father. I'm so sorry that you've ended up in this situation because of me."

Janon embraced Anika tenderly and whispered to her, "You're not to blame for your father's actions, Anika. We face this challenge together and we will find a way out."

Gronak, Fiona and Lea agreed with Janon and expressed their support for Anika. The group had already overcome many adventures together and they would face this new challenge together as well.

Anika smiled gratefully and suggested, "Let's keep moving. We need to find a way out of these catacombs and stop Reyve and Xalis before they cause more havoc."

The group continued their journey through the dark catacombs. On the walls, they discovered numerous eerie symbols, including stone coffins and skulls arranged in a sinister pattern. The gloomy atmosphere and the creepy motifs created a chilling mood in the underground passages.

Eventually, they reached the end of the corridor and stepped into a large, round room. The walls were adorned with countless runes and symbols arranged in a fascinating pattern. Janon was visibly impressed by the room and couldn't take his eyes off the mysterious symbols.

He immediately began studying the runes and deciphering their meanings. Anika laughed softly and said jokingly, "Don't be surprised, this is how he always is when he finds something interesting. He can spend hours researching ancient writings."

Janon, without diverting his attention from the runes, replied with a mischievous smile, "I can't help it, Anika. These signs might give us clues about the history of this place and possibly about the rune crystal we're searching for."

Fiona examined the mysterious signs and runes on the wall attentively and suddenly, she had a realization. She carefully retrieved the book from her bag, which she had found in the abandoned villa. The pages of the book were marked by years of dust and age, but the writing and symbols were still well preserved.

Fiona eagerly flipped through the pages until she reached a section with exactly the same runes and symbols as those in the enigmatic room. Her heart raced with excitement and she knew she had discovered something valuable.

Without hesitation, Fiona went to Janon and asked him to look at the discovery. Janon took the book in his hands and began studying the writings and symbols closely. A spark of excitement appeared in his eyes and he could hardly contain his joy.

"Where did you get this book?" Janon asked as he continued reading. Fiona replied, "We found it in the Lost Forest, in an old villa forgotten by time."

Janon studied the writings carefully and after a while said, "This is the solution." Fiona couldn't contain her curiosity any longer and asked excitedly, "The solution to what, Janon?"

Janon explained with enthusiasm, "This room is a kind of guide or pointer to a powerful artifact. This artifact is said to have the unique ability to tame and control evil magic."

Fiona looked at Gronak and Lea, excited by this discovery. "Did you hear that? This must be the rune crystal Sawil told us about. The rune that can help us stop Xalis."

Lea nodded in agreement and Gronak was visibly excited about the prospect of stopping Xalis. "That sounds promising. But what does the description of the artifact say, Janon?"

Janon pondered for a moment as he re-read the writings. "If I understand this correctly, you need to place your hand on this symbol and then perform magic. But unfortunately, I'm not very knowledgeable about magic, so I can't tell you more about it."

Fiona smiled gratefully at Janon and said, "I'll give it a try." Carefully, she placed her hand on the rune symbol on the wall and closed her eyes, focusing on her magic. She let her energy flow into the symbol and felt a connection forming between her and the rune.

The center of the room began to glow gradually and the light manifested itself as a map of the surroundings. On the map, a small green light was marked at a spot in the mountains. Fiona opened her eyes and saw the map floating in front of her.

Janon, recognizing the significance of this place, quickly pulled out his own map and searched for the marked point. With a pen, he marked the location on the map and said excitedly, "That's it! That's the place we're looking for. The shrine and the artifact are there in the mountains."

Fiona carefully removed her hand from the rune symbol and the map slowly disappeared. She took a deep breath and smiled with relief. "That was quite exhausting. I couldn't have held that much longer," she admitted.

Lea looked at the marking on the map that Janon had drawn and noted, "It's in the middle of the mountains. It's going to be a difficult journey, but we're ready to face the challenge."

Fiona was deeply grateful to Janon for his help and said, "Thank you so much, Janon. Without you, we would never have found this shrine."

Janon handed Fiona the map and replied, "You've saved us and it was a pleasure to help you. I hope you reach your goal and can stop Xalis."

Gronak remarked, "We should leave here quickly before more trouble arises. The path to this shrine will surely be difficult, so we need to hurry."

The group continued their way through the catacombs when suddenly strong tremors shook the ground and walls. The tremors grew more intense and the ruin seemed to be falling apart.

Gronak shouted in panic, "We need to get out of here quickly; the ruin is going to collapse!" The group ran down the only corridor they had not yet explored. The walls became cracked and dust clouds swirled around them as the ceiling began to crumble dangerously.

"Come on, everyone, hurry up!" Lea shouted, pushing the group forward. The tremors grew more violent and the ruin seemed to be collapsing in on itself. The group ran for their lives as the tunnel ahead of them caved in.

At the end of the tunnel, they saw a faint light and ran toward it. The air was filled with falling dust and debris, but they didn't give up.

Suddenly, a massive boulder broke loose from the ceiling of the catacombs and crashed down toward Anika with devastating force. The entire group froze in shock as the threatening mass approached, but Janon acted in a desperate act of love. With all his strength and without a thought for his own safety, he shoved Anika aside to protect her from the falling rock.

The boulder struck Janon with relentless force, crushing his entire lower body. A bone-chilling scream of agonizing terror filled the air and pierced the hearts of the entire group. Janon cried out in pain, his voice filled with the horrific torment that overcame him.

Anika couldn't grasp what had just happened and she screamed in horror and despair, "Janon!" Tears streamed uncontrollably from her eyes as she helplessly watched Janon pinned beneath the enormous boulder, suffering unimaginable pain. Her heart broke in that terrible moment and the whole group witnessed Janon's selfless sacrifice for the woman he loved.

Gronak and Lea tried with all their might to lift the boulder to free Janon, but it proved too heavy. The ruin around them continued to crumble and time was running out. The group was trapped in a desperate situation, knowing they needed to save Janon as quickly as possible before the entire ruin collapsed on them.

Janon spat blood, his body convulsing with agonizing pain and his screams echoed through the catacombs like a mournful lament. Yet, even amid this unimaginable torment, he cried out with desperate resolve, "Keep going, run! Don't let yourselves be stopped!" His voice was weak but filled with unshakable will.

Anika knelt in despair and deep sadness before Janon, tears streaming uncontrollably down her face. Her sobs testified to the profound despair that had seized her. "No, I don't want to be without you, Janon. I love you!" she cried with a broken heart.

A faint smile crossed Janon's pain-wracked face as he experienced his final moments. With his last strength, he pulled out a small box from his jacket pocket and handed it to Anika. A final, loving look from his eyes met hers before he closed them forever and the suffering and pain finally ceased.

The cry of grief and pain that Anika let out tore through the air. "No, don't leave me alone, Janon!" she sobbed desperately, clutching the box tightly in her hands. It felt like the last remaining piece of Janon she had and her heart was shattered by his tragic sacrifice.

The ruin seemed to be on the verge of collapsing. Gronak cried out desperately to Anika, "We need to get out of here now, Anika! We have no more time!"

Anika, however, did not respond to Gronak's words. Her gaze was vacant and filled with tears as she clutched the box Janon had given her. She seemed trapped in her grief, unable to move.

Gronak realized they had no more time and acted swiftly. He lifted Anika onto his broad shoulders and carried her while shouting, "Run, everyone, run!"

The group followed Gronak and at the last moment, they reached the exit of the ruin. They found themselves in one of the remaining buildings of the monastery, just in time before the ruin collapsed in on itself. The catacombs and the room with the mysterious runes were now forever lost, buried beneath the debris of history.

Lea looked through a hole in the wall and could see Reyve in the distance, continuing to destroy the ruin with his wyverns. The powerful creatures caused massive destruction and Lea realized that this was the reason for the collapse of the catacombs.

She quickly turned to the others and said with concern, "This madman is destroying the entire ruin with his flying beasts! No wonder the catacombs have collapsed."

The attacks seemed to continue for a while, but after a few minutes, they stopped and Reyve flew away with his wyverns. The group breathed a sigh of relief, grateful to have escaped the attacks, while simultaneously mourning Janon, who had been left behind in the catacombs.

Lea approached Anika to comfort her as she slowly came out of her state of shock. Anika broke into a torrent of tears of grief and despair, her voice filling the room as she screamed and cursed Reyve.

"I will kill that bastard, I will make him suffer just as he made me suffer. I won't rest until I have personally killed him and avenged Janon's death," Anika swore with a determination that burned her words into the air. Her fist struck the ground and her face was twisted with rage.

Lea, understanding the anger and pain in Anika, embraced her without a word and held her tightly. It was a hug that spoke more than words ever could. After a brief moment of silence, the embrace ended and Anika looked at Lea with a hint of gratitude in her eyes.

"Thank you, Lea," Anika said with sorrow in her gaze. It was a thank you for the support in this darkest moment when the world had fallen apart for her.

Anika looked at the box Janon had given her at the last moment. With trembling hands, she opened it, revealing a ring. The names "Janon" and "Anika" were lovingly engraved on the ring. The meaning of the ring was immediately clear and tears welled up in Anika's eyes once more.

Gronak stepped closer and whispered to Anika, his face filled with compassion. "Janon told me yesterday that he wanted to ask you after this adventure if you would marry him." His words struck Anika like a stab to the heart and her emotions burst forth.

"Why him? Why, Janon!" she sobbed, holding the ring in her hand. The grief and pain were overwhelming and she felt betrayed by this merciless world.

Without another word, Anika turned away from her friends and walked quickly toward the door. She opened it and stepped out into the blinding daylight. With a heavy heart, she said, tears on her cheeks, "I will leave you now, my friends. Thank you for everything you've done." Then she ran out of the building and left the ruin, alone and filled with sorrow, searching for answers and perhaps a way to cope with her loss.

After a few minutes of painful silence, Gronak suggested they continue and focus on the shrine marked on Janon's map. The deep emptiness left by Janon's loss seemed insurmountable, but they knew they had to press on. Fiona and Lea exchanged glances and Fiona nodded in agreement. "You're right, Gronak. We should move on."

During their journey to the marked destination, silence reigned among the three remaining friends. Each of them needed to first process what had happened and come to terms with Janon's loss. The grief was deep and weighed heavily on their hearts.

Gronak eventually broke the silence and encouraged them with a trembling voice that could not hide the pain in his chest. "Don't let your heads hang low. We need to keep our goal in sight. Only then can we stop Reyve and Xalis. We owe it to Janon."

Fiona and Lea looked up and agreed. The grief and loss would always accompany them, but they knew they could not let Janon's sacrifice be in vain. "You're right," Fiona said with a mix of sorrow and concern. "Let's find this shrine and turn Janon's sacrifice into our hope."

Eventually, they arrived at a steep rock face that rose almost vertically. The wind-swept path had led them here and the significance of this place was unmistakable. This spot was marked on Janon's map and they hoped they would find the shrine here that Sawil had spoken of.

Lea, who was considered an experienced climber, took the lead. "Let's carefully climb up the rock face and reach the cave entrance," she suggested. The others agreed and they began the arduous ascent. The rock was rough and uneven and every grip and step had to be chosen with care. The tension in the group was palpable as they worked against the uncertainty of their future.

Finally, they reached the cave entrance, hidden in the rock face. Darkness swallowed them as they stepped into the narrow cave. The torches they had brought flickered in the wind, casting only a faint light that barely penetrated the darkness. The cave walls were covered in shiny, damp stones and the smell of moss hung heavy in the air.

Gronak, who led the way, groped through the darkness, followed by Fiona and Lea. They eventually reached a large chamber, illuminated by a faint glow. The source of this light was the shrine they had been searching for. It stood in the middle of the room and appeared to be made of an obsidian-like stone. Ancient symbols and script adorned its surface and they seemed to be written in a language none of them understood.

Fiona approached the shrine, fascinated by the strange energy emanating from it. "This is it," she whispered, as if afraid to disturb the shrine's magic. "The shrine Sawil described to us. The rune crystal we've been searching for must be here somewhere."

Lea also moved closer and gently touched the smooth surface of the shrine. "It feels like there is an immense power sleeping here," she remarked. "But how are we supposed to find or activate the rune?"

Gronak, observing the shrine from a distance, said, "I believe we need to look around and search for clues. The crystal certainly won't be obvious."

The group began to search the room, inspecting the walls, floor and the shrine itself, hoping to find something that would aid them in their quest for the powerful rune crystal.

Fiona examined the stone slab behind the shrine and noticed that the same symbol appeared on the slab as in the ruin they had explored earlier. She hesitated for a moment, then carefully placed her hand on the stone slab. She closed her eyes and focused her magic as she tried to establish a connection. Her hand began to glow and she slowly transferred her magical energy into the slab.

A powerful magical aura pulsed around the shrine as it began to slowly open. The massive stone blocks moved aside and the rune they had been searching for was revealed. The rune crystal in the shrine was the center of attention. It was bathed in a deep green and radiated an intense glow that bathed the room in a mysterious light.

Lea gazed at the rune crystal with wide eyes, overwhelmed by its beauty. "This is it!" Lea exclaimed excitedly. "The rune Sawil meant. We've found it!"

The crystal itself was a hand-sized stone with a powerful rune engraved in its center. It was surrounded by a circle of smaller symbols, which were also carved into the stone. The runes seemed to be written in an ancient and unknown script and their meaning remained a mystery.

Gronak gazed at the rune crystal with fascination. "I've never seen anything like this. I can actually feel its magic," Gronak remarked, intrigued.

Step by step, the group approached the shrine and the closer they got, the more they felt the eerie presence that filled the room. It was completely dark and only the faint green light of the rune crystal illuminated the space, casting long shadows on the walls. The air was heavy and stuffy and it seemed as if something ominous lingered in the atmosphere.

Fiona moved closer to the shrine and slowly extended her hand to touch the crystal. As she approached the rune, she noticed it was surrounded by a faint greenish light. Her fingers touched the smooth surface and at the moment her skin made contact with the crystal, something unexpected happened. The rune crystal in the center of the shrine suddenly blazed with light, sending radiant beams that filled the entire room.

Lea let out a surprised cry. "Look at that! The crystal is practically pulsing with power, as if it's coming to life!"

The group felt the immense power of the rune crystal surrounding them and knew they needed it to confront Xalis and avert the impending danger. Fiona carefully picked up the crystal and the moment she held it in her hand, she felt a powerful magical energy flowing through her body. An incredible sense of connection and strength surged through her and she knew that this rune was crucial for their mission.

Fiona looked at her companions and smiled excitedly. "This is it! This rune will help us defeat Xalis, I can feel it. We should return to Sawil as quickly as possible to learn more about the rune and its significance. Maybe he can also help us activate this powerful source of magic."

The group returned with the rune crystal to the hermit, who was visibly pleased that they had found the rune. He invited them into his modest home and they took their seats at the rustic wooden table. The hermit politely asked to see the crystal and the adventurers placed it carefully on the table.

Sawil pondered for a moment and sighed softly before he straightened up and walked to a dusty shelf in the corner of the room. He rummaged through the books, seemingly searching for something specific. Finally, he pulled out a very old book covered in faded symbols and runes. He leafed through it carefully, murmuring quietly to himself as he searched the pages.

After a while, he found what he was looking for and an expression of awe passed over his face. He turned the book towards the adventurers and pointed to a page where the rune was depicted. "This is it," he said softly.

The group listened intently to his words, asking what he knew about this rune. The hermit cleared his throat and began to speak with reverence. "This rune crystal is a powerful symbol of protective magic, capable of weakening dark magic. In the past, there was a powerful sorcerer named Malachai who tried to subjugate the world with dark magic, just like Xalis. The people fought desperately against him and sought a way to combat his sinister power. Eventually, they discovered the power of protective runes."

He paused briefly to let the tension in the air settle before continuing. "The protective runes were kept in various locations around the world to ensure they did not fall into the wrong hands. The people relied on these runes to protect their world from Malachai's dark magic."

Sawil leaned back in his chair and looked at the crystal on the table. "There is, however, a way to completely neutralize dark magic, but it is extremely dangerous. Unfortunately, I cannot tell you in detail how it is done, as it is described in the ancient texts of the lost temple. These texts might provide the answers to your questions."

Fiona could no longer contain her curiosity and asked Sawil with a questioning look, "What kind of temple are you talking about and where can we find it?"

Sawil leaned back in his chair and gazed into the distance as he chose his words carefully. "This temple," he began, "contains ancient knowledge that could be crucial for combating dark magic. Unfortunately, no one has found the temple for several hundred years. All we know is that it is hidden somewhere in the wasteland. But you must be cautious, as this area is a vast desert filled with dangers."

At this point, Lea interrupted, sounding concerned, "A desert? That sounds like an inhospitable environment. How are we even supposed to find the temple?"

The hermit nodded in agreement and continued, "Yes, it will be a dangerous journey and there is no easy way to get there. But you are the chosen ones and you are prepared to do whatever it takes to defeat Xalis and his dark magic. The ancient texts contain clues about markings and signs that might guide you. But remember, the desert is a place of loss and confusion. You must keep your unity and trust your instincts."

Gronak, who had been silent until now, looked up and said resolutely, "We will find this temple and gain the knowledge to stop Xalis. Thank you, Sawil, for your help and your wisdom."

Gronak, Fiona and Lea stood up, thanked the hermit Sawil warmly and expressed their gratitude for his support and the valuable information about the lost temple. Sawil responded with a warm smile and said, "May luck and the protection of the protective runes be with you on your journey."

With a sense of hope and a clear goal in mind, they left Sawil's modest home and set out for the wasteland that stretched beyond the majestic mountains. The sun was slowly setting on the horizon as they carefully checked their supplies and prepared for their dangerous adventure.

As they set out, they began to make plans and discuss their approach. Gronak spoke to his companions. "We should look for these markings and signs that Sawil mentioned. They might be the key to finding the temple."

Fiona, ever curious and eager for knowledge, agreed and added, "Yes and maybe we can learn more about Xalis along the way. The more we know, the better prepared we will be."

Lea, who shone with her wisdom and intuition, said thoughtfully, "Don't forget that we will be traversing dangerous terrain. We must stick together and watch out for each other. Sawil emphasized that the desert is a place of loss and confusion. Our strength will be our unity."

Together, they set out on the arduous path, determined to overcome every obstacle to halt Xalis and his dark magic. The majestic mountains appeared almost magical in the twilight as they ventured into the unknown, ready to face the challenge ahead.

Chapter 9: The Wasteland

Gronak, Fiona and Lea had struggled their way through the mountainous and harsh terrain, hoping to finally reach the wasteland. The environment around them had steadily changed and the dry air cut through their throats. The ground beneath their feet was parched and cracked, as if nature itself had given up here. There were barely any signs of plants or animals and the silence enveloped them like a grim cloak.

"This really doesn't look good," Fiona murmured as she gazed over the lifeless landscape. "Have you ever seen anything so desolate?"

Lea furrowed her brow and looked anxiously at the bleak scene. "I've heard that the wasteland is not for the faint-hearted. We need to be careful and stick together, just as Sawil advised us."

Gronak, who was silently scanning the horizon, nodded in agreement. "It won't be easy to find our way. There are no roads or paths here to rely on."

"Maybe we should use the sun as a guide," suggested Lea, pointing to the sky. "If we keep an eye on it, we won't lose our direction so easily."

Fiona agreed. "Good idea, Lea. Let's keep track of it and hope this barren place doesn't swallow us up."

After days of traveling through the harsh landscape, Gronak, Fiona and Lea finally reached the edge of the wasteland. An endless desert stretched out before them, covered by gray clouds, while a warm wind swirled the hot sand around their feet. The desolate scenery made

Fiona stare uncertainly into the desert. "So, which way should we go?" she asked, her eyes searching.

Gronak hesitated for a moment before answering. "I suggest we go that way. But be on guard, we could easily get lost."

The sun beat down mercilessly on them as they set out on the supposed path. The ground was so hot it seemed to burn through the soles of their boots. No signs of life were visible, only the endless sand stretching to the horizon.

"Remember, water is precious here," Gronak warned the others as he lifted his bottle to his lips. "We need to ration it wisely if we want to make it through."

The three sipped cautiously from their water reserves and ate sparingly from their supplies. Each step in the desert seemed to take an eternity, as the heat drained their strength.

Deep in the wasteland, Gronak, Fiona and Lea saw a dust cloud rising in the distance. Lea squinted her sharp eyes and quickly realized that a massive creature was approaching them. The ground shook beneath their feet as the beast drew closer and the tension in the group was palpable.

"What the hell is that?" Fiona shouted as she gripped her weapons tightly.

Lea furrowed her brow and analyzed the approaching threat. "That's no ordinary monster. That's a sand viper. And it's enormous!"

Gronak, with a grim expression, added, "Let's be ready. Sandvipers are dangerous and we need to defend ourselves well."

The Sandviper approached relentlessly. The desert air was filled with its menacing growl. As the creature came closer, it was at least ten meters long and its shiny scales sparkled in the sun. The Viper's eyes were huge and glowing yellow and its long, sharp teeth glittered dangerously.

"That's not a small snake, that's a damned beast!" Fiona exclaimed nervously.

The three friends formed a defensive line, their weapons firmly in their hands. Gronak stepped forward. "It's a Sandviper, but we can defeat it if we act smartly."

The Sandviper burst from the sand, its scales glistening in the desert heat and its eyes sparkled with fury. With a loud growl, it turned toward the adventurers and attacked.

Gronak drew his massive sword and boldly charged at the Sandviper, his determination reflected in his eyes. Fiona focused her magic for an icy spell, while Lea aimed to weaken the monster with skillful, precise shots. Yet their weapons seemed ineffective against the Sandviper's thick armor. The creature lashed out wildly with its massive tail, sending Gronak and Fiona flying through the air, landing with a thud on the hot desert sand.

"Focus your attacks on its weak spots!" Gronak shouted as he struggled to his feet.

Fiona nodded and began hurling icy projectiles at the Sandviper's eyes, hoping to impair its vision. Lea, adept with her bow, aimed at the soft spots between the scales. But the Sandviper was agile and deftly deflected the attacks. Gronak desperately tried to pierce through the armor with his sword, but it seemed hopeless.

The desert heat intensified the friends efforts, as the Sandviper growled menacingly, baring its teeth and launching a counterattack.

Lea, dodging the creature's attacks skillfully, remembered an old legend she had heard from a desert tribe. "Listen to me! We need to make the Sandviper bite itself. That puts it in a trance and then we can strike!"

Gronak and Fiona listened intently while continuing to withstand the Viper. "But how the hell do we do that?" Gronak shouted, narrowly avoiding another powerful tail strike.

Lea thought quickly. "We need to provoke it to swing its tail at us. If we can make it bite its tail, we're one step closer!"

Lea lured the monster towards her with skillful movements. Her heart pounded loudly as the huge Sandviper, with glowing red eyes, charged at her. With a precise sidestep, she barely escaped the whipping tail that crashed to the ground with immense force. The Sandviper, seemingly irritated by Lea's escape, turned and tried to catch its prey.

Gronak, closely observing the situation, saw the opportunity. With a powerful leap, he grabbed the Sandviper's outstretched tail and pulled it toward the monster's head. The ground trembled under the clash of titans, as Gronak, with all his strength, tried to overpower the Viper.

"Lea, now!" he shouted, holding the thrashing tail tightly.

Lea reacted instantly. With a precise shot, she aimed her arrow at the Sandviper's head. The arrow pierced the shiny scales, hitting right between the creature's glowing red eyes. A bone-chilling scream filled the desert air as the Viper cried out in pain.

The Sandviper seemed confused and tried in vain to free itself from Gronak's grip. It snapped wildly at Gronak, but at the crucial moment, he deftly dodged. In a desperate act, the creature bit down with full force on its own tail as Gronak and Lea retreated.

An earthquake-like roar filled the air as the Sandviper sank to the ground. The desert heat seemed to intensify with the monster's fall.

Meanwhile, Fiona focused on her magic. Her hands glowed with icy energy and she felt the power of the element rising within her. The air around her seemed to freeze as she summoned numerous sharp ice crystals that sparkled in the blazing sun.

"This is your end, you giant monstrosity!" Fiona shouted, hurling the icy projectiles with impressive precision at the unprotected head of the Sandviper. The ice crystals pierced the creature's scales, leaving glittering trails.

The Sandviper, struck by the icy missiles, began thrashing wildly. Its monstrous body convulsed in pain, but the ice shards had already taken their deadly toll. With a final, strangled cry, the Sandviper fell to the ground, its body twitching a few more times before its eyes closed for good.

The three friends, exhausted but victorious, let a moment of silence fall over the desert. Fiona lowered her hands, the magic fading and she took a deep breath.

"That was close," Lea said, her bow still drawn. "Good thing I knew that old legend."

Gronak nodded in agreement as he examined the Viper up close. "You never stop learning, especially in these forsaken lands."

Fiona smiled slightly. "Let's move on. We still have a long way to go and who knows what else awaits us."

The three friends gathered their strength, packed their gear and continued their journey. The defeated Sandviper lay behind them and the wasteland stretched ahead, full of mysteries and challenges.

The sun beat down mercilessly on Gronak, Fiona and Lea as they wandered through the desolate wasteland. Their supplies dwindled with each step and the prospect of water and food grew increasingly bleak. The heat sapped their strength and the worry lines on their faces deepened with each passing day.

But then, just as they were about to lose hope, a small green spot appeared in the distance. Exhausted and filled with new hope, they pressed on toward this miraculous place. As they drew closer, the vision of an oasis in the middle of the desert became clearer.

The friends stood still as they gazed at the place surrounded by tall palms and trees. The lush greenery and the shade cast by the leaves seemed like an illusion in this hostile environment.

Gronak, seeing the exhaustion in his companions' eyes, said with relief, "This is our salvation. An oasis! Let's pray there's really water and food here waiting for us."

The three cautiously approached the oasis, hearing the soothing sound of water. When they finally arrived, a sight opened before them that filled their weary bodies with new energy a clear, sparkling lake, fed by a small waterfall.

Fiona took a deep breath, feeling the cool breeze from the lake on her skin. "Water! It's like a gift from the gods."

Lea filled her water container and looked around. "I thought we were done for. We're really lucky. Hopefully, we can find some food here too."

The trees and shrubs around the lake offered plenty of fruits and berries. The friends greedily reached for the juicy delicacies, savoring every bite. The sweet refreshment and the nutrients they desperately needed revitalized their tired bodies.

Gronak looked into the distance and said gratefully, "This is like a little paradise in the midst of this hostile desert. May this place give us the strength and energy to continue our journey."

As they replenished their strength and supplies, they began to share their experiences.

Fiona, gazing at the sparkling lake, said, "Who would have thought we'd stumble upon such a jewel in the middle of the desert? It reminds me how important it is to never lose hope."

Lea, popping a handful of berries into her mouth, agreed. "It shows that even in the most unlikely moments, miracles can happen. We should remember that we are not alone on our journey."

Gronak, contemplating the clear water of the lake, added, "It also teaches us to respect nature. It may be relentless, but it also holds surprising gifts. Let's set up camp and rest here; who knows when we'll get such an opportunity again."

The sun slowly dipped toward the horizon as Gronak, Fiona and Lea built their small camp from palm leaves. Their weary bodies seemed to find some rest as they began to check and repair their gear. Supplies were carefully sorted and every move was made with deliberate thought.

When everything was finally prepared, they settled under a shady palm. The cool breeze from the lake caressed their heated faces and a feeling of relief spread. Fiona, sinking to the ground exhausted, began the conversation. "I'm so grateful we found this place. I wonder how much longer we could have lasted."

Gronak, while checking his weapons, agreed. "Sawil wasn't exaggerating when he warned us about the wasteland. And our journey is far from over."

Lea, leaning back and watching the palm leaves sway in the wind, voiced another concern. "I wonder how Anika is doing. She ran off so angrily. I'm really worried about her."

Gronak looked seriously into the distance and replied, "Janon's death hit her really hard. You could see the desire for revenge in her eyes."

Fiona, concerned for her friend, looked at Gronak. "I just hope she doesn't put herself in danger."

Gronak tried to reassure them. "She'll manage. Anika has survived so many adventures, she's good at taking care of herself. But still, I'm worried. Revenge and anger can cloud your judgment."

Lea nodded thoughtfully. "That's true. When I saw Olaf, all I could think about was what he did to Elena and I acted rashly. Thankfully, everything turned out okay. Thank you for being there with me, friends."

The group was silent for a moment, as the shadows of the palms grew longer and the silence of the oasis was only broken by the gentle lapping of the lake. Then Gronak resumed the conversation. "We need to consider how to proceed. Our mission is not yet accomplished and the wasteland surely holds many more dangers for us. Let's discuss our next steps together."

So they sat together, sharing their experiences, planning their next moves and continuing their mission. Amidst the green oasis, surrounded by the shade-giving palms, their unity proved to be an anchor in the merciless wilderness of the wasteland.

The days of rest in the oasis had been like a brief dream and as Gronak, Fiona and Lea set out again, they were greeted by the harsh reality of the wasteland. They wandered for hours through endless sand dunes, their steps accompanied by the silence of the desert. Here and there, they saw sparse plants, but most were withered and animals seemed to avoid this inhospitable place. The burning sun beat down relentlessly on them, their bodies exhausted and their throats parched.

After hours of wandering, they finally saw the outline of a city in the distance. But the hope for refuge or salvation faded as they drew closer. The city lay in ruins, the buildings crumbled as if witnesses to a past catastrophe. The streets were covered in rubble and ash and the wind carried a scent of despair.

Lea looked at the remnants with a sad expression. "What happened to this place? It looks like no one has lived here for ages."

Gronak, his eyes keenly observing the surrounding ruins, replied, "It seems this city fell victim to a terrible tragedy. Everything is in ruins."

Fiona peered into the destroyed buildings, only to discover empty, burnt-out rooms. "It's horrible. As if a fire consumed everything."

The few remnants of furniture and household items that hadn't been destroyed by time were either rotten or gnawed at by birds and rodents. The silence that hung over the city was almost palpable and the emptiness seemed to echo in every shattered building.

Gronak pulled his weapon closer and cautioned, "We must be careful. There may be no one left here, but that doesn't mean there aren't any dangers."

They walked through the crumbling streets, their steps muffled by the debris. The memories of past inhabitants seemed to linger in the dilapidated walls, telling a sad story of loss and destruction. Amidst this bleak scene, they remained vigilant and alert, ready for any possible threats lurking in the ruins.

Gronak scoured the remnants of the buildings, searching for clues or signs about the fate of this once-thriving city and its residents. Meanwhile, Fiona and Lea picked their way through the rubble-lined streets, looking for survivors or useful items.

As the day drew to a close and darkness began to fall, they decided to set up camp on one of the higher buildings. The elevation would at least provide some protection from the unpredictable dangers of the wasteland. Together, they built a makeshift camp and lit a small fire to prepare their meager meal the little that remained of their supplies.

But suddenly, a low rumble pierced the stillness of dusk. It was a sound of pounding feet coming from afar, breaking the atmosphere of calm. The three friends, alerted by this unfamiliar noise, drew their weapons and positioned themselves, ready for whatever was approaching.

Gronak peered into the encroaching darkness. "What could that be? A creature or something else?"

Fiona looked tense. "I don't know, but I have a bad feeling about this."

Lea directed her gaze toward the approaching darkness and cast a worried glance at her friends. "Hopefully, it's nothing hostile. Let's be ready, whatever it is."

The stomping noise drew inexorably closer, growing louder and more menacing. Their campfire cast flickering shadows on the surrounding ruins, heightening the tension among the friends. The uncertainty about what was coming weighed heavily on their shoulders.

Slowly and ominously, the sound approached and the friends saw an army of undead advancing toward them. The creatures were decayed, distorted shadows of their former human forms. They shuffled and stumbled toward their targets, their faces expressionless, their eyes empty, devoid of any emotion. Time and decay had marked their pale skin, their clothes were torn and dirty.

Some of the undead carried rusty swords and decayed clubs, while others had only their bare hands as weapons.

Some bore open wounds oozing foul blood, while others had rotting bones showing where tissue should have been.

The noise surrounding these undead beings was eerie and unsettling. No sound came from their mouths, no breathing, no sighing. They moved relentlessly and unceasingly forward, as if they felt no pain or sensation of harm.

Gronak, with a tense look, broke the uneasy silence. "What are these creatures? They look like they were once human."

Fiona kept her weapon ready, her expression fierce. "I've never seen anything like this. These are no ordinary undead."

Lea, her gaze fixed on the approaching threat, swallowed hard. "We need to defend ourselves. These things won't back down."

The friends prepared for battle, their thoughts filled with a will to survive. But as they braced themselves against the eerie army, the uncertainty of how to combat beings so grotesquely altered weighed heavily on their shoulders.

At the moment the undead were only a few meters away from the group, Gronak broke the silence and charged forward. His sword swung wildly, slicing and hacking, while Fiona unleashed her magic to annihilate the creatures. Flames swirled through the air, followed by blinding lightning that either set the undead ablaze or tore them apart. Lea aimed with her bow, her arrows finding their marks with deadly precision, while she shouted instructions to support Gronak and Fiona, whether for dodging or attacking.

The undead, numerous and relentless, surged at the friends. Gronak led his weapon, landing each strike precisely as he defended against the oncoming creatures. His sword sliced through the air, severing rotting limbs and leaving the undead in pieces.

Fiona, surrounded by an aura of magic, sent destructive forces into the crowd. Flames flickered, lightning split the air and the undead fell burning or shattered into fragments on the ground.

Lea, skilled and focused, drew her bow repeatedly, her arrows hitting their targets with deadly accuracy. "Gronak, to the right!" she called out, pointing to a group of undead approaching from the side. Her arrows pierced the decaying bodies as she simultaneously guided her friends to coordinate their attacks.

The battle raged on and the friends fought with united strength as the undead creatures relentlessly charged at them. Each strike, spell and arrow was a desperate attempt to withstand the horde of decay and corruption.

Amidst the ongoing onslaught of the undead, there seemed to be no end in sight. Gronak was grabbed by one of the beings, but with a powerful blow of his sword to its face, he freed himself at the last moment.

Lea called for a plan as Gronak gathered his thoughts. "Fiona, Lea, behind me!" he roared, as he prepared himself. His eyes locked on the advancing horde as he focused on his strength and combat skills. With a powerful leap, he landed among the undead and began to move like a wild whirlwind. Fiona and Lea used this distraction to stay behind him and attack the creatures from the rear.

The plan unfolded and the friends fought as a coordinated unit. Gronak whirled through the undead, his sword dancing among them, while Fiona and Lea carried out their attacks with arrows and magic precise and deadly.

After a grueling period of fighting, they had defeated all the undead. The friends stood exhausted, their breaths heavy and their clothes covered in blood and dirt. Yet a spark of triumph lay in their weary eyes.

Gronak looked at his friends with concern. "Are you two unhurt?"

"We're fine, Gronak," Fiona said. "But you're injured; I'll heal you quickly."

After Fiona had tended to Gronak, he said to the others, "We need to find out what's going on here. So let's search the city once more, but be careful."

As the friends continued to roam the city, they deepened their search, hoping to find clues that would help them break the dark curse hanging over the abandoned city. Every house was meticulously searched, every room thoroughly examined in hopes of finding a solution.

In the decaying walls of an old library, they came upon a hidden room shrouded in dark shadows. A cold breeze of past tragedies seemed to blow here. An old table stood in the center of the room, covered with layers of dust and neglect. On this table lay a yellowed piece of paper, atop which rested a weathered skeleton.

Gronak, Fiona and Lea approached the table cautiously, their eyes fixed on the yellowed paper. Fiona carefully drew the note closer and began to read, while Lea checked the room for any potential dangers. "It seems someone wrote down the fate of this city in their last breaths," Fiona murmured, trying to decipher the fragmented words.

The note revealed the terrible truth about the curse that plagued the city. A powerful necromancer had unleashed dark forces upon the city, transforming its inhabitants into undead warriors. The writer's final wish was that the necromancer must be defeated to lift the curse.

"This is it! The necromancer is the key," Gronak declared with a hint of hope in his voice. "If we can find and defeat him, we might lift the curse and free the people."

Armed with this new knowledge and a plan in their minds, the three friends continued their search. They fought their way through the dark, deserted streets, each step accompanied by the oppressive silence of the cursed place. Slowly, they approached an imposing church, its gothic towers looming darkly against the overcast sky.

Lea, with her bow firmly in hand, was the first to approach the church. "We need to be careful here," she warned quietly as she surveyed the surroundings.

Fiona nodded in agreement. "It could be a trap. The necromancer might not be alone."

Gronak squared his shoulders and drew his sword. "Prepare yourselves. We will bring down this necromancer and end this curse once and for all."

The building was steeped in shadows and surrounded by an aura of decay. A sinister presence greeted them with a suffocating sense of dread as they entered the old church. A sharp stench of rot and corruption filled the air as they cautiously made their way into the gloomy halls.

At the far end of the somber room stood a figure the necromancer. His mere presence seemed to intensify the darkness. His face was pale, almost lifeless and his eyes appeared as black gates to another world. His tattered clothing, marked by years of decay, cloaked him in a mantle of darkness. A chain with rusted, menacing symbols hung around his neck, heralding an ominous power.

In the skeletal fingers of the necromancer rested a staff, enveloped in a greenish glow. An eerie energy seemed to emanate from the staff, distorting the air around him and sending heavy pressure waves through the room. It was as if he held the very essence of death in his hand.

Gronak, with an expression of outrage, charged forward. "How could you kill innocent inhabitants in such a cruel manner?"

Lea joined him, her voice piercing. "You will be held accountable for your deeds!"

The necromancer rose majestically, his deep voice echoing menacingly through the church. "I am Norax, a servant of the mighty Xalis. I was sent to spread terror and chaos and you will be my next victims."

The friends were shocked by these words, but there was no time to think. The necromancer's dark aura seemed to suffocate the atmosphere as the tension between the friends and this servant of evil reached its peak.

The necromancer raised his icy voice, drenched in a dark magic that made the blood in their veins freeze. His words seemed like spells that could fill even the bravest warriors with fear and dread. The air crackled with an overwhelming aura as the ground shook and skeletal warriors rose from the void.

Gronak and Lea, ready for battle, did not hesitate. They threw themselves into the relentless onslaught of the undead, their weapons striking wildly at the bones as they desperately tried to take down as many foes as possible. But the number of enemies seemed to increase endlessly, with new undead creatures constantly emerging from the ground.

In a moment of respite, Fiona asked her friends for time. Reaching into her pouch, she retrieved the magical rune. She closed her eyes and focused on the rune crystal, directing all her strength and determination to this one moment. She felt the energy radiating from her, merging with the magic of the rune crystal. The darkness the necromancer spread around him clashed against the power of the rune.

The creatures, undead and hungry for destruction, surged forward to crush any resistance. Gronak and Lea fought valiantly, but their strength was overwhelmed by the seemingly endless wave of undead creatures.

The confrontation reached its climax as Fiona, surrounded by her aura, amplified the magic of the rune crystal. Her battle against the necromancer's darkness was intense, the powers clashing and the room trembled with the concentrated energy in the air. Meanwhile, Gronak and Lea desperately tried to hold their ground against the unstoppable horde of undead, which continued to spread with no signs of exhaustion.

Fiona felt her energies waning as she relentlessly opposed the overwhelming darkness of the necromancer. But she did not give up; her resolve held firm and she felt she could succeed. Suddenly, a surge of new strength coursed through her and she knew Gronak and Lea had helped her. By defeating some of the undead, they had weakened the necromancer's magic, granting her a moment of relief.

As the necromancer's darkness seemed to weaken, Fiona felt that the time for action had come. She raised her hand, clutching the rune crystal tightly and unleashed the full power upon the necromancer. A tremendous wave of magical energy crashed down on him and the necromancer screamed as he was struck by the power of the rune crystal. Fiona knew she had weakened him; her magic was finally having an effect.

Gronak and Lea seized the opportunity and intensified their attacks against the undead creatures. With renewed determination and taking advantage of the necromancer's weakened magic, they struck with all their might at the undead army. The rune had diminished Norax's power, allowing them to defeat one undead after another. Piece by piece, the undead fell to dust until finally, the last of them succumbed to the curse and disintegrated.

With only Norax left, his power greatly weakened by the rune crystal, Gronak felt the decisive moment. He charged forward, sword firmly in hand and with a powerful swing, he severed the necromancer's head. A chilling scream filled the church as Norax collapsed and eventually turned to dust.

The group now stood at the edge of the battlefield, breathless and exhausted from the fierce fight against the undead and the powerful necromancer. The air was filled with a mixture of silence and the gentle rustle that came from the restored calm of the city.

Fiona, still holding the crystal, slowly approached her friends. "We did it," she said with a touch of relief in her voice. "The curse is broken."

Gronak, his sword still stained with the necromancer's remnants, nodded in agreement. "It was a hard fight, but we have freed the city."

Lea, now holding her bow loosely, looked at the scattered remains of the undead. "The inhabitants can finally rest in peace."

With the necromancer's death, the dark power that had ruled over the city was gone. The rotting bodies of the undead that remained in the city turned back to dust and the city began to heal slowly. The curse was lifted and a hint of life returned to the once-darkened alleys.

As Gronak, Fiona and Lea took a moment of respite, their eyes fell upon a hidden door in the back of the church. Curiously, they entered the gloomy room behind it. The air was heavy, filled with dust and a suffocating pressure. Candles and incense burners dimly lit the room and on an old table lay some dusty books.

The grim walls were adorned with eerie images that radiated an aura of darkness. A shabby, old throne stood on a pedestal and in front of it lay a skeleton on the floor, its bones almost reduced to dust. A ghostly heaviness hung in the air, raising the group's hairs.

Lea was the first to pick up one of the books from the table and began to leaf through it carefully. Her eyes scanned the yellowed pages, searching for clues or information. Fiona approached the skeleton cautiously, her curiosity accompanied by a sense of awe, while Gronak thoughtfully sat on the throne and surveyed the room with a serious expression.

"How can there be so many secrets in one room?" Lea murmured as she continued to flip through the book, checking entries and looking for any possible clue about the curse.

Fiona, examining the skeleton more closely, noted, "This skeleton seems to have been here for an eternity. It's as if it's a witness to past tragedies."

Gronak let his gaze wander around the room as he spoke thoughtfully. "This room practically screams secrets. I wonder what was practiced here in the past?"

The tension in the room was palpable as the group examined the space and its mysterious objects more closely, searching for answers about the past of this cursed city.

Suddenly, Fiona noticed something about the skeleton. In its lifeless hand, it held a map. Carefully, she picked it up and unfolded the yellowed parchment. The map depicted a part of the wasteland but was otherwise blank. Fiona sensed a faint magical aura surrounding the map. Her eyes sparkled with curiosity as she focused her own magic on the map. A small X appeared, accompanied by text in a very old runic language.

Although Fiona couldn't read the text, she was fortunate. Sawil had once given her a book that taught the art of rune translation. Concentrated and focused, Fiona translated the text on the map and couldn't believe it. The mark indicated the location of the temple, that ancient place they had been desperately searching for.

A thrill of excitement and relief flowed through the group. "This is it! This is the temple we've been looking for!" Fiona exclaimed with enthusiasm.

Gronak, who had been carefully studying the map, nodded in agreement. "Finally, we have a concrete lead. Let's set out immediately and follow the X on the map."

Lea, with a hopeful smile on her lips, said, "It seems like we've solved the riddle. The temple will hopefully provide the answers we seek."

With renewed hope and a clear objective, Gronak, Fiona and Lea left the gloomy church. The city, once shrouded in darkness, seemed to be slowly recovering. The ruins appeared less menacing as the sun began to break through the clouds, a glimmer of hope in this cursed wasteland.

The group left the city limits and set out on their journey. The path through the wasteland was dangerous and full of challenges, but their determination was strengthened. With the map in hand and the goal of the temple in sight, they traversed the endless expanses, ready for the adventures and trials that lay ahead. Each step brought them closer to the ancient place that might hold answers to their questions.

Chapter 10: The Old Temple and Its Knowledge

Gronak, Fiona and Lea had set out to find the ancient temple in the wasteland after the battle against the necromancer and his undead. However, after a two-day journey through relentless heat and dry land, they were suddenly caught in a fierce sandstorm.

The heat of the wasteland had exhausted their bodies when the sandstorm unexpectedly struck. The sky quickly darkened and the wind began to tug at their garments while swirling a cloud of sand and dust around them. The sky vanished behind an impenetrable wall of sand grains whipping around them.

"Gronak, I can barely see anything!" Fiona shouted, her voice swallowed by the storm as she clung tightly to his arm to avoid being swept away by the storm.

Lea, squinting her eyes, desperately tried to keep the sand out of her eyes. "Stay close together! We have to try not to get lost!"

The storm raged around them and the world seemed to sink into a churning chaos of sand and wind. Every step forward felt like a battle against nature itself, which threatened to overwhelm them with its unchecked power.

Gronak tried to keep his bearings, but the swirling sand made it nearly impossible. "Follow me, hold on tight!" he yelled against the storm, struggling to maintain a direction.

The air was filled with a biting smell of dust that irritated their airways and further obscured their vision. Their skin felt like it was being scraped by tiny grains of sand and the harshness of the storm made them struggle with every movement.

"We need to find shelter!" Lea shouted, her voice overshadowed by the force of the wind. "Over there, maybe there's something that can offer us protection!"

They fought their way against the storm, gritting their teeth and taking steps with the hope of not being swallowed by the sand. Yet even in their determination, the natural force of the storm seemed overwhelming.

The storm had tugged at them, but they continued to push through the opaque chaos, always with the goal of reaching the ancient temple in mind. The uncertainty of whether they were even heading in the right direction gnawed at their nerves. Every step was a battle against the elements trying to overpower them and drag them into the sandstorm.

"We have to hold on!" Gronak shouted, struggling against the wind to be heard over the howling of the storm.

Fiona nodded in agreement, rubbing the sand from her eyes. "We have to keep going. Hold on tight, or you'll get lost!"

Lea looked around, trying to find orientation amid the swirling sand and dust. "I can barely breathe through all this sand!"

They pressed on, step by step, until the sun finally broke through the clouds and the storm subsided. The air was filled with a sense of relief as the sandstorm gradually eased and the sun sent its warm rays through the thinning clouds. Gronak wiped the sand from his eyes and took a deep breath, while Fiona and Lea helped each other shake the fine sand from their garments.

"We made it," Fiona gasped, her gaze shifting to the sky, which seemed to be clearing from the dark storm clouds.

"The storm was more intense than expected," Lea murmured, surveying the surroundings as she tried to get her bearings.

As they wiped the dust from their faces and looked around, they suddenly found themselves facing a breathtaking sight. A gigantic crater stretched out before them, deeply carved into the earth and surrounded by majestic sand dunes standing like guardians around the crater's rim.

Gronak raised an eyebrow as he looked at the crater. "That's impressive."

Lea stepped closer and felt the smooth stones encircling the crater. "Look over there. A temple!"

In the midst of the crater stood a monumental temple of gray stone, rising majestically and seeming untouched by the centuries of sand and wind.

"This must be the temple we're looking for," Gronak said with conviction in his voice.

"It's almost as if this crater hides a secret," Fiona noted, looking at the tall sand dunes that created a strange silence around the place.

The steep slope of the crater lay before them, a challenge that would test their courage. Gronak examined the descent and sensed the tension in the air.

"This won't be easy," he warned, carefully placing one foot after the other as he began to descend the steep incline.

Fiona nodded and focused on placing each handhold securely. "Let's proceed slowly and cautiously. No taking risks."

Lea, with a firm grip on the rocks, looked down intently. "This is damn high, friends. One wrong step and it could be the end."

The descent was arduous and slow, the scorching sun burning on their skin while the dust impaired their vision. Every handhold was crucial, every step had to be carefully considered to find their way down safely.

As they neared the base of the crater, they felt the heat of the day on their skin, while the dust swirled around their feet and bathed the surroundings in a diffuse light.

The group approached the majestic temple, perched in the midst of the crater. The gray stones of the structure were marked by past grandeur and mysterious runes were engraved into them, surrounding the building with a mystical fascination.

"These runes... they look like the ancient writings from the shrine back then," Fiona noted as she examined the ornate symbols on the stones. Gronak studied the runes with interest. "Then we must be on the right track."

The entrance to the temple was blocked by a massive metal door that radiated an aura of mystery and secrecy. Lea leaned closer to the door, feeling the coldness of the metal on her skin. "This door stands between us and the knowledge. How are we supposed to open it?"

On the door itself were runes engraved in ancient script, forming a text that posed a riddle. Fiona frowned as she tried to decipher the meaning of the words.

"It says, 'You who seek knowledge, be warned. Those who wish to gain knowledge must face a hard trial. Only those who succeed shall gain access to the knowledge,'" Fiona translated with a focused look.

Gronak stepped closer to the rune-covered door and examined it carefully. "A trial, then. But what kind of trial could it be?" he murmured thoughtfully.

Fiona frowned as she pondered. "It could be a challenge that tests our resolve, whether mentally or physically."

Lea, concerned about the unknown that awaited them, glanced back and forth between the other two. "That sounds really dangerous."

Gronak nodded seriously and added thoughtfully, "We expected no easy task ahead. But this knowledge is crucial to defeating Xalis. We must pass this trial, whatever form it takes."

Fiona stepped closer to Lea and placed a reassuring hand on her shoulder. "This could be the key to victory and saving everyone. And together, we've overcome everything so far."

Lea let her thoughts wander for a moment, then clenched her fist. "You're right. Let's do our best and master these trials."

Gronak stepped forward and placed his hand on the heavy door, which opened with a loud, creaking sound. A cold draft met them as they entered the dark entrance of the temple. The floor was covered with a layer of dust and weak light filtered through narrow slits in the high ceiling.

"Stay alert," Gronak warned as they drew their weapons and cautiously continued into the temple. Each step echoed in the gloomy silence and the feeling of being watched hung over them like a veil. But their resolve remained unbroken as they advanced through the temple's corridors, leading deep into its interior.

Fiona held her torch high to bring more light into the dark corridors, while Lea and Gronak stayed by her side. The dust swirled with each of their steps, enveloping them in a hazy atmosphere.

"It's dark down here," Lea remarked, her voice muffled by the surroundings. "I wonder when the last time someone was here was."

Fiona nodded in agreement and tightened her grip on the torch. "Sawil mentioned that no one had found the temple for hundreds of years."

Gronak peered into the darkness of the corridors. "Watch your surroundings. There may be dangers down here that we need to be prepared for."

The group reached an open passage leading into a room shrouded in complete darkness. The blackness swallowed the light from their torches, making the room appear like an impenetrable veil.

Cautiously, Gronak, Fiona and Lea continued their steps into the room, their eyes searching in the darkness for signs of danger. Although the room seemed quiet and deserted, there was a palpable tension in the air.

Suddenly, a dull sound broke the silence behind them. As they turned, their gaze was captured by a massive stone wall that slowly and inexorably closed off the entrance. The grim grinding of the rock and the muffled echo of its movement filled the room as the exit was blocked.

Gronak kept his cool and spoke calmly to the others. "The situation is getting serious. Be ready." His words echoed in the silence as the group prepared for possible challenges.

The darkness enveloping the room was suddenly pierced by a magical force. Along the walls, torch sconces ignited by themselves, casting a flickering orange light that illuminated the room and revealed its architectural splendor.

The room revealed an impressive expanse, punctuated by the flickering flames. The depth of the room almost vanished into the darkness, but the flickering torchlight pierced it, unveiling the majestic splendor. Massive columns rose up on either side, their imposing size a testament to the masterful craftsmanship of past eras. Each column was adorned with intricate carvings that shimmered in the pale torchlight, reflecting the beauty of bygone times.

"Wow, this is amazing," Lea remarked as she marveled at the room. Her eyes traced the patterns of the columns, losing themselves in the play of light and shadow. But Gronak, ever vigilant, reacted less enthusiastically.

"Don't be fooled by the grandeur," he warned the others. "I don't like this at all. Something is lurking here, I can feel it."

Fiona agreed, a trace of concern in her voice. "You're right. I also have a bad feeling about this sudden turn of events."

A thunderous rumble filled the room as a massive gate at the other end opened seemingly by magic. Slowly and majestically, two imposing figures stepped through, accompanied by an aura of power and danger.

The first to enter was a truly gigantic warrior over two meters tall. His stature was massive, clad in golden armor that covered him from head to toe. Every step he took radiated power and invincibility. With a formidable and threatening presence, he strode to the center of the room, his presence filling the space with an aura of dominance.

Beside him moved a smaller, initially less threatening figure. But with each step she took closer, her presence became increasingly evident. She was a woman in silver armor, her helmet resembling a dragon's skull. This warrior-like appearance gave her a menacing and almost mystical aura, which was not diminished by the imposing stature of the warrior.

In a deep, threatening tone, the large warrior began to speak. "My name is Kronos and my partner here is Shyra. We are the guardians of this temple and will allow no one to pass who is unworthy of taking the knowledge of this temple."

Shyra, the smaller woman in silver armor, laughed derisively. "Look at them, the three want to fight us. We haven't had a fight in several hundred years and now only three. I'll kill them quickly alone, okay Kronos?"

Kronos placed a calming hand on Shyra's shoulder. "Wait a moment, you should not underestimate your enemies." Shyra seemed slightly annoyed. "Yeah, yeah, fine. I'll be careful."

The tension in the room was palpable as the guardians' words filled the space. The steadfastness of Kronos and the challenging attitude of Shyra hinted at immense power and experience. It was clear that the group was facing a serious challenge, as the temple guardians seemed both physically and mentally prepared to defend their position.

The atmosphere in the room was tense as Shyra moved slightly forward and raised her hand. A storm of lightning surrounded her hand and suddenly a splendid spear materialized, which she grasped with impressive skill. Her gaze was powerful as she prepared for battle.

Gronak turned to his friends. "Get ready, this is going to be a tough fight."

Fiona began to prepare her magic, but suddenly she was struck by a shock. Her face turned pale as she spoke with a trembling and strained voice. "I... I can't cast any magic."

Shyra let out a loud laugh. "Yes, that's right. Magic doesn't work in this room. It's all about pure strength and skill here."

The realization that magic was useless in this room brought a moment of uncertainty to the group. It was an unexpected twist that rendered their usual tactics and abilities useless. The temple guardians had set clear rules, making this confrontation a purely physical battle.

The group reacted immediately to the threatening situation. Gronak and Lea positioned themselves protectively in front of Fiona, ready to defend her. "Don't worry, we'll protect you," Gronak assured Fiona while keeping a firm eye on Shyra.

Shyra took another step forward and sneered. "Oh, so there are only two real fighters among you. This is really no fun." Her tone was mocking and challenging at once.

Suddenly, her demeanor changed and a diabolical laugh filled the entire hall, creating a suffocating atmosphere. "Come on then! I'll kill you and tear you apart!" she declared with a malevolent determination that intensified her words.

The challenge was clear and the tension rose. Gronak and Lea prepared for the fight, while Fiona, although unable to use her magic, focused on being supportive wherever she could.

Shyra charged towards the group with impressive speed, her spear held high. The challenge in her eyes was unmistakable, but Gronak remained calm.

"Don't pretend to intimidate us. We are not easily overwhelmed!" Gronak shouted back, his voice firm and full of courage. As Shyra struck with her spear, he reacted swiftly, parrying the attack with his sword, the blade clashing against the shaft of the spear.

Lea, standing by Gronak's side, was undeterred. With skilled movements, she attempted to support Gronak in close combat with her daggers. However, Shyra proved to be nimble and adept, evading the attacks with graceful ease. It almost seemed superhuman how effortlessly Shyra parried the duo's attacks.

Gronak swung his sword again, this time with even greater force. The attack was powerful and targeted. But Shyra, while engaged with Lea, noticed Gronak's mighty strike and reacted quickly.

With a swift step to the side, she drove her spear firmly into the ground, just in time to block Gronak's sword attack. The clash of the sword against the spear produced a thunderous sound and for a moment, the entire hall seemed to shudder from the impact.

Gronak and Shyra stood face to face, a charged moment filled with tension. Gronak launched another powerful sword strike, but Shyra, moving with almost unnatural speed, elegantly dodged and countered with a precise thrust of her spear.

Her movements were smooth and calculated and while Gronak fought with raw strength and determination, Shyra seemed to be a tactical master. Her spear danced through the air as she evaded Gronak's attacks and responded with quick counterattacks.

Gronak tried with all his experience and strength to overwhelm Shyra, but she proved to be agile and foresighted. Every blow he delivered was skillfully deflected or avoided. It seemed as though Shyra anticipated each of his moves and reacted before he could even complete them.

Despite Gronak's persistence and fighting spirit, Shyra appeared to be a step ahead. Her movements were precise, her attacks well-considered and her defense nearly impenetrable. The superiority of her skills became increasingly evident and Gronak struggled against an opponent who was superior in this respect.

The opportunity that arose as Gronak challenged Shyra did not leave Lea idle. She seized the moment when Shyra focused all her attention on Gronak to attack from behind. Lea crept silently forward, her daggers tightly gripped and tried to launch a surprise attack on Shyra.

But Shyra, who seemed to always be aware of her surroundings, sensed Lea's approach. Before Lea could strike, Shyra deftly turned around and delivered a lightning-fast kick directly to Lea's stomach. The sudden attack caught Lea off guard and threw her back with great force. A painful impact left her dazed for a moment.

Gronak, who had been keeping an eye on the scene, immediately reacted to Shyra's swift and precise counterattack. With an energy-charged charge, he surged forward and slammed into Shyra with full force. The sudden collision was strong enough to knock Shyra back, but it seemed insufficient to force her to the ground.

Shyra, although thrown back by Gronak's attack, showed no signs of weakness. She wavered briefly but managed to stay on her feet, her silver armor gleaming in the dim light of the temple. Her stance was firm and determined and she appeared ready to continue facing the challenge, undeterred by her opponents' attacks.

Gronak and Lea had just managed to get back on their feet when Shyra, despite being knocked back, displayed a seemingly superior composure. Her words pierced the tense silence of the temple. "You guys really have some skills. How about we have a bit more fun now?"

A menacing crackle filled the air as Shyra's spear suddenly began to spark. Lightning danced along the blade and an electric crackle permeated the room. With a fearsome motion, Shyra struck her spear against the ground.

A massive shockwave rippled through the room, its roar causing the ground to tremble and everything within its radius to quake. Gronak and Lea were engulfed by the untamed energy, a painful jolt coursing through their bodies as if struck by an invisible force.

Gronak tried to move, but a paralyzing numbness surged through his body. "I'm paralyzed!" he shouted, frustration evident in his voice.

Lea, also hit by the shockwave, felt the inability to move. "Me too, damn it!" she exclaimed, a mix of anger and concern in her voice.

Shyra approached slowly, a diabolical grin on her lips. "Well, it seems our little game is already over. But don't worry, I won't kill you right away."

Her words were a foreboding warning as she moved slowly and threateningly toward Gronak. Her gaze was filled with superiority and triumph as she looked over the paralyzed fighters with an almost supernatural confidence.

As Shyra raised her spear to deliver a deadly thrust, a series of explosions suddenly rocked the room. Several bottles exploded near Gronak and Shyra and thick smoke began to fill the space.

Amidst the smoke, Fiona appeared, having ignited a series of improvised explosives. The smoke and confusion gave her a moment of surprise, allowing her to intervene in the fight.

Shyra, irritated by the sudden interference, turned to Fiona and angrily shouted at her. "How dare you meddle in a warriors' fight, you miserable bitch!"

Without hesitation, Shyra charged at Fiona, her speed and power frightening. Fiona, shocked by the sudden attack and the speed of her opponent, desperately tried to dodge, but seemed powerless against the speed and precision of Shyra's assault.

Everything happened so quickly. Shyra, filled with rage, drove her spear with brutal force directly into Fiona. A horrific scream of pain tore through the air as the spear pierced Fiona's body. A moment of sheer terror and despair enveloped the room.

Fiona recoiled in pain, her eyes widening in a moment of shock. The unimaginable agony coursed through her body as the spear struck her fragile form.

But Shyra was not finished. With terrifying brutality, she kicked Fiona with full force. The cruel kick hit her with incredible power and Fiona was hurled violently against the wall, the impact causing her to collapse heavily to the ground.

Fiona writhed in unbearable pain, her breath coming in shallow, painful gasps. Her body was weakened and blood flowed from her in a dreadful stream, staining her clothing and the ground around her.

The scene was marked by horrific terror as Fiona struggled in pain and despair, her body severely battered by the brutal attacks. The power and violence with which Shyra had struck her were evident in Fiona's agonizing screams.

The sight of Fiona's suffering and torment cut Gronak to the core. A mix of anger and despair surged through him as he lay helplessly, witnessing the cruel scene unfolding before his eyes. But at that moment, an immense power manifested within him.

With unwavering determination, Gronak tried to free himself from the paralysis. His strong will to save Fiona drove him and with every fiber of his being, he fought against the numbness. An uncontainable resolve flowed through him and slowly, but with unyielding will, he managed to overcome the paralysis.

Meanwhile, Shyra approached Fiona, her words dripping with scorn and disdain. "You are weak and worthless. I will now take my revenge on you and punish you for your arrogance."

At the moment Shyra was about to strike, she was suddenly pierced from behind. Gronak's sword had driven with terrible force through Shyra's chest. A moment of surprise and confusion appeared on Shyra's face as she looked down at the sword that had penetrated her. "How can this be? You were paralyzed!" she stammered, incredulous at the sudden turn of events.

Gronak responded with a fury that erased any doubt. "No one harms Fiona. Protecting her gave me the strength to break through this paralysis." His gaze was filled with an unspeakable will as he pulled his weapon from Shyra's body, causing her to sink to the ground.

Seeing Shyra fall lifeless and defeated, Gronak felt a mix of relief and concern. Lea, who was also able to move again after Shyra's death, sprinted to Fiona, who lay bleeding heavily on the ground and wasted no time.

With swift movements, Lea pulled a strong healing potion from her belt and emptied the entire bottle over Fiona's severe wound. Fiona let out a pained scream as the potion took effect. However, the wound began to slowly close, the healing power of the potion already showing its effect.

Gronak, ready to eliminate the threat once and for all, spoke to Lea. "Please stay with Fiona. I'll deal with Kronos." Lea nodded silently, her eyes full of concern for her injured companion, as Gronak turned to Kronos, who remained motionless in the center of the room.

Kronos's massive form remained in an eerie calm as Gronak approached him. His eyes flashed with determination as he prepared to confront Kronos and end the battle.

Amid the oppressive silence, Kronos rose, his voice calm yet carrying an unwavering superiority. "Remarkable that you freed yourself from Shyra's paralysis. In the end, her arrogance was the cause of her downfall. But don't get your hopes up; I am not so careless."

Kronos extended his arm sideways and as before with Shyra, lightning crackled around his hand. Suddenly, a massive hammer materialized, emanating a menacing presence in his grasp.

The hammer was colossal and seemed to embody a terrifying power. Yet Gronak faced Kronos with ironclad determination. With a clear mind and firm resolve, he moved around Kronos, positioning himself so that Fiona and Lea were out of attack range.

Lea, her voice filled with confidence and support, called out to Gronak. "You've got this, Gronak! We believe in you!" Her words pierced the room, carried by hope and optimism. The friendship and unity of the group were, in that moment, their greatest source of strength.

Amidst the crushing tension, Gronak stood battle-ready before Kronos, the air almost vibrating from the charged atmosphere between them.

Suddenly, the ground beneath Kronos began to tremble, a thunderous roar escaping him. The tremor spread like a wave across the room and Gronak felt the threatening power radiating from Kronos.

Every step Kronos took toward Gronak seemed to make the ground quake. His form appeared monstrous and the force of his movements made the surroundings shudder. Gronak felt the overwhelming presence and the unimaginable power emanating from this being.

Kronos swung his mighty hammer and the air was sliced by the massive movement as the hammer descended toward Gronak. But Gronak reacted instantly, nimbly dodging the blow to escape the impending danger.

The impact's tremor coursed through Gronak's body deep into his bones as the massive hammer strike from Kronos was narrowly avoided. The air quaked and the ground showed the imprint of the massive hammer in the form of a deep crater.

Gronak was stunned by the immense power Kronos unleashed, but despite the shock, he remained steadfast. With an iron will reflected in his eyes, he attacked Kronos, but his sword merely bounced off the guardian's massive armor, inflicting no damage whatsoever.

Shocked by this result, Gronak became reckless and in that moment, Kronos seized the opportunity. With a swift, powerful punch, he struck Gronak, who was hurled backward by the force of the blow. Gronak, heavily struck, felt the harsh impact and found himself with his back against one of the massive columns. The injury weakened him, but his will remained strong and unyielding.

Kronos swung his powerful hammer again with tremendous force. Gronak instinctively leaped aside just in time before the hammer crashed down with devastating force onto the column. The column could not withstand the attack and collapsed under the hammer's impact.

The room shook from the force of the collapse, dust and debris filling the air. Gronak quickly sought cover behind the remnants of the once-proud column. His heart pounded heavily with tension. "If I don't think of something quickly, he'll finish me off," he thought anxiously. "He's incredibly strong, but also slow. However, his armor is like a fortress."

Kronos, with his hammer in hand, stood calmly as he searched the room for Gronak. His form was menacing and the heavy steps he took made the ground tremble. His armor seemed nearly impenetrable, making the prospect of direct attacks appear hopeless.

Fiona, watching the fight with Lea, felt the urge to support Gronak. But her injuries were still too severe and she turned to Lea. "Help him, Lea. I'll manage," she said with her last strength, encouraging Lea to focus on Gronak.

Lea, still shaken by Kronos's power and size, slowly regained her composure. "You're right," she said. "Gronak can't do this alone."

Gronak, waiting behind the column for Kronos, searched for an opportunity for a surprise attack. With all his strength and determination to defeat Kronos, he seized a crucial moment. He leaped onto the column's remnants and launched an attack on Kronos, his sword firmly in hand and his eyes fixed on Kronos's head.

But Kronos, having anticipated Gronak's movements, reacted swiftly. He leaned aside and Gronak narrowly missed his target. Kronos seized the opportunity and grabbed Gronak by the leg while he was still in mid-air. With tremendous force, he swung Gronak through the air and hurled him with brutal violence onto the hard temple floor.

A bone-chilling scream escaped Gronak as the impact forced him to the ground. Pain surged through his body and blood flowed from his mouth. The unbelievable force of the impact made him scream in agony as he lay dazed on the floor, struggling to rise. Kronos's power and strength were overwhelming and Gronak felt helpless against the superhuman might of his opponent.

Lea, having silently crept up on Kronos, attempted to attack him from behind with her daggers. She leaped onto his neck and thrust one of her daggers directly through the small slit in his helmet, aiming for his eye. Kronos screamed in pain as the dagger pierced his eye and, with a powerful movement, threw Lea off of him.

At the moment Kronos repelled Lea, Gronak, using his last ounce of strength, had managed to stand and seized the chance to attack Kronos. Kronos noticed Gronak's attack and swung his hammer to put an end to it. The tension in the room was palpable as the confrontation between Gronak and Kronos reached its climax.

But Kronos's vision was severely impaired by Lea's attack and Gronak knew this. He knew he had to seize this moment. As Kronos's hammer swung toward Gronak, he skillfully ducked underneath it. With full force and desperation, Gronak delivered a decisive sword thrust. He aimed for an unprotected part of Kronos's armor, located in the armpit.

Gronak swung his sword with all his might and severed Kronos's arm. Kronos's arm and hammer fell to the ground, while a torrent of blood gushed from his shoulder, staining the floor around him a deep red.

Kronos's knees touched the hard stone floor of the temple, his massive form bent with exhaustion. A hint of admiration was in his voice as he spoke. "Incredible, you have defeated me. Now, finish it."

Gronak, his breath heavy and labored, lifted his gaze to Kronos. Exhaustion was evident in his eyes as he replied with strained voice. "Can't you just let us pass? Isn't that enough for you?"

Kronos shook his head with regret, a faint expression of respect in his gaze. "No, the gate will only open for you once you have defeated both of us. Finish it and claim the knowledge you seek."

Gronak nodded in understanding. "You were by far the strongest warrior I have ever encountered," a blend of admiration and exhaustion marked his words.

Gronak removed Kronos's helmet and raised his sword. He swung his powerful blade with force, severing Kronos's head with a single strike.

Lea approached Gronak with deliberate steps, her eyes shining with admiration and respect. "You were incredible, Gronak," she said, her voice filled with deep admiration for his bravery and strength.

Gronak responded to Lea's praise with a mix of humility and gratitude. "But without your help, I couldn't have landed the decisive blow. We did this together."

Fiona, who had fought her way back to her feet despite her exhaustion, carefully approached her group. "Thank you both. Without your support, I wouldn't be here now."

Before Gronak could react, Fiona unexpectedly embraced him tightly. "And you, take better care of yourself. I almost lost you, you big idiot," she whispered softly, with a touch of concern in her voice as she held him affectionately.

Gronak, touched by Fiona's concern and warmth, simply smiled and returned her embrace. In that moment, he felt a strong bond and mutual care that made their group an unshakable unit.

Lea eventually broke the brief silence as she noticed, "Look, the gate is opening. We can proceed." Her voice sounded full of excitement and relief as she pointed to the slowly opening gates.

The group entered the corridor that had opened before them. The walls of the corridor were adorned with intricate reliefs and ancient runes that seemed to tell a story. The soft crunching under their feet echoed in the silence of the temple as they ventured deeper into the ancient structure. Suddenly, a faint humming sound came from afar, catching their attention.

"Do you hear that?" Lea inquired, pausing briefly to listen more intently.

Fiona also listened closely. "Yes, I hear it too. It's a faint noise, almost like a voice calling to us."

The group followed the sound and entered a vast chamber adorned with majestic statues and intricate reliefs depicting past wars and legendary battles, a chronicle of ancient heroics. In the center of the room stood an elevated pedestal upon which rested a strange artifact. It was a box of unusual beauty, decorated with diamonds and gemstones that glowed mysteriously in the darkness.

The group approached the glowing artifact slowly, its rays becoming more intense as they drew nearer. Suddenly, a mysterious voice cut through the silence and spoke to the group. "Welcome, travelers. I am the Keeper of Knowledge."

Before them, a spectral figure materialized from light, taking the form of a beautiful woman. With long white hair and a noble tunic, she radiated an aura of power. The group was awestruck by this unexpected sight as the Keeper of Knowledge gazed at them with penetrating eyes.

The Keeper spoke with a gentle voice. "I have been expecting you, heroes of destiny." Gronak responded skeptically. "Heroes of destiny? What do you mean by that?"

A warm smile appeared on the Keeper's face as she replied. "You are the heroes from the prophecy, chosen to halt the evil in this world."

Gronak and the other members of the group exchanged uncertain glances as the meaning of these words slowly sank in. The Keeper took a step closer and explained. "Many eons ago, this prophecy was recorded and now the time has come for the heroes to rise and fulfill their destiny."

Fiona, surprised by this information, felt the urge to learn more. "So you knew we would come and that we needed help to defeat Xalis?" she asked with a hint of wonder in her voice.

The Keeper answered Fiona with her gentle, soothing voice. "Yes, I did. I have been waiting for hundreds of years for your arrival to guide you in defeating the dark lord Xalis."

A quiet sense of astonishment filled the group as the meaning of these words reached them. The Keeper of Knowledge had been expecting them, preparing them and was ready to guide them on their dangerous path.

Gronak, eager for knowledge about Xalis, turned to the Keeper and asked. "Can you tell us more about Xalis? What kind of being is he? What powers does he possess?"

The Keeper nodded and began to tell an ancient story about Xalis is rise and fall. "Xalis was once a high mage of an old, long-gone civilization," she began. "But his lust for power corrupted his soul and he turned to the dark side. He practiced increasingly ancient and forbidden magic and his power grew stronger."

The group listened intently as the Keeper continued. "One day, he turned against the Mage Circle and killed them all. After that, he began a reign of terror that drove many peoples to the brink of destruction."

The Keeper continued. "One day, however, Xalis was sealed away by a group of brave warriors with an ancient artifact. For hundreds of years, peace prevailed and people forgot the terrible deeds that Xalis had committed." A shadow of relief appeared on the listeners' faces.

"But there was a dark sorcerer who learned about Xalis from ancient legends," the Guardian continued. "He gathered all sorts of information about the Dark Lord and became obsessed with emulating Xalis and worshiping him like a god."

A silence fell over the group as the Guardian continued her tale. "The dark sorcerer founded a cult and gathered followers with the same goal. They wanted not just to worship or revere Xalis, but they sought a way to break the seal that imprisoned Xalis to free him once again."

"Years passed and they developed powerful magic to break the seal," she went on. "On a Blood Moon night, all the cult's followers gathered around a magical circle and performed the ritual. The earth trembled, dark clouds gathered and a massive crystal rose from the ground, within which Xalis was imprisoned."

Her voice grew serious as she continued. "The cult continued the ritual and managed to shatter the crystal." A tense silence spread as the Guardian's words conveyed the dark turn of events.

The Guardian continued calmly but with a serious expression. "Once Xalis was free, all the dark sorcerers gathered around him and fell to their knees. They told him that he had been sealed for over a thousand years and that they had freed him. Arrogant as he was, Xalis thanked them for this act. His laughing, diabolical echo filled the air before he gradually killed the assembled cult."

The group remained stunned as the Guardian described the grim development of events. "The desperate cult asked Xalis why he did this," the Guardian continued. "But he only explained that they had fulfilled their service and that he no longer needed them. Without hesitation, he killed each one of them. He then went to his old fortress, which had remained intact all these years, as no one had dared to lay a hand on it."

"And then he began sending out his monstrous minions to spread death and destruction just like in the old days," she continued.

The group was equally shocked and overwhelmed by the revelations. The cruel story of Xalis is rise and his merciless tyranny had cast a gloomy silence over them. The inhumanity and extent of his malevolence left a bitter aftertaste of disbelief.

Gronak was deeply enraged by the tales. "How can a single person be so demonic?" His voice trembled with indignation. "We have to stop him! This cruelty must not continue!"

Fiona agreed with a serious expression. "He killed even his followers without hesitation. If we don't stop him, the whole world will fall victim to his destruction." The concern in her voice was palpable as she considered the threatening prospect posed by Xalis is unchecked power.

Lea was visibly worried. "But if he is so powerful, how can we stop him? The Elder told us back then that the artifact that sealed Xalis was unique." The worry in Lea's voice was clear as she contemplated the daunting prospect of the upcoming battle.

The Guardian smiled and continued. "That is unfortunately true, but there is still hope. Xalis is seal is broken, but his power has not fully returned yet. But time is running out."

Fiona, visibly relieved by this information, asked further. "Can you help us destroy Xalis once and for all?"

The Guardian responded to Fiona. "You carry the Holy Rune Crystal with you. This crystal is very powerful and will help you defeat Xalis. However, the Rune Crystal alone is unfortunately not enough to accomplish this. Come to me, Fiona."

Fiona took a step forward towards the Guardian and looked expectantly into her eyes. The Guardian pointed to the box behind her. "In this box is the Book of Wisdom and Power. It holds ancient knowledge and powerful spells.

There you will also gain the knowledge to use the Rune correctly to neutralize Xalis is dark powers. But the book not only hides knowledge; it is also an artifact that greatly enhances the magic of its user. With this power, I am confident you will defeat Xalis and save the world."

Fiona slowly approached the magnificent box and opened it with careful hands. As the lid lifted, she discovered an ancient book adorned with fine gold decorations. The book was made of the finest parchment and inscribed with antique characters in a glowing, mystical color.

The group was fascinated by the grace of this artifact and Fiona turned to the Guardian with reverence and thanked her for this incredible gift. As Fiona gently opened the book, a blinding light suddenly enveloped her. The pages of the book began to turn on their own, as if invisible hands were moving them gently. An energy, warm and exalted, flowed from the pages and surrounded Fiona, who felt safe in this light. She felt a force entering her that gave her an unimaginable strength.

The book revealed to her a method to amplify the power of the Rune Crystal. It explained that she needed to focus on her concentration and her inner energy to enhance the Rune with her power. But that alone would not be enough. Fiona also had to use the elements around her to further channel the crystal and intensify her magic. Only then would she be able to direct the concentrated rune magic at Xalis.

Overwhelmed by this revelation and new knowledge, Fiona carefully closed the book. She turned to Gronak and Lea, whose eyes were full of expectation. "This is it. With this knowledge, we can destroy Xalis," she said with a firm expression of determination in her voice.

Fiona looked gratefully at the Guardian. "I thank you from the bottom of my heart for your knowledge and help. This book will surely assist us." The Guardian smiled with hope and addressed the group. "Promise me, heroes of the prophecy, to stop Xalis."

Gronak stepped forward. "We will do everything in our power to stop Xalis." Lea nodded in agreement. "Count on it, together we will defeat Xalis."

The Guardian smiled and spoke to Gronak and Lea. "I also have a gift for you." She asked them to stretch out their hands and when they did, she gently placed her hands on theirs. A brilliant light flared from the Guardian's hand and Gronak and Lea felt an immense energy flowing through their bodies.

As the Guardian removed her hand from Gronak and Lea, they looked at their palms in fascination. Several rune symbols had appeared there. They looked at the Guardian with wonder, asking what these symbols meant. The Guardian smiled softly and explained. "This is my gift to you, symbols of power. They are inseparably linked to you and enhance your physical strength."

Gronak felt the newly acquired strength and beamed. "This power is incredible! I feel like I could uproot trees!" Lea smiled gratefully and joyfully. "Thank you, Guardian. This power is amazing; we will use it wisely."

It was as if an indescribable power had merged with their very being. An energy that strengthened them not only physically but also mentally. The Guardian had transferred a part of her own power to them, a gesture that instilled trust and hope in the hearts of the two heroes.

The Guardian looked at the three heroes of the prophecy and spoke with calm determination. "Now go, heroes and fulfill your destiny. Xalis is fortress lies further to the northwest and the journey is still long and dangerous."

The group bowed gratefully to the Guardian and made their way to the temple exit. As they reached the room where they had previously fought the two powerful guardians, they noticed something strange. The room was completely undamaged.

Lea frowned, visibly confused. "But why are there no signs of a battle? And where are the bodies of the guardians?" she asked as she examined the room closely.

Suddenly, a familiar female voice came from a corner of the room. "We are over here."

The group turned abruptly toward the voice and froze as they unexpectedly saw Kronos and Shyra at one of the massive columns. Surprise and concern were reflected equally on the heroes' faces.

Shyra, who now appeared less aggressive than before, slowly approached the group. "So you made it and you really seem to be the heroes from the prophecy," she noted with a hint of recognition in her voice.

Gronak, bewildered to see them again, could not hide his confusion. "But how is this possible? We killed you."

Shyra, irritated by his statement, replied. "'Killed'? You merely took advantage of a small lapse in attention."

Kronos chuckled briefly. "Small? You got carried away again and that cost you your lives."

The group looked at each other in astonishment as Fiona approached the two. "But how can this be? You stand here as if nothing has happened."

They listened intently as Kronos began to explain. "We do not exist in the world of the living. We were summoned by the Guardian to protect this place. We cannot leave this place or even die ourselves. If we are defeated, we are summoned again to continue guarding this place."

The heroes were equally impressed and astonished by this revelation about Kronos and Shyra's true nature. Kronos continued his speech, his voice filled with centuries-old wisdom. "Listen, heroes of the prophecy. Shyra and I are the heroes who sealed Xalis back then."

Gronak, Fiona and Lea were overwhelmed by this new realization. It was incredible to comprehend that they were speaking with the heroes from a long-forgotten time.

Kronos continued his story, his words carrying a deep respect for the past. "Our leader, Sir Thorfinn, was the one who used the artifact to seal Xalis. Unfortunately, his soul was also sealed during the ritual, which is why we were left as just two after the battle. After our deaths, the Guardian protected our souls and bound them to this place, waiting for the new heroes."

Shyra abruptly interrupted Kronos. "Did you hear that! You must kill that bastard Xalis and avenge Thorfinn's sacrifice!"

Kronos looked somewhat embarrassed and apologized for Shyra's words. "Please forgive her; she has a very impulsive nature, but she and Thorfinn were together, so she is very sensitive about this topic."

Shyra remained silent and only wrinkled her nose before abruptly turning away and leaving. It was clear that she was struggling with her own emotions and had difficulty showing them.

Gronak called after Shyra. "We will avenge Thorfinn, you have our word!"

Kronos smiled faintly and tried to calm the situation. "Don't worry, she can be kind too and she respects you, even if she doesn't show it."

It was evident that Shyra was deeply affected by the past and had a strong connection to Thorfinn. The group felt the seriousness of the situation and understood how important it was for Shyra to seek justice for Thorfinn.

The group thanked Kronos and left the temple, ready for their journey through the wasteland towards Xalis is fortress in the northwest.

As they continued on their way, Gronak spoke to his friends. "That was incredible. Shyra, Kronos and the Guardian. The knowledge and power they've given us."

Lea, visibly still reeling from the events, responded. "I can't believe the guardians were the heroes of the past and they were damn powerful. And the story of the Guardian. I need to process all of this."

Fiona, meanwhile, was deep in thought as she flipped through the Book of Power. "This book is incredible," she murmured enthusiastically to herself. "Spells I've never heard of, rituals from ancient days and this magical power it grants."

She spoke more and more about the fascinating contents of the book as Gronak and Lea listened attentively. The descriptions of ancient spells and powerful rituals sparked their interest and fueled their imagination. Fiona was fascinated by the variety and depth of the magic described in the book.

After days of arduous travel, the group finally reached the end of the wasteland. A hint of relief was visible on everyone's faces. The desolate and barren landscape of the wasteland was now behind them and a sense of relief spread as they faced a new chapter of their journey.

Gronak sighed with relief and smiled at his companions. "We finally made it. That desert was really exhausting."

Lea, relieved that the barren landscape was behind them, agreed. "I was afraid we'd never get out of the wasteland. All the sand and heat were really annoying."

Fiona smiled in agreement. "It feels good to leave this part of the journey behind. But remember what the Guardian said; we still have a dangerous path ahead of us."

The group felt a new surge of energy and motivation as they prepared to tackle the next stages of their journey. They had overcome the wasteland and felt ready for the new challenges that lay ahead.

Chapter 11: The Dwarf and His Companion

As the three left the wasteland behind and reached the mountains, they noticed a sudden change in the air temperature. It became colder and colder with every step they took up the mountain. The once warm sun was now obscured by a cold, gray cloud cover and the wind was blowing snowflakes into their faces.

They felt their bodies being assaulted by the cold and were grateful that Sawil had given them warm clothing back then. Ice and snow were visible everywhere and in some places, small waterfalls cascading from the rocks formed ice formations. They had to move cautiously as the snow and ice on the rocks made their steps slippery and uncertain.

The mountains around them appeared majestic and powerful but also threatening and unforgiving. The wind howled through the rocks and the echo of its sounds amplified the sense of loneliness and disorientation. They knew they were in a dangerous and unpredictable environment and had to stay alert.

The group made their way slowly through the frosty terrain, their steps muffled by the crunching snow under their boots. Lea pulled her hood tighter around her face as she tried to shield herself from the icy wind. "This cold is really brutal," she remarked, rubbing her hands to keep them warm.

Fiona, whose breath appeared in small white clouds before her, nodded in agreement. "Yes, the wasteland was hot, but this is a whole different challenge." She blinked as a snowflake hit her eye and smiled slightly. "But at least we prepared for these temperatures."

Gronak, who was laboriously making his way over smooth rocks, muttered to himself. "This icy cold really makes moving difficult." He leaned on his hiking stick to avoid slipping and looked around. "But this landscape is impressive. Dangerous, but impressive."

The mountains around them seemed like rugged sentinels watching over the land. A dull rumble echoed in the distance as ice detached from the cliffs and thundered into the valleys. "We need to be careful," warned Lea as they walked along an uncertain path. "These ice chunks can easily hit us."

Fiona stopped and looked up at the sky, where the clouds had thickened into an impenetrable gray. "I hope we have enough protection against a snowstorm. The Guardian warned us that these mountains can be unforgiving."

Suddenly, they heard a dull crunching sound above them. Instinctively, they ducked as an avalanche of snow and ice broke away from the rock faces and plunged into the valley. They held their breath until the thunder of the snow slowly faded and a white veil settled over the land.

Gronak took a deep breath. "That was close. These mountains are full of surprises." He looked around and added, "Let's keep moving before we get caught by another natural disaster."

The three adventurers continued through the rugged mountain landscape when suddenly a bone-chilling roar filled the air. Lea, Fiona and Gronak pricked up their ears, exchanged a fleeting glance and recognized the sound the roar of a colossal creature. Without hesitation, they hurried toward the noise, their steps driven by tension and curiosity.

The closer they got, the sharper the sounds of blades hitting hard flesh and the desperate cries of two fighters battling the beast became. When they finally reached the scene, they were met with a chaotic sight.

A dwarf of impressive stature swung a massive hammer with formidable force against the snow troll, which lashed out at him with mighty blows. Beside him stood a woman with a taut bow, skillfully shooting arrows at the monster while maintaining her position.

The snow troll was an imposing yet terrifying creature. It was at least three meters tall and had a massive build covered by a thick, snow-white fur coat. Its eyes were dark and malevolent and its sharp teeth were enormous. Its limbs were long and powerful, each finger equipped with deadly claws that posed a lethal threat to any opponent.

Its breathing was heavy and irregular and with every breath, the troll's exhalation steamed like a cauldron. Its roar was deafening, causing the ground to tremble. Anyone who came too close could feel the heat and intensity of its rage. Overall, the snow troll was a being that inspired both fear and respect.

Gronak, Fiona and Lea exchanged hurried glances before diving into the fray. Lea drew her bow and employed her own accuracy, while Fiona cast a spell to weaken the troll. Gronak, on the other hand, let out a battle cry and attacked with his sword to assist the dwarf.

Amid the raging battle, the dwarf shouted to them, "Help us, strangers! This damn troll is stronger than he looks!"

Fiona called back, "We're here to help! Cover us!" Her magic erupted in a dazzling light, briefly weakening the troll and allowing the dwarf to deliver a devastating blow with his hammer.

The woman at the dwarf's side skillfully aimed her arrows at the troll's weak spots and shouted to the newcomers, "Thanks for the support! We need to coordinate our attacks to have a chance!"

In the midst of the fierce combat, the snow troll charged with brutal force at the brave fighters. The enormous dwarf, armed with his massive hammer, rushed forward to block the troll's first blow, while the skilled archer shot arrows at the beast from a safe distance.

The troll, its furious eyes fixed on the woman, leaped toward her in a terrifying motion. With lightning reflexes, she dodged to the side, her arrows continuing to fly relentlessly at the massive creature. The troll shook off the projectiles and let out a bone-chilling scream before turning its attention back to the fighters.

Gronak, brave and battle-hardened, charged into the fray and swung his mighty sword at the snow troll. A battle between a giant and Gronak erupted, the troll roaring angrily and striking back with overwhelming force. Despite his relentless efforts, Gronak's attacks seemed to have little effect on the troll's thick skin, which absorbed every blow. As the troll attacked Gronak with its enormous fists, Gronak's sword was forcefully knocked away, landing several meters into the snow.

Fiona unleashed a powerful lightning spell on the troll, but even that seemed to have little effect. Lea, skilled with her knife, ventured close to attack the troll, but her strikes also appeared ineffective.

The troll loomed like an insurmountable Goliath, its strength and resilience making it nearly impossible to defeat. Gronak drew his axe and continued to fight bravely, striking the troll again and again. Eventually, the axe broke under the immense force of the blows and Gronak was forced to use his bare hands as weapons. With relentless determination, he attacked the troll, his blows raining down on the massive head of the beast. The troll staggered back and eventually fell to the ground.

The dwarf seized the opportunity and charged at the troll with all his fury, repeatedly striking its head with his massive hammer until the troll lay lifeless on the ground. The creature's body now lay motionless, covered in a mixture of blood and snow. The group gasped for breath, their clothes smeared with the traces of battle, as they brushed the snow off themselves.

Gronak, Fiona and Lea cautiously approached the two strangers who had fought the snow troll. The older dwarf, with a gray bushy beard and a patched leather cloak, looked relieved at the end of the battle. His smithing tools clinked softly as he moved and he seemed glad that the danger had passed.

The young woman at his side wore a cloak marked by the strains of battle and carried a heavy, well-used axe in her hand, with a bow slung across her back. A disheveled ponytail stuck out from her hair as she briefly assessed the newcomers.

"Thank you," said the dwarf with a gruff accent, patting Gronak firmly on the back. "I am Grimgor Ironbeard, a smith from the deepest caverns of the mountains. And this is my apprentice, Sigrid."

Sigrid seemed about to say something but fell silent abruptly. Instead, she pulled her cloak tighter around herself and avoided direct eye contact, glancing at the snow with slight discomfort.

Gronak stepped forward and nodded warmly. "We are on a journey and happened to be nearby when we heard the battle. We couldn't just stand by."

Fiona added, "When we saw the troll, we knew you needed help urgently."

Grimgor nodded gratefully. "That's right. This damned troll ambushed us while we were on our way to our forge."

Lea stepped closer and looked at Sigrid. "You fought bravely. That was a formidable opponent."

Sigrid nodded briefly but still avoided direct eye contact. "It was close, but fortunately, we all came out unscathed."

Gronak, Fiona and Lea offered to accompany Grimgor and Sigrid on their way and Grimgor gratefully accepted the offer. Together, they set up camp and began preparing dinner. The flames of the fire danced in the darkness of the mountain night as they gathered around the campfire to warm up and share their stories.

Grimgor spoke of his smithing skills, detailing how he created his works and his search for materials for his weapons. Sigrid mostly listened in silence, her gaze shifting between the flames and her companions.

Gronak recounted the many dangers they had overcome on their long journey and the challenges they had faced. Fiona added that their goal was to reach the fortress of Xalis, whom they needed to stop, which visibly impressed Grimgor.

"Xalis? That's no small feat, to stop the leader of darkness," Grimgor commented, focusing his gaze on Gronak and Lea. "You must possess powerful weapons to face such a threat. May I take a look at them?"

Curiously, Grimgor examined Gronak's and Lea's weapons, his experienced hands gently brushing over the blades to assess their quality. Sigrid watched him attentively, her eyes full of expectation, as Grimgor evaluated the weights of the weapons and their balance.

Grimgor leaned back and surveyed Gronak's and Lea's weapons with a satisfied nod, recognizing the quality and skill behind their creation. His eyes gleamed with interest as he considered how he might further enhance them.

"These weapons are impressive, but with the right magic, they could be even more powerful," Grimgor began, his voice full of confidence. "I have mastered the art of enchantment and rune-smithing for many years. With my expertise, I could imbue them with special powers that would give you a decisive advantage in future battles."

Sigrid, who had been silent until now, nodded in agreement. Her eyes sparkled with curiosity as she listened to her mentor's words.

"Runes and enchantments can strengthen weapons and armor, enhance their properties and aid you in battle," Grimgor continued, emphasizing his experience. "I could forge new weapons and armor with these powers or enhance your current weapons, depending on what you prefer."

Gronak and Lea exchanged a brief glance before Gronak responded. "Upgrading our weapons and armor sounds promising. What do you need for that, Grimgor?"

The dwarf smith scratched his bushy gray beard thoughtfully and looked at the group with a critical eye. "To forge such powerful items, I need extraordinary materials," he explained. "First, I need a snow troll's tooth. Fortunately, we already have that. Then I need a bone and feathers from a thunder harpy and finally, scales from a fire salamander."

Lea frowned as she considered the requirements. "That sounds like a demanding collection of materials."

Grimgor nodded seriously. "Yes, these materials are rare and difficult to obtain. But with them, I can forge the most powerful runes and enchantments, turning your weapons and armor into true artifacts."

Grimgor held up a parchment-like list with detailed sketches and notes about the sought-after materials. His rough fingers traced the drawings as he explained the descriptions. "Here, you see what you need to perfect your weapons," he began, his deep voice filled with gravity.

He pointed to the sketches and continued, "The snow troll's tooth is already in our possession. But the thunder harpies, known for their cunning, nest high up in the mountains. And the fire salamanders dwell in the deepest and hottest regions of the lava caves."

A hint of challenge lingered in Grimgor's gaze as he looked at the group. "It won't be easy to outwit these creatures and obtain the required materials. But I'm sure you'll manage."

Gronak and Lea exchanged a determined glance before Gronak replied. "We will do our best to acquire these materials. The powerful equipment you promise us is worth the effort."

The old dwarf smith scratched his bushy beard thoughtfully once more and then nodded firmly. "Be cautious. These creatures are dangerous. But bring me these materials and I will forge the most powerful weapons you have ever seen."

Lea beamed with anticipation. "That's a great offer, Grimgor. We accept it gratefully and will set out to find the materials."

Fiona, who had been listening until now, spoke up. "We will retrieve these materials together. These weapons will surely be of great use to us in our battle against Xalis."

After finalizing the plans for the upcoming quest for the materials, the group settled around the campfire and enjoyed a well-deserved meal. The crackling of the fire and the aroma of the food filled the air as they discussed the best way to tackle the challenge ahead.

Gronak leaned forward with curiosity and asked Grimgor, "Do you happen to know a dwarf named Hemli?"

The old dwarf smith raised an eyebrow in surprise. "Hemli, you say? Yes, I know a Hemli. How do you know him?"

Fiona answered with a smile. "We met Hemli in a crystal cave, along with many other dwarves. We helped him defeat a golem. In gratitude, he helped us escape the cave."

Grimgor laughed heartily. "Ah, old Hemli! A true miner, always in search of new ores and treasures."

He leaned back, reminiscing. "Hemli and I are old friends. I haven't seen the old fellow in ages, but I'm glad to hear he's doing well."

The group exchanged cheerful stories as they gathered around the fire. The memories of their encounter with Hemli and the dwarves in the crystal cave brought a certain warmth to the cold mountain night. They were pleased to have been of help and enjoyed the connection to one of Grimgor's old friends.

Night fell and the chill of the mountain air seeped through the group's sleeping bags. The dwarf's deep snoring echoed through the rocks, causing Sigrid to pull her hood tighter around her face to avoid the noise. Fiona and Lea whispered quietly until fatigue eventually overtook them. Meanwhile, Gronak lay awake, his thoughts on Grimgor's magical weapons and their upcoming journey to the fortress of Xalis. The worry about the dangers ahead occupied his mind.

With the first light of morning, the group slowly rose from their campsite. Grimgor had already started gathering the necessary materials from the snow troll to prepare for enchanting the weapons. The rising sun bathed the landscape in a warm, golden light, enveloping the rugged mountains in a soft glow.

Gronak still felt somewhat dazed from the fight with the snow troll. The efforts of the previous day had left their mark. Sigrid approached him and handed him her axe. "Here, take my axe," she said kindly. "Yours didn't survive the battle yesterday." Her words sounded sincere and Gronak thanked her as he took her axe. The weapon felt light and well-balanced in his hand, ready for new challenges.

Meanwhile, Grimgor had gathered the others and patiently explained the exact materials he needed for enchanting the weapons. In a calm voice, he outlined the process. "The troll's tooth will be used for the axe, the bones and feathers of the thunder harpy for the bow and the scales of the fire salamander for the sword and armor."

Fiona and Lea nodded in agreement, their eyes shining with interest and admiration for Grimgor's skills. They were impressed by the clarity of his explanations and the depth of his knowledge. The idea of how the weapons would be enhanced with magic and ancient dwarf techniques sparked their curiosity and excitement.

"The art of enchanting and rune forging are ancient dwarf traditions that I have perfected over the years," Grimgor explained proudly. "The combination of powerful materials and the right runes will make these weapons unparalleled artifacts."

The group was fascinated by the possibilities before them and thanked Grimgor for his explanations. Their trust in the dwarf smith and the prospect of these powerful, enchanted weapons strengthened their determination to obtain the required materials.

The group packed up their gear and began the arduous climb through the snow-covered mountains. Each step took them higher and the icy cold seemed to intensify with every meter. The snow crunched under their feet as the wind howled around the rocks, causing their cloaks and hoods to flap wildly. In the distance, the growls and roars of wild beasts echoed, a foreboding sign of the dangers that lay ahead.

Hours passed until the group finally reached the base of a steep mountain. Their eyes wandered upward to a rocky ledge where a massive harpy nest was perched. The air was clear and fresh, but the biting wind cut through their clothing and made them shiver. Fiona and Sigrid trembled from the cold, holding their coats tightly around themselves as they focused on the sight of the nest.

Grimgor looked around, contemplating the best approach. His eyes scanned the surroundings as he scratched his beard. "We must be extremely cautious," he warned. "Harpyies are very dangerous, especially when they attack in groups."

Gronak nodded in agreement. "I suggest we approach slowly and try to hide to surprise them. A direct confrontation could be risky."

Lea focused on the steep path leading to the nest. "We should sneak up from behind quietly. That might improve our chances of not being noticed."

The group moved cautiously and silently up the steep mountain, their progress aided by every available rock ledge and indentation in the landscape. The closer they came to the nest, the more clearly they could see the full splendor and size of the harpy nest. It looked like a dense tangle of branches and twigs hanging from a ledge, almost like a giant, round ball in shape and structure. The sounds of the harpies, their shrill screeching and scolding, emanated from the nest.

Gronak motioned for the others to come closer and whispered in a hushed tone, "Let's attack all at once. Be ready."

The group slowly and with utmost caution approached the nest, which clung to the rock wall like a honeycomb. The wind whistled around them, driving the snow before it and making their clothing flap. Fiona prepared her fire spells while Lea drew her bow and Gronak gripped his sword tightly, ready for the impending attack.

When they were within range of the nest, Fiona decided to lure the harpies out of their hiding place. She aimed at the nest and unleashed a flame spell that instantly set the tangle of branches and twigs ablaze. The sudden burst of fire made the nest flare up and the harpies' panic was immediately palpable as they stormed wildly out of the burning nest, searching for an escape route.

Harpies are winged creatures with a menacing aura. Their eyes are sharp and gleaming like a predator's, while their beaks are long and curved like an eagle's. Their feathers are a shimmering brown that seamlessly transitions into a deeper black and they have sharp claws on their feet and hands.

When a harpy starts to fly, the movement of its wings fills the air with a thunderous flapping. Their scream is deafeningly loud and piercing, enough to make one's blood freeze in their veins.

When facing a harpy in combat, it is difficult to predict their attacks, as they can strike with both their claws and their beak. Their speed and agility in the air make them hard to hit and their keen survival instinct keeps them dodging and escaping repeatedly.

Lea did not hesitate as the harpies flew out of the burning nest. Her practiced hands sent arrows flying accurately and several harpies were hit by her shots, screaming in pain. However, this attack alerted the remaining harpies, who then dived wildly towards the group.

Gronak stepped forward bravely, swinging his sword wildly to defend himself against the attacking creatures. With each powerful movement, he tried to fend off the screeching harpies. Sigrid and Grimgor stood side by side, using their skill and strength to keep the approaching harpies at bay.

As the harpies realized the group was becoming too dangerous, they began swirling wildly and charging up. Suddenly, a blinding bolt of lightning shot from their beaks, heading straight for the group. But Fiona reacted quickly, concentrating her magic and forming a protective spell. An invisible, shimmering shield materialized around the group to intercept the incoming lightning.

The blinding bolt struck Fiona's protective shield and shattered in all directions, leaving the group unharmed. The harpies screamed in fury and disappointment, their anger palpable in the air. Their eyes glowed with hatred as they prepared to attack again.

With a blood-curdling scream, they swooped down on the group, their sharp claws and beaks ready to inflict severe damage on their enemies. The sky echoed with their horrific screams and the wild flapping of their wings as they charged at the group with menacing speed.

Their massive wings whipped the air and their eyes sparkled with furious excitement. Fiona concentrated, her hands whirling in an elegant dance of magic as she unleashed her wind powers to keep the harpies at bay.

Lea aimed her bow again and rained arrows down on the attacking creatures. Some of the projectiles hit their mark, causing painful screams and making a few of the harpies recoil. Gronak stepped forward and roared, his voice full of confidence. "They're getting tired; this is our chance, so hold your ground!"

The harpies attempted to use their magic again, but Fiona was prepared. She blocked the attacks and fended off the creatures' immense energy. In a desperate last attempt, the harpies dived to the ground to strike with their deadly claws and beaks, but Gronak acted swiftly. He ducked under their attacks and thrust his sword directly into the chest of one of the harpies, which immediately fell lifeless to the ground.

The remaining harpies realized their fight was hopeless. They took off and flew high into the sky, retreating to safer territories. The group breathed a sigh of relief as the harpies flew away.

Sigrid knelt down and began to carefully collect the harpy's feathers. Her fingers glided over the shimmering plumage as she ensured none of the precious feathers were damaged. Grimgor, on the other hand, focused on the lifeless body of the harpy. His skilled hands pulled out a small knife and began to precisely cut a suitable bone from the carcass.

As he held the feathers and bone in his hand, Grimgor inspected them closely. He twirled the feathers between his fingers, gently tugging at them to check their firmness and then placed the bone on a stone. With a targeted hammer strike, he tested the bone's strength.

After a moment of intense scrutiny, Grimgor nodded in satisfaction. "These are really good feathers and the bone is strong enough. I can work with this." The others looked relieved that their efforts had paid off.

As they took a short break, Gronak seized the opportunity to ask Grimgor about the fire salamanders. "Where could we find the fire salamander's cave?" The experienced dwarf thought for a moment and finally replied, "Not far from here, there's a cave where fire salamanders often dwell. Be warned, though, they are dangerous creatures. If we're not careful, we could easily be burned to ashes."

The group decided to follow Grimgor's advice and set off towards the fire salamander's cave. Yet, the determination of the three was unbroken and they were ready to face any challenge.

The group trudged persistently through the serene scenery of the snowy mountains, the crunching of snow under their feet accompanying their journey. The mountains, in their majestic tranquility, offered a captivating backdrop, complemented by the clear air and bright sky. Between the rock formations and the narrow path, their way led further uphill.

On the way, Lea, out of curiosity, started a conversation with Sigrid. "Tell me, Sigrid, how did you end up becoming Grimgor's apprentice?"

Sigrid's gaze turned to Lea, her eyes bearing the heavy burden of past events. "It... it was a few months ago when Xalis creatures suddenly attacked my village out of the blue."

The silence that followed her words was almost tangible. But then Sigrid found the strength to continue speaking. "They burned everything down, the buildings and the people; they were all slaughtered like cattle. My parents and my little brother were killed too."

Lea could hardly conceal her horror and sorrow. "How did you manage to survive?"

Sigrid looked into the distance, as if she were reliving that moment. "I was out in the forest gathering mushrooms that day. I heard the screams from afar and ran back to the village as fast as I could. I hid at the edge of the forest and had to watch helplessly as the monsters destroyed my family and my village. I fled towards the mountains, hoping to find shelter there. That's how I came to Grimgor's forge."

Grimgor joined the conversation, his deep voice full of compassion. "The poor girl stood at my door in the middle of the night, completely frozen. After she told me everything, I offered her a place to work and live. I needed an apprentice anyway and I could give her a new perspective."

Sigrid looked at Lea, a hint of gratitude in her eyes. "If Grimgor hadn't taken me in, I would probably be dead by now. I'm really very thankful to him."

Lea was moved by the story. "That's truly awful. You were really lucky. I'm glad you made it through."

Fiona added, her voice tinged with bitterness, "Xalis has brought so much suffering to the land. It's really terrible."

Gronak clenched his fist, determination reflecting in his eyes. "We won't let him get away with it, I promise you, Sigrid."

Sigrid smiled, a hint of contentment in her smile. "Thank you, your words mean a lot to me."

As they climbed higher, the surroundings transformed. The sky remained bright blue, while the vegetation gradually disappeared, leaving only bare rocks as their companions. Each step took them deeper into the rugged solitude of the mountains.

The cave they finally arrived at seemed like a dark cleft in the rock wall. An ominous heat emanated from the entrance, melting the nearby snow. Glowing stones framed the entrance, casting a scarlet light that illuminated the interior of the cave. The atmosphere was foreboding and the group could almost feel the looming danger.

"This seems to be the place," Gronak said, observing the cave with a tense expression. "It's going to be hot and dangerous in there. Be careful; it could get perilous." His words were filled with seriousness and he turned to the others. "Let's proceed cautiously and be prepared for whatever awaits us."

Gronak proceeded cautiously, his sword firmly in hand, while the others prepared to endure the heat and dangers of the cave. Fiona focused on protective spells to shield her companions from the cave's intense heat. Lea and Sigrid tightened their bows, keeping a keen eye out for any movement.

"Stay vigilant, I have a bad feeling about this," warned Gronak as they ventured deeper into the dark cave. His gaze swept over the glowing crystals on the walls, which resembled smoldering coals, casting a dim, warm light. The heat enveloped them as they pressed further.

Grimgor, illuminating the path with a glowing crystal, muttered softly as he drew the sparkling stone from his pouch. Its gentle light pierced the darkness, revealing the cave's vastness. They seemed to be entering a world of reddish glow and shadowy crevices, while the faint smell of sulfur and smoke reached their senses.

The expanse of the cave offered numerous hiding places and crevices, perfect shelters for the fire salamanders. Here and there, they could see small lava pools shimmering in a glowing, liquid red. The heat radiating from them was intense, making proximity unbearable.

"Watch out for the lava pools," warned Grimgor, his gaze fixed on the glowing liquids. "If you fall in, you're dead instantly." The group moved cautiously onward, their senses sharpened and alert for possible dangers.

They followed a path winding into the cave's depths, progressing carefully. The heat intensified and they could hear the crackling of flames. Eventually, they reached an open chamber where a group of fire salamanders had gathered around a glowing stone.

"There are some over there, lying on the ground," Lea noted, pointing to the creatures.

Grimgor warned the group to be cautious again. "You must be very careful. Their fire attacks are as hot as a dragon's. One wrong move and we're dead."

Fire salamanders are dangerous creatures that live in heat and lava. They are impressively large, with scaly skin and eyes that look like glowing coals. The heat emanating from their bodies is so intense that it vaporizes everything nearby. Their long tails are lined with sharp spikes, capable of inflicting devastating damage.

When threatened, fire salamanders use their powerful fire breath, which burns everything in its path. Few objects or materials can withstand this fire. Their strength and ruthless behavior make them some of the most dangerous creatures in the area.

The fire salamanders noticed the intruders and reacted instantly. Their massive, red-scaled bodies whirled around, their glowing eyes locking onto the intruders. The salamanders' tongues lashed through the air as flames shot from their gaping mouths. The acrid smell of burning flesh filled the cave as the salamanders attacked aggressively.

Fiona felt the charged energy in the air and shouted, "Be ready, they're attacking!"

The fire salamanders unleashed a powerful blast of flames, which surged toward the group like a raging wave, threatening to engulf everything in its path. Panic erupted, but Gronak reacted swiftly, throwing himself in front of Fiona, Lea, Grimgor and Sigrid. With his shield, he tried to protect them from the devastating attack.

The fire struck Gronak's shield, crafted from one of the most resilient materials. It wavered, swirled and raged, but held firm. The heat began to penetrate the shield, burning Gronak's skin. Fiona immediately recognized the danger and concentrated on healing him to alleviate the burns.

"Hold on, Gronak!" she called out, focusing her energy on mitigating the worst of the burns on his skin. "Thanks, Fiona, I couldn't have held out much longer," he shouted back, wincing in pain. The flames battered the shield, but Gronak stood steadfast as Fiona worked to provide him relief.

The flames danced wildly, sparks swirling around the group, but Gronak remained steadfast thanks to Fiona's aid. The fire salamanders fought with their consuming breath, which threatened to engulf the companions. Exhausted from their initial powerful attack, the fire salamanders briefly ceased their devastating fire breath.

However, the respite was short-lived. The fire salamanders began gathering their strength again to unleash another deadly flame attack. Grimgor quickly threw a handful of smoke bombs in their direction. The sudden fog enveloped the salamanders, confusing them and obscuring their vision, preventing them from aiming accurately.

Fiona seized the opportunity and concentrated her magic. She felt the icy power coursing through her veins. Raising her arms, which began to glow, she summoned the cold from within. An icy whirlwind formed around her as she built up the power. The fire salamanders noticed the impending magic and tried to hide, but it was too late. Fiona unleashed the spell and an icy beam shot from her hands.

The icy beam struck the fire salamanders, which were now covered in frost. The cave's heat was neutralized by the cold and the once-dangerous creatures were frozen into statues. A moment of silence spread before the frosty veil slowly settled to the ground. The group stood victorious among the frozen salamanders, relieved at the outcome of Fiona's powerful spell.

In the silence following Fiona's mighty ice spell, Gronak stepped forward, his axe firm in his hand. With palpable determination, he raised the axe and brought it down with tremendous force on the frozen salamanders. A powerful blow echoed through the air, shattering the icy creatures into a thousand pieces. The cave reverberated with the sound of his axe and the ice statues crumbled into a clattering rain of shards that fell to the ground.

Gronak turned to the others, a broad grin on his face. His powerful swing had destroyed the enemies with such force that it seemed the entire cave had trembled. "That should be enough to forge our weapons," he declared proudly, raising his axe triumphantly. The others nodded in agreement, impressed by Gronak's immense strength.

Fiona, exhausted from the powerful spell, felt a deep sense of relief. She was tired but happy that she could protect her friends and contribute to the victory. A gentle smile crossed her face as she received approving looks from her companions.

As the ice slowly began to melt, the remains of the fire salamanders became visible. Some of the glowing red scales clung to the frozen bodies, while others had already fallen to the cave floor. Grimgor and Sigrid cautiously stepped forward, their eyes focused on the valuable remnants. Together, they began collecting the scales and other useful materials.

Grimgor, deftly handling his small knife, carefully cut off the shiny scales and gently placed them in a special pouch he carried with him. He made sure the scales remained undamaged and none were lost. The scales themselves were of an intense red color, glistening in the dim light of the cave. They felt smooth and hard, a clear indication of their high quality.

Satisfied with his haul, Grimgor nodded to the others, signaling that the mission was successful and it was time to leave the cave. The group, laden with the precious materials, began their arduous journey back. Exhausted from the intense battle and the strenuous expedition, they breathed a sigh of relief. Yet their exhaustion was filled with the awareness that they now possessed the valuable resources to forge their weapons and armor, preparing optimally for the upcoming fight.

The cave was finally behind them. Exhausted but triumphant, they collapsed onto the cold ground outside. Breathing was heavy, but each inhale filled their lungs with the refreshing air of freedom. "That was one hell of a journey, guys," sighed Fiona, leaning against the rock wall, tilting her head back and closing her eyes.

"But it was worth it," said Grimgor, sinking down beside the others. He reached into his pouch and pulled out the shiny scales he had fought so hard to get from the fire salamanders. "Look here, my friends! This is our treasure!"

The group gathered curiously around Grimgor. "Wow, they look like they were forged from fire itself," marveled Gronak, taking one of the scales in his hand. His finger slid over the smooth surface, which was warm and glowing under the sun.

"Shall we take them to the forge right away?" suggested Lea, examining the scales as if they were precious jewels. "I can't wait to see what will come of them!"

Grimgor nodded, his face beaming with anticipation. "Yes, but first we need to get down the steep path." He stood up and began packing his gear. "The snow will soon get thicker. Let's move before we get stuck in the frost."

The group slowly rose, their limbs tired from the arduous journey through the cave. They gathered their backpacks and checked their equipment before setting off for Grimgor's forge. The snow crunched under their boots as they walked along the narrow path by the mountainside.

"Can you believe we actually did it?" Lea asked Gronak, stretching her stiff limbs.

"It was tough, but we make one hell of a team," replied Gronak with a smile. "And these scales will give us legendary weapons!"

The group laughed and as they walked, they shared stories of their adventures. The hardships of the past days were palpable, but their hope, joy and the treasure they had found propelled them forward.

When they finally reached Grimgor's forge, it looked rather unremarkable compared to the majestic mountains and forests surrounding it. It was a small, weathered building protruding from the trees, surrounded by a wrought-iron fence. A few ravens sat on the roof, cawing loudly as they pecked at each other. A small chimney rose from the roof, with a plume of smoke blending into the sky.

The entrance to the forge was made of solid wood and adorned with carvings of dragons and other mythical creatures. The door was old and creaked with every movement, as if it hadn't been opened in years. In front of the door was a small shed where a few horseshoes and other tools were stored. A sign reading "Grimgor's Forge" hung above the door.

Around the forge were several rusty armors and weapons, evidence of the blacksmith's work. A small stream flowed nearby and the water sparkled in the sunlight. It was a peaceful and quiet place where one could recover from the strains of adventure.

As Grimgor opened the door to the forge, Gronak, Fiona and Lea stepped inside. "Make yourselves at home, friends." The heat from the forge hit them immediately and the air smelled of molten metal and coal. Grimgor led them through the workshop and showed them his work area.

Heavy metal tools hung on the walls and several forges fueled by charcoal were visible on the floor. The room was filled with heat and smoke and the smell of hot metal and burning coal hung heavily in the air.

In the center of the room was a large anvil surrounded by several tools, including hammers, tongs and chisels. On the wall behind the anvil was a large assortment of metal plates, rods and other materials. Grimgor's workbench was on the right side of the room, covered with a variety of tools and materials.

In one corner of the forge was a large pile of scrap and old metal, while on the opposite side of the room were several shelves with finished pieces and items. Various trophies and awards adorned the walls, including some from Grimgor's previous battles.

Overall, Grimgor's forge was an impressive place, filled with the heat and energy of smithing and the creativity and craftsmanship needed to create such masterpieces.

Grimgor led the group into his forge, which was filled with glowing forges, anvils and tools. "Welcome to my world," he said proudly, gesturing to the various smithing tools. "I will show you how these scales and other materials will become something incredible."

The adventurers looked around curiously as Grimgor began to lay out the fire salamander scales. "These will be the basis of your armor. Heat-resistant and protective," he explained, pointing to the glowing scales. "We will also use the tooth of the frost troll, the scales and the bones of the thunder harpy for the weapons. But we need to work them properly so that they are not only stylish but also functional."

Gronak looked fascinated at the tooth of the frost troll. "How will you put all this together, Grimgor?"

The blacksmith smiled. "That, my friend, requires precision and patience." He took the tooth and began arranging the various elements on the anvil, while guiding the group through each step. "This will become your axe. The tooth will serve as reinforcement and give it magical abilities."

Gronak furrowed his brow as he watched. "But how will you ensure that the armor and weapons don't become too heavy?"

Grimgor nodded understandingly. "That's a good question. The balance between protection and weight is crucial." He explained how he would skillfully combine the materials to provide protection and strength without compromising the wearer's mobility.

The next few days were spent observing Grimgor at work. The forge echoed with the sounds of hammering and the hissing of hot metal as he and Sigrid worked on every detail with great care. The scent of hot iron and coal hung heavily in the air as the adventurers watched in fascination as raw materials were transformed into armor and weapons.

"I never thought blacksmithing was so complex," murmured Lea as she watched Grimgor carefully incorporate the troll tooth into the weapon.

Grimgor smiled as he worked the glowing metal with his hammer. "There's much more to it than it seems at first glance. But the result will be worth it, I promise you."

Days passed and slowly the armor pieces and weapons took shape under the skilled hands of the blacksmith. Everyone in the group was captivated by the craftsmanship evident in every movement of Grimgor and Sigrid.

By the end of the week, the armors were completed and the weapons were sharpened to a fine edge. The forge echoed with the final hammer blows as Grimgor proudly presented the armor and the razor-sharp weapons. "Here they are, custom-made for you," he declared proudly, wiping the sweat from his brow.

Gronak was the first to reach for the fire sword. His eyes lit up as he examined the sparkling ruby on the hilt. "This is... this is impressive," he murmured, running his hand along the gleaming blade. The light from the forge danced on the surface, making the sword appear to be aflame.

Lea admired the fire sword. "It's really something special, Gronak. It will serve you well."

Gronak nodded in agreement before picking up his new ice axe. The ebony handle felt smooth and solid in his hand. He marveled at the cool aura of the blade, which still radiated a pleasant warmth as he held it. "This is better than I imagined," he said with a smile, swinging the axe gently through the air to feel its weight and balance.

Lea couldn't resist taking a look at the blade. "It looks sharp and you can really feel the magic in the weapon."

Gronak laughed and set the axe aside to focus on the armor. He lifted the heavy leather and felt the solid construction as he donned it. The metal plates and scales fit together perfectly, giving him a sense of protection without restricting movement. "It fits like a glove," he remarked with satisfaction, turning around a few times to test its mobility.

Lea stepped forward with a smile as it was her turn to receive her new weapons and armor. Grimgor proudly presented the thunder bow. "This is for you, Lea." The bow was crafted from dark, flexible wood and adorned with golden embellishments that ran along the bow in intricate runes. The bow seemed light yet sturdy enough to deliver swift and precise shots. As Lea placed her fingers around the smooth grip, she felt an almost instinctive connection.

"That's wonderful," she said as she admired the bow and gently drew the string to feel the tension.

Grimgor also handed her a quiver filled with arrows made from the feathers of harpies. "With these arrows, you'll be able to make even more precise shots," he explained as he handed over the quiver.

Lea took the quiver and examined the arrows. "They really look impressive. Thank you so much, Grimgor."

But that wasn't all. Grimgor then revealed the armor for Lea. The leather armor was crafted to allow freedom of movement, cut in various layers yet sturdy enough to provide protection. It was made from thick, strong leather and adorned with golden buckles, giving it an elegant touch. The hood attached to the armor promised additional protection against rain and wind.

Lea held the armor up in admiration. "This is really well thought out and beautifully made, Grimgor. I feel safer just by wearing it."

Grimgor nodded in satisfaction. "It will protect you when you need it. I'm glad you like it."

Gronak, Fiona and Lea stood before Grimgor and Sigrid, overwhelmed by the quality and beauty of their new gear. They expressed their heartfelt thanks for the help in crafting their weapons and armor.

Grimgor chuckled softly, his beard twitching. "No, no, I thank you. Without your bravery, we would hardly have been able to defeat the troll. You safely led us to the forge. We owe you that."

A shadow crossed his face as he became more serious. "But be warned. Beyond the mountains lies Xalis is territory; his fortress is not far off. His power knows no bounds. Promise me that you will be careful and put an end to him."

Gronak, with a look of determination, responded unwaveringly. "We promise, Grimgor. Together, we will defeat Xalis, once and for all."

Fiona nodded in agreement. "We have overcome so much. And with your weapons, we are stronger than ever. We will make the impossible possible."

Lea looked at Sigrid firmly and spoke with a confidence that resonated in her voice. "We will avenge what he has done to you and your family. And for all the others whose lives he has destroyed."

Sigrid lowered her gaze, grateful for Lea's words and nodded quietly. A meaningful moment followed as Grimgor and Gronak shook hands. It was more than just a gesture of farewell. It was a silent pact between the seasoned blacksmith and the brave warriors, a promise sealed with a firm handshake.

With warm smiles, the friends bade farewell to the blacksmiths. Their steps were forward as they left the forge and set off westward through the majestic, snow-covered mountains to confront Xalis and his terrors.

The sun was slowly dipping toward the horizon as they continued their journey through the mountains. The air was cold, but their resolve warmed their hearts. They knew they faced great challenges, but with their new weapons and armor, they felt empowered and ready for the unknown that awaited them.

Chapter 12: An Unexpected Encounter

The group continued their cautious trek through the icy mountains, which now gently descended. The biting winds of the high altitudes eased and a more pleasant climate enveloped the adventurers as they neared the end of the mountain range. Each step was marked by determination as the group approached the next stage of their perilous journey.

Lea, with her exceptionally sharp eyes, noticed something in the distant expanse. She paused for a moment to peer through the crystal-clear air. "There's something over there," she announced to her companions, pointing to a spot on the distant horizon.

The others strained to look into the distance. Gronak, trying to decipher the blurry outlines, spoke up. "Yes, I see a massive, dark cloud, but I can't quite make out what it is."

Lea, her face clearly showing tension, said with unwavering confidence, "That's a castle. I'm certain it's Xalis is fortress." Her words pierced the calm mountain air and an aura of certainty surrounded her as she pointed to the distant silhouette of the castle, ominously rising on the horizon.

The group slowed their pace as they collectively regarded the distant silhouette of the castle, which loomed on the horizon. The castle towered threateningly into the sky, shrouded in a gloomy cloud that lay like an impenetrable veil over the land. The atmosphere grew more oppressive with each step as the adventurers approached the foreboding fortress.

Gronak frowned, his expression marked by concern. "That must be the place Grimgor mentioned. Xalis is fortress. We should prepare ourselves for the unexpected." His words echoed through the air and the group felt the gravity of the impending challenge.

Fiona nodded in agreement, her eyes reflecting serious concern. "We need to proceed with extreme caution. Xalis is powerful and we don't know what else might await us on the way."

Lea spoke with a forceful tone. "We're ready. We carry the finest tools that Grimgor could forge. Let's storm this fortress and hold Xalis accountable." Her words were filled with an unwavering resolve as she focused on the threatening castle that was now drawing closer.

The mood in the group grew increasingly serious as Fiona attempted to calm the tension. "Perhaps we should get closer first and calmly devise a solid plan for how we want to proceed," she suggested. "We've learned so much during our journey and are much stronger now than at the beginning. I'm confident that we can defeat Xalis."

Lea vigorously agreed with Fiona and laughed. "Absolutely! With Grimgor's mighty weapons, the holy book, the rune and the support of our friends we've met along the way, we simply cannot lose."

Gronak, however, remained silent and gazed worriedly into the distance where Xalis is fortress lay. In his gaze was the weight of the impending task and he was fully aware that the endeavor ahead would be anything but easy. His silence spoke volumes about the challenge that lay before the group.

The group carefully descended the steep slope and slowly entered a forest, which transitioned the landscape from open plains to a denser, tree-lined area. The forest itself did not appear immediately threatening, but the increasing density of the trees and the rustling foliage created an atmosphere of uncertainty. The place seemed perfect for an ambush.

Gronak, recognizing the potential danger of the new surroundings, sharpened his senses. "Stay alert," he warned the group as they cautiously moved through the forest. "In Xalis is territory, we never know what might be lurking. Enemies could be hiding everywhere."

The group proceeded cautiously through the forest, always prepared for a possible attack. Lea, with her keen eyes, scanned the treetops for any signs of danger. Fiona sensed the magical energy in the air and kept an eye out for possible magical illusions.

Suddenly, they heard a faint rustling in the underbrush. The group froze, preparing for a potential attack. Gronak lifted his axe, Lea nocked an arrow in her bow and Fiona concentrated her magic, ready to unleash it if needed. The tension in the air was palpable as the adventurers braced for what the opaque forest might throw at them.

A fluffy, brown dog suddenly sprang from the dense undergrowth and stood before the group. Its tail wagged happily and its eyes radiated trust. A moment of silence fell over the adventurers as they regarded the unexpected guest.

The dog seemed to pose no threat. On the contrary, it appeared extremely friendly and approachable. Fiona and Lea, who had a particular fondness for animals, couldn't resist and approached the dog to pet it affectionately. The dog immediately responded to the attention and visibly enjoyed the affection from the two women.

Fiona smiled as she touched the soft fur of the dog. "He's so cute! I wonder where he came from?"

Lea nodded in agreement and said, "He must have gotten lost. But don't worry, little friend, you're with friends now." The initial tension of a possible attack in the forest gave way to a warm atmosphere as the group unexpectedly gained a furry companion.

Gronak, watching his friends cheerful moment, also smiled. Yet, there was a trace of concern in his gaze. He couldn't help but wonder where the dog had come from and why it was so close to Xalis is fortress.

"It's nice that you've found a new friend," Gronak said as he stepped closer. "But don't you find it a bit odd that such a friendly dog appears so near Xalis is fortress? We should perhaps be cautious and consider where it might have come from."

The women looked up and exchanged thoughtful glances. The cheerful atmosphere was briefly interrupted by the reality of the impending adventure. They had learned to be wary and not to take unexpected things at face value.

Fiona continued to stroke the dog's head and said, "You're right; this isn't a wild dog. Someone must own him. We should stay alert." The reminder of the dangers that might lurk near Xalis is fortress kept the group cautious, even in moments of apparent harmlessness.

The group stood in the clearing, thoughtfully observing the friendly dog. Lea also gathered her thoughts and said, "Maybe he's a survivor from the times when Xalis is minions roamed the land. Perhaps he hid and is now looking for a new home."

Fiona nodded in agreement and added, "That could very well be the case. But what do we do with him now? Xalis is fortress is certainly no safe place for a dog."

Gronak, who looked worriedly at the dog, said, "That's true, we definitely can't take him to Xalis is fortress. Maybe it would be better if we left him here. The surroundings could be dangerous for him."

Fiona and Lea agreed that it would probably be best for the dog if he stayed here. The group set off again, but the dog stubbornly followed them. The women looked at each other, unsure of how to handle the persistent companion.

"Well, if he really wants to come along, maybe it's okay," Lea suggested, looking at Gronak. "What do you think?"

Gronak chuckled softly and said, "Why not. As long as he doesn't hinder us and keeps an eye on the surroundings. But don't forget to stay vigilant."

The determined group continued their journey through the forest, accompanied by the dog, who cheerfully bounded ahead. The dense tree canopies formed a natural roof over their heads and the soft forest floor cushioned their steps. Suddenly, a desperate call pierced the silence of the forest, cutting through the clear sky. "Paco! Paco, where are you? Come to me!"

The dog immediately reacted to the familiar name, his ears perked up and his tail wagged with joy. Without hesitation, he dashed toward the calling voice. The adventurers exchanged surprised glances as the dog raced through the underbrush, leading the way.

Fiona, with a keen look, suggested, "Maybe we should follow him. If there are indeed people here, they might need our help." The group's eyes met as they grasped the significance of the situation.

Gronak, recognizing the seriousness of the moment, agreed. "You're right, Fiona. Let's hurry."

The group continued their hurried pursuit of the swift dog through the dense forest. "Man, is that little guy fast," Gronak commented. His eyes followed the dog, who darted like a swirling spot through the underbrush.

Lea, appearing calm and composed, reassured the others with an encouraging tone. "Don't worry, I've got him in sight. Just follow me." Her sharp eyes remained fixed on the dog, who skillfully led them through the thicket. The group hurried after Lea, navigating obstacles and weaving through the dense rows of trees.

Finally, they reached a small clearing where an elderly woman stood. She radiated a calm and deep connection with nature. Her silver-gray hair was loosely tied in a bun, with a few strands gently falling around her face. The lines on her forehead and around her eyes spoke of the traces of a rich life, full of ups and downs.

Her eyes reflected both wisdom and kindness. A few laugh lines framed her eyes. Still, there was a hint of sadness in her gaze, as if she carried deep scars from a difficult past.

The woman wore simple but well-maintained clothing that emphasized her connection to nature. She was dressed in a long robe of earthy colors and light leather shoes, perfect for the surroundings. Over her shoulders hung a plain fabric cloak that fluttered gently in the wind.

The dog, Paco, ran joyfully to her, his tail wagging with exuberant joy. The elderly lady radiated relief and spoke lovingly to the dog. "Paco! There you are, my dear. I was so worried."

The three friends observed the joyful reunion between the elderly lady and Paco. Fiona addressed the elderly lady, who had not noticed them until now. "Excuse me, is this your dog? We found him earlier and he followed us."

The elderly lady, who had seemed absorbed in her own thoughts, turned to the group with surprise. A hint of confusion was in her gaze as she spoke. "I'm sorry, I didn't notice you. Yes, that's Paco, my beloved dog. And who are you, if I may ask?"

Gronak stepped forward and responded with a mix of pride and seriousness. "We are warriors on a mission to stop Xalis. Our path leads us straight to his fortress."

The mood of the elderly woman became contemplative and serious. A warning reflected in her eyes as she addressed the group earnestly. "Are you sure you want to do this? Xalis is no ordinary man; he is a demon in human form. You should leave quickly if you value your lives."

Fiona replied with measured calm. "Thank you for the warning. Don't worry, we will fight him and bring peace to the land. Xalis will no longer cause harm."

Gronak and Lea nodded in agreement as Fiona politely addressed the elderly lady. The lady, whose eyes delved deeply into those of the three adventurers, revealed a mix of interest and admiration. In a calm voice, she said, "I see in your eyes that you are determined. Such resolve is rare in these times."

Lea, driven by her natural curiosity, politely asked a question. "May I ask what you are doing alone with Paco in the forest, especially so close to Xalis is fortress?" The lady responded to Lea's question with a counter-question. "Would you be so kind as to take me to my home? I would be happy to tell you everything you want to know."

The group exchanged glances and agreed unanimously. "Of course, we will accompany you to your home," Fiona said with a warm smile. There was a sense of connection and willingness to help in the air as they prepared to follow the lady and learn more about her story.

The lady was noticeably pleased with the group's company and they set off together. During the walk, she revealed a little about herself. "I haven't introduced myself. My name is Martha and I have lived here all my life in this valley. This is Paco, my loyal companion."

Fiona responded warmly. "We're very pleased to meet you, Martha." Driven by her ongoing curiosity, Lea couldn't resist and asked further. "Do you live with Paco alone in the forest?"

Martha shook her head slightly. "No, my dear. I live with my husband in a cottage not far from here, just outside the forest." Gronak, intensifying his gaze, directed a serious question at Martha. "Alone in this area? Aren't you afraid that Xalis is minions might find you?"

The atmosphere was momentarily dampened and Martha took on a thoughtful expression before answering with a trembling voice. Her words carried the heavy burden of past traumas. "We are too old and too weak to flee. When Xalis is minions ravaged the valley, they ruthlessly killed everything that stood in their way. The people fought stubbornly, but unfortunately, without success. Desperate, all the survivors tried to flee as long as they could, but there was no escape for us. We hid in the cellar and hoped for a miracle. The fear of death choked us as we waited in darkness and silence for an end. When the screams died down, we dared to look outside. Everyone was gone, many houses lay in ruins or burned fiercely and everywhere were the bodies of our friends and neighbors. Since that day, however, there have been no more attacks; the valley was as if swept clean."

Gronak's anger was reflected in his face as he looked at Martha intently. "Those bastards will pay for this!"

"That must have been terrible for you. I can hardly imagine it," Fiona said with a somber tone. Lea, visibly upset, assured her, "We will put an end to this, I promise you."

Martha smiled sadly at the group. "Thank you for listening to an old lady." Her gaze conveyed not only gratitude but also deep sorrow for what had been lost. At that moment, the group's journey seemed not just a mission against evil but also a journey through the ruins of Martha's past.

The group continued on their way, accompanied by Martha and the cheerful Paco, whose barking filled the forest. As they moved through the dense greenery, Lea suddenly heard a distant noise. Her sharp eyes scanned the forest boundaries to determine what it might be.

Gronak, puzzled by Lea's reaction, asked worriedly, "What's wrong, Lea? Did you spot something?" Lea looked around in confusion and then shook her head. "No, I thought I heard something, but it seemed to be just an animal. It's not audible anymore, so everything is fine."

The group continued their journey, remaining alert to potential dangers in the forest. Paco trotted happily ahead and Martha led the group to her home. Meanwhile, Fiona, Lea and Gronak attentively observed their surroundings, their senses heightened, ready for any unexpected encounter. The rustling of leaves and the chirping of birds were accompanied by a latent feeling of tension, as if the forest itself was watching their journey with a certain reluctance.

After a while, the group reached the edge of a town marked by devastation and partially extinguished flames. Fiona could hardly conceal the expression of shock on her face. Her eyes lingered on the remains of a once-thriving community now scarred by the hand of destruction. "This is dreadful. It's a miracle that nothing happened to you," she whispered as her gaze swept over the ruins.

Martha nodded regretfully, her eyes reflecting the sorrow of the story she carried. "Fortunately, our house was on the outskirts of town and suffered only minimal damage in the end." She led the group through the scarred streets to a small, old house that, despite the circumstances, seemed to retain a touch of charm. The walls bore signs of past splendor, now covered in cracks and soot. The fence, once standing proudly, now lay broken and destroyed on the ground.

Paco seemed to recognize the home. His tail wagged happily as they opened the heavy wooden door. The interior of the house told stories of survival and perseverance. The traces of the past were clearly visible: shattered windows, peeling paint on the walls, yet amid this decay lay a certain warmth. A fireplace, surrounded by memories and the familiar surroundings created a contrast to the bleak scene outside.

The group entered the house and the faint scent of the past mingled in the air. Martha pointed with a touch of nostalgia at the furniture, once filled with life.

Martha politely asked the group to take a seat. "Please, make yourselves comfortable. I will just quickly go to my husband Richard. I'll be right back," she said with a smile that could hardly hide the strain of past days.

The atmosphere in the house carried a subdued mood as the group sat down. The furniture, once part of a harmonious home, was now marked by the passage of time and the burdens of past events. The faint smell of the past and present hung in the air. Pictures on the walls spoke of better times, when the town was full of life and laughter. The creaking of the floor revealed stories of countless steps that once echoed through the house.

Gronak and Fiona took their places on the aged chairs around the old wooden table, while Lea tenderly attended to Paco, who was joyfully by her side. The three waited patiently, their gazes fixed on the closed door behind which Martha had briefly disappeared. The tension in the air was palpable, with the silence only interrupted by the soft sounds of the crackling fire.

Minutes stretched on and eventually, Martha returned with a heavy, desperate expression on her face. Lea looked at Martha with a hint of concern in her eyes and finally dared to ask, "May I ask what is happening with your husband?" Her words floated gently in the room, which seemed filled with memories and losses.

Martha sat down with a sigh at the worn wooden table and began to share her story. "You see, my husband

Richard is very ill. After the devastating attack by the minions, he desperately tried to bury the bodies of the residents. He felt it was his duty to give the dead their final rest. Day and night, he worked, digging countless graves to provide each person with a dignified resting place. But the burden became nearly unbearable for him in his older years. Exhaustion overcame him and high fever eventually left him bedridden. Since then, I have been scouring the area in search of healing herbs that might cure him. Fortunately, I have Paco; he has a keen sense and helps me in the search. But even for me, it becomes more difficult each day."

A hint of sadness lingered in her voice as she shared her words. The group listened with deep sympathy, while Fiona responded empathetically. "We are truly sorry, Martha. One can hardly imagine how difficult this must be for you." Her words floated as a gentle comfort in the room, marked by Martha's fate and the deep bond with her ill husband.

Lea looked at Fiona with hope. "Can't you heal him with your magic, Fiona?" Fiona's eyes filled with sadness as she gently explained, "Unfortunately, no. Magic can heal injuries, but it is powerless against diseases. That requires knowledge of alchemy and herbalism, of which I only have limited understanding. Additionally, I lack the necessary resources." Lea's gaze fell with dejection and Gronak also seemed moved by the gravity of the situation.

Fiona turned back to Lea and said, "But even if I can't heal him completely, we can alleviate his suffering and speed up his recovery. For that, I need specific herbs." She pulled out an old book from her bag and flipped through it. "Look here. These three herbs are needed to make a potion that will surely help him recover." Lea and Gronak mirrored Fiona's enthusiasm and even Martha seemed relieved at the prospect of help.

Martha examined the ingredients and said, "I have Kobold root and Fairy tulips right here in the house." Fiona beamed with joy, "That's great, then we only need the Shadow plant. Unfortunately, I have no idea where we can find it." Lea smiled at Fiona and explained, "I know where to find Shadow plant. In my village, we used it often. The plants grow on rocky mountain slopes, especially in shaded areas. They're hard to spot, but I have a good eye for them."

Gronak jumped up from his chair, "Perfect, then we should head out immediately and get that Shadow plant. Don't worry, Martha, we'll help you and your husband." Fiona and Lea smiled with excitement and also stood up.

"Yes, exactly, we'll help you," said Lea and you could see the joy in their eyes as she looked directly at Martha. A hint of hope and camaraderie filled the room.

Martha was deeply touched by the trio's willingness to help. "Are you really sure you want to help an old lady?" Fiona placed her hand on Martha's shoulder and soothingly replied, "Of course, Martha. We'll make your husband well again." A moment of connection occurred as Martha wiped tears from her eyes. "I thank you from the bottom of my heart. I will accompany you. I know this area well and know of a place that matches Lea's description. We should be able to find it there."

The group carefully checked their equipment and then set out together with Martha and Paco. The dog seemed to share in the excitement, running eagerly between the group members. The solidarity that emerged between the travelers and Martha gave the tense atmosphere a new energy as they set off to find the healing herbs for Richard.

After an hour of trekking, the group reached a rocky plateau. The surroundings were marked by stark beauty and the path led them through a mountain pass, surrounded by imposing rock walls. Lea pointed to the steep rock faces and explained, "Right up there in the crevices, we should be able to find the Shadow plant."

Fiona looked worried and remarked, "The walls are very steep, it could be quite dangerous." Lea smiled and tried to reassure Fiona. "Don't worry, I've done this often enough before. I can manage."

Before Fiona could further voice her concern, Gronak spoke up. "Don't worry, Fiona. If Lea says she can handle it, we should trust her." Fiona visibly relaxed and Gronak added, "You can do it, Lea. We believe in you." A sense of confidence ran through the group as they prepared to climb the steep rocks and find the coveted Shadow plant.

Lea cautiously made her way to the majestic rock wall, accompanied by Paco, who stood loyally by her side. The majestic scenery of nature surrounded them as Gronak, Fiona and Martha observed the events from a safe distance. The sun cast its warm rays over the scene as Lea stopped in front of the imposing rock wall and looked up, searching for a suitable crevice.

After carefully examining the wall, she finally found a promising spot and began to climb it with impressive agility. Paco seemed excited with joy, his tail wagging happily, while the others watched Lea's progress intently. Every handhold, every secure step was silently admired by the nature around them.

After climbing several meters and reaching the crevice, Lea dedicated herself to finding the sought-after shade plant. Minutes passed, during which nature maintained its own silence. Finally, Lea carefully descended, her face showing a mixture of frustration and regret. She looked at her friends and said quietly, "Unfortunately, there was nothing up there. I'll try again over there."

Martha called out to Lea, "Please be careful, my child!" Lea set off again towards the rock wall, followed by the tense gazes of her friends, who watched her with hope and well wishes.

Lea prepared to climb at another spot, the mountain air cooling her skin as she accepted the challenge of the rock wall. Paco suddenly seemed to sense a change in the atmosphere. His fluffy ears perked up and his eyes fixed on a point in the distance, as if alarmed by an invisible danger.

Lea noticed her animal friend's unrest. Confused, she looked at Paco and asked, "What's wrong with you, Paco?" At that moment, as she spoke these words, she felt Paco jump against her with great force, pushing her aside as if he wanted to protect her from something terrible.

The group, watching the events from a safe distance, froze in shock. Lea landed roughly on the rocky ground, while Paco stood protectively in front of her. A scream of pain pierced the mountain air as Lea realized what had happened. Paco lay motionless on the ground, a crossbow bolt protruding from his body and blood streamed heavily from the wound.

Lea was shocked by this sudden and threatening situation. Her heart pounded wildly as she helplessly looked at Paco. Martha, who had followed the dramatic incident, desperately called out her beloved dog's name. "Paco!" The mountain air seemed to fill with tension and concern as nature witnessed this unexpected turn of fate.

Martha wanted to run to Paco, but Gronak held her back. "Stay here, Martha! Lea, come here, we're being attacked!" he shouted, his voice tense as the group prepared for the imminent attack.

Lea, slowly emerging from her state of shock, stood up and ran to Paco. The loyal dog lay severely wounded and bleeding on the ground, but his breathing signaled that he was still alive. With trembling hands, Lea lifted Paco, while out of the corner of her eye, she noticed several arrows flying towards them.

With skillful evasive movements, Lea avoided the dangerous projectiles and rushed to her friends. She quickly laid Paco down gently and Martha knelt, crying, over her beloved dog. Gronak, feeling the rage rise within him, shouted into the mountain landscape, "Who did this? Show yourself immediately!" The surroundings remained silent and an oppressive silence settled over the scene as the group waited with tense anticipation and sorrow for further developments.

In a dark moment, a menacing voice cut through the tense air as the stranger began to speak. "Honestly, I'm surprised to see you here. I thought I had already killed you. But you're like pesky insects. This time, you won't escape me!"

Lea instantly recognized the hated voice. "Reyve, you miserable bastard!" she shouted with a mix of disgust and anger and as Lea uttered the name Reyve, Gronak and Fiona felt a growing tension grip the atmosphere. A wave of rage surged through Gronak, who was determined to put an end to this threat.

Suddenly, Reyve appeared atop one of the rocky slopes, his sinister laugh echoing threateningly through the air, creating an ominous backdrop. His appearance intensified the already tense situation as he revealed himself.

Reyve's malevolent laughter pierced the air, sending a shiver down the spines of those present. "That's right, it's me. And this time, it will be our last meeting. You annoying maggots won't bother me again."

Fiona, faced with this threatening announcement, addressed Reyve directly. "How did you know we were here?" Her voice was tense, but the spark in her eyes revealed her curiosity.

Reyve, displaying his typical arrogant superiority, replied. "Xalis ordered me to guard this valley and one of my goblin scouts spotted you in the forest and reported to me immediately." His words dripped with arrogance as he divulged information about the group.

Lea suddenly remembered the strange feeling in the forest that she couldn't initially place. "So that was a damn scout. Damn, why didn't I notice it right away?" Self-reproach tinged Lea's voice as she recalled the moment of unease in the forest.

Fiona tried to calm Lea, speaking in a gentle voice. "Don't worry, Lea. What's important is that we stop Reyve now." Her gaze remained fixed on Reyve, readying herself for the impending confrontation. The tension in the air was palpable as the group prepared for the upcoming battle.

Reyve's mocking grin spread across his face. "So you want to stop me? What a joke." He snapped his fingers and several armed goblin warriors emerged from the shadows. The group was shocked by this numerical superiority and readied themselves for combat.

The goblin warriors were small but nimble creatures. With green, scaly skin and hideously grinning faces, they exuded a malevolent aura. Armed with swords and makeshift armor, they were numerous and agile, ready to follow their leader into battle. Their eyes gleamed with greed and brutality as they advanced towards the group.

A shrill whistle cut through the air and in that moment, Reyve's mighty wyvern appeared. Reyve smoothly mounted the winged dragon and rose majestically into the sky. "You will die here and now! Trico, you know what to do." With these words, the wyvern unleashed a massive fireball upon the group.

Fiona reacted instinctively, summoning a powerful shield. The fireball exploded and the ground shook from the impact. Yet, the shield held firm, defying the destructive force of the flames.

Gronak drew his massive sword and roared, "Goblin or not, they won't stop us!" Lea smoothly drew her bow, her gaze fixed on the approaching threat, ready to face the onslaught of goblin warriors and the fire-breathing wyvern. Amidst the raging battle, the group demonstrated impressive courage, standing against the overwhelming power of their enemy.

As the dust slowly settled, the friends saw the image of the goblins rushing towards them. Gronak spoke with a serious, commanding voice. "Fiona, you protect Martha with your magic. Lea, you're with me. We're attacking the goblins."

The two women nodded in agreement. "Got it!" they confirmed with a determined look. Martha, standing behind Fiona, looked at her worriedly and apologized, distressed. "I'm sorry for being such a burden."

Fiona smiled reassuringly and placed her hand on Martha's shoulder. "Don't worry, Martha. We'll handle this. Just stay in cover." With these comforting words, Fiona turned to face the impending goblin attack, ready to use her magical powers to protect her friends. Amidst the tension and chaos, the group showed their readiness to face the challenge ahead.

Gronak, with a serious look and his sword firmly in hand, charged determinedly at the oncoming goblins. His massive presence radiated superiority as he plunged into the raging battle. Lea positioned herself at a distance, drawing her bow to fire precise arrows and provide Gronak with cover.

Fiona focused her magical abilities on creating a protective shield to fend off the incoming goblin arrows. The air was filled with the danger of the approaching enemies. Gronak, now in the thick of the action, delivered powerful blows and skillfully deflected the attacks.

Lea, her movements fluid and precise, shot targeted arrows at the goblins, ensuring they couldn't advance unchecked. The coordination between the friends demonstrated their well-practiced combat unit. Meanwhile, high above, Reyve circled on his wyvern, watching the scene and laughing mockingly.

"Let's see how long you can keep this up!" he taunted condescendingly, his gaze full of arrogance as he watched his fighting friends. But the group, filled with determination, defied the taunts and fought together against the advancing threat.

Reyve's hand, extended towards the group, radiated a menacing aura. "Even though it's fun watching you in your death struggle, it's time to end this. So, let's finish this, Trico you..." Suddenly, Reyve was struck by a painful blow to the stomach. Confused, he looked down at his body and saw an arrow deeply embedded in his abdomen. "What the hell, who was that?"

A powerful voice broke through the tension from the opposite rock wall. "The only one meeting his end today is you, Reyve!" The battle came to a halt and all eyes turned to Reyve. He clutched his bleeding stomach, spat blood and lost his balance before falling from the wyvern and hitting the ground with a dull thud.

The goblins became agitated as the group realized a new player had entered the fray. The mysterious figure on the rock wall initially remained hidden in the shadows. In this moment of confusion, Fiona, Lea and Gronak seized the opportunity to regroup and strengthen their defense.

The unknown figure finally stepped into the light, hooded and exuding an aura of mystery, a skilled archer moving deftly among the rocks. Reyve, still on the ground and coughing up blood, struggled to rise. "Who the hell are you?" he wheezed, as the tension in the air thickened like a dense fog.

The stranger pulled back the hood, revealing their face. As Gronak, Fiona and Lea looked up at the rock wall, they could hardly believe their eyes. Lea expressed her astonishment, "That's... that's Anika." Fiona agreed, "Yes, it's her."

Anika stood majestically atop the rock wall, her long blonde hair tousled by the wind, as she looked down at Reyve. With agile movements, she gracefully leapt from rock to rock, descending towards the battlefield. Reyve, slowly getting back on his feet, noticed Anika and taunted, "If it isn't the little merchant's daughter. So you're still alive."

The goblins were about to make their way to Reyve when he bellowed to his army, "You handle the three of them and I'll take care of this little wretch here." The goblins and the wyvern turned their attention back to the group, launching a renewed attack. Reyve, with a smug grin, focused solely on Anika as the center of the upcoming battle.

Gronak roared, "Let's show this goblin scum what we're made of! Anika, you got this!" The group quickly found themselves at the heart of the chaotic skirmish, fighting against the overwhelming number of goblins and the fierce assaults of the wyvern.

Reyve turned to Anika again, mocking her. "Why have you come to me? Shouldn't you be hiding in some hole, cowering in fear?" Anika glared at Reyve with deep-seated contempt and replied angrily, "I'm here for revenge!"

"Revenge?" Reyve asked, visibly puzzled by Anika's presence. Without hesitation, she drew a dagger and slowly approached Reyve. "I will avenge the life, hope, future and love you destroyed!" Reyve drew his sword, readying himself for the imminent confrontation. "I don't know what you're talking about, but if you want to die,

I'd be happy to..." Reyve faltered as he felt a strange change in his body. "What's happening to me?"

The scene was charged with intense tension as Anika advanced on Reyve, the unspoken promise of vengeance hanging in the air. The imminent fight seemed to be taking a turn, with Reyve, despite his superiority, sensing an inexplicable threat.

A mysterious smile spread across Anika's face. "Feeling your predicament now? The arrow that hit you was poisoned. But don't worry, it's not deadly; it's meant to paralyze you. I want to kill you myself, you bastard!" Reyve's sword fell soundlessly to the ground as he looked at Anika, who was approaching with determined steps. Panic reflected in his eyes as he recognized his absolute helplessness.

Reyve, once so arrogant, turned his gaze to his goblins and cried out desperately, "Help me, you worthless scum!" Some goblins at the rear heard his plea and rushed to Reyve's aid. The scene seemed to be turning into a dark drama as the balance of power rapidly shifted.

The battle raged relentlessly and amidst the chaos, Gronak and Lea fought tirelessly against the attacking goblins. Fiona stood firm, fending off the powerful attacks of the wyvern, doing everything in her power to protect her friends, Martha and the injured Paco. The air was filled with the sounds of steel clashing and the thunderous roar of the charging wyvern.

Lea, her senses sharpened, suddenly noticed that Anika was in danger. Gronak, sharing the same concern, shouted over the noise of the battle to Lea. "Go help her, Lea! I've got this! I'll distract them so you can get to her unnoticed." With his blazing sword, Gronak struck the ground forcefully, causing a tremor that sent the goblins around him tumbling to the ground. "Now, Lea, hurry!" Gronak called as the dust settled around him.

Lea nodded gratefully to Gronak and skillfully darted around the fallen goblins. Her movements were fluid and with impressive speed, she maneuvered behind the goblin army. The path to Anika seemed clear, but the intensity of the battle around her created a scene marked by wild attacks and the dull roar of the rearing wyvern.

Four goblins were only a few meters away from Anika and Reyve. Reyve grinned triumphantly. "Well, you might be able to paralyze me, but not all my warriors." Reyve laughed arrogantly as Anika readied herself to defend against the approaching threat.

In this crucial moment, Lea proved to be lightning-fast and skillful. She drew her bow, nocked an arrow with precise dexterity and released her arrows, hitting the goblins with deadly accuracy. The creatures fell lifeless to the ground and a moment of relief swept through the tense atmosphere.

Anika and Lea exchanged glances. Lea, glad to have intervened in time, asked, "Can you handle the rest on your own?" The two women stood amidst the battle, with the goblin threat seemingly subdued for the moment.

Anika looked at Lea gratefully and said with a hint of relief, "Yes, thank you, Lea. I'll take care of Reyve." Reyve, enraged by the assistance, shouted furiously, "Trico, take care of the elf girl!" The wyvern turned menacingly towards Lea.

Anika looked at Lea with concern, her eyes reflecting her worry for the brave elf. But Lea, her face adorned with a confident smile, said reassuringly, "Don't worry, I can handle this. You take care of Reyve." Lea ran away from Anika and Reyve, ensuring that Anika would not get caught in the impending fight.

The majestic wyvern, soaring into the air, dived towards Lea with a tremendous roar. Lea, her senses at their peak, deftly avoided the wyvern's massive claws with agile movements. Simultaneously, she aimed her bow precisely and released deadly arrows towards the charging beast.

Anika's eyes burned with an insatiable desire for revenge as she turned her gaze back to Reyve. Her expression grew even more serious, tinged with a dark loathing. "So, Reyve, now we are alone." The coldness in her voice revealed the deep resentment she held towards the villain.

Without hesitation, Anika moved determinedly towards Reyve. In her hand rested a dagger, its blade embodying her deep, painful anger. With a firm grip on the dagger, she began to strike at Reyve repeatedly. Remarkably, she aimed for non-lethal body parts, a clear intention to make Reyve suffer rather than granting him a swift death.

Reyve, still paralyzed, could only emit painful sounds. "What the hell is this? If you want to kill me, why don't you just do it?"

Anika's gaze grew colder with each blow, her eyes reflecting the deep hatred and destructive resolve within her. "You want death? You don't deserve a quick death. I will make you suffer, just as you made me suffer!" Each strike seemed to be a reckoning for the torment Reyve had inflicted upon her.

Reyve could only scream in agony, his attempts to fend off Anika's devastating revenge proving futile. Meanwhile, the battle against the remaining goblins and the wyvern raged around them, yet this dramatic scene between Anika and Reyve formed the emotional core of the conflict.

Anika allowed her deep anger to rise, delivering another powerful stab with her dagger. But to her surprise, Reyve managed, with a final burst of strength, to block the dagger with his hand. The metallic sound of the impact echoed through the air. The dagger now lodged in Reyve's hand and with the remaining strength his paralysis allowed, he flung the blood-soaked blade aside. Anika's eyes widened at the impressive willpower Reyve displayed in this hopeless situation.

Reyve stood there, blood dripping from his hand, exhausted yet glaring at Anika with narrowed eyes. "What did I do to you that you hate me so much?" Despite his own suffering, Reyve tried to find an answer in Anika.

Anika's fist clenched with unprecedented force as she fixed her gaze on Reyve. "Hate doesn't even begin to cover it! You took from me what was most important in the world. You took my husband, Janon. You killed him and now you will be executed by me!" Anika's voice trembled with unmistakable resolve and painful loss.

Despite his severe injuries, Reyve let out a mocking laugh. "Janon? You mean that little loser who traveled with you. Weaklings don't deserve to live anyway. His death is no loss." The contemptuous words revealed Reyve's heartlessness and added a bitter note to the already charged atmosphere.

Upon hearing these scornful words, Anika's gaze froze into icy coldness and the anger within her boiled like an uncontrollable fire. With terrifying fury, she took a deep breath and let her fist crash down on Reyve's face with devastating force. The impact was so intense that Reyve staggered to the ground, blood spurting from his mouth. Anika's wrath had been unleashed in that powerful blow.

Reyve lay on the ground, helpless and marked by Anika's vengeance. In an impulsive burst of rage, she leaped onto him and began screaming wildly at him. "You miserable bastard! My Janon was no loser. He was the best man in the world and you killed him!" Every scream seemed to carry a wave of immense pain and bitter fury.

Anika struck Reyve repeatedly with all her might, her face drenched in tears of grief and anger. "You don't deserve to live! I will make sure you can never harm anyone again!" Each blow seemed to be a form of redemption, as if Anika was trying to rid herself of the burden of her emotional torment through this physical retribution.

Filled with pain and rage, Anika continued her revenge against the helpless Reyve. Every strike seemed to echo all the pent-up grief and despair that simmered within her. The scene unfolded as Anika held Reyve accountable for the senseless killing of her beloved.

Reyve lay on the ground, severely injured and gasping, his face contorted with pain. Despite the apparent misery surrounding him, a smug grin seemed to flicker across his face, as if he found satisfaction even in the midst of defeat. Anika's expression betrayed disgust and contempt. "What are you smirking about?" she asked in a scornful tone.

Reyve whistled twice and turned his gaze to Anika, filled with arrogance. "I won't give you the satisfaction you're looking for." His words sounded like a final act of defiance, as he refused to grant Anika the satisfaction she sought.

Anika's gaze showed confusion as she heard Reyve's words. The wyvern, which had previously been engaged in battle with Lea, responded to Reyve's whistles. Lea called out to the winged beast, "Hey, I'm your opponent!" But the wyvern ignored Lea's presence and instead began to prepare a powerful magical attack.

Lea looked at Reyve and suddenly realized what the creature intended. Without hesitation, she sprinted toward Anika to protect her from the impending danger. The wyvern unleashed a massive energy beam, which hurtled toward Anika with destructive force.

Anika stared in the direction of the powerful magical attack, her eyes reflecting both shock and a sense of helplessness. Reyve laughed derisively, taunting, "Well, if I'm going to die, I'm taking you with me." The immediate threat of the impending colossal magical assault was mirrored in Anika's eyes.

A tremendous explosion shook the surroundings. Clouds of smoke rose, accompanied by flying debris. The tremor in the earth caused Gronak and Fiona to glance worriedly at the affected area. The remaining goblins, who had survived the battle, also turned anxiously and stared at their fallen commander.

Amidst the chaos, the nearby rock wall near the explosion collapsed, burying everything beneath massive boulders. The air was thick with dust clouds, shrouding the scene in an impenetrable fog. For a moment, a heavy silence prevailed, broken only by the faint crackling of settling stones. Nature had responded to the magical explosion with a devastating force that swallowed everything in its vicinity.

The goblins screamed in panic and quickly fled. The fear of uncontrolled magic drove them into the darkness. Fiona, whose thoughts lingered on Lea and Anika, called out anxiously to Gronak, "Gronak, we need to get to them quickly!"

Gronak, equally marked by concern, shook his head. "We need to deal with the wyvern first." His gaze remained fixed on the persistent threat posed by the creature.

Fiona gathered her magical power into an impressive attack. "I'll handle it," she declared confidently, though her voice was tinged with deep concern. Her hands began to glow as she channeled the energy for the upcoming spell.

The wyvern turned toward Gronak and Fiona as it sensed the sudden threat. But it was already too late. Fiona unleashed a powerful bolt of lightning, which struck the wyvern directly with blinding light. The creature staggered and finally crashed to the ground, convulsed by the concentrated energy.

Gronak immediately charged toward the fallen wyvern. He brought his sword down with a powerful strike into the creature's head. The wyvern twitched once more before finally lying lifeless.

Exhausted, Gronak sank to the ground, his breath heavy from the strain of the battle. Breathlessly, he turned to Fiona. "We did it, Fiona. Now we need to take care of our friends." His eyes reflected both exhaustion and the relief of having triumphed over the mighty wyvern.

Fiona looked over to Martha, who knelt motionless before Paco. With a concerned expression, she approached the grieving woman, who was only a few steps away. The sorrow in Martha's eyes was unmistakable.

When Martha finally raised her gaze, a wave of despair seemed to wash over her. Tears filled her eyes and her voice broke as she spoke the painful truth. "Paco is dead. My Paco is gone." The words hung heavily in the air, the loss echoing in Martha's broken voice.

Fiona found no words of comfort. The grief and despair surrounded her like an impenetrable fog. Martha, with a trembling hand, gestured toward Gronak and then, with a voice strained by barely contained emotion, said to Fiona, "I'll be fine. Go to your friends and help them." Fiona nodded silently and hurried with a heavy heart to Gronak, who was already waiting for her.

Together, Fiona and Gronak made their way to the site of the devastating explosion. When they arrived, an unsettling silence filled the air. In a desperate attempt to call out to their friends, their voices were met only by their own echoes. The lack of a response weighed heavily on them.

Gronak began moving the massive rocks aside to search through the rubble. Fiona stood by his side, assisting him in this hopeful endeavor. The gravity of the situation hung over them like a leaden shroud as they dug through the debris, searching for any signs of life.

The thought of potentially losing their friends overwhelmed Fiona. Tears streamed down her face as the grim mood deepened with each passing second. The uncertainty of what they would find beneath the rubble weighed heavily on their shoulders.

Suddenly, a faint sound emerged from the debris. A glimmer of hope pierced the darkness. Gronak, infused with a sudden surge of energy, reacted immediately. He began clearing away the stones, his voice ringing out with encouraging words. "Hold on, I'm going to get you out!" Hope filled the air as they prayed to find their friends unharmed.

After what felt like an exhausting eternity of digging, Gronak's gaze finally penetrated the darkness of the wreckage. There, he recognized the injured forms of Lea and Anika. With swift movements, he pulled the two women from the grim tangle of stones and gently laid them on the ground. Both were severely injured, their bodies covered in blood.

Fiona rushed to the two women, her heart pounding with worry. She immediately began the healing process, her concentration fully focused on restoring her friends. Time seemed to stand still, each second stretching into an eternity as Fiona worked tirelessly to ease their wounds.

Finally, Lea and Anika slowly opened their eyes. Fiona burst into tears of joy as the realization that she hadn't lost her friends overwhelmed her. "We thought we'd lost you. I'm so happy," she whispered through her tears, her hands continuing to glide gently over their injured bodies, healing them.

Gronak couldn't suppress a smile. "You were really lucky to survive that, but I'm damn glad you did." The relief over their friends safety overwhelmed the group and they took a moment to savor their gratitude and joy.

Anika let her gaze drift to Lea. Lea, equally filled with joy and relief, met her eyes with a warm smile. In a calm voice, she began to explain, "When I saw that the wyvern was about to attack both of you, I ran and pulled you aside at the last moment before the attack hit. When I noticed the rocks coming down on us, all I could do was hope everything would turn out okay."

Lea's words broke through the emotional dam within Anika, releasing a wave of relief. Overcome with emotion, she broke into tears, washing away the dust and blood on her face. Without hesitation, she hugged Lea tightly, as if in that moment, she could shake off all her worries and fears. With a deeply emotional voice, Anika said, "You almost died because of me. Why did you do that? If anything had happened to you, I could never have forgiven myself."

The two friends shared a tender moment of gratitude and connection, observed by the other members of the group with quiet relief. In that moment, the world seemed to stand still and the strong bond of friendship between Lea and Anika was only further strengthened by this experience.

Lea returned Anika's embrace with sincere warmth and spoke softly to her. "You and I share the same experience, the same pain. I know exactly how you felt, driven by hatred. But my friends were there for me, supporting me, catching me when I fell. And you are our friend too. That's why I supported you, no matter how dangerous the situation was. Please, don't blame yourself."

Lea's words reached Anika, who lowered her gaze as tears continued to stream down her cheeks. A moment of silence followed, filled with the weight of past events and the depth of their emotions.

"But I couldn't kill him. That bastard robbed me of my revenge in the end!" Anika's words were laced with frustration and disappointment. The mix of anger and sorrow was evident in her voice, as if she had lost control of the situation. The darkness of failure and the missed opportunity seemed to weigh heavily on her.

The group remained silent for a moment, the heavy emotions filling the air. Lea's words of understanding and comfort seemed to bring a gentle ray of light into Anika's dark emotional state and the friends stood ready to support each other in the challenges ahead.

Gronak placed his strong hand reassuringly on Anika's trembling shoulder. His words, spoken with deep respect, cut through the air. "He's dead. He can't hurt anyone anymore and that's thanks to you. If you hadn't come, we might have been his next victims." His words were both an acknowledgment of her bravery and an attempt to lift the burden of self-doubt from Anika's shoulders.

Fiona knelt gently beside Anika, her eyes shining with gratitude. With a warm smile, she said, "That's right. Thank you for helping us. Without you, we would have been in serious trouble. You saved us." Her words were not just an expression of gratitude but also an acknowledgment of Anika's courageous actions in a critical moment.

Lea stood up and respectfully extended her hand to Anika. "You were very brave. Janon would have been proud of you." Lea's words elevated Anika's courageous act to a higher plane and her gaze reflected a mixture of pride and understanding for the challenges Anika had overcome.

Anika looked up at Lea and wiped away her tears. The heavy veil of sorrow seemed to be slowly lifting. She took Lea's hand and rose to her feet. A faint but uplifting sense of togetherness enveloped the group. In that moment, they felt the bond between them, strengthened by the trials they had endured together and the support each had received.

Fiona approached Lea. "I'm afraid I have something else to tell you." Lea looked at Fiona, confusion and a creeping sense of unease in her eyes. "Paco didn't make it. He died during the attack," Fiona said, her voice heavy with sorrow, the words hanging in the air. The news pierced through the room, leaving behind a painful silence.

The news from Fiona's lips filled Lea with a deep sadness. An expression of disbelief spread across her face as she struggled to grasp the reality of the words. Without saying much, she immediately ran to Martha, who was holding Paco's lifeless body in her arms.

When Lea saw her beloved companion in Martha's embrace, the floodgates of her emotions broke. "Why? Why did this have to happen?" she whispered brokenly. A brief silence hung in the air, punctuated only by Lea's sobs. She gently stroked Paco's body, as tears streamed down her cheeks. "Thank you, Paco. You saved me from that attack. Without you, I might be dead. Thank you."

Gronak, Fiona and Anika slowly approached and silently observed the scene. Lea asked Martha if she could carry Paco and Martha agreed. Together, they walked to Martha's house. The journey back was marked by a somber atmosphere. No one spoke a word; the shock and the wounds of the battle weighed heavily on the group's hearts. Each step seemed accompanied by the palpable void that Paco's death had left behind.

When they arrived at Martha's house, Gronak suggested digging a grave for Paco. Still deep in mourning, Martha pointed to a spot behind her house, where Gronak immediately began digging. Lea grabbed a shovel as well and helped Gronak clear the earth.

The silence was broken only by the dull sound of shovels and the rustling of leaves. Each of them channeled their grief into the physical effort of digging. The earth flew in high arcs out of the grave as the sun slowly set on the horizon.

After a while, when the grave had reached a suitable depth, they laid Paco to rest with respect and care. Martha whispered her final goodbyes and Lea expressed her gratitude for his heroic deed.

Gronak carefully filled the grave and Fiona created a small memorial with flowers and an improvised cross made of branches. The group gathered around the freshly covered grave and stood in silent reflection.

Martha thanked everyone for their help and offered them a place to stay in her house for the night. The group gratefully accepted. Lea looked at her friends. "I'm going to stay here for a bit," she said, her voice slightly subdued. "I'll stay with Lea. You all go on inside," Gronak said to the others.

Martha led Fiona and Anika into the house, where an oppressive silence prevailed. In the kitchen, Martha silently began to prepare a simple meal as darkness slowly fell outside. The atmosphere reflected the weight of the recent events.

Anika, unable to contain her curiosity, turned to Fiona. "What were you looking for in that rocky place?" Fiona, surprised by the question, flinched slightly before answering, "Oh no, we forgot to get the Shadow Herb!"

"Shadow Herb?" Anika asked, her brow furrowing slightly in confusion. Fiona nodded thoughtfully. "Yes, we were searching for Shadow Herbs to cure Martha's husband. Unfortunately, we had no luck finding any and then we were ambushed by Reyve."

Anika gently opened her bag and searched through it with the utmost care. "Ah, here it is. I knew I still had some Shadow Herb," she announced with relief. With a deliberate hand, she handed Fiona a bottle of the precious substance. "I hope this is enough for the medicine."

Fiona took the bottle with a joyful smile, her eyes shining with relief. "Yes, this is more than enough. Martha, look, we have Shadow Herb and can treat your husband." The joy over this unexpected turn of events filled the room.

Martha, who had been lost in her thoughts until that moment, turned around, her face lighting up with happiness. "Thank you, Anika. Thank you so much." Fiona immediately set to work preparing the potion for Richard. In the kitchen, an atmosphere of hope and confidence emerged as the women worked together to create a remedy for Martha's husband.

Meanwhile, Gronak and Lea stood silently in front of the freshly dug grave. Gronak turned his empathetic gaze to Lea and gently placed his hand on her shoulder. "How are you doing, Lea?"

Lea, her eyes fixed on the grave, sighed softly. "I think I'll be okay. You know, many years ago, I had a dog that looked very much like Paco. Elena and I played with him every day and it was a really wonderful time. When he passed away one day, Elena and I were very sad and all those memories and feelings came flooding back with Paco."

Gronak looked at Lea with understanding and waited a moment in silence before gently asking, "Shall we go back inside?"

Lea nodded wordlessly, a silent agreement passing between them. The walk back was accompanied by a quiet melancholy as their thoughts lingered on memories of past losses.

When Gronak and Lea entered the house, they were greeted by a pleasant aroma from the kitchen. Anika stood focused by the pot, still busy preparing the meal. Gronak, puzzled by the absence of Fiona and Martha, cast a searching glance at Anika. "Where did they go?"

Anika, holding a wooden spoon, looked cheerfully at the newcomers. "They're with Martha's husband, giving him the medicine Fiona just made."

Lea, surprised by this information, turned to Gronak. "But we didn't find any Shadow Herb."

"By chance, I had some with me and when Fiona told me why you were out, I immediately gave her the herb," Anika explained joyfully as she stirred the pot. The relief of having restored Richard's healing remedy was evident on her face.

Gronak, visibly relieved, smiled. "That's fantastic news." The weight on their shoulders seemed to lighten slightly as the unexpected salvation in the form of the Shadow Herb was secured.

After some time, Fiona and Martha emerged from the adjoining room. Everyone looked at Fiona with anticipation. She spoke hopefully, "The medicine seems to be working on Richard. Now, he just needs plenty of rest and patience to recover." Martha, standing beside Fiona, had clear relief written all over her face.

After they all enjoyed the meal that Martha and Anika had prepared, they began to set up their sleeping places. The mood was subdued, shaped by the day's events and intense emotions, from the sorrow over Paco to the hope for Richard's recovery.

Lea, lost in thought, turned to Anika. "Do you know what you're going to do next?" Anika thought for a moment before answering, "I think I'll stay here with Martha for a while and help her out. Knowing you, you'll probably set off for the Fortress of Xalis first thing in the morning, right?"

Gronak agreed and added, "Exactly, we'll head out early tomorrow. The fortress isn't far now." The anticipation of the upcoming journey hung in the air, accompanied by a mix of determination and uncertainty.

The day had been an emotional rollercoaster. Exhausted from the events, everyone eventually lay down and closed their eyes, seeking to recover from the intense happenings, in anticipation of the new morning and the path that lay ahead.

The next morning dawned and Gronak, Fiona and Lea were already up early, packing their gear and preparing for the departure. The atmosphere was filled with a mix of hope and tense expectation.

Martha, standing before the group of heroes, spoke earnest words to them. "Please stop Xalis and put an end to the terror he has inflicted on so many people." The gravity of her words reflected the urgency of their mission.

Fiona stepped forward and took Martha's hand. She looked her firmly in the eyes and assured her, "We will do everything we can to stop Xalis, we promise you that. And when it's done, we'll come back to you and tell you everything." Her determined words were a commitment that extended beyond the task ahead.

Gronak agreed cheerfully. "Exactly! And in the meantime, please take care of our friend Anika." The concern for their friend was evident in his words, a testament to the bond within the group.

Lea and Anika stood a few feet away, embracing each other in farewell. "Take good care of yourself, Lea," Anika said, her voice a mix of worry and encouragement. Lea looked at her friend and smiled warmly. "Of course, I'll take care. And when it's all over, we'll come back to get you." The words carried a clear commitment to return and a shared future.

Anika returned the smile and grinned at Lea. "Alright and then we'll have a real celebration." The anticipation of reuniting and sharing their successes was reflected in her words.

After a heartfelt farewell, in which Lea and Anika parted from each other with a warm embrace, Gronak, Fiona and Lea continued on their way. The menacing towers of the fortress already loomed on the horizon, serving as a constant reminder of the tasks and trials that awaited them.

The path to the fortress promised not only scenic challenges but also lurking dangers. Yet, the group was determined, both physically and mentally, to stop Xalis and restore peace to the world. Every step was accompanied by a blend of courage and hope.

Chapter 13: The Ruler of Darkness

Gronak, Fiona and Lea had been continuing their journey for an entire day, drawing ever closer to the dark fortress of Xalis. The path led them through a desolate, depopulated land marked by an atmosphere of devastation and decay.

The trees, which had once proudly lined the way, had lost their leaves and now stood bare and lifeless against the sky. The branches appeared as skeletal fingers reaching upward to grasp the last remnants of life. The ground they walked on was parched and cracked, as if no raincloud had touched the thirsty earth for ages. No blade of grass, no flower dared to show itself in this inhospitable environment. Nature seemed trapped in a state of perpetual stagnation.

The few houses that crossed their path presented a mournful picture of decay. Their once proud facades were now scarred by time, the windows shattered, the doors hanging and creaking halfway off their hinges. The wood that had once offered protection and comfort was now permeated with rot and decay. No smoke rose from the chimneys, no sound emerged from the deserted walls. The silence weighed heavily on the abandoned houses like a cloak of forgetfulness.

The oppressive silence was only occasionally broken when the wind rustled through the bare branches of the trees, carrying a grim whisper through the air. No birdsong, no rustling in the underbrush enlivened the desolation. It was as if the world itself was holding its breath, anticipating the impending doom that was about to descend upon it.

Lea looked around the desolate surroundings with a sorrowful gaze as they drew closer to the fortress. "The closer we get to the fortress, the worse it gets," she murmured quietly. "Hard to believe that people once lived here."

Fiona nodded in agreement, also looking around with concern. "Martha told me this was once a beautiful and fertile land," she said with a heavy voice. "It's terrible what Xalis has done to it."

Gronak, whose gaze was fixed on the grim fortress, replied in a serious tone. "If we don't stop this bastard, soon the whole land will look like this. We can't let that happen."

Eventually, they reached another abandoned ruin which they chose as a refuge for the night. The ruins of this small town spoke of past splendor, now, however, it lay in ruins. The creaking of rotting wood beneath their feet and the faint rustling of the wind were the only sounds in this deserted wasteland.

The three of them looked around the deserted town while searching for shelter for the night. Among the crumbling buildings and overgrown alleys, they finally found a somewhat intact hut that Gronak deemed suitable for the night.

The walls of the hut were covered in cobwebs and the furniture appeared as if it had been destroyed by time. Nevertheless, it was the best place they could find to protect themselves from the encroaching night.

The three began preparing the hut for the night. Gronak and Lea set about lighting a fire in the old hearth while Fiona prepared the food Martha had packed for them.

The crackling of the fire filled the silence of the night as they gathered around the warming light. They ate in silence, enjoying the heat provided by the fire, while outside the darkness slowly descended over the deserted town.

Lea carefully pulled a shiny necklace from her pocket and examined it in the flickering glow of the fire. The orange-red crystal hanging in the middle of the necklace shimmered in the gentle light, almost like a glowing jewel in the darkness of the abandoned hut.

Fiona, glancing curiously at Lea, couldn't help but notice the unusual necklace. "Where did you get that necklace, Lea? This is the first time I've seen it," she asked as her gaze fell on the radiant crystal.

A smile crossed Lea's face as she continued to examine the necklace. "Anika gave me this necklace when we said goodbye," she explained. "She told me it would bring me luck in the fight against Xalis."

Gronak observed the warm glow on Lea's face as she looked at the necklace. He felt the joy emanating from her and couldn't help but voice his thoughts. "You really care about Anika, don't you, Lea?"

Lea looked up from the necklace and gazed at Gronak with a loving smile. "Yes, I do," she replied thoughtfully. "It's hard to explain, but I feel a deep connection with her. We've been through similar things and that bonds us together. I'm really glad she's still alive and waiting safely with Martha."

Gronak and Fiona exchanged smiles as they absorbed Lea's words. It was clear that the bond between the three was growing stronger and the assurance that Anika was safe gave them all hope and comfort in this dark time.

After they had finished their dinner, Gronak and Lea sat by the fire and began checking their gear. Gronak focused on feeling the weight of his sword as he drew it from its sheath. His experienced hands glided over the blade to ensure it was sharp and ready for use. He then put on his armor piece by piece, ensuring that each part was intact and would provide full protection in battle.

Lea, meanwhile, attended to her bow. She carefully checked the string, pulling it taut and releasing it to make sure it was tight enough to shoot her arrows with precision. With practiced hands, she also inspected the condition of the arrows to ensure none were damaged and that they wouldn't fail her in the heat of battle.

Meanwhile, Fiona sat slightly apart, absorbed in the Holy Book she had found in the old temple. She read softly to herself, her eyes following the sacred text as her mind seemed filled with deep contemplation. In the words of the book, she sought wisdom and guidance for the trials ahead, hoping to support her friends with her magic.

In the stillness of the night, all three were deep in their thoughts when Gronak finally broke the silence. His voice pierced the darkness of the room. "Tomorrow is the day," he began, his gaze fixed on the fire that softly illuminated the surroundings. "We will finally reach Xalis fortress."

Fiona, who had been absorbed in the Holy Book until then, slowly closed it and turned to Gronak with a worried expression. "This will be our greatest challenge," she said with a serious face. "One mistake and everything will have been for nothing."

Lea, who had set her bow aside, also turned her gaze to Gronak. A hint of fear was in her eyes, but her voice was steady as she replied. "Even though I'm a bit scared, I'm confident we can do this. For Anika, Elena, Martha and for all the other inhabitants of this land." Her words were filled with determination and she hoped they would also inspire courage in her friends.

Gronak smiled with confidence as he heard his friends words. "Exactly," he agreed, his voice full of assurance. "We will stop this monster and free the land. So many are counting on us; we simply can't afford to lose!"

The three friends sat by the fire late into the night, discussing plans for the coming day. They analyzed every possible step, every potential danger and every strength they had on their side. It was a calm and starry night, accompanied only by the crackling of the fire and the soft whisper of the wind.

As it grew late and the flames of the fire began to die down, the friends made their way to their sleeping places. Together, they lay down to find rest and gather strength for the day ahead. With their thoughts filled with hope and their faith in each other, they eventually fell asleep, ready for the challenges the morning would bring.

The next morning, the three friends set out once more and continued their journey to the fortress. The sky was clear at first, but soon clouds gathered and darkened the heavens. A gentle wind began to blow, which soon grew into a stormy gust.

Suddenly, the rain began, initially timid, then growing into increasingly heavy showers that cloaked the landscape around them in a dull gray. The road they walked on quickly turned into a muddy trail, making their steps difficult.

After a while of laborious progress, they saw the towering, black fortress. Lea pointed to a hill nearby. "We should have a good overview of the area from up there," she suggested, her voice almost drowned out by the rain.

Gronak and Fiona nodded in agreement and together they made their way to the hill to gain a strategic advantage and devise a plan for how best to approach Xalis and his fortress.

When the three friends reached the hill, they were met with an imposing sight. The dark, foreboding fortress of Xalis loomed before them, its massive walls a penetrating black. The fortress seemed as if it had been born from the shadows themselves, a grim manifestation of power and evil.

The walls were high and thick, crowned with ominous towers whose spires reached threateningly into the sky. Skeleton warriors patrolled the parapets, their dark armor glistening in the rain and their eyes glowed like those of a predator in the darkness.

At the immense gate stood two powerful ogre guards, their massive forms seeming like fortresses unto themselves. Their skin was a dark gray, their muscles were immense and their massive clubs rested heavily on their shoulders.

The black fortress radiated an aura of terror and menace that seemed to darken the air around it. Yet, despite the formidable opponents and the seemingly insurmountable walls, Gronak, Lea and Fiona knew they had no choice but to face the monster Xalis and his fortress bravely.

Gronak furrowed his brow as he weighed their options. "The fortress is really well guarded," he murmured finally, scratching his beard thoughtfully. "If we simply go through the main gate, we'll be spotted immediately and we'll have to fight our way through hordes of monsters."

Lea, with her sharp eyes, scanned the area and spotted something. "Look over there," she said, pointing to a small window in the fortress. "If I climb up there, I can drop a rope down for you. That way, we can get in unnoticed."

Fiona nodded in agreement. "That should work," she concurred. "The side of the fortress also seems less guarded. This seems to be the best option."

Gronak examined the proposed route and nodded slowly. "We can sneak from rock to rock up ahead," he suggested, pointing to a possible path. "Thanks to the rain, we should be able to do it unseen."

After a brief discussion, the three heroes set off to sneak up to the fortress. Moving cautiously from rock to rock, they skillfully avoided the watchful eyes of the fortress guards. The roar of the heavy rain enveloped them and obscured their movements, as the rain continued to pour relentlessly.

By skillfully using natural cover and the distraction of the rain, they managed to advance unnoticed. The sounds of their steps were swallowed by the noise of the rain and the guards seemed to notice nothing.

Eventually, they reached the massive wall of the fortress. They were now only a few meters from their goal, ready to venture into the darkness of the fortress and confront their enemy.

Lea prepared to climb the steep wall of the fortress. Gronak carefully handed her a rope, expressing his concern. "Be careful up there, Lea."

A confident smile touched Lea's lips as she reassured her friends. "Don't worry, I've got this."

With determined grips, Lea began to climb the wet and slippery wall, inch by inch. But the rain, which had previously concealed her movements, now became an obstacle. The wall was slippery and treacherous and Lea struggled to make progress.

Despite the adverse conditions, she pressed on courageously. Eventually, she reached the small window that would serve as her entry into the fortress. With her last ounce of strength, she pulled herself through the window and climbed inside.

Lea took a deep breath, her heart pounding in her chest as she prepared to secure the rope to a sturdy pillar. Her fingers trembled slightly with tension as she carefully tied the knots. Every move had to be perfect, as her safety and that of her friends depended on it. With one final check of the rope's security, she swung it down to Gronak and Fiona, who waited patiently below.

Gronak and Fiona grabbed the rope and began to climb the steep wall of the fortress. Each pull was deliberate, each grip firm and determined. Their eyes were fixed on their goal as they slowly but steadily approached the window that Lea had painstakingly reached.

When they finally reached the window and climbed into the fortress, Gronak could not hide his admiration. "That was truly impressive, Lea," he praised her with pride in his voice, as he checked his gear to ensure everything was intact.

Fiona turned to Lea with a relieved smile, wringing out her soaked cloak. "I was really worried you'd slip and fall," she admitted, her eyes full of gratitude for Lea's skill.

The group took a brief moment to dry off and organize their equipment. Every moment of calm was precious in the grim surroundings of the fortress, yet they knew they couldn't afford to waste any time.

As they left the small room accessed through the window, they carefully and quietly made their way down a dark corridor. Each step echoed in the silence and the tension in the air was palpable.

Eventually, they reached an imposing staircase that descended into the darkness of the fortress. With cautious steps, they made their way down the stairs and entered a vast hall filled with a somber silence.

Gronak noticed the massive door next to the stairs and paused for a moment to listen. "That must be the main gate," he whispered softly as he looked around. "Let's hope the ogres don't hear us."

Lea looked at the magnificent yet ominous hall with a hint of fascination and unease. "Look at this," she said quietly to her companions, "the room is enormous. But it's also really cold and eerie." Her eyes swept across the shadowy corners of the hall as she realized how deep they had now penetrated into the enemy's stronghold.

The hall stretched out before them in a dark and menacing expanse. The walls were made of black stone, which, in the dim candlelight, radiated an ominous grandeur. The floor, made of white marble, was pristine, yet under the circumstances, it felt like a cold tomb. Red carpets ran through the room, as if marking the path to their dark ruler.

The flickering candlelight cast ghostly shadows on the walls, illuminating the symbols of dark magic in a grim light. Everywhere were signs and runes engraved, exuding an aura of evil and power.

The atmosphere in the hall was oppressive and threatening. Every breath seemed burdened by an invisible weight and the silence was only broken by the crackling of the candles and the dull echo of their footsteps.

Fiona looked around with a questioning expression as a gnawing feeling of unease grew within her. "Actually, I'm worried about something else. Have you noticed that we haven't encountered a single guard in the fortress yet?"

Gronak nodded gravely, his expression concerned. "You're right, Fiona. I've noticed that too and I don't like it at all. We need to stay alert. We can't afford to make any mistakes now."

Lea pointed forward and whispered softly, "Look, up ahead, there's a large gate. That must lead to the throne room."

The group slowly approached the imposing staircase that led to the throne room's gate. The stone steps appeared weathered and menacing as they advanced. But the moment they set foot on the first step, they felt a dark shadow form around them.

The group stood frozen in surprise as a threatening change suddenly occurred in their surroundings. The dim corridor, which had previously muffled their steps, seemed to come alive as black hands formed from the shadows, reaching out for them. The shadows seemed impenetrable; Lea and Gronak tried in vain to defend themselves.

Lea was suddenly completely enveloped by the shadow and a blood-curdling scream escaped her as she was seized by invisible forces. The darkness seemed to suffocate her as she desperately sought help. Her voice echoed through the gloomy corridor, but her screams were swallowed by the void.

Gronak fought desperately against the black hands that held him, but they seemed to overpower him with unstoppable force. Despite his strength, he was eventually completely engulfed by the shadow. A dull thud sounded as he fell to the ground, his screams mingling with Lea's as he writhed in pain.

Fiona watched her friends in panic, her thoughts spinning wildly in her head as she was surrounded by shadows. She felt paralyzed, unable to act or help her friends. The sudden darkness around her shook her to the core and a feeling of helplessness and despair took hold of her.

Gronak writhed in pain as the shadow continued to envelop him. Suddenly, everything around him went black and he found himself in a room without light or sound. The silence was deafening and the darkness suffocating.

Gronak tried to get his bearings, but all he could feel was the cold and emptiness of this eerie place. He didn't know how he had gotten here or how he could escape. The fear for his friends and the uncertainty about their safety made his heart race as he remained trapped in the darkness.

Suddenly, Fiona appeared before him. He felt searing pain coursing through his entire body and he couldn't move, as if his muscles had suddenly failed him. "Fiona, please, help me!" he pleaded, but his words seemed to vanish into the void. The desperation in his voice was clear, but Fiona just stood there with a blank stare that broke Gronak's heart.

"Fiona, what's wrong with you?" he cried out again, but it was as if she couldn't hear him or was no longer herself. Gronak could only watch helplessly as the situation before his eyes worsened.

In that horrific moment, Reyve suddenly appeared behind Fiona. His presence was like a nightmare and Gronak could see the horror in his eyes. Without a word, Reyve plunged his sword through Fiona and Gronak had to witness her being struck before his very eyes.

A blood-curdling scream tore from Gronak's throat as he desperately tried to rise and rush to his friend's aid. But his muscles refused to obey him, leaving him motionless on the ground, unable to act or even lift a finger. The helplessness that washed over him was unbearable as he watched Reyve complete his gruesome deed.

Reyve laughed mockingly as he pulled his blood-stained sword from Fiona's body. With one final, agonized gasp, she collapsed lifelessly to the ground, her blood slowly spreading across the cold stone floor. The crimson tide seemed to permeate the room and Gronak could almost feel the icy breath of death hanging in the air.

A sense of shock overtook Gronak as he watched his friend lose her life before his very eyes. His muscles were paralyzed and he could do nothing as the horror unfolded in front of him. The helplessness choked him and a curse of impotence weighed on him like a leaden shroud.

Gronak stared into Fiona's lifeless eyes, which now reflected only the emptiness of death. But before he could utter a single word of farewell or grief, something inexplicable happened. Suddenly, he felt the ground beneath him begin to sway and his gaze was lost in the emptiness of the room.

A dizzying sense of void enveloped him and he felt as though he were falling into nothingness. The world blurred before his eyes and then... there was nothing. Everything turned to darkness and Gronak lost consciousness as he plunged into the void.

All at once, Gronak found himself back in his home village, but it was no longer a place of peace and safety. The village was ablaze, with black smoke rising menacingly into the sky. The villagers lay lifeless on the ground, their bodies consumed by the flames or torn apart by the monsters.

Monsters roamed the streets, their malevolent eyes glowing in the flickering light of the fires. They destroyed everything Gronak had held dear, as if they took pleasure in spreading chaos and devastation.

Gronak roared at the monsters, but they didn't even acknowledge him. They continued their work of destruction, as if controlled by invisible strings, unable to respond to human voices or emotions.

The powerlessness that seized Gronak was overwhelming. He could only stand by and watch as everything around him went up in flames, as everything that had once meant so much to him was reduced to rubble and ash. His heart ached with grief and rage, but he was powerless against the overwhelming force of evil that had descended upon his village.

When Lea opened her eyes, she found herself in her home village, which was being ravaged by the horrors of the attack. The air was thick with the stench of burning houses and the sounds of battle. Elven warriors fought desperately against the advancing monsters, their swords flashing in the light of the flames.

In the background, Lea heard the terrifying screams of women and children echoing from the burning houses. The piercing wails cut through the night, shattering Lea's heart into a thousand pieces. She felt the despair and pain of those she knew and loved.

Lea tried to stand, but her muscles wouldn't obey. A wave of frustration and fear washed over her. "Damn it, why can't I move?" she cursed softly, struggling in vain against the invisible force that held her captive.

Her gaze wandered to the villagers, who were frantically trying to escape certain death. "Run! Get to safety!" Lea called to them in a trembling voice, but her words were lost in the noise of battle and destruction. She felt helpless, trapped in a nightmare from which there was no waking.

As the monsters advanced relentlessly, they slaughtered every villager one by one. Lea broke into tears, her cry of despair drowned out by the brutal sounds of the massacre. She felt powerless and impotent in the face of the terrible fate that had befallen her village.

When Lea closed her eyes and opened them again, she found herself hanging, bound from the ceiling. Panic seized her as she realized she still couldn't move. She shook desperately at her restraints, but they were too tight.

Her eyes scanned her surroundings and they widened in horror at what she saw. Olaf stood nearby, a dark aura of evil surrounding him and before him lay Elena, her body drenched in blood, motionless on the ground.

Lea screamed at Olaf, her voice filled with rage and despair. "Leave Elena alone, you miserable bastard!" she shouted with clenched fury, her eyes burning with tears and anger.

Olaf sneered at Lea, his eyes glinting with malicious delight as he produced a baton. A cold shiver ran down Lea's spine as she dreaded what was about to happen next.

Lea was forced to watch helplessly as Olaf repeatedly struck Elena. Each blow hit Lea like a hammer to the heart. Her sister's screams tore through her soul, shaking her to the core. Every cry of pain seemed to rattle Lea's bones and her fury grew beyond measure.

Lea fought with all her strength to free herself, but her bonds held her mercilessly captive. She tugged and twisted, her muscles straining with effort, but it was in vain. She could only watch as her sister's suffering grew worse and worse.

Anger and sorrow were etched on Lea's face, her eyes blazing with wrath and her cheeks stained with tears. But despite her spirit and strength, she was powerless against the cruelty unfolding before her eyes.

Meanwhile, the shadows tried to overwhelm Fiona, yet whenever they approached her, they seemed unable to touch her. It was as if they sensed an invisible barrier around her, keeping them from reaching or engulfing her.

Fiona looked at her friends, who lay on the ground in pain, trapped by the shadows. Her heart ached at the sight and her despair grew with each passing moment.

"Gronak, Lea, can you hear me? Talk to me!" Fiona cried out in desperation, her voice filled with hope and fear.

She prayed fervently that her friends could hear her, that they could stand together even in this darkest of hours.

In the darkness of the room, Fiona suddenly heard a voice that seemed to come from all directions. Confused, she looked around, but there was no one to be seen. The voice was both menacing and mesmerizing, filling the room with an eerie presence.

"I'm surprised my shadows can't attack you," the voice echoed through the room. "No one has ever managed that before. I'm very impressed."

Fiona felt a chilling cold within her as she heard the words. Her thoughts raced as she tried to grasp the meaning behind them. Anger surged within her as she remembered her friends, who might now be in grave danger. "You can keep your praise!" Fiona shouted into the room, her voice defiant yet tinged with fear. "What have you done to my friends?"

The voice laughed arrogantly, its words cutting through the air with a sinister coldness. "Your companions have fallen victim to my shadow creatures," it announced triumphantly. "They are currently enduring hellish torments, reliving their deepest fears and nightmares over and over again."

Fiona's heart pounded faster as she realized the horrifying truth. Her friends were in the clutches of this unknown enemy, trapped in an endless nightmare from which there was no escape. Her thoughts swirled and a wave of despair threatened to engulf her.

The voice paused briefly before continuing in a threatening tone. "By the way, you should hurry if you want to help your friends," it warned. "Otherwise, they will soon die from the torments my shadows are inflicting on them." With those words, the voice fell silent, leaving Fiona alone with her despair.

Fiona felt paralyzed by fear and helplessness. The despair threatened to overwhelm her as she looked at her fallen friends, writhing in pain on the ground. Tears welled up in her eyes, but she forced herself to stay focused. She couldn't give up, not now, when her friends needed her the most.

Fiona knelt beside Gronak and desperately tried to wake him. She shook him, called his name, but Gronak didn't respond. His body was curled in pain on the ground and his eyes remained closed, as if he were trapped in a deep sleep.

Lea, too, lay beside him, her breathing shallow and irregular. A wave of despair crashed over Fiona as she realized that her friends weren't waking up. Tears filled her eyes as she felt helpless, unable to do anything to help them.

The shadows around Fiona continued to approach menacingly, yet strangely, they hesitated to attack her. A sense of fear seemed to emanate from Fiona, causing the shadows to waver, as if they were afraid of her.

Suddenly, Fiona noticed a faint green light emanating from her bag. Her hand trembled as she opened it and discovered the familiar rune crystal. It was her last hope to save her friends.

Tears blurred her vision as she clutched the crystal tightly, focusing all her magic into it. A pulsating green glow surrounded her as she poured the power of her hope into the crystal.

The light from the rune crystal grew more intense, radiant and a bright green glow filled the room. Fiona felt a wave of hope wash over her as she faced the shadows that held her friends captive.

With trembling hands, she placed the crystal on Gronak's body, then on Lea's. The warm glow of the rune transferred to her friends and a strange hissing sound filled the air.

The shadows that had enveloped Gronak and Lea began to scream as the bright light of the rune pierced through them. Fiona felt the darkness around her recede as the shadows gradually began to dissolve. With each passing moment, the threat diminished until the shadows finally vanished completely, as if they had never existed.

Gronak and Lea lay unconscious before Fiona, their chests rising and falling heavily with the rhythm of their breathing. Fiona felt panic rising within her as she once again tried to wake her friends. She gently shook Gronak's shoulder while carefully supporting Lea's head.

Suddenly, Lea's eyes snapped open, panicked and drenched in sweat and she began to scream. "Elena! Olaf! I will..." Her voice trailed off and her eyes appeared confused, as if she were still trapped in a nightmare.

Fiona held her friend and tried to soothe her. "It's okay, Lea. Elena is safe, you're with us. You're safe now." Her words were calming, but Lea still seemed to be under the influence of the terror she had experienced, her panic clearly visible.

Gronak slowly opened his eyes and when he saw Fiona, tears of joy welled up. "Fiona, is that you?" His voice was weak but filled with relief.

Fiona turned to Gronak with a smile, her eyes radiating comfort and reassurance. "Yes, Gronak, I'm here. Everything is okay. It was just a nightmare," she reassured him gently, placing a comforting hand on his shoulder.

A look of relief spread across Gronak's face and he took a deep breath. His smile was faint but genuine. Yet despite his outward calm, the traces of the horrors he had witnessed were still etched on his face.

"Thank you for saving me, Fiona," Gronak said, his voice a mix of gratitude and exhaustion. "I don't know how much longer I could have held on without you. Without your help, I would have been lost." His words were sincere and Fiona felt the depth of his gratitude in every sentence.

After Gronak and Lea had calmed down and gathered their strength, Fiona sat with them to explain what had happened. She shared her experience with the mysterious shadows and the menacing voice that seemed to come from nowhere. Gronak and Lea listened intently as they tried to process the events.

Once everything had been discussed, the three of them stood up together. A sense of tension hung in the air as they looked towards the gate at the top of the stairs. This was their moment, their chance to confront the evil that threatened them.

Gronak turned to his friends and spoke with a determined voice. "Let's end this, once and for all!" His gaze was strong and he exuded a resolve that spread to his companions.

Fiona and Lea nodded silently, a sign of their resolve. Together, they began their ascent up the stairs to the gate, ready to face the unknown and fight for the survival of their world.

When they reached the top, the heroes stood before the ornate gate that marked the entrance to the throne room. The atmosphere was tense as Fiona spoke to her friends. "Please, draw all your weapons. I will enhance them with my magic. We can't leave anything to chance."

Gronak unsheathed his massive sword and also grabbed the axe that was fastened to his belt. Lea, with her bow in hand, also drew the familiar knife she always carried. Worry was etched on her face as she prepared for the battle.

Fiona focused, channeling her magic. A mystical blue light enveloped the heroes' weapons as she infused them with her power. The light pulsed with a certain force, indicating that they were ready for battle, to face the evil ahead.

Gronak and Lea could feel the power emanating from their weapons. It was as if a spark of determination and strength flowed from the enhanced weapons into their veins.

Gronak looked at his companions and spoke in a firm voice. "The moment has come. We don't know what awaits us beyond the gate, but no matter what happens, we must stop Xalis." His words were filled with the courage to defeat the evil.

The two women nodded, their eyes reflecting confidence as they prepared to confront the enemy. Gronak stepped forward to the massive gate and pushed against it with all his might. His muscles tensed as he tried to open the gate.

The gate slowly opened and an icy breeze blew against the group as if the room itself was trying to push them away. Gronak shoved the gate fully open and the group now stood at the entrance of the vast chamber.

The throne room stretched out before them, dark, cold and menacing. Majestic columns rose to the very high ceiling, casting the interior into shadow. The oppressive atmosphere was palpable, as if it sought to crush the group.

On either side of the room were narrow, yet very tall windows through which they could see the rain and storm outside, pounding relentlessly against the glass. The sound of the rain and thunder filled the throne room with an eerie backdrop, intensifying the tension within the group.

At the end of the room stood a massive throne, upon which a dark presence sat, shrouded in the shadow that dominated the room. The figure on the throne remained hidden, its face and intentions concealed from the group's sight.

The throne room was illuminated only by the eerie light of the lightning outside, casting threatening shadows across the room. Each flash of lightning briefly illuminated the outlines of the mighty columns and the throne before the darkness swallowed them again.

From the darkness came a slow clap, followed by a voice as sinister as death itself. "I am quite impressed that you made it this far," the voice echoed, filled with a malevolent presence. "And especially you, young lady, for managing to free your friends from the grasp of my shadow creatures," the voice continued.

Gronak broke the silence of the room with a powerful shout into the darkness. "Show yourself, Xalis! We know you're here!" His voice echoed through the throne room, charged with the tension of the impending battle.

The dark figure on the throne began to laugh diabolically, a malevolent sound that filled the air. "Such arrogance you display, my warrior friend," the voice mocked. "But allow me to introduce myself properly."

A snap pierced the darkness and suddenly hundreds of candles along the walls and in the grand chandeliers ignited. The warm light of the flames cut through the gloom, illuminating the room and revealing the majestic columns and the throne.

The group looked toward the throne, where a man sat, cloaked in a black robe that seemed to swallow his form in the flickering candlelight. His pale skin appeared even more ghostly in the glow of the flames and his dark hair fell ominously over his shoulders.

It was his eyes, however, that captured the group's attention. Red, glowing eyes, so dark and menacing that they felt as though they were staring into the depths of hell. The eyes of the dark sorcerer Xalis burned with malice and a lust for power and every movement in his face exuded a sinister aura.

His thin, pale lips curled into a cold smile that heightened the tension in the air. Xalis sat on his throne like a ruler of darkness and decay and the group could feel the malevolence radiating from him, an impenetrable aura that surrounded him.

Xalis is arrogant gaze pierced through the room's darkness as he looked down at the three heroes, a cynical grin on his lips. Slowly, he rose from his throne and spread his arms wide, a commanding gesture that emphasized his dominion over the fortress. "Welcome to the Fortress of Asasel," Xalis began, his voice dripping with conceit, "and as you rightly said, I am Xalis, Lord of Darkness and the future king of this land."

Gronak clenched his fist in anger and took a step forward. "King, you say? You monster, you don't deserve to carry that title!" His voice trembled with rage.

Lea, too, refused to hold back and called out firmly to Xalis. "Exactly! A king is kind to his people. But you kill indiscriminately and ravage the land with your monsters! So many innocents have already died because of you. We won't allow this to continue!"

The heroes' words echoed through the throne room, filled with courage and determination. But Xalis seemed to absorb their words with a mixture of mockery and superiority, his smile unchanged and his red eyes glowing with malice.

Xalis stood tall before his throne and looked down upon the three heroes, his grin a sign of his perceived dominance. "So, you say you won't allow it?" he sneered. "I believe you're overestimating your situation."

Fiona stepped forward boldly and spoke with a voice blazing with anger. "I don't think so, Xalis! We've come to destroy you once and for all!"

Gronak stepped beside her and added in his powerful voice, "We're going to finish what Thorfinn couldn't. You will die here today, you bastard!"

As Xalis heard the name Thorfinn, his mood shifted abruptly to fury. "That damned Thorfinn!" he growled. "If that bastard hadn't sealed me back then, I would have..." His voice choked with rage and he clenched his fists in anger.

Xalis paused his words and began to speak calmly, though his eyes still burned with wrath. "But it doesn't matter," he began, "the artifact that sealed me is no more. And without it, there's no being alive that can challenge my power."

Lea pointed at Xalis and replied firmly, "We're not here to seal you. We're here to kill you today, to protect this land and all its people."

Xalis grew increasingly enraged by his intruders. "You little worms have some nerve. But I've had enough," he snarled darkly, "the only ones who will die here today are you!"

As Xalis spoke with malicious arrogance, a dark, black aura enveloped him, radiating a menacing presence. The sorcerer's red eyes glowed dangerously and his words echoed through the throne room, causing the three companions to tremble.

"Do you really think you can stand against me?" Xalis boasted, his grin full of conceit. "I am the Lord of Darkness, my power is invincible and you will soon learn what it means to be in my grasp. You'll wish for death before I'm done with you!"

The malice in his voice pierced the air, sending a cold shiver down the spines of Gronak, Fiona and Lea. They felt the ominous power emanating from Xalis and knew they were preparing for a battle of epic proportions.

Determination flared in Gronak's eyes as he readied himself for combat. "It begins," he muttered quietly, gripping his massive sword tightly. He looked to his companions and nodded. "Get ready!"

The three heroes assumed their fighting stances, prepared to face the dark lord. The air in the throne room was tense and Xalis is black aura filled the space as he extended his arm toward the group, his grin brimming with confidence.

The black aura enveloped the three heroes, forming a pulsating sphere of darkness around them. Xalis laughed triumphantly, believing he had finally defeated his foes. "This is pure dark magic; it will burn you from the inside and inflict torments worse than death."

But suddenly, a bright green light pierced through the darkness of the sphere, causing it to crack and crumble piece by piece until it eventually collapsed entirely. Xalis stared in disbelief at Gronak, Fiona and Lea, who stood unharmed and resolute amidst the remnants of the black sphere. Confusion and irritation flickered across his face as he tried to comprehend what had just happened.

Fiona still held the rune crystal firmly in her hand, its glow continuing to emit an aura of protection and power. Xalis could feel the energy emanating from the crystal and his frustration over the failure of his plan intensified.

"How did you escape my darkness?" Xalis asked, his voice laced with irritation as he eyed the three heroes suspiciously. His tone was threatening, but there was also a hint of uncertainty as he struggled to understand how they had eluded his grasp.

Fiona extended the rune crystal in her hand toward Xalis. In her other hand, she firmly held the sacred book, its pages infused with centuries-old knowledge and divine power. A magical green circle of protection formed around Fiona, shielding her and her companions from Xalis is dark machinations.

The rune crystal began to glow ever brighter as Fiona combined her magic with the power of the sacred book. The light radiating from the crystal shone with an intense divine power, pushing back the surrounding darkness of Xalis and holding him at bay. The oppressive darkness that had once surrounded them slowly receded before the brilliant glow of the crystal, filling the room with a sense of hope.

Fiona's gaze locked onto Xalis, her eyes blazing with determination. Her voice was clear and resolute as she spoke. "Your mistake was underestimating us!" Her tone was filled with confidence and strength. "We are stronger than you ever imagined and we will stop you, no matter the cost!"

A radiant circle of light began to form around Xalis, its glow intensifying with each passing second. The green circle of light tightened around Xalis, restricting his movements. His eyes widened in confusion as he stared down at his feet, feeling the divine power of the light circle envelop him. He struggled against the invisible bonds, but the strength of the circle held him fast, giving him no room to escape.

"What is happening?" Xalis muttered with a mix of confusion and anger as he desperately tried to break free from the magical barrier. His movements became more frantic as he felt the invisible restraints binding him, yet the power of the light circle was too strong, leaving him no chance to flee. The dark power that had made him seemingly invincible now seemed powerless.

In this critical moment, a mighty beam of light erupted from the rune crystal, engulfing Xalis completely. The blinding green light pierced through the darkness of his aura, burning away every trace of shadow. Xalis is eyes widened in shock and pain as he felt the relentless force of the light sear his skin.

Xalis was forced to his knees as the pillar of light neutralized his dark powers and rendered him powerless. The black aura that had surrounded him, the source of his strength, vanished entirely. A sense of exhaustion washed over him, his limbs feeling heavy and weak as though all energy had been drained from him.

"What in the hell have you done to me?" Xalis roared in desperation. His voice echoed through the room, filled with anger and frustration as he realized that his dark powers had been broken. He tried to resist the power of the light, but every attempt was in vain. The light held him in its unyielding grip, merciless and all-encompassing.

Fiona stood before him, her eyes shining with inner strength. "We've thwarted your dark plans with the rune crystal, Xalis," she said with unwavering determination. "You underestimated the power of the light and now you will face the consequences."

Gronak gripped his sword tightly, his eyes glinting with tension and fury. In a voice filled with anger, he shouted at Xalis, "Your black magic can't save you now. We will make you pay for all the suffering you've caused! You will answer for your crimes!"

A brief silence fell over the throne room as the circle of light around Xalis disappeared and he knelt seemingly defeated on the floor. But then, he began to laugh, a laugh full of arrogance and condescension that grew louder, filling the room.

His laughter echoed through the hall as he slowly stood up, his face taking on an expression of pure madness and unrestrained power. "So you think that just because you've banished my dark magic, I'm now defenseless?" Xalis sneered with a malevolent grin. "Let me tell you something. Before I even attained my black magic, I was already considered the strongest sorcerer in the land. So, if you think I'm now an easy opponent, you're sorely mistaken!"

A menacing pause followed as Xalis continued his speech. "However, I must commend you. You have achieved what no one before you has. Not even the three would-be heroes who sealed me away back then could withstand my black magic."

Xalis is words were filled with an unyielding pride in his powers and a threatening undertone that made it clear he was far from being defeated. The heroes felt the looming danger emanating from him and knew that the battle was far from over.

Xalis concentrated magic in his hands and formed powerful fire magic, which manifested into dangerous fireballs. With a sinister smile, he hurled the burning projectiles at the heroes to destroy them.

Fiona reacted in an instant and stepped in front of her friends, raising her hands to create a protective shield. An aura of glowing light surrounded her as she repelled the flames rushing toward them. The shield trembled under the force of the attack, but it held firm, protecting the group from the destructive flames.

Gronak saw the opportunity and called out to Lea. "It's our turn now!" Gripping his sword tightly, he charged at Xalis with Lea by his side, ready to confront the dark sorcerer. Their footsteps echoed loudly through the throne room as they approached the enemy, their courage unwavering despite the looming danger.

Gronak swung his mighty sword with all his strength, aiming to pierce through Xalis and defeat the dark sorcerer. At the same time, Lea nocked several arrows on her bow and skillfully released them at Xalis, hoping to break through his defense.

But the heroes were surprised when they saw both the arrows and Gronak's sword bounce off an impenetrable magical shield surrounding Xalis. The shield seemed to effortlessly deflect every attack and the heroes' efforts appeared to be in vain.

Xalis laughed, unimpressed by the heroes' attack. His voice echoed through the throne room, full of arrogance. "You must have thought it would go differently, didn't you?" he mocked. "You're not the only ones who can create a shield. My magic is invincible and will destroy you all." His grin was full of superiority as he challenged the heroes.

Despite their relentless efforts, Gronak and Lea seemed powerless against Xalis is powerful shield. Each of their attacks was easily deflected by Xalis, as if he could foresee their every move.

Gronak's muscles tensed as he swung his sword again, but each time he struck, he was thrown back by an invisible barrier. Lea's arrows bounced off the barrier without causing any damage. Frustration began to build within them as they realized that their previous efforts had been in vain.

The two heroes exchanged a discouraged glance as the certainty that they were in a hopeless situation solidified within them. Yet despite the frustration and despair in their hearts, they did not retreat. They were ready to keep fighting until they found a way to defeat Xalis.

Fiona's mind raced as she searched for a solution to overcome Xalis is impenetrable shield. She knew they needed a more powerful force to stand against the dark lord. With a concerned look, she called out to her friends. "Gronak! Lea! Fall back!" Fiona shouted with an urgent seriousness.

Gronak and Lea understood the significance of her words and withdrew from the uneven battle. Together, they gathered around Fiona, pondering how they could proceed against Xalis.

Xalis, meanwhile, remained unimpressed in front of his throne, his eyes gleaming with superiority as he wondered what the three heroes planned to do next. He grinned as he awaited their attempt to challenge his superior power.

Gronak felt the exhaustion in his muscles as he turned to Fiona, breathing heavily. His eyes searched hers for a spark of hope. "Do you have a plan, Fiona?" he asked, a hint of desperation in his voice.

"Yes, I have a plan. I'm going to enchant your weapons once more. That should be enough to break through his powerful shield," Fiona said confidently in the face of Xalis is overwhelming strength.

The tension in the air was palpable as Fiona concentrated her magic. Every muscle in her body was tense as she placed her hands on Gronak's and Lea's weapons. An intense glow surrounded the swords and arrows as they were infused with the concentrated power of her magic. The glow grew ever brighter and one could feel the weapons being charged with new energy.

Xalis watched the process with increasing discontent. His face, which had previously radiated arrogance, darkened as he realized what the group was attempting. A look of pure rage overtook his features and his hands clenched into fists. "That little witch!" he growled angrily to himself, as he felt his control over the situation slipping away.

Xalis gathered his magic and directed it at Fiona, who was in the midst of performing her enchantment. A moment of inattention, a split second of weakness and Xalis fired a concentrated beam of his destructive magic at Fiona.

For Gronak and Lea, a scene of horror unfolded as they helplessly watched time seem to slow down. The deadly beam pierced Fiona's right chest, leaving a deep wound from which blood flowed profusely.

The screams of agony shattered the silence of the throne room as Fiona collapsed to the ground under the immense pain. The floor became soaked with her blood and the desperate cries echoed throughout the room. Gronak and Lea were paralyzed by the horror they were witnessing.

Lea did not hesitate for a second and immediately rushed to Fiona on the ground, her heart pounding with panic as she tried to stop the bleeding. With trembling hands, she pressed firmly on the wound, but the blood seemed unstoppable. "Hold on, Fiona," she whispered with a broken voice, her eyes full of tears.

Gronak turned to Xalis with an inhuman rage, his muscles tensed with fury. "You will pay for this, Xalis!" he roared. His eyes gleamed as he prepared to confront his enemy.

Xalis stood there grinning at Gronak, his gaze full of arrogance. He seemed confident in his power, savoring the anger of his opponent. The aura around him pulsed with strength and he appeared ready to repel any attack.

Gronak charged at Xalis in a fit of rage, his blade raised for a devastating strike. With a powerful leap, he launched himself into the air to attack his foe. At the decisive moment, he brought his sword down.

However, Xalis once again conjured a shield, his magic forming an impenetrable barrier around him. Yet as Gronak's blade struck the shield, it began to crack the force of the attack was too great for Xalis is defense. The barrier crumbled under the pressure of Gronak's relentless assault and a moment of hope sparked in the hearts of the heroes.

Xalis immediately recognized the danger and deftly dodged Gronak's attack, his body swift and agile like that of a predator. At the same time, Xalis noticed that Fiona had managed to enchant the weapons just in time. A look of surprise flashed across his face, followed by a moment of fury. His eyes blazed with anger as he realized the heroes were stronger than he had anticipated.

While Gronak and Xalis were locked in a fierce battle, Lea desperately turned her attention to Fiona. She rummaged through Fiona's pockets, her hands hurried and impatient as she searched for a healing potion. But her search was in vain and a moment of panic threatened to overwhelm her.

Desperate, Lea instead grabbed some healing herbs she found in Fiona's pouch. She applied them to the wound, which was still bleeding heavily, her hands trembling with tension. The herbs seemed to bring some relief to the wound, but the blood flow wouldn't relent.

Lea tore a strip of cloth from her sleeve, attempting to make a makeshift bandage. Her heart pounded with effort, but she didn't give up as she frantically tried to stabilize Fiona, giving her a chance at recovery as she gasped in pain.

Lea glanced over at Gronak and saw her friend fighting with all his might against Xalis. Her heart clenched as she watched Gronak take heavy blows, but also strike back hard. However, every hit he landed seemed not to faze Xalis, which only deepened Lea's concern.

Gronak looked visibly weakened and injured, his breath labored, his face streaked with sweat and blood. Yet despite his exhaustion, he fought on fiercely, his resolve unbroken.

Lea felt torn between helping Gronak and tending to Fiona, who lay on the ground struggling for her life. She was desperate and didn't know what to do. The situation seemed hopeless and fear threatened to overwhelm her.

In that moment, Lea heard Fiona's faint voice. Her eyes filled with tears as she looked down at her friend, who lay on the ground, her face contorted in pain. "Lea, please help Gronak," Fiona asked in a trembling voice. "I'll manage."

Lea swallowed hard, her throat dry with fear and desperation. She knew Fiona desperately needed help in this situation, but she couldn't abandon Gronak. An inner battle raged within her as she tried to make a decision that could determine the fate of her friends.

Lea felt a mix of anger toward Xalis and relief that Fiona was still alive. Determination flared within her as she decided to rush to Gronak's aid. "I'm going to help Gronak now. Please, don't push yourself too hard, Fiona," she said firmly as she stood up.

With a determined gaze fixed on Xalis, Lea charged forward. But Xalis noticed her movement and reacted immediately. He unleashed several fireballs that shot toward Lea. She skillfully ducked and dodged the attacks, all while planning her own counterattacks.

With practiced hands, she drew her bow and fired arrows at Xalis. The dark lord deftly avoided most of the arrows, but one struck his leg, causing him to stagger briefly.

Meanwhile, Gronak slowly fought his way back to his feet. His body ached, but his resolve to defeat Xalis remained unbroken. With a furious roar, he launched another attack, his sword gripped tightly in his hand.

Fiona, in the meantime, battled intense pain as she tried to heal her own wound. Every attempt was marked by agony, but she didn't give up. With each passing second, she bravely fought against the pain to help herself and support her friends.

Gronak and Lea fought side by side against Xalis as he bombarded them with powerful magical attacks. The air was filled with lightning, fireballs and energy waves emanating from Xalis is powerful aura.

Despite their combined resistance, Xalis maintained the upper hand. His attacks were relentless and seemed unstoppable. Gronak and Lea fought desperately, but their strength was slowly waning.

Xalis laughed triumphantly as he watched the two exhausted warriors before him. "I truly underestimated you, but I am far beyond your capabilities. However, I'll give you one last chance to escape your hopeless situation alive," he declared, his voice dripping with superiority.

Gronak and Lea watched intently as Xalis continued. "Join my army. Fight for me and you will become even more powerful than you are now."

A moment of silence followed as Gronak and Lea contemplated the dark lord's words. But their resolve was unwavering. "Never!" Gronak shouted, his voice filling the room with strength. "We will never fight for you, Xalis! We would rather die than submit to your dark power!"

Lea nodded in agreement. "We will fight together and win, no matter what sacrifices we must make. Your reign of terror ends here and now!"

Xalis laughed mockingly as he heard Gronak and Lea's words. "Fools! Very well, if you wish to die here, so be it," he sneered, his voice brimming with triumphant arrogance. Suddenly, Xalis began to float, his form rising majestically into the air. Gronak and Lea looked up at him in shock, wondering what he was about to do.

Black lightning made of pure magic crackled around Xalis, filling the air with a menacing tension. The room began to tremble as dark energies coalesced around the dark lord.

Gronak and Lea could feel the pressure of Xalis is magical power testing their limits. Despite the looming threat and the overwhelming superiority of their opponent, they stood firm, ready to fight for good and for their friends, even if it was to be their last battle.

Rain pounded relentlessly against the windows of the throne room and the thunder outside made the scene even more terrifying. The low rumble of the storm echoed through the chamber as Xalis continued to gather his magic, preparing to unleash his devastating attack on Gronak, Lea and Fiona.

Lea reached for her bow and aimed at Xalis. She released the arrow, hoping to weaken the dark lord even slightly. But the magic he had amassed was so powerful that the arrow simply bounced off, as if it had struck an impenetrable barrier.

In Gronak and Lea's eyes, pure fear was reflected as they saw the devastating attack coming. The darkness emanating from Xalis seemed to swallow everything and they knew they could hardly stand against such power.

Fiona, despite being in unimaginable pain, realized what Xalis was planning and desperately tried to rise. Her body trembled with effort and her face was contorted with agony, but she refused to be deterred from her goal of helping her friends and stopping the evil before them.

Fiona began to gather her own magic. With the last of her strength, she focused on activating the power of the sacred book she carried. Her hands shook with the strain as she clutched the book tightly.

Xalis noticed Fiona's desperate attempt and sneered. "It's too late, little mage. You and your friends will perish and there's nothing you can do." His voice dripped with scorn and arrogance, as he seemed to revel in his dominance.

Fiona ignored Xalis is taunts and despite her excruciating pain, she retrieved the sacred book. Blood dripped from her hand onto the pages as she slowly opened it. As if guided by a higher power, the pages began to flip on their own until they suddenly stopped.

Fiona's eyes began to glow and a white aura formed around her. The air around her seemed to hum with energy and a sense of purity and hope filled the room. It was as if the very essence of light enveloped her, infusing her with divine power.

Fiona extended her left arm toward Xalis as the white aura around her grew stronger. The power of the sacred book flowed through her and she felt an immense strength rising within her.

Xalis was visibly impressed by Fiona's resolve, though he still laughed at her attempt to defy him. His dark form trembled slightly in surprise as he recognized the extent of Fiona's power, but his arrogance made him believe he remained invincible.

With a grim expression, Xalis unleashed a concentrated bolt of magic, a lightning strike that shot across the room. His malevolent energy was so intense that it seemed to darken the air around him as the bolt surged relentlessly toward its target.

Fiona, her eyes fixed on Xalis, had gathered all her magic in her left hand. With a determined expression, she simultaneously fired a powerful beam of light from her hand. The beam of pure light pierced the room with its radiant energy as it shot directly towards the dark lightning. The intensity of her light stood in stark contrast to the darkness of Xalis attack.

The two opposing attacks collided in a clash of light and darkness. A massive crackling filled the room, accompanied by an explosion of pure energy as the forces struggled for dominance.

The surroundings trembled as the two powerful magical attacks clashed. The impact sent shockwaves through the throne room, the walls quaking under the unimaginable force emanating from the opposing energies. Cracks formed in the stone walls as the structure of the room seemed threatened by the sheer power of the collision.

The window panes rattled ominously under the pressure, some even shattering from the tremendous shock. Shards flew through the air, accompanied by a mournful howl of wind rushing through the broken openings. Cold rain entered the throne room, leaving damp spots on the floor that amplified the glow of the spells.

Gronak and Lea stood in stunned silence, their eyes wide as they watched the menacing spectacle unfold. The intensity of the battle between light and darkness was overwhelming and they could only watch in awe and growing concern as the forces of magic shook the throne room. The threat of uncontrolled energy was palpable and they knew they had to act to save their world.

Fiona, still gravely injured, fought bravely against the weight of the effort. Every breath seemed a struggle and despite her injuries and blood loss, she persevered as she stood against Xalis. Her robe was stained with dark blood, her face twisted in pain, but her eyes still glowed with determination. With every fiber of her being, she resisted the power of the Lord of Darkness, her willpower unbroken.

Lea felt the pressure of desperation as she saw Fiona suffering under Xalis attacks. A hint of fear tinged her voice as she called out to Gronak. "Gronak! We have to do something; Fiona can't hold out much longer." Every word was laced with a trace of panic as she watched her friend's struggle.

Gronak's reaction was immediate. His eyes blazed with tension as he drew his mighty axe from its sheath and turned to Lea. His voice was powerful and charged with energy. "We attack Xalis!"

A deep growl escaped his throat as he hurled the axe with impressive force at Xalis. At the same time, Lea drew her bow and released her thunder arrows with a precise shot at the dark mage. The air was filled with the courage of the two heroes as they stood against the evil.

The weapons sliced through the air with unprecedented force, filling the room with tension. The icy axe and the flashing arrows struck against the impenetrable magical barrier that surrounded Xalis. A massive explosion of ice and lightning erupted, filling the room with a deafening roar and causing the ground to tremble.

The massive explosion caused by the clash of magical forces had devastating effects on the surroundings. A portion of the ceiling collapsed under the force and massive stone blocks came crashing down. Gronak, weakened by exhaustion and caught off guard by the sudden danger, couldn't react in time.

The stones rained down on him and although he tried to shield himself, he couldn't withstand the onslaught. A heavy chunk struck him with great force, hurling him to the ground. Dust swirled around him as he lay motionless, buried under the rubble. Lea screamed in horror as she saw her loyal companion hit by the falling stones.

Xalis is expression betrayed his surprise at the sudden attack from Gronak and Lea. His face was momentarily shadowed by irritation and his concentration wavered as the force of the attack struck him. The powerful impact caused him to recoil as he struggled to regain his composure.

In this critical moment, Fiona noticed Xalis is distraction. Despite her severe injuries and agonizing pain, she gathered her remaining strength and concentrated all of her remaining magic into one final desperate assault against the Lord of Darkness.

A brilliantly bright beam of light emanated from Fiona's hand, filled with a power that seemed to come from the depths of her despair. Every spark of her magic was like a cry for justice, a final stand against the darkness that surrounded her. This beam was stronger than ever before, shining and radiant in its purity and it relentlessly pushed back Xalis is lightning with unstoppable force.

By the time Xalis realized the unexpected strength of Fiona's final attack, it was already too late. A look of surprise and horror flashed across his face, but he couldn't escape the relentless stream of light. The concentrated energy struck him with unyielding force and he was thrown back by the power of the beam. A massive explosion erupted, a fusion of radiant light and dark lightning that filled the room. Xalis crashed to the ground, his once-proud smile long gone, as he hit the hard floor with a dull thud. The Dark Lord lay motionless, defeated by the power of the light that brought him down.

Meanwhile, Fiona's entire body trembled, her muscles strained from the effort and her skin pale with pain. Every breath was a challenge, her body exhausted from the relentless battle and the loss of blood. Dark red blood flowed continuously from her wound, a steady stream that soaked her clothing and stained the floor beneath her. With each passing second, her strength waned until she barely had the energy to remain standing.

Her heartbeat echoed in her ears, a dull thudding that seemed to overwhelm her consciousness. It was as if time itself was trapped in an endless cycle of pain and exhaustion. Fiona fought desperately against the impending darkness, against the void that threatened to consume her. Finally, as the world around her began to blur and everything faded into darkness, she lost consciousness and collapsed to the ground.

Lea looked on in panic at her friends, who lay incapacitated on the ground, while Xalis, severely injured, lay on his back, gasping for breath. The strain of his powerful attack had exhausted him, but despite his injuries, he still seemed dangerous.

Then Xalis slowly opened his eyes and Lea could see him trying to rise with great effort and pain. A spark of terror shot through her as she realized that the Dark Lord was still alive. His gaze was full of rage and fury and Lea knew that she and her friends were in an extremely dangerous situation.

Lea felt the fighting spirit rise within her as she prepared to face the Dark Lord once more. Her hand gripped the bow tightly, her eyes gleaming with determination.

Xalis was gravely wounded, but his power seemed undiminished. Every fiber of his being radiated anger and wrath as he slowly approached Fiona, who still lay on the ground, severely injured and bleeding.

With practiced hands, Lea drew her bow and aimed at Xalis as he moved slowly toward Fiona. Her heart pounded wildly with excitement and fear as she released the arrow.

Xalis sensed the incoming attack and abruptly turned to Lea. His eyes sparkled with superiority as he dodged the arrow with a smooth motion. A dark grin appeared on his face as he prepared to attack Lea.

Suddenly, Xalis conjured a black sword out of thin air, which materialized in his hands. With a menacing look, he charged at Lea, his voice dripping with contempt. "You little elven brat won't stand in my way!" he snarled in a sinister tone as he swung his sword.

Lea quickly drew her dagger from her belt pouch and readied herself for battle. Her grip on the dagger was firm, her eyes burning with determination. She knew she had to face the Dark Lord, no matter the cost.

Skillfully, Lea dodged Xalis is heavy sword strikes and launched counterattacks of her own. Her dagger flashed in the dim light of the throne room as she aimed for the vulnerable spots on Xalis is body. With every move, she tried to weaken the Dark Lord and inflict damage.

As Lea deftly evaded another attack and drove her dagger deep into Xalis is thigh, a bone-chilling scream tore through the air. Xalis let out a cry of pain that filled the room, followed by a growl of rage. But before Lea could pull the blade out, Xalis suddenly grabbed her by the throat.

Lea felt his iron grip close around her neck and she was brutally lifted off the ground. The dagger slipped from her hand as Xalis hoisted her up and she kicked desperately in the air, trying to break free. But his grip was relentless and he slowly began to choke the life out of her.

Panic gripped Lea as she felt the darkness slowly envelop her mind. She struggled to break free from his iron grasp, her fingers clawing desperately at his arm, but she could barely breathe. Her heart raced with fear and her senses began to fade as the world around her turned into a darkening fog.

Xalis looked at Lea with grim hatred and burning anger in his eyes, his voice filled with fury. "You three have annoyed me long enough!" he snarled menacingly. "How dare you even think to challenge me, Xalis!"

With a dark premonition, Xalis gathered his sinister magic in his hand and bolts of lightning began to surge through Lea's convulsing body. A deafening scream of agony echoed through the hall as Lea cried out in pain, writhing in his grasp.

Gronak, slowly regaining consciousness, heard the cries of his companion. His eyes widened in horror as he witnessed the dreadful scene unfolding before him. The hall was filled with the burning darkness of Xalis is magic and Lea struggled desperately against the torment being inflicted upon her.

Lea convulsed in pain, but Xalis held her mercilessly, his fingers like iron claws around her delicate neck. With a malevolent grin, he gathered the last of his magical reserves and placed his other hand on her abdomen.

An eerie wave of pressure surged through Lea's entire body and in that horrific moment, she was hurled away from Xalis with tremendous force. Her body flew through the air like a ragdoll, crashing into a massive pillar in the hall with bone-shattering impact.

The collision was of such incredible force that the massive pillar began to crack, fissures spreading across its surface like veins, forming a web of brittle stone. A thunderous crash resounded through the hall as the stone gave way under the relentless power of the collision.

The sound of splintering stone mixed with the sickening crack of breaking bones as Lea screamed in pain, her voice piercing and filled with anguish. Her body seemed to descend to the ground in slow motion, every movement accompanied by unbearable suffering.

When she finally hit the hard floor, Lea convulsed in pain, a slowly spreading pool of blood surrounding her motionless form. She appeared fragile and vulnerable amidst the chaos left in the wake of Xalis is ruthless assault.

Gronak, deeply shaken by the sight of his beloved friend, desperately tried to rise, but his muscles were too weak to obey. Despite his wild desire to rush to Lea's aid, he remained powerless on the ground, unable to protect her.

Xalis walked slowly and with eerie calm toward Lea, who was struggling to breathe. Each breath seemed a battle, her chest rising and falling in desperate attempts to draw air into her lungs.

Gronak, lying helplessly on the ground, looked at Xalis with an expression of despair. His voice trembled with rage and horror as he commanded the Dark Lord. "Leave her alone, you bastard!"

Unmoved by Gronak's words, Xalis now stood beside Lea, who was still gasping for breath in her death throes. A wicked grin spread across Xalis is lips as he turned his gaze to Gronak. His eyes gleamed with malice.

Suddenly, Xalis raised his foot and brought it down with full force on Lea's back. A bone-chilling scream of death pierced the silence of the hall as Lea crumpled under the brutal blow. Her screams reverberated through the room, seeming to cut the very air, while Gronak felt the blood in his veins turn to ice. The cruel brutality of Xalis is actions left no doubt that he knew neither mercy nor weakness.

Xalis continued to kick Lea, his blows filled with contempt and cruelty. Each kick felt like a hammer blow to Gronak's heart, as he helplessly watched his beloved friend being mercilessly abused. Lea's tear-filled eyes met his gaze and in her desperate look, he could read the fear and pain that pierced her soul.

A malicious laugh escaped Xalis throat as he raised his sword, which gleamed menacingly in the dim light of the hall. With an almost eerie calm and precision, he lowered the blade and drove it through Lea's back. A blood-curdling scream shattered the silence, accompanied by another torrent of tears and blood.

Gronak roared in despair and agony, but his cry lost its strength as he gazed into Lea's lifeless eyes. In that moment, he realized that the spark of life had left her, that her soul had been irrevocably consumed by this cruel act of violence. The silence that followed the end of her screams was filled with Gronak's excruciating loneliness and the irreparable loss he would never forget.

Xalis vile laughter echoed through the hall as he looked at Lea's motionless body lying in her own pool of blood. His grin was an expression of perverse satisfaction with his cruel work, as he felt triumphant.

His eyes slowly turned to Fiona, who lay unconscious on the ground. "Now it's the annoying mage's turn." A diabolical glint flickered in Xalis eyes as he slowly moved toward her, the power over life and death in his hands.

Gronak, desperately trying to rise, suddenly felt something unusual. The rune mark given to him by the Keeper began to glow in his palm, a sign of divine intervention and a reminder of his destiny.

A wave of unbridled power surged through Gronak, stronger than anything he had ever experienced before. With a mighty effort, he fought his way to his feet, his body infused with the divine energy that now flowed through and strengthened him. The determination in his eyes reflected an unyielding will to save his friend and the world from the dark threat.

Gronak grabbed his sword and stood ready to face Xalis. His voice echoed through the room as he challenged, "I am your opponent, Xalis! Let's settle this like real men!"

Xalis was surprised by Gronak's sudden surge of power. A dark smile curled his lips as he responded, "I didn't think you'd get up again. But if you're so eager to die in front of your friend, I'll grant you your wish."

The tension in the room was palpable as the two adversaries faced each other. Gronak's sword ignited in his hand, enveloped in a powerful aura. He fixed Xalis with a bold stare and prepared himself, ready to fight for his friend's survival.

Xalis black sword also began to shroud itself in a dark and threatening aura. The power of darkness seemed to course through him as he prepared to face Gronak. The atmosphere was tense and a fight to the death seemed inevitable.

Xalis and Gronak stood facing each other, heavily wounded, their breaths labored and their bodies bearing the marks of the previous battles. The tension in the room was extreme as the two fighters prepared to face off one last time.

With determined gazes, Gronak and Xalis launched their attacks. Their swords sparkled in the light of the lightning outside as they clashed with each other. The impact of their blades was so powerful that the ground beneath their feet seemed to tremble and a dull sound echoed through the throne room.

A long and grueling sword fight erupted between Gronak and Xalis. The swords whirled through the air as the two warriors fought with all their strength and skill. Every strike was precise, every defense a matter of split seconds. As the intense battle raged on, the storm outside continued to roar, with thunder shaking the throne room.

Xalis slowly began to gain the upper hand. With skillful dodges and swift counterattacks, he forced Gronak into a defensive position. A well-aimed strike hit Gronak, who was thrown to the ground after a hard collision.

Gronak fought bravely, but the superiority of his opponent was insurmountable. Exhausted and breathing heavily, he sank to his knees, feeling his strength waning. The pain of his injuries coursed through his body and he knew he had little energy left to continue the fight.

Xalis stood confidently over Gronak, his dark aura emanating a menacing presence. He regarded Gronak with a hint of recognition in his eyes. "You fought well, I'll give you that," he remarked with a mocking tone. "But now, it's over for you."

Gronak lifted his head and looked at Lea, who lay lifeless on the ground and at Fiona, who was gravely injured and unconscious. A sense of helplessness washed over him as he realized the extent of the destruction around him. With a heavy sigh, he turned to Xalis, his gaze filled with both fear and sorrow.

A wave of frustration surged through Gronak and he slammed his fist on the ground in anger. "I'm sorry, my friends," he muttered quietly, his voice filled with pain. "I failed to protect you."

Xalis reveled in Gronak's frustration and laughed arrogantly, his grin full of arrogance and malice. It seemed as if he was savoring every second of this triumphant moment, basking in the humiliation of his opponent.

In the decisive moment of his supposed victory, as Xalis stood triumphantly over Gronak, relishing his perceived superiority, something unexpected happened behind him. Lea's body was suddenly enveloped in a faint, orange light that gently pulsed around her. It was as if an invisible force surrounded her, tenderly beginning to heal her wounds.

The injuries that had previously marred her body slowly began to close as the warm light around her gently glowed. A soft, steady pulsing filled the room, as if the light itself was marking the rhythm of her returning life.

Suddenly, out of nowhere, Lea's heart began to beat again. It was as if a spark of life had returned to her and she took a deep breath as her lungs filled with air. The surprise was reflected in her wide-open eyes as she slowly regained consciousness and became aware of her surroundings.

A wave of confusion swept over her as she looked around and realized she was alive again. The relief of escaping death mingled with her growing anger. Her gaze fell forward, where Xalis stood triumphantly over Gronak, his sword raised, ready to deliver the final, deadly blow. The sight ignited a spark of panic in her and she knew she had to act to save her friend.

Lea, aware that she needed to move quickly, stretched out her hand with the last of her strength and grabbed her bow, lying next to her on the ground. She painfully pushed herself up, her expression a mix of fury and concern for Gronak, as she drew the bowstring and aimed it at Xalis.

Meanwhile, Xalis grinned at Gronak one last time, his voice dripping with malice. "When you die, I might heal your little mage friend, just to torture her over and over again," he taunted before swinging his sword down in a deadly attack on Gronak.

Filled with rage and frustration, Gronak looked up at Xalis, bracing himself to face the lethal blow. But to his astonishment, he noticed Xalis abruptly pausing, his sword trembling in his grasp.

Confused and alarmed, Xalis felt an inexplicable force surge through him, his body shaking from the effort. "What the hell! Who dares...?" his words were suddenly cut off as pain seemed to overwhelm him.

Lea had aimed precisely and shot Xalis with an arrow directly in the back. As Xalis turned in surprise and irritation, he saw Lea standing unsteadily and covered in blood, her bow drawn and her gaze fixed on him.

Surprise and disbelief painted themselves across Xalis face. "But how did you...? You were dead, you little elven brat!" he stammered, trying to comprehend the sudden turn of events.

Lea ignored his question and instead focused on her next move. With steely determination and hatred in her heart, she fired another arrow, this time striking directly into Xalis heart.

Xalis spat blood, his eyes widening in disbelief as he looked at Lea. The presence of the young elf bewildered him deeply. Gronak, watching the scene, was equally astonished by Lea's sudden reappearance. But he knew he had to act now to protect her and stop Xalis.

Despite his severe injuries, Xalis tried one last time to gather the remaining magic within him. A glowing fireball began to form in his hand, a menacing manifestation of his remaining power.

Lea saw the imminent attack coming, but her strength was spent and she had no means left to defend herself. With one last glance at Gronak, she collapsed from exhaustion, unable to continue the fight.

Xalis raised his hand to unleash the devastating attack when he suddenly felt a jolt that threw him off balance. Surprised, he paused and looked down in shock.

Lea lifted her head, her eyes widening in astonishment at what was happening. She realized that Gronak, despite his severe injuries, had managed to muster the last of his strength to stand up.

With a desperate surge of strength, Gronak plunged his sword with all his remaining might into Xalis is chest. The blade pierced through the darkness as it drove into the body of the Lord of Darkness.

A blinding light ignited around the sword and Xalis was engulfed in flames. A bone-chilling scream of agony tore from his throat as the flames consumed him. The heat licked at his body while he roared in a mix of pain and despair.

Gronak pulled the sword from Xalis is body and stared down at the once-powerful Lord of Darkness. "In the end, you were the fool, Xalis! You will never harm anyone again!" he declared with determination in his voice.

Xalis, now forced to his knees, was horrified by the unexpected turn of events. His proud face was twisted with confusion and rage. "I am the fool?" he mocked, his frustration growing in the face of his hopeless situation. "You are the fools if you think you will walk away from this alive!"

His words were a final, desperate attempt to assert his power as he faced his inevitable fate. The flames that surrounded his body slowly died out. The darkness swallowed the once-mighty Xalis.

Xalis let out a powerful scream that shook the surroundings, sending a shiver down Gronak and Lea's spines. His body trembled with darkness as he was engulfed in flames once more. But this time, the flames were not ordinary; they were pitch black and seemed to reflect the essence of his corrupt power.

"If I die, I'll drag you to death with me!" Xalis shouted with rage, the darkness enveloping him, his words laced with a sinister aura.

Suddenly, Xalis exploded with immense force, unleashing a massive shockwave. Gronak and Lea were thrown back with tremendous power, crashing hard to the ground. The thunder of the explosion echoed through the room, intensifying the gravity of the moment.

The dark fortress, which had witnessed Xalis is sinister reign for years, trembled to its very foundations under the unstoppable force of the devastating attack. The mighty walls, once thought to be insurmountable, cracked and collapsed in on themselves. The thunderous crashing was deafening as massive stone blocks plummeted to the ground, driven by the furious forces of destruction.

Dust, rubble and smoke swirled through the air in thick clouds, stirred by the falling debris. The dark fortress, once so majestic and menacing, was now engulfed in an infernal firestorm unleashed by Xalis.

The firestorm enveloped the fortress in a boiling cauldron of flames, seemingly striving to pierce the heavens themselves. The flames raged in vivid colors, from furious red to searing orange, roaring with a deep, ominous black. The sky above the fortress was shrouded in the darkness of the smoke and the world was swallowed by this apocalyptic inferno.

In this moment, as the dark fortress teetered on the brink of its inevitable demise, Gronak rose with the last reserves of his strength. He looked around and realized he had to act immediately. He grabbed the unconscious Fiona and the collapsed Lea. He held Lea under one arm while carrying Fiona over his shoulder. Together, he ran with the two women out of the burning fortress.

The air was filled with the sounds of destruction, with the shrill cries of the desperate structures collapsing in on themselves and the crackling and roaring of the all-consuming flames.

Gronak fought his way through the swirling smoke and the burning remains of the fortress, his body marked by exhaustion and battle. But he knew he had no time to pause. He kept running, his lungs burning from the effort and his heart beating in sync with the relentless chaos behind them.

Eventually, they reached the outer walls of the fortress and stormed into the open. There, at a safe distance from the fortress, he turned around and saw how the once-proud symbol of darkness was now sinking into a true inferno. The dark fortress, which had spawned so many terrors, was now a place of flames and destruction.

Lea slowly opened her eyes and saw the inferno around her. The flames were still roaring high, but something in the air had changed. The ominous aura of Xalis seemed to be fading and a sense of relief spread through her.

She looked up at Gronak, whose exhaustion and bliss were evident on his face. "Is it over, Gronak?" she asked with a weakened voice, her eyes filled with hope and exhaustion.

Gronak turned his gaze away from the fortress and smiled, exhausted but happy. "Yes, Lea," he replied, his voice tinged with relief. "We really did manage to stop Xalis."

A surge of joy passed through Lea and tears of relief ran down her cheeks. She smiled with happiness and felt a deep gratitude for her friends and for the victory over evil.

Slowly, the sky also began to clear and the sun's rays broke through the dark clouds. The land was illuminated by a warm light that signaled hope and a new beginning. The darkness receded before the light and the world seemed to be recovering from the terrors it had endured.

The group had defeated the mighty Xalis, but they paid a high price for their victory. The dark fortress, which had once been a stronghold of darkness, was no more. Their victory had driven away the darkness, but they bore the wounds of their heroic struggle and the memory of the cost they had paid.

Exhausted and heavily injured, but with a sense of fulfillment and pride in their heroic deed, Gronak and Lea looked back at the remains of the dark fortress. They had achieved the impossible together and saved the world from a grim threat.

However, the joy of victory was short-lived. Gronak took a brief, exhausted breath before addressing the pressing reality. "We can't waste any time now," he said in a serious tone. "Fiona is still in danger. We need to get back to Martha and Anika immediately so they can help her."

Lea looked at Fiona, who still appeared weak and injured and immediately recognized the urgency of the situation. "You're right," she agreed, her voice filled with concern. "Let me down, Gronak. I can walk on my own and that will get us back faster."

The concern for Fiona grew immeasurably as Gronak and Lea saw the severity of her wounds. The blood flowing from the injuries intensified the urgency of the situation. Every heartbeat seemed louder, every breath harder, as they became aware that every second was precious. The awareness that Fiona's life was hanging by a thread drove them on.

Gronak, with his strong body, carried Fiona gently as if she were made of glass. Every movement was cautious and deliberate, to avoid risking any further injuries. His muscles tensed under the weight of the responsibility he bore and his eyes reflected the determination to save his friend.

Lea, her steps hasty and energetic, led the way to Martha's house. Her heart pounded against her chest as she tried to cover the distance as quickly as possible. Every stone on the path seemed like an obstacle they had to overcome to save Fiona. Her thoughts were a jumble of worry and fear.

Every step was marked by urgency and concern, knowing that Fiona's life might depend on their swift response. Every moment of delay felt like an eternity as they were determined not to waste any time. The hope that Martha and Anika could help them was the only thing driving them in this race against time.

Chapter 14: The End of a Journey

Gronak and Lea hurried as fast as they could, their steps driven by worry and determination. Despite their own injuries and exhaustion, they did not take a break. Every moment counted and they were ready to save Fiona at any cost.

After what felt like an eternity, Lea saw Martha's house appear in the distance. She stopped and breathed a sigh of relief. "Gronak, I see Martha's house. We're almost there!" she shouted, her voice full of relief and hope.

Gronak, at the end of his strength, held Fiona firmly in his arms and felt a wave of relief at the thought of their imminent arrival. His heart pounded against his chest as he struggled to mobilize his weary muscles to cover the last stretch of the journey.

Lea ran ahead, her steps hasty and energetic. "I'll go ahead to the house to get everything ready!" she called back. Gronak nodded in agreement, his thoughts full of gratitude for Lea's support. He held Fiona gently to him and continued his arduous trek, knowing they would soon reach help. The hope of saving Fiona drove him forward, despite the pain and exhaustion plaguing his body.

Lea gathered her last reserves of strength and sprinted to Martha's house, her lungs burning from the effort as she neared the sanctuary. The hope of rescue and help for Fiona propelled her forward, even though her legs felt as heavy as lead and each step was a battle against fatigue.

When she finally arrived, she opened the door, exhausted and breathless. Martha, who was standing by the cauldron cooking something and Anika, who was reading a book, were startled by the sudden opening of the door.

Anika looked at Lea, who stood at the door, completely exhausted and wounded. Her eyes widened in dismay as she recognized the state of her friend. "Lea, you look awful! What happened and where are Gronak and Fiona?" she asked with deep concern for her friends.

Lea breathed heavily, her chest rising and falling in an irregular rhythm. Tears streamed down her battle-scarred cheeks as she met Anika's worried gaze. "Gronak is coming with Fiona. Fiona is in danger; we need to tend to her immediately," she replied with a trembling voice, her words filled with fear and urgency.

Martha immediately understood the gravity of the situation and went without hesitation into the next room to prepare everything. She gathered bandages, herbs and other supplies needed for treating Fiona's injuries. Every moment counted and she needed to ensure she was ready to act as soon as Gronak and Fiona arrived.

Shortly afterward, Gronak came through the door with the severely injured Fiona in his arms, his face marked by exhaustion and concern. Martha called to Gronak, "Bring Fiona in here and lay her on the bed; I'll take care of her right away." Her voice was calm as she prepared to treat Fiona's injuries.

Gronak nodded and moved quickly, carefully placing Fiona's body on the bed. He felt the weight of responsibility on his shoulders as he was careful not to cause her further harm. Martha and Anika immediately rushed to Fiona's side to stop the bleeding and tend to her wounds. They worked in unison, putting everything into saving Fiona's life.

Martha carefully cleaned the wounds while Anika handed over bandages and helped treat the severe injuries. Time seemed to stand still as they worked feverishly to save Fiona's life. Every move was precise and every moment was filled with hope for a miracle.

Gronak and Lea sat at the table, slowly recovering from the hardships of the past hours. The tension in the air was palpable as they waited for news of Fiona's condition. Time seemed to stand still and every second of waiting felt like an eternity.

Lea looked up at Gronak with tear-filled eyes. "I hope we made it in time," she whispered, her voice laden with worry as she leaned against him.

Gronak lovingly embraced Lea, sensing her fear and despair. "All we can do now is pray and hope for the best," he said gently, his words full of comfort and reassurance, even though he too was filled with worry inside.

After several agonizing hours of waiting, Anika emerged from the adjacent room. Her expression revealed nothing as she slowly approached Gronak and Lea. The silence in the room was suffocating and the two friends waited anxiously for her words.

Gronak and Lea looked at Anika with concern, their hearts racing with anticipation and fear. The uncertainty about Fiona's fate weighed heavily on them and they desperately hoped for good news.

Anika sat down wearily at the table with Gronak and Lea, her face serious and concerned. The strain of the last few hours was evident, but she spoke in a calm voice. "Martha and I did everything we could. Fiona has lost a lot of blood and is still not out of danger. All we can do now is hope she survives."

Gronak felt relieved that there was still hope for Fiona, but his concern for her remained unchanged. "I thank you from the bottom of my heart, Anika," he said sincerely, his eyes full of gratitude. "Without Martha's and your help, we wouldn't have had any chance of saving Fiona. You are our salvation."

Lea nodded in agreement, her eyes glistening with tears of relief and gratitude. "Yes, thank you, Anika," she added, her voice filled with emotion. "You did everything possible. Now we must pray for Fiona and hope she pulls through."

Anika smiled at their kind words, but her eyes showed signs of exhaustion and worry. "It's the least I could do for what you've done for us," she replied gratefully. But after a brief pause, her expression grew more serious as she looked back and forth between Gronak and Lea. "But now, tell me what happened out there. Not only does Fiona look bad, but you both look like you've been through hell."

Gronak and Lea shared the whole story with Anika, from the moment they reached the fortress to the horrors of the shadow creatures, the battle against Xalis and the collapse of the fortress. Anika listened in shock as they vividly recounted every moment.

Her eyes widened in horror at the dangers they had faced, but also in joy that they had managed to come out alive despite everything. "What you've been through is incredible!" Anika said, her voice choked with tears of joy. "I'm so happy you survived. You are true heroes."

Gronak then looked at Lea with a questioning expression. "But there's something I don't understand, Lea. Xalis killed you right before my eyes, yet you were alive later. How did you do that?"

Lea returned Gronak's gaze with a look of confusion. "Honestly, I have no idea," she admitted quietly. "When Xalis tortured me, the pain was so overwhelming that everything went black and I was engulfed in eternal darkness. No light, no warmth and no pain anymore. Just nothing! But suddenly, I saw a bright light and I felt my heart start beating again. I can't explain it."

Anika looked at Lea with interest. "May I see the necklace I gave you?" she asked unexpectedly.

Lea was puzzled by Anika's question, but she retrieved the necklace from her clothing. As she examined it, she was astonished by what she saw. The red-orange crystal, once so vibrant and radiant, had lost its color and was now just black.

Lea looked at Anika with wide eyes. "What happened, Anika?" she asked, a hint of concern in her voice.

Anika smiled gently and began to explain. "You know, this necklace was given to me by my father many years ago," she began. "He told me it might save my life one day. Back then, I thought it was just a good luck charm and didn't pay much attention to it."

Her gaze briefly shifted to the fire in the cauldron before she continued. "One day, when Janon and I met an old mage, he was fascinated by the necklace. Of course, I asked him what was so special about it. He explained to me that the crystal is a Phoenix Crystal. These crystals are very rare and extremely valuable. He told me that the crystal has the power to bring back to life those who have died. But it only works once, after which the crystal loses its power."

A joyful smile spread across Anika's face as she looked at Lea. "That's why I gave you the necklace, so it could save your life in an emergency, just like you saved mine back when we fought Reyve."

As Lea realized the meaning of Anika's words, all the emotions she had suppressed came flooding out and tears streamed down her cheeks. "You saved my life. Without you, I'd truly be dead now," she sobbed, her voice filled with gratitude and overwhelming emotion.

Anika stood up, sat down beside Lea and lovingly took her in her arms as Lea continued to cry. She held Lea tightly, allowing her to release her emotions freely.

Gronak, who had been quietly observing the touching scene, felt the intensity of the emotions in the room. His face showed a mix of relief, gratitude and respect for the deep bond between Lea and Anika. He remained seated, giving the two women their moment of closeness and comfort.

A short while later, Martha emerged from the adjacent room. She glanced at Gronak and Lea and spoke in a calm but firm voice. "Fiona needs rest, time and a good dose of luck now." Her words were filled with hope.

Martha moved toward the cauldron and began selecting ingredients for a meal. Her expression was hopeful and she radiated a confidence that spread to the others. "I'm going to make you all something to eat now," she announced. "And tomorrow, the world will look different."

Gronak and Lea nodded in agreement, grateful for Martha's presence and her comforting words. The prospect of a warm meal and Martha's confidence allowed them to breathe a little easier and hope that things would turn for the better.

The days passed slowly in the land. Martha tended to Fiona with love and care, day and night. She monitored her recovery with the utmost diligence and dedication and every small improvement brought new hope for the future.

Gronak took on the responsibility of providing for the group. He went hunting regularly to gather food for everyone and took care of minor repairs and damages to the house. His skills as a hunter and craftsman were invaluable to the group and his dedication remained tireless, despite his concern for Fiona.

Meanwhile, Lea and Anika had developed a close bond. They spent much time together, sharing their thoughts, hopes and fears. In the quiet moments, they found comfort and strength in each other's company and their friendship became a source of solace and support during these difficult times.

One day, Martha's husband, Richard, also recovered from his illness. The entire group was overjoyed that Richard had regained his strength. His recovery brought an additional wave of hope and happiness into the house and they all celebrated his return to health.

Yet, as the joy over Richard's recovery spread, Fiona still lay unconscious in bed. Despite Martha's tireless care and the love of her friends, Fiona's condition seemed unchanged. The uncertainty of Fiona's fate weighed heavily on them and their thoughts remained with their dear friend, whose recovery was still uncertain.

But one day, as the sun slowly sank behind the hills, casting a golden glow across the sky, Martha suddenly emerged from the house and called out to Gronak, who was chopping firewood. "Gronak! Quickly, come here! She's awake!"

The ax fell from Gronak's hands as he heard Martha's words. Without hesitation, he ran into the house to Fiona. His heart raced so fast he could hardly catch his breath. When he entered the room, he saw Fiona greeting him with a weak smile.

Gronak rushed to her bedside and held her hand tightly. Tears of joy streamed down his face as he spoke to her. "I'm so happy you're alive, Fiona. Every day I prayed you would wake up." His voice cracked with emotion as he held her hand, as if afraid to ever let her go again.

Fiona gently let her hand glide over Gronak's cheek, locking eyes with him. "I'm endlessly grateful to you, Gronak, for saving me from certain death," she spoke with a voice full of deep-felt gratitude.

A delicate smile played on her lips as she added, "And besides, who would take care of you if I weren't around?" It was a light-hearted joke that instantly lifted the heavy atmosphere in the room, causing both of them to laugh.

Overwhelmed by a flood of emotions, Gronak embraced Fiona with tender care. In a soft whisper meant only for her ears, he shared something that made her smile even broader and happier.

Lea and Anika also rushed into the room as soon as they heard that Fiona had awakened. Their eyes sparkled with joy when they saw their friend conscious again. Lea immediately ran to Fiona's bed and hugged her tightly, tears of relief and happiness streaming down her cheeks.

The friends decided to celebrate Fiona's recovery and their victory over Xalis that very day. The atmosphere was filled with gratitude and joy as they reminisced together about all the challenges they had overcome.

A few days passed and it was finally time for Gronak, Fiona, Lea and Anika to begin their journey back home. They packed their belongings and prepared for the trip back to their homeland.

Fiona carefully packed her bag, but when she searched for the magical book and the rune, she couldn't find them. "Lea, have you seen the magical book and the rune?" she asked in puzzlement.

Lea sighed heavily and shook her head regretfully. "Unfortunately, all the weapons and equipment we had were lost when the fortress collapsed," she replied, her voice tinged with disappointment.

Fiona looked at Lea reassuringly and placed a hand on her shoulder. "Don't worry," she said gently. "What matters is that we stopped Xalis and that we made it out alive." Her words were full of comfort and confidence and Lea felt a bit of relief.

The four adventurers bid farewell to Martha and Richard, grateful for their help and support. With one last look back, they set out to complete the final leg of their adventure.

They chose the safer trade routes, even though they were longer. But the extra time seemed a small price to pay to ensure the safety of their journey.

After many days of walking and overcoming obstacles, they finally arrived in the trading town where they were to pick up Elena. The joy was immense as they entered the bustling streets of the town and approached the tavern.

The door of the tavern swung open and the group stepped inside. The sounds of conversation and laughter filled the room and the scent of fresh beer and delicious food hung in the air.

Elena, who was standing at the counter cleaning glasses and mugs, turned around as she saw the group enter. A beaming smile lit up her face when she spotted Lea. She dropped everything and ran toward her sister in joy.

"Lea!" Elena cried, her eyes shining with happiness. She clung tightly to Lea, tears of joy in her eyes. "I'm so glad you're back, big sister," she whispered, her voice choked with emotion. Lea returned the hug warmly, feeling the warmth and relief of finally being reunited with her sister.

The tavern keeper also approached the group, greeting them warmly and inviting them to sit and share their stories. Together, they recounted their journey, the dangers they had faced, the battles, the challenges and finally, their triumph over Xalis.

The innkeeper, impressed by their adventures and bravery, decided to host a grand celebration for the victory over Xalis. The joyous news of the dark lord's death was announced and the town rejoiced in their liberation from his tyrannical rule.

Many people flocked to the tavern to personally thank Gronak, Fiona and Lea, expressing their admiration. They were celebrated as heroes and the friends felt honored and humbled by the recognition.

The next day, after the festivities had died down and the town slowly returned to normal, the friends set out on their journey once more. The memories of their adventures and the joy of their victory accompanied them on their way.

A few days later, they reached a crossroads where their paths diverged. One direction led to the Forest of the Elves, while the other led toward Gronak and Fiona's village. The decision they had to make hung heavy in the air as they stood together at the crossroads.

Gronak looked at his friends, a solemn expression on his face. "Now is the moment of farewell," he said quietly, his voice filled with emotion. He knew it was time to say goodbye.

Lea hugged Gronak and Fiona tightly, tears in her eyes. "I will miss you both so much," she whispered, her voice choked with emotion. "Thank you both for everything you have done for Elena, my village and me." Her words were heavy with gratitude and sorrow. She knew that without her loyal friends, there would be a great void in her life.

Fiona hugged Lea warmly in return, her own voice fragile with emotion. "We will miss you too, Lea," she said softly. "But you will always be a part of our family, no matter where your path takes you."

Gronak held Lea close, his heart heavy with the pain of parting. "Take good care of yourself, Lea," he said with a hint of melancholy in his voice. "You will always be a sister to me, no matter how far apart we are."

The three friends stood silently for a moment, wrapped in the stillness of their farewell. Yet they knew that this was not the end of their friendship, but rather the beginning of a new chapter in their lives.

Gronak gently let his gaze drift to Anika, his face marked by curiosity. "What are your plans now, Anika?" he asked calmly.

A radiant smile spread across Anika's face as she looked directly into Gronak's eyes. "I will stay with Lea," she announced with a broad smile that made her eyes sparkle. Lea joined their conversation, her eyes shining with happiness. "That's right, we've decided that she'll live with Elena and me," Lea confirmed proudly, her voice filled with warm affection.

A faint blush rose to Anika's cheeks as she felt the warmth of their acceptance. She smiled gratefully at Lea, her eyes glowing with joy and relief at the decision made.

Gronak and Fiona exchanged knowing smiles, their suspicions confirmed. They had already guessed that Anika would choose this new adventure. The bond between the two women was strong and deep and they knew that Anika would be in good hands with Lea.

After the emotional farewell, the group went their separate ways. Gronak and Fiona set off towards their village. The path led them through dense forests and across green meadows as the sun slowly sank on the horizon.

Fiona glanced back at their friends, who were slowly disappearing into the distance. "I already miss them, Gronak," she said softly, her gaze full of longing.

Gronak placed a comforting hand on Fiona's shoulder. "We'll see them again soon, I'm sure," he assured her with a gentle smile.

405

Fiona smiled and nodded. "You're right," she said quietly. "Let's go home first." Her heart was heavy with the pain of parting, but she knew that together with Gronak, they could face the journey ahead.

Several days passed before Gronak and Fiona finally caught sight of their home village from afar. The sun bathed the landscape in warm light as they slowly approached their destination. The joy in their hearts grew with each step they took closer.

The excitement grew as they neared the village. Their faces were beaming and their steps quickened with anticipation.

A group of children spotted Gronak and Fiona from afar and recognized them immediately. With joyful shouts, they ran directly into the village to spread the news of their return. The message spread like wildfire through the village and the residents prepared to welcome them.

By the time Gronak and Fiona reached the village edge, half the village was already there to greet them. People of all ages had gathered, their faces radiant with joy and relief. Tears of happiness were shed as Gronak and Fiona were warmly welcomed by their friends and family members.

The mayor, a respected man with a friendly demeanor, stepped forward to greet Gronak and Fiona as well. His words were filled with gratitude and pride as he praised the two heroes for their bravery and honored their victory over Xalis. The villagers cheered and applauded as they listened to the mayor's words, expressing their appreciation for Gronak and Fiona.

To celebrate their return and the victory over Xalis, Walter, the innkeeper and close friend of the two heroes, organized a massive village festival. The villagers flocked to the festival grounds, which were adorned with colorful banners and filled with cheerful music. The scent of roasted meat and sweet treats filled the air as people gathered to celebrate together.

The festival lasted for several days, marked by exuberant joy. There were dances, music and games for all ages and people laughed and celebrated together. Everywhere you looked, there were beaming faces and the atmosphere was filled with a palpable sense of unity and joy.

Gronak and Fiona were surrounded by villagers who offered their congratulations and expressed their admiration for their heroic deeds. There were hugs, pats on the back and warm words of gratitude as people showed their appreciation.

Slowly, peace returned to the land and the stories of Xalis, who had once struck fear into the world, became legends. The names of the three heroes Gronak, Fiona and Lea were written into the history books and passed down from generation to generation as symbols of bravery, sacrifice and the triumph of good over evil.

The End